Then
lurki
stripp

Just why she didn't weep or scream in terror
she'd never know. Maybe it's true

Hunkered low over his saddle, the lone cowboy
drilled her with such angry, laser-bright blue
eyes, she knew he was bad. He had to be Cole
Knight, one of the neighbours her daddy
regularly cussed out. Even after he realised she'd
spotted him, he didn't avert his predatory gaze or
smile or even bother to apologise.

He was as bad as any bandit.

"I've heard all about you," she said. "You're
known to have a nasty, vengeful disposition.
You're a gambler, too, and you've got a bad
reputation with girls."

"Did your daddy tell you all that?"

When he edged his mount closer to hers, she
instinctively backed hers up. He smiled and let
his hot, sinful eyes devour the length of her
body. "You're not scared of me, now, are you?"

Also available from **Ann Major**

THE HOT LADIES MURDER CLUB

ANN MAJOR

THE GIRL
=== with the ===

GOLDEN

SPURS

MIRA

MIRA is a registered trademark of Harlequin Enterprises Limited,
used under licence.

First published in Great Britain 2008.
MIRA Books, Eton House, 18-24 Paradise Road,
Richmond, Surrey, TW9 1SR

© Ann Major 2004

ISBN: 978 0 7783 0274 2

63-0908

MIRA's policy is to use papers that are natural, renewable and
recyclable products and made from wood grown in sustainable
forests. The logging and manufacturing processes conform to the
legal environmental regulations of the country of origin.

Printed and bound in Spain
by Litografía Rosés S.A., Barcelona

To all my soul mates out there, especially in Texas, who wanted to grow up and become cowboys, only to have their mothers warn them, "Make up your mind, girl, because you can't do both."

ACKNOWLEDGEMENTS

I must thank Tara Gavin for her friendship, support, trust, talent and faith.

And Karen Solem, who is a genius.

And Nancy Berland, who is also a genius.

And Dianne Moggy and everybody at MIRA Books for the wonderful job they are doing!

And Kelly Nemic.

And all my ranching friends who tell me stories – the Joneses, the Bateses, the Telleses, Becky Rooke and my aunt Mabel.

And Amber Maley, who works in the sheriff's office at Rockport, Texas.

And Lady Liddington, who was my best friend from junior high through university.

PROLOGUE

Smart Cowboy Saying:

Just 'cause trouble comes visiting doesn't mean you have to offer it a place to sit down.
                                            —Anonymous

Prologue

The devil had dealt from the bottom of the deck one time too many.

An eye for an eye, the Bible said. Or at least Cole Knight had heard somewhere the good book said something like that. To tell the truth, he wasn't much of a Biblical scholar. But he loved God, he loved the hot, thorny land under his boots that by all rights should have been his, and he loved his family—in that order. He was willing to die for them, too.

Maybe that was overstating the case. In fact, Cole Knight wasn't much of anything. Wasn't likely to be, either. Not if Caesar Kemble and his bunch had their way.

But where was it written you couldn't kill a man on the same day you buried your good for nothin' father and set things right? Especially if that man was the cause of your old man's ruin? And yours, too?

Hell, it was about time somebody stood up and demanded justice. The Knights had as much right—more right—as the Kembles to be here.

Cole Knight *belonged* here. Trouble was, he didn't own a single acre. The Kembles had stripped him to the bone.

The feud between the Kembles and the Knights went

back for more than a hundred and forty years. It had all begun when the first Caesar Kemble, the original founder of the Golden Spurs Ranch, had died without a will, and his son Johnny Kemble had cheated his adopted sister, Carolina Knight, out of most of her share. The Knights were direct descendants of Carolina Knight, whose biological father, Horatio Knight, had been a partner of the original Caesar Kemble. When Horatio and his wife had been killed in an Indian raid, Caesar had adopted their orphaned daughter.

As if being cheated hadn't been bad enough, four more generations of Kembles had continued to cheat and collude and steal even more land from the Knights. Not that the Knights were saints. Still, the Knights' vast holdings, which had once been even bigger than the Kembles', had shrunk to a miserable fifty thousand acres. Then worst of all, not long ago, Cole's father had lost those last fifty thousand acres in a card game.

Thus, Black Oaks had faded into oblivion while the Golden Spurs had become an international agribusiness corporation with interests in the Thoroughbred horse industry, the oil and gas industry, cattle ranching, recreational game hunting and farming. The Golden Spurs developed cattle breeds, improved horse breeds and participated in vital environmental research. The Kembles owned hundreds of thousands of acres and mineral rights to vast oil and gas reserves and were Texas royalty, while the Knights were dirt.

Cole had already been to the barn to saddle Dr. Pepper. No sooner had Sally McCallie, the last hypocritical mourner, waddled out of the dilapidated ranch house than Cole was out of his sticky, black wool suit and into his jeans and boots. A few seconds later his long, lean body was stomping down the back stairs into the sweltering, late July heat and the rickety screen door was banging shut behind him.

There was finality in that summertime sound. Thrusting

his rifle into his worn scabbard, he seized the reins and threw himself onto Dr. Pepper. His daddy was dead, his bloated face as gray and nasty under the waxy makeup as wet ash, and Cole's own unhappy boyhood was over.

It was just as well. Not that he had much to show for it. He'd had to quit college after his older brother, Shanghai, who'd been putting him through school, had unearthed some incriminating original bank documents and journals, which proved Carolina had been swindled. When Shanghai had threatened to sue the Kembles, Caesar had run him off or so people had thought. His disappearance was something of a mystery. Shanghai had left in the middle of the night without even saying goodbye. Without Shanghai's help and with an ailing father to support, Cole hadn't had money to pay tuition much less the time to spend on school.

Twenty-four and broke, Cole was the last of the line and going nowhere. At least that's what the locals thought. Like a lot of young men, he seethed with ambition and the desire to set things right. He wanted the ranch back, not just the fifty thousand acres, but the rest of it, and there was nothing he wouldn't do to get it.

Too bad he took after his old man, local folk said. Too bad his brother Shanghai, who'd shown such promise as a rancher, had turned out to be as sorry as the rest of the Knights when he'd abandoned his dying father.

Cole felt almost good riding toward the immense Golden Spurs Ranch. Finally he was doing something about the crimes of the past and present that had made his soul fester. Partly he felt better because he couldn't get on a horse without relaxing a little. Cowboying had been born in him. It was as natural to him as breathing, eating and chasing pretty girls.

For the past three years, Cole had wanted one thing—to get even with Caesar Kemble for cheating his daddy out of what was left of their ranch and for running his brother off. Those acres weren't just land to Cole. They'd been part of him. He'd dreamed of ranching them with his brother someday.

Not that his daddy had given much of a damn that the last of the land that had once been part of their legendary ranch had been lost.

"Leave it be, boy," his daddy had said after Cole had found out the ranch was gone. "It was my ranch, not yours. Maybe Caesar and me was both drunk as a pair of coons in a horse trough filled with whiskey, but Kemble won Black Oaks fair and square with that royal flush."

"The hell he did, Daddy. The hell he did. You were drunk because he *got* you drunk. Caesar Kemble knew exactly what he was doing. What kind of fool plays poker drunk?"

"I'm not like you, boy. I play poker for fun." But his old man's explanation didn't mollify Cole.

"Black Oaks wasn't just yours. You didn't have the right to gamble it away. It was mine and Shanghai's."

"Well, it's gone just the same, boy. You can't rewrite history. You're a loser, born to a loser, brother of a loser. History is always written by the winners."

"I swear—if it's the last thing I ever do, I'll get Black Oaks back—*all* of it."

"You'll get yourself killed if you mess with Caesar Kemble. That's what you'll do. My father was a hothead like you and he went over to have it out with the Kembles and vanished into thin air. Don't get yourself murdered, boy, or run off, like Shanghai did."

"As if you care—"

His easygoing daddy hadn't cared much about anything other than partying and getting drunk.

With his Stetson low over his dark brow and longish black hair, Cole followed a well-worn dirt pathway through sandy pastures choked by huisache, ebony and mesquite. Dr. Pepper trotted for at least a mile before Cole's heart quickened when he saw the billowing dust from the herd rising above a stand of low trees like yellow smoke to dirty the sky.

The vaqueros and Kemble's sons, who worked for the Golden Spurs, had been gathering the herd for several days in the dense thickets that had once belonged to the Knights. Rich as he was, Caesar, who like Cole, loved cowboying more than he loved anything—including cheating at cards—would be out there with his men and sons. Cole hoped to catch him alone in some deep and thorny thicket and have it out with him once and for all.

Yes, sirree, that's just what he hoped until he saw Lizzy Kemble through the dense brush. Somehow the sight of the slim, uncertain girl on the tall black gelding struggling to keep up with the vaqueros and her younger, more able brothers, cousins and sister stopped him cold.

Lizzy was fair-skinned and didn't look like the rest of her family, who were a big-boned, tanned, muscular bunch—a bullying bunch, who thought they were kings, who lorded it over everybody else in the four counties their ranch covered.

The spirited horse was too much for her, and she knew it. Her spine was stiff with fear. Anybody could see that. Her hands even shook. She was covered with dirt from head to toe, and her hat was flat as a pancake on one side, which meant she'd already taken a tumble or two.

She might have seemed laughable to him if her eyes weren't so big and her pretty, heart-shaped face so white. She looked scared to death and vulnerable, too. Sensing her fear, the gelding was stamping the ground edgily, just itching for trouble.

Cole shook his head, ashamed for the girl and yet worried about her, too. What the hell was wrong with him? He should be glad Caesar Kemble's teenage daughter was such a miserable failure as a cowgirl.

He had a mission. He should forget her, but Cole couldn't stop watching her, his gaze fixing on her cute butt in those skintight jeans and then on the long, platinum, mud-caked braid that swung down her back.

Not bad for jailbait.

His former glimpses of her in town hadn't done her justice. She'd grown up some since then, gotten herself a woman's soft, curvaceous body and a woman's vulnerability that appealed to him much as he would have preferred to despise everything about her. It didn't matter that she was a Kemble, nor that the Kembles had been swindling the Knights for more than a hundred years. Something about her big eyes made him feel powerful and want to protect her.

He forgot Caesar and concentrated on the girl, who didn't seem like she fit with her clan at all. She was Caesar's favorite, and despite the fact she seemed the least suited to ranch life, the bastard wanted to make her his heir. All of a sudden Cole's quest for revenge looked like it might take a much sweeter path than the one he'd originally intended.

But then that's how life is. You think you're fixed on where you're going and how you'll get there—then you come to a tempting fork in the road that shows you a much sweeter path.

Lizzy Kemble, who was seventeen, had more important things to do than ride a horse all day long in this godforsaken, hot, thorny country—even if it *was* her family's immense ranch. And not on just any horse—Pájaro!

Why had Daddy insisted she could ride Pájaro? The horse had a bad reputation. Why did Daddy always have to challenge her?

"Challenges build character, girl."

Daddy had the sensitivity of a bulldozer. You'd better do what he said or get out of his way.

Lizzy Kemble was tired, bored, saddle sore, sunburned and scared to death she'd fall off again. Not to mention her imagination was running wild. Every time she got lost in a thicket, she conjured some wild bandit up from Mexico or a drug runner lurking behind every bush just waiting to snatch her.

She wished she was home talking on the phone or reading a book. Why couldn't she have been born to a normal city family who thought it was natural to hang out in malls?

Indeed she wished she was anywhere except on this monster called Pájaro, getting her fair skin burned to a crisp and scratched up on thorns while she choked on dust and horse flies. Not to mention the bruises on her bottom. Pájaro had thrown her twice already.

She was thinking that Pájaro was a bad name for a horse because it meant bird in Spanish, and the last thing Lizzy, who'd been run away with before, needed was another horse that could fly.

The herd was deep in these horrible thickets made of thorns and cactus. She'd never been on this particular division of the ranch, and she hoped she'd never set foot on it again. Because the land here was too wild and rugged for pens or helicopters, the cattle simply melted into the thickets. Yes, Black Oaks was the only division where a real, old-fashioned roundup was still necessary.

If she had to do this, oh, how she wished she was on her gentle mare, Betsy! But Betsy had gone lame, so here she was trying to stay on this black monster with a wide chest and shiny-muscled back, whose hooves tapped so lightly over the earth, she was gut sure that at any moment he would bolt or fly.

The thicket grew denser and Lizzy strained to find her daddy's sweat-stained, battered Stetson bobbing above the bawling herd. She saw Uncle B.B. riding tall, as handsome as a prince. Much as Lizzy wished she could give up and go home, she couldn't. Not with her black-haired brothers, Hawk and Walker, and her sister, Mia, who was a natural born cowgirl if ever there was one, making bets about the exact hour Lizzy would chicken out.

She was used to people regarding her with secretive, speculative glances when they thought she wasn't watching. She supposed they did so because everybody—her siblings, her aunts and uncles, even her mother—was jealous of her since she was Daddy's favorite. She hated the way her father's favoritism caused her problems on every level.

Hawk had said he'd give her an hour in the heat and thorns at best; Mia had said two. When Lizzy had heard Walker and her cousin, Sam—who never laughed at her—laughing, too, she'd made a bet of her own that she'd make it the whole day, even if every second of it was torture. Hawk and Mia had really smirked at her then, which was why she had to stick it out.

She'd show Hawk and Mia and Daddy, too. She'd show everybody, even Mother, who took such pride in Mia—she'd show them, she was a true Kemble if it killed her!

But even though she was Daddy's favorite, she didn't feel like a Kemble, and she never had. She often felt she'd been born into the wrong family.

On the Golden Spurs taking part in roundup was a sacred family tradition. Every family member was expected to participate alongside the hands. Even Aunt Nanette flew in from Montana to help work cattle and prepare the camp lunch. Of course, the lunch was always fancier than their normal fare when bossy, stylish Aunt Nanette took charge. She hired half a dozen caterers and had them flown in by private jet from Dallas.

For a hundred and forty years, Kembles had been working this land. They'd endured bandit raids, Union soldiers, drought, the Depression, inheritance taxes and now, in the twenty-first century, family dissention and constant lawsuits. They'd come close to selling out and giving up on the ranch dozens of times. Then oil and gas had been discovered, and there was too much at stake to sell out.

"As long as the family sticks together, the ranch will survive," was the family motto.

Being a Kemble was like being part of a football team or being a believer in a cult religion, or maybe it was worse, more like the Mafia, because it was family. There was a do-or-die feel to being a Kemble. You were supposed to feel your Kembleness in your bones, to dedicate your entire life to the ranch. Or you were the worst kind of traitor.

So Lizzy felt terrible that she'd been born with this weird feeling that she didn't belong here and that she lacked the talent to ever be a rancher. This lack in herself filled her with self-doubt. She wanted to please her father by becoming the perfect cowgirl more than anything, but she didn't think she ever could. As if he sensed this, her father, who was not normally intuitive, had done everything in his power to turn her into a proper Kemble.

"Keep your eye on me, honey," Daddy had said only this morning when she'd begged to stay home. "And you'll be fine."

Easier said than done. Daddy was everywhere at once.

The sun was a fat red ball low against the horizon, but that didn't mean her daddy would order the cowboying to stop anytime soon. She was tired of the hot rivulets of wet dust running down her face and throat. More than anything she wanted to wash her pale, curly hair so it was no longer matted with dirt and sweat. She'd been in the saddle so long, her butt felt numb and her legs ached. Her throat was dry from all the blowing dust. She probably had chiggers, too.

Nearby a calf escaped, and Hawk waved his cowboy hat and whooped at it. There was laughter and *gritos* as he and his terrier, Blackie, galloped toward the squealing calf in pursuit. Lizzy jumped forward causing Pájaro's hooves to tap skittishly.

"Easy, boy," Lizzy said. Phobic about dogs, Pájaro danced backward. Tensing, Lizzy pulled back on the reins. She hated it when horses did anything except walk in a straight line. She'd been bitten, thrown and kicked too many times to remember, and that wasn't even counting today.

It had all started on her fifth birthday when she'd begged Daddy for a doll, a beautiful Madame Alexander doll in a gorgeous velvet black dress, but he'd given her a dreadful Arabian mare named Gypsy instead. Daddy had told Lizzy the best way to make friends with the huge, snorting beast was to give her an apple. Only when she'd tiptoed fearfully up to the mare with the crescents of apple in her palm, the brute had snorted and then bitten off the tip of the little finger on Lizzy's left hand. Mia had grabbed the apple and fed the beast expertly. Not that Daddy had even noticed her doing so.

At the plastic surgeon's, Lizzy had cried and cried about wanting a doll instead of a biting horse. Not that her daddy had had the least bit of sympathy.

"Don't be such a big crybaby, Lizzy. She knew you were afraid."

How do you not be afraid when you are?

Ever since Gypsy, Lizzy had had problem relationships, you might say, with horses and cows—with any large animal, really.

But she loved her daddy. And her daddy was determined to make a cowgirl of her or kill them both trying. So, here she was, out in the blazing sun, in thorny brush country, getting herself all sore and sunburned to make her daddy proud.

"You were born to this life, honey," Daddy was constantly saying, but there was always a lack of conviction in his voice that scared Lizzy deep down and made her wonder why he was trying so hard to prove she belonged.

Even though he took her everywhere, constantly instructing her about the operation of the ranch, somehow, she never quite felt a true kinship with the Golden Spurs. It was as if her life were a puzzle, and a big piece in the middle was missing.

"Why can't I do the cowgirl stuff then?" she had asked him.

"Because you're stubborn and you've made up your mind you can't. Change your mind, and you'll change your result."

And so their discussions went, if you could call them discussions. Daddy, who never listened, always did ninety percent of the lecturing, and if she said anything, that just kept the unpleasant conversation going.

Sometimes she made small improvements in her horsemanship. But who wouldn't have, considering how many hours had gone into her training? Sometimes she went for months without a mishap, but she always backslid.

No father ever spent more time grooming an heiress for the running of his empire. Before she'd been old enough for school, he'd carried her with him everywhere, whether on horseback or in his pickup or in the ranch's plane. He'd taken her to San Antonio to the board meetings, introducing her to everyone important, who had anything to do with the ranch. He'd taken her to feedlots, to auctions. He'd let her play at his feet when he'd worked in his office.

Sam and her siblings had begged her father to take them, but almost always, he'd insisted upon Lizzy going because ranching came so naturally to the rest of the brood. He'd taught her to shoot and to ride, but she disliked guns and horses. The other children had watched her leave with her father for her lessons or trips, their eyes narrowed and sullen with jealousy....

One minute Lizzy was hovering on the edge of the herd, watching her daddy, mother, her uncles, cousins, brothers and her sister do the real work while she tried to stay out of their way and endured the blistering day. Then she saw him—a real live Border bandit…or maybe a drug runner— lurking in the brush, staring holes through her, stripping her naked.

Just why she didn't weep or scream in terror, she'd never know. Maybe it's true what they say about curiosity killing cats.

He was half-hidden in the mesquite and *granjeño* and palmetto fronds. Hunkered low over his saddle, the lone cowboy drilled her with such angry, laser-bright blue eyes she knew he was bad. Even after he realized she'd spotted him, he didn't avert his predatory gaze or smile or even bother to apologize.

No, bold as brass, his narrowed eyes roved from her face to her breasts and her thighs.

Rigid with shock and not a little fear, she glowered back at his harsh, set face.

"Who do you think you are—trespassing, spying on me?" she said, wishing for once that she was carrying a hateful gun like her daddy always advised.

"If your daddy wasn't a thief, you'd be trespassing, honey. This was Knight land for five generations."

English. He spoke English. Drawling, lazy, pure Texas English, but English. "So, you're Cole…"

Naturally she knew that Cole Knight was as bad as any bandit. Worse—if her daddy had his say.

Cole lifted his hat and nodded, his hostile, white smirk mocking her. "Pleased to meet you, darlin'." Not that he looked pleased.

She wasn't about to say she was pleased to meet him.

He had longish black hair, dark skin and radar eyes that saw through a girl.

"I've heard all about you," she said. "You're known to have a nasty vengeful disposition. You're a gambler, too, and you've got a bad reputation with girls."

"Did your daddy tell you all that, *little* girl?"

She refused to give him the satisfaction of admitting it, but she felt herself get hot and guessed her blushing was telling him more than she wanted it to.

"Cole Knight is set on revenge against me, honey," her daddy had told her, and more than once.

"Why, Daddy?" she'd asked.

"Oh, no reason. Just because he's an ill-natured cuss if ever there was one."

"So, you're Lizzy Kemble," the handsome, ill-natured cuss drawled lazily in that pure-Texas accent of his, bringing her thoughts back to the present.

When he edged his mount closer to hers, she instinctively backed hers up. Again he smiled and let his hot, sinful eyes devour the length of her body, taking liberties she'd never given any man—and certainly didn't want to give the insolent likes of him.

He stared until she was practically frothing with fury. Then he shot her another bold smile that made her skin really heat.

"You blush real easy, don't you, *little* girl? I like that."

"Well, I don't like it, and I don't like anything about you, either," she snapped.

"You barely know me."

"I know enough."

"Then why don't you run, *Little* Red Riding Hood?"

"Go away. Just go away!" she said. "Before somebody sees you here."

"You've seen me. Aren't you somebody?"

Before she could stop herself, "I don't count for much around here."

He laughed at that, and some of the strain and anger left his dark face. He was handsome—too handsome for his good and for hers, too, she suddenly realized. This was bad. She wasn't as immune to his charm as she needed to be.

"I know that feeling...not counting for much," he said, his voice low and beguilingly gentle now as he urged his big horse to sidle closer to hers. He tipped his hat back, so that she could see his beautiful, long-lashed eyes better. "It's an awful feeling, isn't it?"

"I've got to go," she said, studying the silky length of his lashes rather too fixedly.

"You're not scared of me, now are you, little girl?"

"No! Of course not!"

"Then stay. Relax. I'm not the big bad wolf. I'm just your neighbor. Maybe it's time we got better acquainted."

She was about to say no, but Blackie charged through the brush, yapping his fool terrier head off at a rabbit that was running for his life. Panicked at the shrill barks, Pájaro reared slightly.

When the rabbit and dog sprinted toward the gelding like a pair of bullets, Lizzy screamed, and Pájaro started bucking for all he was worth.

"Keep your head, girl, and quit your screaming," Cole yelled, moving swiftly toward her.

Lizzy hollered again and again.

"Hush," Cole ordered, trying to grab her reins.

"Get away!" she yelled, slapping at his hands with them.

Then Blackie rushed under Pájaro's hooves again, and the gelding tossed his head wildly and reared. Cole grabbed the reins just as Pájaro bolted. The reins flew out of his hands, and Lizzy clutched the saddle horn and the gelding's mane and held on.

Born to fly, Pájaro's hooves pounded the earth as if ten demon terriers were chasing him straight to hell instead of one small dog. Lizzy was equally spooked. No way could she stop screaming now.

Pájaro dashed straight through thorny brush—through mesquite, huisache and *granjeño,* racing for the middle of the herd. Lizzy clung desperately, fighting to hang on. If she fell, she could be trampled. Behind her, she heard Cole shouting instructions, but the cattle were bawling so loudly, she couldn't make out what he was saying.

Ahead she saw a low branch, so she bent low over Pájaro's back. When he raced beneath it, thorns knocked off her hat and shredded the back of her blouse. Pájaro shot through a bunch of cattle, scattering them in all directions. Then he veered away from the herd back into the brush, racing at a full gallop for maybe five minutes.

Her heart was thudding in terror, but still she held on. If anything the monster sped up. The man on the horse behind them seemed to be catching up, which made Pájaro even wilder to outrun them.

Tightening her grip on the saddle horn and the coarse hair of Pájaro's mane, somehow she endured the wild, thundering chase. Suddenly Cole and his horse were racing right beside her.

"Let go!" a hard voice yelled. "I've got you."

Let go? Was he crazy?

Even when she felt Cole's powerful arm around her waist, her knees gripped Pájaro's flanks and she held on to the saddle horn for dear life. But her strength was nothing compared to Cole's, who yanked her off with seeming ease.

Her hands were ripped off the saddle horn, and for a fleeting horrible second she was airborne between the two flying horses. Pájaro veered to the left, and Cole pulled her in front of him on his horse.

"I've got you," Cole repeated over and over against her ear.

Panic tightened her stomach even as Cole pressed her tightly against his body as he reined in his mount.

"There. You're okay. You're safe," he muttered between harsh, rasping breaths as the thudding hooves slowed. "You're okay."

"I want down. I don't care if I have to walk all the way home, I don't want to ever ride a horse again."

"That's understandable," Cole said soothingly.

"This is all your fault! You shouldn't have chased me!"

"Then I'm sorry. I'm sorry," he said in that same calming tone.

Her daddy would never have been so reasonable. When she fell off a horse, he always hollered or used a stern voice to order her back on.

Cole dismounted and helped her down. Still, terrified, her heart continued to race as he circled her waist with his hands and lowered her from the horse. When he continued to hold her, she was so upset, she lacked the sense to push him away.

Her choked breaths erupted in burning gasps. Her knees were so wobbly she could barely stand, and her eyes burned with unshed tears. She was scared and too mortified for words.

"I—I probably look a mess."

"There now," he said. When he drew her close, she forgot her fear of him and clung. He was breathing hard and fast, just like she was. But he was holding her gently, caressing her and letting her cling.

"If you want to know, that scared the hell out of me, too," he said.

"I'm not scared."

"Then maybe you wouldn't mind loosening your hands just a little. Your fingernails are slicing little hunks out of my back."

"Oh… Of course…"

"You're so much braver than me," he whispered reassuringly. "If anything would have happened to you…"

A callused fingertip caressed her muddy cheek as he pulled a twig out of her dusty curls.

Never before had she been babied when she was afraid, and even though she knew she should push him away, she couldn't let go of him even when she stopped shaking. It was simply too pleasant to be soothed and comforted by someone so strong and solid…and nice.

She didn't care what Daddy had said about him. Cole Knight had saved her life, and he was so *nice* he wouldn't make her ever get on a horse again if she didn't want to. He had a gentle voice, and he smelled real good, of leather and spice and his own clean male sweat. He didn't seem to mind that she was so dirty.

Cole was a full head taller than she was, and the skin above the top buttons of his white shirt was way darker than hers, and his hand that slid against the bare skin of her spine where her blouse was ripped into shreds was way rougher than hers. He was old, much too old for her, probably at least twenty-two. Old, and too experienced with girls. Worst of all, her daddy hated him. Still, he was…nice.

Finally they both got their breath. She glanced up at him, thinking he'd release her. But he didn't, and somehow that was unbearably exciting.

She tilted her head a little to better study the mystery of Cole Knight, not that she could see much more than the sensual line of his mouth and his hard jawline. Still, he had a nice, kissable mouth. The mere thought of her lips against his caused a violent shiver to dart through her stomach.

How could she be attracted to him?

She wasn't. It was just that she'd nearly died. Cole had saved her. Maybe it was only natural to feel some temporary affectionate bond with a man who saved your life even if he was your natural born enemy.

Cole bent his head and stared down at her lips with the same scary, burning intensity she remembered from the thicket, only now, her heart skittered faster.

The wind was warm on her face, but his stillness and watchful silence as he held her caused butterflies to dance in her stomach. Her heart was beating so fast it felt like it might burst. She'd never come close to such a wild dark thrill as Cole Knight, never dreamed of it even.

Until this moment, in his arms, she'd been a child. Even before he lowered his face to hers, she lifted her lips and parted them, half-hoping he would be as bad as people said and steal a kiss from her.

Instead his mouth grazed her cheek so softly she could barely feel his breath. Still his gentle kiss left her aching. Without thinking, she wistfully traced a fingertip across her mouth. His eyes watched her, and maybe they dared her. Before she even knew what she was doing, her fingertip left her lips and traced the shape of his.

His mouth was hard and warm. Just touching him there had her body thrumming and sent heat through her like a lush wild wave. Her other hand inched up his wide chest and flexed around his neck. Then with an unfathomable yearning that bordered on pain, she pushed her innocent body into his, until her breasts were flat against his hard chest.

"Oh, God." He groaned, sucking her fingertip inside his lips for a moment before his black head dipped closer to hers. "You smell sweeter than the sweetest rose."

She stood on her tiptoes, hoping, aching for more.

It was worth nearly getting killed on a horse—well worth it—to be here like this with him.

The moment went on and on, endlessly. Just when he might have kissed her, a horse with Lizzy's daddy on its back thundered out of the brush. When a swarm of her relatives followed, shouting and cursing, Cole pushed her away from him.

Caesar pulled his stallion up in front of her, his face purple as dust whirled around them.

"Lizzy, what in the hell are you doing?" Caesar's horse thrashed closer. "Get away from that devil, girl!"

Uncle B.B.'s handsome face was as stern as her father's. Even Aunt Nanette and her sons, Bobby Joe and Sam, who were Lizzy's age, looked grim and unforgiving.

Lizzy lifted her chin and stepped in front of Cole to shield him from her family. Not that Cole was the type to cower behind a woman even for a second. He seized Lizzy's hand firmly in his and swung her along beside him.

Oh, how she liked his doing that. Standing beside him gave her a new confidence, and she squared her shoulders. To her surprise, her voice was quiet and level, a woman's voice. "Daddy…he saved my…"

Her father's bushy, amber eyebrows snapped together as he stared at her fingers knotted in Cole's. His lips thinned as he hunched forward in his saddle.

Lizzy recognized the signs his temper was on the rise and, removing her hand from Cole's, nervously rubbed her bare arms, which were sunburned and bloody with scratches. Tatters of her blouse fluttered against her exposed rib cage.

"Daddy, he didn't hurt me. He didn't tear my blouse. Mother—he saved my life."

As if mortified by Lizzy's conduct, Joanne looked away.

Caesar's blazing eyes remained fixed on Cole. "*You, boy!* Yes, Knight, I'm talking to *you! You* get the hell off my land!"

"You stole this land, Kemble. You and yours. You drove my brother away! But you can't bully me."

"*You* stay away from my daughter!"

Cole smiled lazily. "Well, I'd say that's more her choice than yours, wouldn't you?"

Cole's gaze softened as he regarded her, and Lizzy felt herself melting like hard chocolate on a hot stove.

"Of all the impudent—" To his men Caesar roared, "Boys, throw this damn trespasser off my land!"

"My land!" Cole snapped.

When Kinky Hernandez, Daddy's loyal foreman, along with half a dozen vaqueros, materialized out of the thicket, Cole's expression darkened. His low voice was hoarse, almost a growl, as he reached out and squeezed Lizzy's hand one last time. "Maybe you're not calling all the shots anymore, old man."

"He's right, Daddy! Leave him alone! I'm all grown up! You can't tell him or me what—"

"Get on your horse, boy—"

Cole whistled, and his big horse trotted up to him like a trick horse in a rodeo. Before he swung his long leg over his saddle, Cole glanced down at Lizzy with another hot look and a smile that cut off her breath and filled her with unbearable joy.

He tipped his hat to her. "See ya 'round, little girl," he said in that gentle tone that mocked her father and made butterflies fly in her stomach.

"See ya," she whispered, bringing her fingertips to her lips, unable to say more, not even goodbye.

Dismounting, her mother slipped up beside her. "If you're smart, you'll forget you ever met that no-good scoundrel," she said. "No telling what he would have done to you if we hadn't—"

He would have kissed me...maybe. The thought made Lizzy ache.

"He's the son of thieves and ingrates—troublemakers and gamblers, the whole lot," her father asserted. "I ran his no-good brother off a few years back when he threatened to sue me, and I'll do the same to this one—if you don't leave him the hell alone." He drew in a savage breath at Lizzy's dazed expression. "Take her back to the house, Joanne. Talk some sense into her."

Lizzy barely heard them. She was too busy watching Cole ride away, too busy wondering if she'd ever see him again.

Even when her mother took her by the arm, she turned her head, still watching the spot where she'd glimpsed the last of his broad shoulders.

"Forget him, girl. He's a Knight and you're a Kemble. He doesn't want you. He wants our land. And he'll do any-thing—he'll use you in any way—to get it. He wants the ranch—not you!"

Oh, if only, if only she'd listened.

BOOK ONE

Smart Cowboy Saying:

Letting a cat out of the bag is a lot easier than putting it back.
                              —Anonymous

One

Eleven years later
South Texas
The Golden Spurs Ranch

Pawing and snorting, hooves clattering on concrete, Domino exploded out of the barn as if a dozen of Satan's meanest horse flies had flown up straight from hell and stung him on his powerful rump.

"Whoa, boy! What's lit into you?"

It was late April. The last of the wildflowers sweetened the warm air that smelled of grass, cattle and horse.

Caesar Kemble leaned back in the saddle and pulled in on the leather reins. "You're mighty anxious for our morning ride, aren't you, fella? More anxious maybe than me. Which is saying one helluva lot."

A few yards away in front of the blazing sea of wildflowers that surrounded the vast ranch house, dozens of spurs sparkled like golden Christmas ornaments in the branches of the thin-leafed, thorny mesquite tree.

Caesar scowled. "Damnation!"

To some, the tree was a pretty sight against the glow of the sky this time of year, but he hated that tree. Hell, he should have cut the damn thing down years ago. Trouble was, the Spur Tree had stood there for more than a hundred years and was part of the ranch's tradition. Not that the spurs had anything to do with something as joyous as Christmas. They represented loss and pain and death and suffering—but courage, too. When a man or a woman left the ranch, their spurs were hung on the tree.

It had taken a lot from a lot of men to hold on to this ranch. His daddy's spurs hung there. So did Jack's, his oldest brother's.

The tree was more than a tree. It had a strange power, more power than most churches. Many a time Caesar had watched a vaquero who was feeling low come and stand in the shade of the Spur Tree for a spell.

Caesar lowered his Stetson to avoid looking at the tree. He was king of these million acres that bordered the Gulf of Mexico on the east and spread out to the west, at least he told himself he was. And he ruled with more authority than many true kings governed their kingdoms or generals commanded their armies. From his birth, there had always been people trying to steal his empire from him.

Jack, his older brother, had been the golden boy, the heir apparent, Daddy's favorite, until he'd broken his damn fool neck in a fall off a bronc in the dunes near the bay. Nobody had ever crossed Jack. Nobody had ever dared say maybe Jack should have had better sense than to ride off alone on an animal like that in the first place.

Coming to power after Jack's death, Caesar had become a helluva lot more spoiled than Jack had ever been. He was used to being obeyed—instantly. Just like Jack, he hated being crossed. Maybe that was the reason that thorny tree stabbed such a big hole in him. His enemies weren't just outsiders.

Children—you thought they were yours—until they com-

mitted the unforgivable crime of growing up and showing you different.

He'd had such grand plans for his children, especially Lizzy, his first, *his* favorite. She'd been born a mere hour before Mia. Oh, but how he'd reveled in that small victory.

Free-spirited, softhearted urchin that she was, Lizzy had attempted a defiant grin when she'd slung her spurs at the tree. Yes, the memory of her slim shaking fingers tossing those spurs before she'd left for New York was burned into his soul like a brand.

The crybaby in the family had dared to stand up to him. First by loving that no-good Cole. Then by leaving.

Nor would he soon forget the rainy afternoon of Mia's memorial service three months ago when he'd hung his second daughter's spurs on a branch beside Lizzy's while Mia's husband, Cole, yes, Cole, fifty vaqueros and five hundred mourners had watched. Joanne, who never cried, had sobbed beneath the Spur Tree, while Lizzy, who was ashamed of crying and too wary of Cole, had watched from the nursery window while she rocked Cole's fretful, month-old baby daughter, Vanilla. After the plane crash that had left Mia dead and Cole so dazed he couldn't remember people, not even his little daughter, Lizzy had come home for a while.

For the first time, she'd helped Caesar run things. She'd been surprisingly adept at dealing with the books and figures and computer work. Just when Caesar had begun to get used to having her around, she'd left again.

Yes, sir, the mere sight of that tree was enough to make his temple throb for hours. Ignoring the pain in his head, he jammed his own spurs against Domino's flank and yelled, "Giddyup, boy!"

Horse and rider flew until the Spur Tree was well behind them.

Both daughters had fallen for the same ruthless, vengeful man. Now they were gone for good—one dead and one simply foolish, irresponsible and ungrateful. And he still had Cole to put up with.

Lizzy had damn near gutted him alive by leaving Texas. As if his little girl, who could barely sit a horse, could make it in the cold cruel world without him pulling strings.

I'm all grown up now, Daddy. I'm twenty-three. I've got a college degree. It's time I left home.

You're a big grown-up crybaby, that's what you are.

He'd said that because she hated the fact that she had a soft heart and wept more than most girls her age. Then he'd gone for the guilt button.

You can't leave your daddy now that you're old enough to be of some use to him around here for a change—after all the trouble you've put him to raising you—

Lizzy, who'd been more trouble than most kids, had kissed him on the cheek as he'd turned away from her and said a tear-choked goodbye. *I know I'm a crybaby. I know I was trouble, but I have to grow up sometime. And, Daddy, you were trouble for me, too.*

If only she'd been born a boy. Maybe everything would have been different. Why couldn't she have been more like Sam, his nephew? Hell, for that matter, why couldn't Hawk and Walker have been more like Sam? Sam had loved the ranch so much he'd moved in with Caesar when he was ten and still lived on the ranch, although no longer in the main house.

His sons, Hawk and Walker, were a worthless pair for sure. He'd never been as close to them as he had to Lizzy. Neither of them gave a damn that he'd built an empire for them. Although they were as different as night and day, if he advised or corrected one of them, they stuck together. After Caesar's recent quarrel with Walker over the artist he'd chosen to do the murals depicting ranch life for the new Golden

Spurs museum, Walker had stormed out in a huff. Hawk had followed suit. Who knew where they were keeping themselves these days. And even the board had sided against Caesar, as well, and the painter had stayed.

Now Caesar had his sons' responsibilities to see about in addition to his own. They'd been in charge of organizing the grand opening of the museum and the celebration of the ranch's 140th anniversary, which were scheduled during Thanksgiving week.

The whole thing was ridiculous. Because of various crises the ranch had faced recently, the board had trumped up the museum and celebration to restore faith in the ranch's name. There would be tours, lectures, a big party and a horse and cattle auction during the week-long festivities. Caesar had thought the celebration was ill-timed to say the least, especially since it would be during a holiday, but he'd been outvoted by the family and the board.

If Hawk could just walk off, maybe Caesar could, too. Maybe it was time he did what the damn bunch wanted and turned the ranch over to the smart-ass suits in San Antonio. Let them come down and run the ranch and this ridiculous celebration they'd dreamed up.

But if he did, the ranch would go to hell in a handbasket. Sam, for all his talent, didn't look at the big picture. The board would diversify into more profitable business ventures than cattle. They wanted the Golden Spurs name on cattle equipment, hunting vehicles, leather goods and guns. They were interested in farming and government subsidies and environmental research, but not a single one of them was a real rancher.

"Times are changing faster than you are, Dad," Walker had yelled at him before he'd left.

The board—and even Sam—had made him furious when they'd told him the same thing.

But, hell, had any of them been named rancher of the decade?

Caesar had a cell phone clipped to his wide belt and a phone number in his breast pocket. The girl that went with the phone number was an exotic dancer in Houston. Last Saturday night he'd watched her perform a wanton cowgirl routine on stage with a real live horse.

She was nineteen—younger than his kids and nephews, but old enough, well worth the hour-long plane ride from the ranch. She had implants, big hair, fake eyelashes, but there was nothing fake about those legs of hers that went forever or the megawatt smile she'd flashed him or the promises she'd made with her big blue eyes and soft hands when she'd gotten off her horse and had done that lap dance wearing a silver, sequined cowboy hat and not much else.

He thought about Joanne and the cold, loveless years of their marriage. Maybe it was time he hung his own spurs on the tree and kicked his heels up, too. It had been a while since he'd had any fun with a woman.

He pulled Cherry's number out of his pocket and memorized it. Then he put it back and grabbed his cell phone. His body heated as he leaned forward and nudged Domino with his spurs.

The gelding's walk was a wonderful kind of tap dance. Domino was the best horse Caesar had ever had, a real genius.

It was only nine in the morning, and already the temperature had to be in the high eighties. But that wasn't why Caesar felt as hot as a billy goat in a pepper patch.

Should he call her? He stared up at the deep azure sky unmarked by clouds and felt beads of perspiration pop out on his forehead. It would get way hotter, and so would he.

He punched in her number, and a recording answered. He waited a few seconds, before he got up the nerve to stammer hello.

A woman's soft voice interrupted and said, "Hi there—"

His big hand shook so hard, he punched something and broke the connection. Then he cursed himself for being such an idiot.

Thank God he'd hung up on her. Gulping in a breath, he attached his cell phone to his belt again.

Heartbreak and grief and disillusionment were supposed to age a man, but Caesar knew he looked and felt much younger than he was. Maybe it was all the hard, physical work he'd done on top of the constant mental challenge of running his empire.

Not *his* empire…the family's…and it was a big family, not just his immediate family…a difficult family with more than a hundred members… Which meant there were a lot of calves sucking off a single tit, which meant the ranch had to produce.

The ranch had been established during the first half of the nineteenth century, turbulent years in south Texas. Land in Texas had gone from Spanish rule to Mexican rule to the Republic of Texas rule to American rule and then to Confederate and then back to Union rule in the space of sixty years. During this period of chaos, land titles and old Spanish land grants had been the original Caesar Kemble's for the asking…or as some said now…for the stealing.

Not that the ranch had been easy to defend even back then. Mexican bandits had marauded constantly and stolen cattle. Northern cattle markets had been uncertain. Drought had plagued the ranch, until a constant source of water had been found.

Through all the disasters, generation after generation had bought land and never sold. The challenges in modern times were no less formidable than they had been during frontier times.

The Golden Spurs was constantly being sued. Only Caesar's love for the land had sustained him through these rough and challenging times.

Not too long ago, a lowlife thief had trespassed on Golden Spurs property to steal gas pipes. He'd used a blowtorch to cut the pipe into movable sizes. The pipe had had a little gas in it and had exploded. The injured thief had sued for damages.

Caesar had blown his stack when the plaintiff's attorney had grilled him on the stand. As a result the thief had walked away with a huge settlement.

Ever since, his lawyers worked hard to keep him out of the courtroom. Under tough questioning, even after hours of tutoring from his attorneys, he couldn't be trusted not to speak the truth as he saw it.

So, he stuck to what he was good at—ranching. Cowboying had never been work to him. He'd given the ranch and his family his best years. Not that fifty was old. Still, it was an age when a man thought about his purpose and his legacy, especially when he'd made a helluva lot of sacrifices and had asked others to do the same—and they hadn't.

All his children and his nephews wanted was the money. Right now they were pestering him for a bigger share of the mineral revenues.

As if they needed more money. Oil money was like play money to them. They bought anything their hearts desired—mansions, foreign luxury cars, airplanes, jewels. The money had made even wimpy little Lizzy confident enough to strike out on her own and try to prove she was somebody.

What the hell was that all about? New York? Crazy town. Too far from Texas. Too many people. City people. None of them with a lick of sense. He'd talked himself blue in the face, trying to get her to come home, but she was as stubborn as her mother.

You were somebody the day you were born, girl. You were

born my daughter, he'd thundered yesterday morning when he'd called her.

But, Daddy, that doesn't mean anything.

It means a helluva lot to everybody in this state but you.

That's just the problem. I don't deserve to be famous or rich. I didn't do anything. And you…you're always saying I'm wimpy….

I never ever say that, baby girl.

You do! When you're mad, you do!

Then it's time you saddled up and changed all that.

I wasn't born to be a cowgirl. It's either born in you, or it's not. At least that's what you always said, Daddy.

Hell, was your smart-mouth kid throwing your own pearls of wisdom back in your face?

What the hell's wrong with you? You grew up on a ranch! I taught you everything I know!

Don't you see, this is why I had to go? I can't live my life—with you bossing me around all the time. With you trying to make me into something I'm not. I want to make you proud, Daddy—my own way! I'm not a cowgirl! And I don't want to be rich!

Well, you are. If you marry out of your class, he'll either want your land or your money!

Like Cole, Daddy? Is that what you're saying?

Yes, like Cole, damn it!

Not that Cole was quite as ornery as he'd been before he'd married Mia. Since the plane crash, he'd been annoyingly easy to deal with. There wasn't a more talented cowboy on the ranch. Most of the hands worked in pairs to trap the worst of the bulls that had gone wild, but, hell, just like Caesar's brother Jack, Cole rode alone. He understood bulls, understood their natures. He knew the exact second they'd turn and charge. And he was ready. Not that Caesar ever praised Cole aloud.

As for his own kids—not one of them appreciated what Caesar had done. Not one of them wanted to do an honest day's work. Of late he'd begun to wonder if any of what he'd thought was so damn important mattered at all.

Had all the years he'd spent teaching Lizzy about the ranch and the business been a waste? From the moment she'd been old enough to sit in his lap, he'd taken her with him on mornings when the work would be light. Many an afternoon he'd ridden home with her limp and sunburned in his arms.

He'd hired the best riding teachers, bought her the best rifles. He'd sent her to A&M and forced her to study ranch management, refusing to pay for another major, refusing to listen when she'd said she wanted to study English and be a writer.

Her brothers and sister had been jealous, wanting to know why he spent so much more time on her than the rest of them. The reason was a secret that Caesar hoped he'd take to his grave.

Lizzy wasn't doing all that great in Manhattan. As always, Caesar had his sources. His kids couldn't keep anything from him.

She'd be back. Damn it, she'd be back.

When Caesar was out of sight of the imposing white, red-roofed ranch house, he pulled in on the reins and let his gaze sweep the flat, coastal pasture. The sea of brown grasses seemed to stretch endlessly, but that was an illusion, as much in life is.

He frowned, not that anything was amiss with the brush-choked creek or the prickly pears along the barbed wire fence or the herd of cherry-red cattle grazing placidly. Or with the black buzzards lazing high above him on an updraft.

A red fox stood still in the distance, watching him warily from the edge of oak trees. Caesar breathed deeply, liking the rapport he felt with the wild fox as much as he liked the smell of the grass and the feel of the warm wind against this cheek. After a minute or two the fox scurried back into the thick brush.

Once Caesar had felt safe and confident here, safe in the knowledge that he was in charge, that his kingdom was secure for future generations. No more. The world was changing too fast and there was no one in the litter he trusted to follow him. The ranch and what it stood for was threatened on all sides.

Besides, the family wanting more of the oil and gas money, every month was a new challenge. The Golden Spurs wasn't just a ranch. It was a global, international, multifaceted, family-owned corporation that had diversified into other businesses, and it had to compete globally. The suits in San Antonio and an uppity, younger CEO, Leo Storm, constantly tried to dictate to Caesar.

Not that the problem that had been eating at him ever since Jim, his lawyer, had called last night was global. Another group of local jackals, distant kin of Cole Knight, had discovered yellowed copies of the same documents Shanghai had shoved in his face years ago, claiming the second generation of Kembles had stolen from their adopted sister. Just like Shanghai, the greedy bastards had had the effrontery to call his great-great-granddaddy a betraying thief and a liar, and, thereby, claim not only a large section of the ranch but all the royalties earned on the oil and gas the ranch had pumped out of the ground for the last sixty years—plus interest.

But what really galled Caesar was the fact that the lawsuit was the result of a tip from someone in the family, who'd leaked secret information from the ranch's sealed archives. Walker? Cole maybe?

Cole was at the center of a lot of the recent crises, and yet that very fact made Caesar suspect it was someone else. Cole had married himself square into the family. He was Vanilla's father. He owned considerable stock in the ranch.

If not Cole, it was damn sure somebody.

Who the hell was the traitor?

Caesar was mad, so spitting mad he had one of his headaches. His ancestors would have fought their enemies with six-shooters. But in these new days, killing came at a price. Thus, this was a problem for his high-priced, fast-talking attorneys.

"If anybody calls you, just refer them to me. Act reasonable," Jim had cautioned him just this morning.

"Act reasonable?" he'd thundered. Not that he'd said much more. Jim cost too much. Billable hours, he called it.

Since Jim had assured him there was nothing he could personally do about the problem except make it worse, Caesar had come out here to give himself an hour or two to settle down. He could have driven the pickup, but he preferred to ride Domino when he needed to get himself together. There was a purposefulness to the sounds of hooves on the ground and the movements of Domino through the grasses.

He was glad he'd escaped Joanne. One look at his face and she would have grilled him for sure. She saw too much. She wanted things from him he couldn't give. Besides, she could have been the one who leaked the information.

Funny, he hadn't realized how demanding she'd be when they'd struck their deal and he'd agreed to marry her. He'd thought she was meek and mild. He'd thought she'd be easier.

Caesar was staring across the thorny brush country beneath the hot blue sky when his phone rang. Expecting Jim again, he yanked it off his belt.

"Hi, there." The voice was soft and breathy, and before he could speak, his armpits were damp and his body burned as hot as a smoldering tree stump.

"How'd you get my number?"

"Caller ID, big boy. You called me a while ago. Am I right?" She giggled. "Now don't be shy. Guess what I've got on."

Not much, I reckon. He imagined Cherry in bed, young and voluptuous, naked, with her long white wavy hair flowing over soft pillows. He imagined her breasts and her pubic hair, which she'd told him she'd died hot pink.

"Hot pink…just for you," she'd teased. "And I shaved it into the shape of Texas. Wanna see?"

"Hi, there back," he said, feeling excited and yet easier, too. "So—what are you wearing, honey?"

"Not much more than a burning bush." She laughed.

He envisioned fluffy coils of hot pink hair shaped like Texas and laughed, too.

"I didn't think you would ever call me," she said.

A beep cut into their conversation. "Damn," he muttered. "Gotta get this."

"Don't hang up again," she pleaded.

"I'll call you right back."

"Bye. But don't be too long," she cooed, a pout in her voice. Then she blew him a kiss.

He clicked over to the incoming call, cursing the timing.

A strange, disembodied voice broke up amidst too much static.

He jammed the phone against his ear, trying to get the gist of what the man, if it was a man, was saying.

Two words stung him like poison. *Dead. Electra.*

His heart beat dully as he remembered a girl with long, pale curls lying underneath him, her hair looking like ripples of moonlight on a dark, boiling sea. More images were burned into his brain and heart. Electra running, her long legs so graceful. Electra smiling, her lavender eyes as intense as lasers. Electra, laughing, always laughing, Electra, wild, beautiful, incredible Electra, his love.

"She can't be dead," Caesar said. "Who is this?"

"Dead," the terrible voice confirmed.

Caesar gripped the phone tight in his fist. "Then how? Where? Who the hell are you?"

"Nicaragua," the caller said without identifying himself.

Electra was a damn fool. He'd told her to stay out of hot spots like that. She was nearly forty-eight, old enough to know better. Funny, when he thought of her, she was forever young. She always looked young when he saw her pictures in the newspapers.

Forty-eight was too young to die. How many times had he warned her about those countries? He'd even gone down to Columbia once and rescued her when she'd gotten herself kidnapped.

"How? How did she die?"

"Did you know she kept a journal…so she could write a book? An intimate tell-all?" Laughter.

Caesar remembered the way she used to sit up at night, writing with the lamp shining on her blond curls. Just like Lizzy. His head began to pound. His throat was so dry he couldn't swallow.

"She wasn't a virginal, saintly heroine, was she? Any more than you're the legendary, responsible Texas hero. Or the faithful husband. You ever wonder who else she slept with…or how you rate?"

Hell, yes, he'd wondered. "Bastard! Who the hell are you? What do you want?"

More laughter. "She wrote about you. Did you know that? Does Lizzy know who her real mother is?"

"What the hell do you want?"

"The world is full of shortages. You have so much."

"Who else have you told?"

"Nobody…*yet.*"

"How did she die?" he repeated.

Laughter. "In her bed."

"How?"

"The bitch got what she deserved. Other people you love will die, too, if you don't release more of the oil and gas revenues to the rightful shareholders."

So the bastard had killed her. Moreover, *the lowlife wanted money. Everybody always wanted money.*

Caesar had no doubt he was talking to the traitor.

A warrior's scream rose inside him, like the screams of cattle in a burning barn. He must have made some sound because vultures exploded out of nearby oak tree and circled slowly, as if he were a stricken creature.

"You won't be around forever, old man. When you're gone, whatever will happen to Lizzy?"

Caesar cursed. Then pain, the likes of which he'd never felt before, burst inside his head. His right hand lost its grip on the leather reins, and he cried out.

The pain subsided as quickly as it had come, as it always did. Other than feeling curiously empty as if a part of himself was gone, he felt all right. It was nothing, he told himself. Nothing. He'd had headaches all his life. He was too young for it to be anything serious. Just in case, he pulled an aspirin out of his pocket and chewed it, swallowing the bitter taste.

"Who are you? Who the hell gave you this number?"

Laughter. Peals of it. Then the line went dead.

He had no idea how long he sat in the saddle thinking about Electra, wondering what had happened to her, before the phone rang again. Quickly he answered it.

"Hi there. I got worried when you didn't call right back." Cherry's voice was soft and friendly, but he couldn't talk, couldn't say anything.

"Hey, big boy, are you there? Are you okay?"

Caesar cleared his throat and tried to focus. "I can't talk right now."

"I'm sorry." She sounded genuinely sympathetic. "So, do you want to get together?"

He didn't answer. That he was even considering cheating on Joanne with a woman like Cherry had to be a sign that the tremendous strain he'd been under was taking its toll.

"I don't think that's a very good idea," he said. "Look, I shouldn't have called you—"

"You won't be sorry," her low, sultry voice promised. "I swear. I think this is fate. Your name starts with C—my name starts with C. I looked up your birthday. You're a Taurus and I'm an Aquarius."

What the hell did that have to do with anything?

"I'm free…late, every single night," she whispered, "after I finish dancing. We could unwind…after a long day. I'm off all day Sunday, and I never go to church. Get your cowboy son-in-law or his pilot to fly you up here again."

"You're awful sure of yourself."

"*You* called *me,*" she said.

He remembered Electra and his wild passion for her that had lasted even until now. Sorrow, not lust, gripped his heart.

"You called me back—twice. Don't chase, girl. If I want you, I'll do the chasin'. Frankly, I'm not in the mood."

"Ohhhh!" She sucked in a breath. "Go to hell. Go straight to hell."

When she slammed the phone down so hard she made his ear pop.

She was a pistol.

A woman like her could take a man's mind off his worries. His sorrows…

All things considered, he had half a mind to call her back.

Two

Six months later
Manhattan,
Upper West Side

The cell phone rang just as Lizzy made it up the concrete stairs outside her brownstone with baby Vanilla. Golden leaves fluttered on the trees that lined her street. Not that she paid much attention to the afternoon's beauty.

She was too preoccupied at her front door as she buzzed Bryce, her present live-in, who didn't answer. When he didn't, it was panic time.

Bouncing her fidgety niece up and down instead of searching for the phone, Lizzy hit the buzzer again as waves of uneasiness washed over her. Her brother, Walker, was visiting them. Why wasn't he home?

Lizzy hated the way she overreacted to everything, but when Bryce didn't answer, butterflies whirled in her stomach. Not good butterflies, either.

Lizzy had been trying to make her mark in Manhattan for over five years. She'd started out as a cat- and dog-sitter and then a nanny. Next she'd read manuscripts for her landlord, who was a publisher. But when she'd passed on a couple of shallow novels that had turned out to be bestsellers, her landlord had suggested that she stick with cats and dogs and children. Lizzy was in television production at the moment, but like every other job she'd had here, she wasn't as good at it as she was at dog-sitting. Her boss, Nell, had said, "You didn't really acquire…an…er…broadening…education on the university level, now did you? Besides that, you don't get New York or our audience."

Lizzy's love life hadn't been a roaring success, either, at least not until Bryce. Yes, she had high hopes for Bryce— he was part of her fantasy. A successful woman, at least a woman with a drop of Texas blood in her, always had a man to share her success with. Okay, so for her, the right man had come before the right career.

Lizzy's fantasy was also to be a beautifully groomed, kick-ass career girl, somebody with short, smooth, glossy black hair instead of long, platinum corkscrew curls. She wanted to be a real live heroine with a fantastic wardrobe; a fighter, who might get knocked down, but who could always joke about life's little upsets with snappy, sexy one-liners.

Lizzy most certainly did not want to be somebody who didn't even get jokes half the time, even dumb blond jokes, or somebody who was tongue-tied, shy, repressed and riddled with self-doubt. Most of all she did not want to be a crybaby.

Heck, maybe she should see a shrink again, but that would be admitting she was still a mess.

The phone in her purse stopped ringing.

Love means letting go of fear.

Why had that particular pearl from some dumb pop-psychology book she'd read on the sly sprung into her mind at this exact second? Was it true? If it was, had she ever really been in love?

She'd been crazy-lovesick over Cole, but there had been a darkness in him she couldn't reach. And that had scared her. Maybe that's why she'd finally let Daddy convince her to break up with him. No, the real reason was he was pure country, and since she was no good at any of that, she was determined to be a big-city career girl—not to mention the fact that all Cole'd ever really wanted was a piece of the Golden Spurs.

The phone in her purse rang again and each ring got louder. This time she managed to get the thing out and up to her ear—no easy accomplishment since she was juggling the baby on her hip, her briefcase on one shoulder, a diaper bag as well as her purse on the other, while holding her door keys and buzzing Bryce, too.

"Did I call at a bad time?" her mom asked in a faint, lifeless voice as Lizzy got the big doors unlocked.

"G-great time, Mom," she lied, looking up at the staircase that vanished into the darkness long before it even reached the third floor where she lived.

"How's Vanilla?" her mother asked softly.

Lizzy could hear her mother's white fantailed pigeons cooing in the background, which meant her mother must be in their coop, tending to them. She knew her mom had more on her mind than the baby, but the baby was a safe topic. Hopefully Mom wasn't going to rehash her dad's betrayal and the impending divorce and settlement.

What had gotten into Daddy six months ago?

Sex. Pure raw sex. Bryce had said this in that definitive, annoying know-it-all, male tone that drove her crazy and made her doubt herself—and him—in the wee hours of the night.

Men want more sexual partners than women. Everybody knows that, honey. And more juice…

More sexual partners? Juice? I, for one, didn't know that. Is that what you want, Bryce?

Lizzy hated being caught in the middle of her parents. In

the past she'd never been close to her mother, who used to be stern and strict and so in control. Now her mother called her in the afternoons, and her father called her every morning, each wanting *her* to reassure *them*.

This morning her father had called before her alarm had even gone off, and he'd sounded anxious.

"You have to come home, damn it."

And really be caught in the middle? No, thank you. "I was just there. I'm still playing catch-up. I do have a life here, you know."

"If something happens, promise you'll come home."

He was anxious. "Daddy, what's wrong?"

"Just promise, damn it."

Both her parents wanted her home. They were living on separate floors of the house and driving each other crazy. They didn't understand about her impossible job at the television station or about Bryce, who wanted her all to himself.

"Bring him to the ranch," her father had bellowed.

Not yet. Not yet. Guys changed when they realized who she was.

When they realized how rich she was.

"Bring him to the museum opening," her father had insisted.

In less than a month the Golden Spurs would celebrate its birth with the opening of a ranch museum. Her parents along with Walker, who'd been the ranch archivist, had hired designers, artists and a sculptor. Before Daddy had quarreled with Walker and Walker had quit, her parents had worked on the project together. Since Cherry had entered the picture, her mother had done most of the work on the museum opening alone.

While the museum and the celebration weren't generating the headlines the board would have liked, her daddy's six-month affair with Cherry and her parents' divorce were the talk of Texas. As soon as possible, her father, a high-profile rancher, who'd once seemed so sane and stolid and respectable—if overbearing—would be free to marry Cherry Lane, the stripper he'd met in a saloon in Houston where he'd gone with other cowboys for a night's entertainment.

"You'll love Cherry when you get to know her," her father had actually had the gall to say once.

Right. A girl who'd tipsily showed a reporter her big diamond ring on her twentieth birthday and bragged she'd bleached her pubic hair silver in anticipation of her honeymoon, saying, "I want to be virginal for him," couldn't be all bad.

Lizzy hoped the only thing she and Cherry had in common was the pale color of their hair. If Cherry quit coloring hers, they wouldn't even have that.

Lizzy wasn't beautiful, or at least she didn't think she was. Nor did she enhance her perfectly proportioned features with layers of heavy makeup and bright red lipstick the way Cherry did. People never said she was pretty. What they said was she had an open, friendly face.

Naturally slim, Lizzy would probably stay that way since she ate mostly vegetables—it broke her heart to think of killing animals for food. She also ran in the park every morning before work because she missed grass and trees more than she wanted to admit. Unlike Cherry, she had small breasts with no plans of enhancing them even if Bryce had made a comment or two.

She knew she should cut her long pale curly hair and attempt a more sophisticated style, but the shorter she cut it, the frizzier it got. So she still tied it back in her cowgirl ponytail.

Of course, she'd intended to learn about fashion when she came to the city. But because she loved roaming the streets of New York on Saturday, she shopped for her clothes at fairs and secondhand shops instead. Thus, with her wild hair and mismatched outfits, she looked more like a gypsy than the sleek career woman of her fantasy.

"How's Vanilla?" her mother repeated in a louder voice, interrupting Lizzy's thoughts.

"Sorry, Mom. My mind was somewhere else." She patted Vanilla's diaper. "Your granddaughter is as heavy as a sack of wriggling lead!" Lizzy hiked up her long blue skirt and started up the stairs.

"She made me laugh. I shouldn't have let you take her—"

"You were too tired, what with everything that's been going on… You needed the rest."

"I just laze around and spend way too much time with the hatchlings. I'm always missing meetings that have to do with the museum."

"It's called depression, Mom." Lizzy's behavior had been similar to her mother's when she'd first come to the city. "You should see someone…talk to someone."

"My little birds are so darling. I can't get packed or meet with the museum sculptor about doing a bust of your uncle Jack. I can't do…" Her voice faltered.

"You need to talk to somebody."

"This whole thing—I—I don't know what's wrong with me. All I seem to do is spend time with my gentle birds. They're so angelic and lovely."

No use to tell her mother what to do. Her mother never listened any more than Lizzy listened when people told her what to do. Her mother hadn't asked about Walker, so Lizzy didn't mention him.

Lizzy paused on the first landing. Mia's pregnancy and sudden, rather mysterious marriage to Cole, followed by her tragic death nine months ago that none of them had been able to handle, had been the beginning of a landslide of terrible events. Was it any wonder her mother couldn't face moving out of the house where she'd raised her family to let someone like Cherry move in?

"How can a ten-month-old feel heavier than a brick?" Lizzy said aimlessly.

"Give my plump little pumpkin head a kiss—"

"Don't you dare call her that. Besides I'm panting too hard to talk and climb and kiss her at the same time."

"Where's Bryce?"

Her heart thumped. She thought, *Good question.* She said, "He should be home any minute."

By the time Lizzy reached the third floor of the brownstone with Vanilla, she was truly breathless. Something in her mother's voice made Lizzy's too-imaginative mind whirl with the sinking feeling that something really was wrong between Bryce and herself.

Fool that she was, Lizzy had told her mother having the baby here for a month would be fun. Too bad she hadn't asked Bryce first. Vanilla had been here a week, and he was sick of her.

Vanilla clapped when she saw the tall oak door to their apartment. Her latest trick was to clap when she was pleased. Usually Lizzy clapped and laughed, too. It was one of their games. As Lizzy fumbled for her keys, Vanilla quit clapping and began to squirm.

"Mom, did you call me for a special reason?"

"No…."

"Everything's okay?"

The pigeons cooed in the background. Her mom said, "It's just the waiting—"

"You'll be fine. The worst is over."

"But I have to leave my home."

"It's hard, I know, but you'll adjust. You have to. We all do. I love you, Mom."

"I wish you'd come home."

Guilt stabbed Lizzy. "I will, when I bring Vanilla back. Right now it's pretty hectic at work. My boss, Nell, keeps the pressure on. I can't seem to do anything right. She keeps pulling my stories."

"Quit. You don't have to work."

And do what? Lizzy bit her lips and swallowed as she remembered Nell telling her nearly the same thing only this morning. Lizzy swallowed again. "Look, I'll call you—"

"No, I'll be fine. You don't need to call."

Feeling even guiltier, Lizzy said goodbye. When she pushed the door of her apartment open, Vanilla's big blue eyes widened, and the baby clapped again. Lizzy kissed her forehead and dark curls. "Gran's missing you. That big ol' rambling ranch house is mighty lonely without you and Dad and Mia…and me, I bet."

Lizzy nuzzled Vanilla's soft hair. Even after a long day at day care, Vanilla smelled baby sweet.

Cole's daughter.

Don't think about him or how changed he is.

Inside the gloom, Lizzy's gaze fixed on the card sitting on the table. On the cover was a leather-clad girl with black wings, standing in a doorway with the words *Dark Entry* above it. Lizzy frowned.

How had that thing gotten back into her house, anyway?

At the office earlier, when Nell had challenged her research—and chewed her out in front of everyone when she'd been unable to defend it to Nell's satisfaction—Lizzy had wanted nothing more than to run home and lie down or play with Vanilla. Suddenly Lizzy felt worse to be here at home.

Dark Entry? Maybe she was overreacting. This was simply an invitation to a Halloween party. Probably something Bryce wanted to go to and she didn't, a thing to be discarded like before. But just looking at it gave her that nagging feeling that she was caught in some strange force field and trouble was brewing.

Swimming in a pool of red light, the picture of the girl in the bondage costume with the black wings seemed to glow like an evil spirit. For no reason she remembered that Bryce had bought her a black teddy, boots, handcuffs, and a whip— gifts she'd stuffed into plastic containers with the rest of the suggestive lingerie he'd given her and stored at the very top of her closet.

Lizzy clutched Vanilla tighter. *Don't think about any of it. You're too tired. Nine hours in the television station.*

Only to have Nell humiliate her and cancel her story. Lizzy needed to work tonight. But how? The baby was turning out to be more effort than Lizzy had imagined when she'd offered to give her mother a break.

And Walker? Why was her brother in town anyway, acting like he was ashamed every time she asked him what exactly his quarrel with Daddy was about? All week she wondered why her brother had chosen this week, of all the confusing weeks in her life, to finally visit her.

Work had been tough lately, and she and Bryce had been at their worst. Bryce, who never watched television, had sullenly slumped in his chair every night, watching sitcoms he normally despised, ignoring everybody.

She dropped her briefcase, the diaper bag and her purse onto the oak floor in the entryway. Lizzy drew a breath, but the air in the apartment felt dense and stifling.

Lizzy didn't like the new little fears tearing at her any more than she liked thinking about her mom. Lizzy blamed herself for what had happened to her parents. If she hadn't abandoned them in her quest for a perfect life here, if she'd taken an interest in all Daddy had tried to teach her, maybe they wouldn't be on the verge of divorce.

She frowned. Her life here *was* perfect. Or rather it was

going to be—so she told herself every morning when she lay awake beside Bryce, their bodies apart on their separate sides of the big bed. She would lie there, doing her affirmations, listening to the city sounds outside her window. After the Texas quiet, even noises like sirens and the clatter of garbage trucks were delightful to Lizzy because they reminded her she was really here—in New York.

She'd escaped. She had a glamorous exciting life and the perfect man to share it with.

Why couldn't she forget about the invitation? Because she didn't understand what it could be doing there—again—on top of a week's worth of mail on her small doorside table.

The same identical invitation had come last week. It was for a Halloween party tomorrow night. She hadn't known the person who'd sent it, so she'd torn it up without showing it to Bryce. And what was wrong with that?

Okay, so the thing had been addressed to Bryce, too. But she was the one who did her mail promptly while he left his for months. People had to call him, to demand money or ask him if he was coming to some event, before he would fly at his stack, agitated and accusatory that he had to deal with it. Someone had obviously called him about the invitation and re-sent the thing.

No way was she going to a party like that!

Lizzy felt a fresh stab of guilt as she considered Bryce. The party-giver must be a friend of his. Was Bryce now sulking as he had after she'd told him about the baby?

"Your family," he'd said in a tone of complaint when she'd called from Texas to tell him she was bringing Vanilla back with her.

"Yes, my family," she'd agreed. "There's nothing I can do about them."

"You were down there for two months after Mia died."

"When you meet them you'll understand."

But would he? She'd been attracted to Bryce because he was so different than they were. He didn't have to dominate everybody in a room. Average in both height and build, he was quiet, reserved and contained. He didn't make demands on her all the time.

Except about the lingerie.

Lizzy drew more quick breaths as Vanilla began to clap excitedly. The invitation, like the lingerie stacked in containers in her closet, threatened Lizzy in some strange way.

She grabbed it, intending to wad it up, only to have Vanilla reach for it, too, squealing delightedly as she began to nibble on it and bat her long lashes up at her aunt. Tug-of-war was a favorite game of hers and Cole's.

Cole... Lizzy's heart thumped in her throat again as she remembered how changed he seemed when she'd last been home. Surprisingly, he and Daddy were actually working together without much of their former friction. Cole had even ridden along with her and her father when her dad had shown her the new state-of-the-art hunting camps and bragged about their corporate clients. Her dad had credited Cole with obtaining the leases.

"No, darling," Lizzy admonished gently, prying the card from her tiny fingers. "Nasty. Garbage." She chucked the wet invitation into the trash can even as she was swept with a guilty feeling for doing so.

Again, she told herself that she and Bryce were perfect together. Bryce was from the country. She was from the country, but they'd both craved more excitement, so they'd escaped to *the city*.

He was from Indiana, a dull farm where nothing ever happened. She was from a huge ranch in south Texas with a fabled history that was like a kingdom unto itself where too much happened. Like all kingdoms, its challenges ruled its owners more than the owners ran the kingdom.

People like her father and mother and Cole were obsessed with land, with its being *more* than land; obsessed with duties and loyalties to the land and to each other. Lizzy knew that somehow the land had ruined her parents' lives and maybe her sister's. She was terrified it would consume her, too.

She hoped New York was far enough away for her to be safe from its pull. She loved being able to lose herself in crowds. Here, she could be a nobody or a somebody. Here, nobody was jealous of her. She could be whatever she wanted to be. She wasn't destined to be anything. Here, the name, Kemble, meant nothing.

Holding the baby, who was watching her face expectantly, Lizzy sagged still a moment longer against the wall in her entryway. Her weary gaze took in the cardboard books, stuffed rattles and bottles scattered about the floor of the living room and second bedroom, as well as her own closed bedroom door.

Vanilla smiled at Lizzy and clapped her hands together again to divert her.

"You're glad to be home, aren't you, precious? You want to get down and crawl."

Lizzy cuddled her closer and brought her cheek against the baby's. How was it that Vanilla, her precious little niece, was already such a true little soul mate? Why couldn't Bryce just enjoy her, too?

"But why didn't you ask me?" Bryce had said during that phone call she'd made from Texas to tell him her baby-sitting plans.

"Because I knew you'd understand. Mother can't face the divorce. She needs to pack. It's only for a month."

"A baby—for a whole damn month! Why can't her father... What the hell's his name?"

"Cole... Knight..."

"Right. Why can't Knight do his part for once?"

"I told you...he was hurt in the plane crash. He's not himself— He doesn't remember...her." She'd hated the way her throat had closed when she tried to talk about Cole. "This is something I have to do."

"Well, maybe I don't!" Bryce had banged the phone down.

She'd been terrified until he'd called back and apologized. "It's just that I wanted you all to myself—like before. Like the first night."

Like the first night. She was embarrassed by that memory. Until that night she hadn't known how lonely she'd been away from home, nor how desperate she'd felt to connect with someone...anyone. She'd been like a cat in heat, wanting Bryce. Not that she'd given into her need that first night.

But he'd known. "You want it bad, baby. As bad as I do," he'd said as they reached the front door to her apartment building. "Let me come up."

Later, several weeks later, when she'd finally let him, she'd wanted him with the same ferocity as that first night. She'd let him make love to her again and again, seeking something from his male body, warmth, love, a sense of belonging...something to make her feel she belonged here...and yet...

She remembered getting up alone afterward, going to the window, staring out into the night for hours, listening to the city that never slept, still wanting...something...as she'd listened to him snore. When he'd awakened that morning, he'd wanted her again, and she'd given herself too enthusiastically, wanting to prove—what? That it had all meant something? That he really was as perfect as she wanted to believe?

Suddenly something heavy crashed in her bedroom.

Bryce? Had he ignored the buzzer when she'd rung from the street? Hadn't he heard her come into the apartment? Why hadn't he come out?

Frowning, she walked to her bedroom door and pushed it open.

His eyes wide and startled looking, Bryce gaped at her from the middle of her bedroom. Behind him two big black suitcases lay open on top of her new glittery, orange Indian bedspread. Empty plastic containers that had previously held Bryce's ties and cuff links, along with all that lingerie that she'd stored on her highest shelves, littered her Oriental carpet.

She gasped. When her gaze flew to a black garter belt lying by the bed, Bryce, who was usually calm, tensed. Hostile, bright gray eyes flicked over the baby. Then he flushed and sighed heavily, clamping his lips shut determined to say nothing. She drew in a breath.

So, it was up to her, she who could never speak up at meetings. Her throat went dry, and the first words seemed to stick there. "Y—you're not leaving—"

"Don't start in on me— Look, I'm sorry— I hoped to avoid this—"

So, it was over. Just like that.

The realization slammed through her before she stopped all thought. Vaguely she was aware of Vanilla clinging even as the baby's bottom lip swelled in infantile disdain for this tense, cruel giant.

If only she, Lizzy, could feel such instinctive disdain at Bryce's betrayal, but she felt—if you could call it feeling—only paralyzing numbness and inadequacy. He was abandoning her just as her father had abandoned her mother.

Lizzy was bleeding to death, only the blood was invisible. Their perfect life together was over. She had tried so hard. *Too hard maybe.*

"Where are you going?" she finally whispered, not wanting to have this conversation in front of the baby.

Bryce was dragging his designer Italian suits out of her closet. For no reason at all she saw Cole, his face white, beneath a brilliant azure sky on that awful long-ago afternoon when she'd broken up with him.

Cole didn't matter.

Bryce stared at her and the baby and then hurled his suits on the floor with such violence Vanilla hid her face against Lizzy's throat. When the baby peeped at him again, her bottom lip was huge and her big blue eyes suspicious.

"Is it the baby?" Lizzy whispered.

Bryce slammed the lid of his suitcase down.

"It's only half-full," she said when he made no answer.

Suitcase latches clicked. "Do you think I can pack— *now? With you here?*"

She kept her voice low so as not to frighten Vanilla. "Is it because I don't want to go to the party? Because I don't dress sexy…because I don't wear that…that lingerie?"

When Vanilla began to whimper, Lizzy soothed her. "It's all right, darling. It's all right." She swayed back and forth with the baby resting on her hip.

"Hell, yes, it's the party. You tore up the first invitation. It's a lot of things." He glared. "Do I have to spell it out for you?"

Like the beginning of all relationships, theirs had been mysterious and wonderful, so wonderful they hadn't asked questions. They'd met in a bar. She'd been out with girlfriends one Thursday night. Everybody had been talking to everybody, but the place had been loud and crowded, and Lizzy, who wasn't any better in crowds than she was at business meetings at work, hadn't felt like talking to anybody.

Until she'd noticed Bryce watching her.

He'd joined their table. He'd been as cool and confident

as she'd been riddled with self-doubt. Her friend Amanda had known one of his friends from Princeton. Then somebody had said something funny. Bryce and she had both laughed when nobody else had—as if it were their own private joke. And she didn't get jokes usually.

He'd bought her a drink. Their hands had touched accidentally. She'd felt a spark. He'd gone still at the exact moment she'd yanked her hand from his.

When relationships end, women no longer want the mystery. They want answers. Why is that?

Nothing was ending. This was a mistake. If they could only talk or have sex, they would sort it all out. But they hadn't had sex. Not for a while.

She stared at the red tie dripping from his closed suitcase. "I—I want to know what's wrong."

"When we met, you were so exciting. You even dressed differently."

"And now I'm boring?"

His gray eyes drilled Vanilla. "I'm going to that party—alone."

"Because I'm boring?"

"You never wanted to talk about it before. Why now?"

"When the baby leaves— When Walker leaves—"

"I thought you were wild…free…exciting. But you have this whole family thing."

"They're in Texas."

"They call all the time. Not to mention half your tribe is living with us."

"So—you think I'm boring—in bed and out of it." Careful to keep her voice low, she stroked the baby's hair.

"Don't make me say things I don't want to say." He looked past her. "I'll come back for my things later—when you're calmer."

"I am calm." She measured out the words very carefully,

her eyes glued to the point of the red tie sticking out of his suitcase.

"But your eyes are wild."

You said you wanted wild.

From the bed he picked up a dark rectangular object about the size of a book. Carrying his black suitcase with the red tie flapping, he strode toward her only to stop and place the rectangular object on the dresser next to where she was standing. "I found this in your brother's things."

"You went through Walker's things?"

"I was packing, looking for my stuff stored in his bedroom." He stopped. "Oh…" His eyes changed, and he let the word hang ominously. "Nell called, too." His smug expression filled her with dread.

She froze. "Nell?"

"I told her I wouldn't be here to give you her message, so she called back and left a voice mail for you." He swallowed.

"You listened to it, didn't you? You're leaving me, and you listened to *my*—"

"Maybe now isn't the time to listen to her message."

"What does that mean?"

"Wait until you've had a good night's sleep. That's all. Don't watch that video, either…not until you're feeling stronger."

"Video?" Too much was being thrown at her. Vaguely Lizzy realized the black rectangular object he'd placed on the dresser was a VCR tape.

"I'm strong!"

Bryce stalked past her with his bags, his long legs carrying him through the apartment to the entryway, out the door. When his footsteps thudded down the stairs, Vanilla looked at her, a tentative smile beginning at the edges of her cherubic mouth. Then the doors three floors below boomed shut behind him, and Vanilla clapped.

"Oh, Vanilla, you are a little rascal," she said numbly.

Vanilla smiled, and Lizzy tried to smile, too, but her lips were quivering too much.

"I'm not a weak, softhearted wimp." Lizzy reached for the cordless phone on the dresser, intending to listen to her voice mail tonight. She could take anything this city and Nell could dish out. She could. Gently she set Vanilla down and got her a container and a lid for her to play with.

Lizzy had six messages. Nell's was the last. It was short and sweet; well, not sweet.

"I'm sorry to do this over the phone—Liz. I should have told you today. I meant to." A drumbeat pounded in Lizzy's throat. "I should have told you before you went to Texas. It just isn't working out... You're too young. Your viewpoint is too softhearted and naive for this city. You don't do the kinds of stories we do. Your research is sloppy."

"What? What?"

Nell's voice hadn't stopped, but Lizzy's mind went blank. When she could think again Nell's brisk voice was saying, "...budgets cuts. I have to let you go. Your severance check will be ready first thing tomorrow. My assistant put your things in boxes. You need to turn in your security badge."

"What? Boxes! No! No..."

Lizzy listened to the message a second time, but that only made the horrible words cut deeper.

Slowly she hung up the phone and picked up the videotape and turned it over in her hands. Vanilla had abandoned the container and lid and had crawled into the living room, over to her green couch. Pulling herself up and patting the cushions, she looked over at Aunt Lizzy, waiting to be congratulated on her accomplishment.

Aunt Lizzy was probably white as a sheet. "Darling, that's wonderfu—" Her voice broke. Babies were so self-confident when they faced their challenges. They didn't quit.

Lizzy was shaking too hard to speak. Still holding the video-tape, she gulped in a breath. Then she went to the couch and sank down beside Vanilla, hoping to draw strength from her.

"Darling, darling, what would I do if I didn't have you?"

Blue eyes sparkling, Vanilla grinned at her impishly.

Lizzy fought back hot wet tears. She wasn't going to cry, and she wasn't going to call home, either, no matter how much she suddenly wanted to talk to her mother—even though Mother had never understood her.

Nobody could know the terrible turn her life had taken. Nobody.

Lizzy wasn't going home to Texas in defeat. Maybe her perfect life was unraveling, but she wasn't going home. She'd get her job back and she'd get Bryce back, too. It was all a mistake. A terrible mistake. All she needed was a plan. Affirmations. She'd do some affirmations.

Downstairs the big doors banged, and she heard the fa-miliar tread of boots on the stairs.

Walker! She'd forgotten about him.

The video!

Her brother was loping up the stairs two at a time as she shoved the tape underneath the cushions of her couch.

Wiping her eyes with the back of her hands, she pulled Vanilla into her lap and fought to look calm and composed.

By the time Walker entered the apartment and called to her, she and the baby were playing an innocent game of patty-cake.

"How's it going, Little Lizzy?"

"F-fine." She swallowed.

Their eyes met, and she knew he knew something was wrong.

Walker could read souls.

He waited for her to say something. When she didn't, he reached for the baby, who started clapping.

Then all he said to Lizzy was, "What's for supper?"

Three

Houston, Texas
Caesar

"Hi there." Cherry's lazy velvet voice caressed Caesar across twenty feet of darkness, but it was as if she reached out and circled his cock with her hand and lowered her head. His groin got as hot as if her talented tongue was already wetting him there.

Not that he was in the mood for sex or her lies. Hell, he'd just flown in from a board meeting in San Antonio. His temples ached with tension. He'd gone to the meeting hoping to iron out the details of the Golden Spurs Ranch Museum opening and the following celebration.

Only Joanne had been there. She'd asked the board to tell him to break up with Cherry or step down. She'd listed various ranch crises and how little he'd done for the ranch lately and how much she'd done. And how much Cole Knight had done as well—damn his rotten soul!

"You have no right to air our dirty laundry to the board," he'd growled when she'd gone on and on about Knight.

"My children own stock in the ranch," she'd said.

"She has no right to be here," he'd yelled at the board, pointing toward Joanne.

Then Leo, the CEO stood up. "I invited her here."

"Who is she—who are you, *any* of you—to tell me what to do?"

"I said, 'Hey, there…'" Cherry's warm, silky voice floated to him again.

"Sorry." He rubbed his aching temples. "My mind's a million miles away."

Break up with her? In a week?

He was furious at the board, at Joanne, at himself, and at Cherry. And he had a hard-on.

So what else was new?

Lately he hadn't thought about Cherry much when he wasn't with her. Why was that? But when he was with her, she consumed him.

Lying naked beside her, he loved her female scent and the dark color of her nipples. He loved the way they lay together afterward, drinking Scotch from the same bottle. The only reason he'd agreed to marry her was that she'd said she wouldn't let him screw her anymore if he didn't. When she'd stuck to her guns, he'd figured he'd get out of the bargain somehow. Then he'd given her a great big diamond and a credit card at her twentieth birthday party to appease her. Ever since he'd felt like his life was hurtling toward some fatal destiny that he was powerless to avoid.

He slammed the door of her Houston studio apartment and stomped toward her.

"Want me to give you some special candy, lover buver?" she whispered.

His groin tightened. Special candy was their secret code.

Caesar flushed as he pitched the wad of credit card bills onto the low table near the bed.

"Did you bring me a present?" she cooed.

He looked around, pained. Sequined costumes, thong panties and bras dripped from chairs. T-shirts and dirty jeans littered the stained, turquoise shag carpet. Lingering in the closed room was a stale smell that he associated with airless rooms and unwashed sheets after too much sex.

Joanne was a neat freak. He used to hate the way she hung up each garment as she took it off—even when he was on fire to have her—and the way she stripped the sheets off the bed seconds after he came.

Caesar's head ached. He'd taken more Tylenol than he should've today, but the tablets weren't cutting it. The pill bottle in his glove compartment was running on empty. He felt old today, way older than fifty. Everybody told him, at least those who dared, that he was looking bad, that Cherry was dragging him down.

He'd given Cherry lots of presents because her joy in receiving them had always been rapturous. For her, presents were an aphrodisiac.

When he spoke, all he could manage was a rough, semiharsh whisper that didn't sound much like himself. "You've been buying yourself quite a few presents lately. More than I can afford."

She laughed. "Oh, is that all that's eatin' you, big daddy? You're rich. I'm poor."

"Land rich. Cash poor."

"If it was the other way around, I'd give you the moon."

Would she? Would she even look at him twice?

"Relax, big daddy. Relax." She sounded young and spoiled and very self-confident.

He knew their affair was as ridiculous as everybody said it was. When he'd agreed to marry her, he'd made himself the laughingstock of the state. Joanne's lawyers were having a field day, and still, he couldn't stop seeing Cherry. He simply couldn't…not when he remembered how he'd felt before he'd met her.

Sheets rustled as she rolled lazily across her bed toward him. Her diamond ring flashed. "Why don't you come to bed? I've gotten real horny lying in this big ol' bed playing with myself."

The room smelled muskily of other men. Not that he'd been here lately. He wasn't so stupid he didn't realize that she didn't crave him a tenth as much as he craved her.

He leaned down and yanked at the chain of the lamp beside the bed. Golden light flooded the messy room and lit up the silver sequined cowgirl hat she'd hung on a nail on a far wall. She'd been wearing that hat the night he'd first laid eyes on her. The rest of her fetching costume had been matching pasties, a G-string and high-heeled, sequined boots.

He pointed to the bills. "We need to talk."

She stretched like a cat. She slept in the nude. Deliberately she pushed the sheets lower to expose her soft, round body. Then she smiled up at him, batting her long lashes.

Don't look at that bright red mouth. But he did. Next he thought about what those lips did to pleasure him and was instantly aroused. She saw, and her smile brightened with childish delight.

"Come to bed, love. Let little mama scratch your itch."

Then she shoved the bills onto the floor and said, "Let little mama prove she's worth every single penny—and way, way more."

He laughed. Within minutes her expert hands had stripped him of his jeans and boots. Soon she lay on top of him, her mouth licking, circling, wetting his tanned flesh everywhere. She started kissing somewhere beneath his ears and worked down across his chest and stomach and then his belly, her tongue dipping into his navel and then moving lower, trailing up and down between his legs…back and forth, and around and around until he burned like a wildfire. When he was breathing hard, she lowered her head, her long silver-blond hair tickling his stomach as she began to nip and nibble at the most erotic places.

Her damn mouth was like a vacuum. He was rock hard. His blood thrummed. His heart pounded. He felt wonderful, too wonderful for words, until the nagging pain began in his right temple.

Then it struck as viciously as a hammer blow. He felt an explosion in his head like his brain had come out of his skull, and then the pain stopped, and he felt different…numb…not in touch with himself…as if he were floating above them. He'd had the same out-of-body sensation when he'd been bucked off a bronc once and suffered a spinal injury. Only those symptoms had cleared after a day or two.

Like before, he couldn't feel his hands or his legs. Only this time he couldn't move anything, not even his lips or his tongue. It was as if his entire body were dead.

With total clarity he wondered what would happen when she figured out he wasn't all right. Who would she call first—the police, or an ambulance? Would this make the papers and cause still more scandal?

Cherry kept licking him, unaware of the change in him for a while, but he couldn't feel her tongue anymore. And he didn't care. He didn't care about anything. Not the ranch. Not Mia. Not Electra.

Her platinum head bobbed back and forth over his hard dark body for what seemed an eternity. Finally she stopped and looked up at his face, and her eyes grew so startled, they blazed in her white face.

With her fists, she pounded his chest. "Move! Say something! Do something!"

But he was made of petrified stone.

"What's wrong?" He knew she was shouting, but her voice was dim. "What's wrong with you?"

She slapped him hard across the face.

He didn't feel her hand, either, or her nails when they dug into his cheeks a little.

She slapped him again. "Say something!"

All he could do was stare at her as she slapped him again and again.

When she began to cry, he thought about Lizzy.

Would this bring her home? Would she finally realize she had to come home? Would she ever forgive him for the disgrace and scandal he'd brought on her name? Or for Cole?

Vaguely he was aware of Cherry sliding off him and reaching for the telephone. To his surprise she didn't call an ambulance or a doctor or even the police.

When he heard the name of the person she called, a chill went through him.

"You got me in this!" she screamed. "You made me hit on him! What do I do?"

He had been set up. When Caesar remembered who'd suggested that first night at the strip joint, his next thought was for Lizzy.

First Electra. Now him.

If Lizzy did come home, would she be next?

Cherry hung up and dialed another number. "You wanna know who I'm calling, I bet." She flashed him a hateful smile. "Well, I'm calling your wife!"

"Hi there—Mrs. Kemble." Brash as she was, even Cherry hesitated for a moment. "It's me—Cherry. *Your* husband's fianceé."

Joanne must have had plenty to say on that score because it was a long time before Cherry could get another word in.

"Y—yes, well, I—I don't care about any of that. He's in my bed…not yours. And he's as still as a stump. Somethin's bad wrong with him. If you don't send somebody to get him out of here, and send him fast, I'll call an ambulance, and,

and the newspapers. And if I do that—all hell will break loose."

Another long silence.

"No, he's not dead, and I don't want no corpse in my bed! Do you hear me? No! I didn't do anything to him. We were making love." Another long silence. "No. No drugs. A stroke maybe… I'm not a doctor. I don't know. Just hurry!"

Lizzy—he had to warn her.

Why in the name of God had he told everybody he wanted her to succeed him? By doing so, he'd signed her death warrant.

He fought to say her name, but his lips felt like cold concrete.

Imprisoned in his own body, he could only stare helplessly at Cherry, who was watching him, too. Her pretty face beneath her straw-white mane was a mask of disgust. Her eyes were cold and soulless. His throat tightened.

She got up slowly. Lifting her sequined cowboy hat off its nail, she put it on. Then she twirled round and round for him just like she had the first night.

"What's going on in that mind of yours, big daddy?" Spreading her long legs, she made a faux bow.

She pitched her hat toward the bed and went to her mirror where she made up her mouth with vivid red lipstick and combed and fluffed her hair.

When she turned around again and smiled at him, she looked more ravishing than ever.

But it didn't matter. He felt nothing, absolutely nothing for her.

Only Lizzy mattered.

And Electra. She would always matter.

He remembered the day he'd stood in the rain and scattered her ashes under the Spur Tree because she'd written in her will that that was her final wish. She'd chosen to be with him in death at least.

Joanne had been furious when he'd had a bronze marker placed beneath the tree with Electra's name on it.

"Jack's spurs are there, aren't they?" he'd said to shut Joanne up.

Electra. Always Electra.

He had to stay alive to save their daughter.

Four

Manhattan

Too much was happening to her.

The phone was ringing, but Lizzy ignored it. She was too busy watching the two naked men writhe on her television screen with a total absorption that would have embarrassed her had she been of sound mind, which after the catastrophic events of today—she was not.

The late-afternoon sunlight was still red and sparkling outside her window, and the air was crisp and cool. It was a gorgeous evening for a walk. The smart Lizzy had known she should have gone with Walker and Vanilla when Walker had been nice enough to invite her, but the self-destructive Lizzy had been depressed at the thought of an activity that might cheer her up. That Lizzy had wanted, no, *needed*, to indulge in her very own pity party.

How could such a gorgeous day have been so terrible?

Finally the phone was silent.

For the first time in her life Lizzy wished she'd listened to her friend Mandy and had gotten into astrology or something useful. Maybe then she would have seen some cosmic warning in her horoscope or palm today.

Your life as you know it, as you dream it, is over now.

Her life was a joke. First Bryce. Then Nell. And now Walker. It's your own fault that you know about Walker.

Curiosity had led her to darker places before this, surely it had, although she couldn't think of any.

Finding out about Walker's private tape collection was the last thing she needed tonight. So why had she played the video the second Walker had left with Vanilla?

Because I'm a glutton for punishment. Because like every other female on earth, I'm like Pandora. If you tell me something is forbidden, I just have to open the box.

She remembered her father being hell-bent on making a man of Walker, as he'd put it. He'd made Walker hunt and ride and participate in rodeos. Daddy had bragged and bragged about how Walker had tamed the wildest broncs or killed the most game while both Hawk and Walker had flushed and looked uncomfortable. She thought about how Hawk had always been so protective of Walker.

The phone started ringing again, and Lizzy felt heavy demands from home. She felt guilty about not answering and torn because she actually wanted to talk to her mother. But if she talked to her right now, she'd tell her everything. Maybe she'd even mention Walker.

Mother—get a life.

Tough talk for a self-destructive wimp.

How many times had Mother called already? Seven? It seemed to Lizzy the phone had been ringing forever as she stared at her television screen where two men, obviously lovers, embraced. Then almost immediately the men lay down together on the bed again, and their bodies began to writhe.

The phone stopped ringing for at least a whole minute. Not that the lovers stopped what they were doing on that bed.

Just because he has a gay video doesn't mean he's gay. Maybe he was just curious and bought it as a joke. Maybe some gay guy with a crush on him had slipped it into his lug-gage... Maybe...

The phone started again. Mother had to be the most per-sistent human being in the world. Lizzy knew it was her mother because she'd checked her caller ID twice before when the phone had rung right after Walker had taken Vanilla down for a walk in the park and to buy take-out Chinese. She'd been hoping, of course, that it was Bryce or Nell call-ing to say they hadn't meant any of it.

As the phone continued to ring, Lizzy wiped at her damp eyes. One of the men was tall and blond, like Bryce; the other short and dark and very muscular like her cousin, Sam. The darker man had seven little daggers tattooed onto his fore-arm. Lizzy knew exactly how many daggers—because she'd counted them twice, maybe to keep her gaze there instead of drifting to the lower part of the men's bodies, which the camera was now focusing upon.

She averted her gaze, but out of the corner of her eye, she was aware of the men's supple, perfect bodies tensing, com-ing closer to some fatal edge. She saw all the parts of their magnificent bodies, yes, *all the parts,* those long rigid parts with the thick purple veins, and suddenly she started thinking about how long it had been since she and Bryce had had sex.

Men liked watching women with each other. Why? Should she be turned on by watching two men? Was some-thing wrong with her because she resented this video? She thought about Bryce...about his leaving her...about her being too dull...especially in bed.

It was all her fault. What would a kick-ass fantasy hero-ine do?

What if...what if she proved to him she wasn't as dull as he thought she was? What if she made him see her as a com-pletely different kind of woman...the way she was seeing Walker in a whole new light?

The men in the video were shouting at each other, soundlessly, because Lizzy had muted the volume.

Look away. Don't watch anymore. Don't torture yourself.

She felt far too insane to take sane advice, even from herself. It made her feel crazy to associate her sweet, wonderful brother with what she was watching. Walker had been so dear and thoughtful before he'd left with Vanilla. He'd sensed something was wrong, but unlike Mother, he hadn't pushed her. He'd simply offered to take the baby out and buy dinner for them. He'd given her space, a precious commodity in Manhattan if ever there was one. Especially, for a Texan used to wide-open spaces.

"You're sure Bryce won't come home starved—"

She mumbled something to Walker about Bryce working late.

"So, if Bryce isn't coming home, are you sure you don't want to come with us?" His eyes had been so kind. As if he knew. "It's a beautiful night."

"Just go. I'm really tired."

He'd lingered at the door, tall and cowboy dark in a plaid shirt and jeans, until she'd said, "go," again.

Walker was all male, tougher than any cowhand she knew. He was! Hadn't her daddy told everybody that over and over again? Walker wasn't... He couldn't be...gay. Not her brother.

But despite her fierce determination to cling to what she wanted to believe about him, her life with him was flashing before her eyes like images on cards. Only now every image had a new meaning as she viewed it with fresh insight.

Walker was as formidably large and male as his brother Hawk and as tough as any man. He could stay on a bucking bronc longer than any of them—but he was so kind and gentle and thoughtful. He never bulldozed over people the way Daddy or Hawk or even Cole sometimes did. He loved art and the theater.

Walker couldn't be gay. Women threw themselves at him. They asked him out on dates.

But he never asked them.

The big glass doors downstairs opened and crashed closed. Even before she heard Walker's heavy boots on the carpeted stairs, she jumped up, took the tape out of the player, rushed to the second bedroom and hid it in a drawer.

As her brother strode up the stairs, she ran into her own bedroom and took the phone off the hook, so it couldn't ring again. If he knew Mother was calling, he'd call her.

By the time Walker walked inside carrying Vanilla, Lizzy was back on the couch with her hands folded primly in her lap.

Vanilla clapped when she saw Lizzy.

Lizzy wished she'd had time to turn the lamp on. She wished she'd grabbed a book or something. It probably looked odd, her just sitting there in the dark.

She steeled herself to look at Walker and felt instantly guiltily disturbed when she did. Instead of his kind, handsome, dark face, she saw those seven tattoos and the joined forbidden parts of those two male bodies.

She took a deep breath.

"You seem in an odd mood," he said.

"I—I'm fine. H-how come you and Daddy… How come you left Texas?"

"Well, I never was Daddy's favorite. Maybe I got tired of always having to prove myself."

"What did you and Daddy fall out over?"

"We had a different vision for the museum."

"That artist painting the murals was a friend of yours in college, wasn't he? You brought him home to the ranch once? Were his paintings too abstract or something?"

"Something like that," Walker agreed vaguely.

Their father had very strong opinions about modern art. If a painting wasn't like a photograph, he thought it was hogwash.

"You hungry?" Walker asked, changing the subject abruptly, but still in that gentle, comforting tone, as he carried Vanilla to her.

"Starved," she managed to say as she took Vanilla, who clapped and smiled some more.

Walker made Vanilla a bottle while Lizzy settled Vanilla in her high chair with a cardboard book. She got plates and silverware out, then brother and sister sat down together at the scarred table she and Amanda had bought at a fair in the Village. Vanilla placed the book aside and guzzled her bottle noisily.

Walker spooned steaming rice and vegetables onto their plates. With her chopsticks, Lizzy toyed with her food. Everything was exactly the same between them as it had been before she'd watched the video, and yet nothing was the same.

"I never did find the knack of eating with those silly sticks, either," Walker said.

Lizzy dropped them with a clatter and picked up her fork. Then she took a deep breath to ward off the panic that threatened to overwhelm her.

He watched her when she set her fork down a few minutes later.

Vanilla pounded her high-chair tray with her bottle, and Lizzy forced a smile.

"You want me to go out and get something else?" Walker said.

"No… No. The food is great…really. I guess I'm not as hungry as I thought I was."

Her stomach churned. No way could she swallow a bite.

"Well, I reckon I'll be leaving in the morning," he said. "Early—before you get up."

"Are you going home?"

"No. I'll call from time to time to see how you're doing. I'll give you my new address when I have one."

It occurred to her he was going through some crisis as bad or maybe even worse than hers. But her own pain and inhibitions wouldn't let her reach out to him.

Maybe that was for the best. She hoped so. Maybe it was better for them both if he kept his secrets and she kept hers. That way, their lives looked perfect…on the surface.

"I'm glad you came," she said, studying him until he looked up and did the same.

He nodded.

She lifted her fork again and then set it down. "Come back anytime."

"New York's a great city. Tell Bryce…"

She bit her lips. Then her hand knocked the fork off the table.

"Hey," he said. "It's okay."

"I know. Everything's fine. Just fine. Perfect."

"Sure."

"He's just working late."

"Sure. You oughtta take him home to meet the folks some time."

She drew a deep, shaky breath and looked away. "I—I will. First thing."

They spoke in generalities until Vanilla started banging her empty bottle on the high chair again and then threw it down on the floor.

Lizzy used that as her excuse to get up. Scooping Vanilla out of the high chair, she gathered her plate and glass and began to wash the dishes. Later, after Vanilla was asleep in her crib, Walker and she finished decorating the table by the door for Halloween. Not that they said much until she came out of the bathroom in her bathrobe and was on her way back to her bedroom to go to bed.

"Your turn to shower," she said a little too brightly before she headed to bed.

He got up off the couch and went to her and pulled her close. "I guess I'd better say goodbye now."

"I'm glad you came."

"I love you, Lizzy. I wish you the best. You take care of yourself. And thank Bryce when he comes home."

She wrapped her arms around Walker and held his solid, muscular body tightly. "You're the most wonderful little brother a girl ever had."

"Little?" He smiled down at her, and when she met his gaze, for an instant she felt incredible pain in his dark eyes.

"I love you," she said simply, not knowing what else to say.

"I know," he said, letting her go, but he looked trapped.

"Wherever you go, don't you do anything wild and crazy."

"The same goes for you."

Houston, Texas
Joanne

It's my fault, Joanne thought coolly as she let out the water and got out of the tub. She reached for a thick towel and wrapped herself in it.

Why had she gone to the board with her demands? Why hadn't she simply told Caesar privately she couldn't face the museum opening with him parading around Texas with Cherry on his arm?

He'd seemed to shrink when the board had taken her side. His skin had gone papery dry and bloodless. She'd gone after the one thing besides Lizzy that mattered to him—his control of the ranch. When she'd said Cole Knight did more than Caesar did to run the ranch, she'd probably made him so furious he'd had a stroke.

Was she crazy? After all he'd done, to even question her

own actions? All his life Caesar had done exactly what he wanted, taken what he wanted. Not that he'd seen in that way. He thought he'd martyred himself for the good of the ranch.

Leaving the bathroom, she headed into the bedroom where her nightgown lay spread in a splash of vivid yellow silk across her huge bed. Even after a long hot bath, Joanne felt alienated and all alone in the luxurious, nondescript hotel room Cole had checked her into. She hadn't spent many nights on her own in such a room where the decor was perfect, if sterile and the same as all other hotel rooms on the floor. He'd offered to call her friends to let them know she was in the city, but she'd said no. Now she felt so alone and afraid she almost wished she was staying with friends.

She slipped the nightgown on and then pulled on the matching robe. No. She wasn't ready to see or talk to anybody yet.

She moved to the window and drew the curtain back with one hand. Even eleven stories above the city, she could hear the roar of the freeway beneath her and see the dazzle of thousands of headlights rushing about in the night. When she'd been a young mother, raising Lizzy and Mia and the boys and Caesar's nephew, Sam, she'd never imagined she'd end up alone and second-guessing herself.

Bad as being on her own was after such a shock, being with anyone else tonight, especially Caesar's family—before she got a grip—would have been worse. Of course, she would have to call Uncle B.B., Caesar's younger brother, or Aunt Nanette, his older sister, but Caesar's relationship with his siblings had been as complex and fraught with as many tensions and jealousies as their marriage. Joanne felt too fragile to deal with them.

Aunt Nanette was a spoiled, bossy hypochondriac who lived like a princess on her feudal ranch in Montana. She took younger lovers, and when she was around, her needs had to come first. Uncle B.B. and his too elegant, extravagant, much-younger wife, Aunt Mona, were every bit as demanding. Uncle B.B. couldn't abide Caesar because he thought he—not Caesar—he should be running things.

She would have to call them eventually, and they would come running because all of them lusted for what Caesar had—power. All of them were constantly at him, demanding a higher return on their holdings. They wanted him to sell land, or give them more oil royalties, or to settle costly litigation.

Caesar, her indestructible Caesar, who could keep them in line, had had a stroke, and Cherry had panicked and thrown him back into her lap. It would be up to her to deal with them.

Tomorrow, when her friends and relatives found out about Caesar, they'd be all over her. Her local relatives would want her to move in with them. And maybe she would. If she hadn't called Uncle B.B. and Aunt Nanette by then, her friends would do it behind her back.

For the first time in a long time she thought of Jack. If only her darling, precious Jack had lived. If only he hadn't thought he was so immortal he could ride wild stallions alone.

But had he been alone?

Joanne would never forget the night Caesar had found her and taken her to Jack's body. Electra had left him by then. That night he'd been so kind and gentle to her, so different than he'd become later. She began to think about that horrible night. At the time it hadn't seemed odd to her that Caesar had been the one to find Jack. After all, he'd been the one who'd refused to give up searching for him until he was found.

She'd never doubted Caesar until years later when someone else had planted the doubt in her mind.

Leaving the window she went to the phone again. When she lifted it, she knew she was being compulsive, but she couldn't stop herself from trying one more time.

Quit dialing. Quit it, damn it. Lizzy won't answer. Not until she's feeling strong enough to talk.

She's not your daughter anyway.

Don't even think that.

You promised Caesar....

He broke his promises, every single one of them.

Joanne had been running on nerves ever since Cherry had called. After that weird, surreal conversation, the worst had been not knowing what was really wrong with Caesar.

By the time she'd arrived in Houston, Caesar was in ICU, looking fragile and helpless underneath coils of tubes that ran everywhere. If she hadn't known it was he, she wouldn't have recognized the still, shrunken body lying in that tiny, windowless room. Only his eyes were the same, and they had burned her with a fierce intelligence that was unnerving even now.

Was he still mad at her? Or did he want to tell her something?

He was completely paralyzed the doctors had said.

"Can he think?" she'd whispered, feeling a weird survivor's guilt. "Is his mind affected?"

"It's too early to tell."

What if he could think?

Horrible thought.

Thank God Cole had been in Houston. She'd called him the minute Cherry had hung up.

She'd sent him over there, and somehow he'd gotten Caesar to the hospital. She hadn't asked for the details, and maybe it would be better if she didn't.

All that mattered was that nobody knew he'd been with Cherry when it happened. And nobody would know—unless Cherry or Cole talked.

The girl had a big mouth. For the moment, however, for some reason, she seemed to be running scared. Joanne wondered if Caesar had told her about the board meeting.

Joanne dialed Lizzy again and listened to the phone on the other end ring until Lizzy's recorded voice answered sweetly, saying her message was very important and that she would get back to her as quickly as possible.

Fear and frustration engulfed Joanne. Sometimes she almost hated Lizzy. From birth she'd been difficult. Not like Mia, who'd fit into their lives so perfectly. Why hadn't Caesar ever seen that? But no, he'd spent all his spare time trying to prove Lizzy was the best. He'd tried to crush Mia.

Joanne set the phone down and walked to the window. This time she opened the drapes, so she could look out without having to hold the heavy curtain. It wasn't dark yet. Her hotel room had a view of the sumptuous pool. Two children about ten years old were laughing and splashing while their parents watched.

What a lovely time in life being a young parent was. She'd been so full of hope back then, so sure she and Caesar would put Jack and Electra behind them.

Joanne liked being up high and able to look out. The ranch was in flat country, and one never had anything like a real view.

"Best room in the house," Cole had said when he'd handed her the plastic card that served as the key.

Odd how life worked out. Her perfect, talented, darling daughter dead. While Lizzy was still very much alive and pulling the same tricks.

Joanne dialed Lizzy again. When the voice mail picked up on the first ring, Joanne suspected that Lizzy knew perfectly well she was calling and had deliberately taken the phone off the hook.

When Lizzy's message finished, it was all Joanne could

do not to blurt, "Your father's had a stroke in that whore's bed. Answer the damned phone. I need you. God, how I need you."

Of course, Lizzy didn't know anything so catastrophic had happened or that Joanne blamed herself and felt crazed. Lizzy was young. Heaven knows, she and Caesar had called her far too often lately. Any girl Lizzy's age had every right to be sick of it.

Joanne bit her lips and pressed the phone against her lips as she inhaled a desperate breath. Then she dialed Lizzy again. "Answer. Please answer. I can't go through this alone."

When Lizzy still didn't answer, she called Cole, who picked up immediately. For all his faults, even when he'd been himself, Cole wasn't one to play games.

"You did say," she began hesitantly, hating herself for feeling so dependent, "that if I needed anything, I should—"

"Are you all right?" he asked.

"I—I'm fine." She attempted polite conversation but managed only false starts, stumbles and stops. "It was hard, seeing him like that," she finally admitted. "I don't think he'll ever be the same."

"I'm afraid you may be right."

"I thought he was…"

"Invincible," Cole finished in his low, flat drawl.

"Yes… It's too early to talk about this, but nothing… I mean the ranch…the family…me…will be the same…if he doesn't get well. There might not be a divorce. I mean how could there be? I certainly never wanted a divorce, and I'm not going to push for it."

Cole said nothing.

How could she like be so frank and friendly with a son-in-law Caesar and she had barely been able to tolerate a year ago?

"I know it's late. I—I called to ask a very specific favor."

"Anything."

"It's Lizzy—I've tried to call her… She won't answer the phone. Anyway, I've decided maybe it's better not to tell her about this over the phone… I wish I could go myself…"

When she told him what she wanted, he was silent for such a long time, she though he would refuse.

"She won't want to hear it from me…or see me," was all he said when he finally spoke.

"I—I know it's not an easy thing to ask," she said, holding her next breath when he didn't say anything else. "But you have an airplane and a pilot—I—I'm sorry. I'm sure you have a million things to do tomorrow."

Besides his crop-dusting business, he ran the Carancahua division. "I did say anything, now, didn't I?"

"Thank you, Cole."

Utterly exhausted, she lay down on her bed and pressed her fingertips against her closed eyelids.

It was funny, how life worked out. She'd hated Cole when Mia had turned up pregnant and said the baby was Cole's. At first she'd thought Mia was lying about him being the father, and then she'd been so sure he was using Mia to get the ranch. But the baby had his blue eyes and black hair. And she knew him well enough now to know he'd never force himself on a woman. Still, nothing about Mia and Cole's relationship had ever made much sense. They'd been so cool and reserved around each other, especially the day Vanilla had been born.

But he'd been so different since the plane crash. When Joanne had been utterly grief-stricken, he'd been kind and comforting. It was almost as if he wasn't the same man. Strangely he didn't remember Vanilla or much about Mia. But he didn't hate them or seethe all the time anymore.

Although Caesar would have been the last to admit it,

Cole had become Caesar's right-hand man. Nobody loved the land more or was better at the hard work that had to be done daily or supervising the hands than Cole. Not even Sam.

Since the accident that had killed Mia, Joanne had felt sorrier for Cole than she had herself. He'd hated the stories people circulated about the man he'd been before the plane crash.

Still, Caesar hadn't trusted him. He was sure Cole would revert to kind and turn on them as soon as he got his memory back.

But would he?

Five

Lizzy was filled with new hope when she woke up before dawn and slipped sleepily out of bed. Switching on her bedside light, she reread her plan and the lists she'd made late last night after doing her affirmations.

> 4:30 a.m.—get up
> coffee
> yoga stretches
> lingerie drawers
> shower—dress
> rework story…
> Nell

Lizzy went over her lists and affirmations and goals until she felt charged. Then she tiptoed silently to her closet, so as not to wake Vanilla, who slept in the corner in her crib with a navy bedspread thrown over it. Ever since she'd been a tiny baby, Vanilla would not sleep in a lighted or a cold room. The only way to get her to take naps during the day or to sleep at night was to put her to bed the way one did a bird—to cover the crib.

With a good night's rest, Lizzy's shock and self-doubt had

dulled a little. She had a plan, didn't she? Goals. A step-by-step list. Several lists, in fact.

The first thing she had to do was get her ladder so that she could reach the French lingerie that Bryce hadn't already taken down. This she did after drinking a cup of steaming vanilla bean coffee. The door to the second bedroom was open. Walker, true to his word, had gotten up even earlier than she had and had already left.

After her sun salutations, she tackled the closet. Trying not to blush, she arranged lacy teddies, bikini panties, corsets, garter belts and bras in her drawers and then stored her cotton jogging bras and panties on the high shelves of her closet. She selected some sexy undergarments, including a corset, to wear today. Next she showered and dressed and reworked her story, until Vanilla stood up in her crib, her head tenting the dark blue bedspread as she began to babble and coo. After that, getting the baby fed, bathed and dressed and both of them out of the apartment—Vanilla to day care and herself to the station—took all her concentration and determination. Lizzy was exhausted by the time she dropped Vanilla at day care.

Lizzy ran all the way to the television station, which wasn't easy since she was wearing the corset. She was racing inside the lobby, rehearsing her speech to Nell in her head, when a hard voice stopped her.

"Your badge please, Miss Kemble."

She whirled, her long red skirts flying around her legs. The security guard, what was his name. *What was it?*

Whatever it was, the tall, dark-eyed man in the black uniform with the balloon belly caught up to her and blocked her path to the elevators.

Owen Jones. That was it.

"Owen, yes…" She smiled. "Owen, I've got to get to my office—"

Usually he was all smiles. Not today. His voice was stern and yet faintly apologetic. "I need to collect your badge."

Lizzy shakily felt for the plastic card pinned to her red sparkly blouse. "I—I really do have to get to my office—"

Not an office really but a cubicle surrounded by short walls. Her desk faced a single window that overlooked the street.

"We need the badge before we can release your things."

"Release my…" The corset cut off her breath, and the scratchy lace on her garter belt was rubbing her thigh raw. "I—I have to see Nell—"

"Miss Bradshaw told me to tell you she won't be in all day."

Lizzy felt a little light-headed. "Of course she's in."

"Your badge, please."

Lizzy drew another tortured breath before surrendering her badge. He had her sign some resignation forms. Then silently he handed her an envelope that contained her severance pay. Without speaking, he led her to a closet which contained four, white store-all cardboard boxes with the name, Liz, scribbled on them in Nell's handwriting.

Nobody had ever called her Liz but Nell.

Three years of dreams and hard work amounted to Nell's telephone message, a final check and four cardboard boxes taped shut.

Lizzy fought tears.

"Do you need help with these?" Owen asked gently.

She turned toward him in a daze of confusion and misery.

"Y-yes—"

So much for her kick-ass, career girl fantasy. Nell wasn't even going to let her in the door.

Two men arrived with dollies. As she walked back to her apartment with them following at a brisk pace, she pulled out the crumpled bit of paper where she'd written her plan for Nell. Tearing it into little bits, she dropped it in a garbage can.

Bryce was number one on the next list.

She slid the list into her pocket. She couldn't tackle Bryce. Not without lunch. Not without advice from a real pro.

Her eyes felt wet, but she wiped them dry with the back of her hand. She told herself she wasn't going to cry. She wasn't.

But she did.

Cole Knight read the screen of his PDA to-do list one last time to make sure he hadn't forgotten anything before he left home. Then he swung his long legs out of his pickup and scowled at the limp windsock. Then he stared down the runway at the clear, blue Texas sky.

Damn. Why couldn't it be raining cats and dogs or fogged in? Hell, he wouldn't have complained about a tornado or two.

He didn't much want to go to Manhattan. In fact he'd rather face demons than square off with Lizzy again.

Much as he'd dreaded the recurrency training he'd taken last week that had included ground school with an IFR simulator, flight training and a flight check, he dreaded her more. He'd passed the recurrency training with flying colors. If the past was any indicator, he'd never get that lucky with Lizzy.

Cole looked way off beyond the fences where a cowboy was pushing a bunch of cows across a pasture. He had better things to do than to fly to New York and bring Lizzy home. He had bulls to test and his crop-dusting business he was still trying to get off the ground to manage. Not to mention he'd been planning to play poker with Eli, Kinky and some of the other hands.

Lizzy always had to tell him off for things he'd done that he couldn't remember and remind him of what a louse he'd been.

He didn't ever feel like fighting with her. She was too damned pretty.

In fact, his feelings for her confused him more than most things since the accident. He had constant recurring visions about her during the day, and at night he dreamed about her. He couldn't smell a rose without thinking about her. In a nutshell, he wanted her, but she despised him for years of offenses he didn't remember and didn't want to.

His recurring dreams and images were like riddles. What had she meant to him? If he'd wanted her so damn much, why the hell had he gotten Mia pregnant and then married her?

Still, somebody had to tell Lizzy about her daddy's stroke and bring her home. With her brothers gone, there wasn't anybody else but him to do it. In the thick of getting Caesar settled in ICU, Cole had given his word to Joanne that if she needed anything, all she had to do was ask him.

Joanne was the one person in the family who'd been really kind to him since the accident and Mia's death. She hadn't blamed him for the accident. Nor for not remembering Mia or Vanilla. Nor for owning Mia's stock. Nor for having feelings for Lizzy instead of Mia. Nor even for still being alive when Mia was dead. She didn't blame him for who he'd been, either. She'd been his main support during the difficult days of the investigation that followed the accident that had killed her daughter.

Cole knew what it was to be on the spot. He had a lot of sympathy for what Joanne Kemble had been through lately, and he admired the way she handled herself when reporters besieged her. Not that he didn't sympathize with Caesar. No matter what he'd done, nobody deserved to end up like that.

Cole knew what it was not to be yourself, too. Even now, when he was so much better, he dealt with flashes and half thoughts, with the inability to focus on a subject, and with walls and closed doors in his mind. A glance at an old photograph or even a chance meeting with somebody he'd known but didn't recognize on the town square triggered weird, jittery feelings that put him on edge and made him sure that soon, soon he'd remember. He couldn't function without his PDA to organize his life.

Then there were the blackouts. He lost time—seconds, minutes, even hours sometimes. He could be driving the truck on a desolate, private ranch road and *awaken* in strange surroundings with no knowledge of how he'd gotten there or what he'd done. Although the blackouts scared him, he'd told no one other than his doctors, who told him not to worry since they didn't interfere with his ability to drive or fly or ride horseback. But he wasn't to fly without another pilot. Nor was he to drive on public roads or highways.

Who was he when he wasn't there? His old hateful self, maybe?

One reason he was leery of going to New York was that he was afraid of blacking out around Lizzy. What if he did something or said something terrible?

Still, Lizzy had to be told and brought home. Joanne had asked him. Even though Lizzy despised him, Cole didn't want her to get the news about her daddy over the phone and have to fly home alone with the baby.

So he was stuck. With a regretful glance at the distant cowboy and his herd, Cole locked the cab door and strode into the office of his private airstrip where he operated his crop-dusting business and kept his Cessna.

Several young mechanics who were hovering over his secretary's desk looked up and then waved and smiled at him and told him that his twin-engine plane was ready to fly. His pilot, John, was in the hangar.

Suz, who was dark-haired and too flirty, looked up, and her hand went still on her ledger as she batted her lashes at him. Next came her slow, warm smile. She pushed her chair back, and her short black skirt crawled up her legs. She wore a tight silk top that was so thin he could see her nipples.

Cole took off his Stetson and tried not to grin or fan himself since his mechanics were watching him. Cole had forgotten a lot, but he remembered the vital stuff, like how to fly and how to cowboy and how to survive. The last men on earth a pilot wanted to piss off were his airplane mechanics. He'd be flying alone soon enough—at least that's what he told himself.

Cole had longish black hair with a few strands of gray, ice-blue eyes, dark skin and a hard jawline. At six feet two inches, he was tall and lean and long-legged and muscular, too. His shoulders were broad, and girls told him his cheekbones were of the slashed variety that wore well over time. Which was good, he supposed, since he was on the wrong side of thirty-five.

The jealous mechanics and the flirtatious Suz made Cole so tense, he willed Suz to go back to her work. Not that he didn't appreciate her interest. He hadn't had a woman since he'd lost Mia. Not that he remembered ever having had Mia. It was Lizzy, only Lizzy who haunted him.

You've got classic bad-boy sex appeal. Cole could almost hear Lizzy's laughing voice. He saw her trace his cheekbones with a fingertip and then kiss the tip of his nose. *Except for your lashes. You have long sissy lashes.*

He remembered his reply, too. *There's not a damn thing I can do about them, darlin'.*

Was that memory real? Or had he made it up?

Ah, Lizzy... Classic good-girl sex appeal. Understated...

She was a little fearful of her wild urges and where they might lead her. He'd only had to touch her to get her all hot and bothered.

How did he know that? Was it true? Or was the memory that got him instantly hot false?

To hell with Lizzy. She was a big, spoiled crybaby, a poor little ranch princess, Daddy's favorite. Caesar had spoiled her, and she'd left him, seeking fame and fortune.

Cole had schooled himself never to dwell on the puzzle of Lizzy. Today, for some reason, the usual tricks weren't working.

Maybe it was for the best. After all, he would have to face her soon. Might as well get his gut in a knot so she couldn't cut him to ribbons.

Jamming his battered Stetson onto his head, he waved goodbye to Suz and headed out onto the tarmac. Climbing aboard his plane, he and John carefully went through their routine in the cockpit and then taxied down the runway, waiting until they were given clearance to take off into that damnably gorgeous blue sky.

According to the latest weather report, it would be smooth flying, all the way to Manhattan.

Smooth flying, that is, until he met up with Lizzy.

Knowing her, she'd give him hell.

Maybe someday he'd remember exactly why she disliked him.

Or maybe, when he was his old self, he'd be dead set against her, too. He'd married Mia, hadn't he?

Why the hell had he done that?

"To get the ranch, pure and simple," old Eli had told him. "To cut Lizzy to the quick. To make old Caesar so spitting mad he'd have a heart attack and die. Probably to make Mia miserable, too. You were a real bastard, Mr. Knight. You were after one thing—revenge against the Kembles, especially

Caesar. And you damn sure got it! You got even more stock for fathering Vanilla!"

Cole hated the cold, ruthless man Eli described. And he was scared that was the real him, that if he got his memory back, he'd be that man again.

Normally Lizzy never stopped by SEX-E-E, the fetish shop, where Mandy worked. The two friends usually met somewhere far more discreet for lunch.

Like Bryce's gifts of sexy French lingerie, the shop wasn't Lizzy's kind of thing, and it amazed her that an honors graduate in English from Princeton, no less, who was the daughter of a wealthy, high-profile family, would choose to work here. And yes, this job was definitely Mandy's choice.

"Okay, I'm going to be a writer when I grow up, if you have to know, kiddo," she'd confessed to Lizzy once at breakfast when they'd been munching bagels after the journalism class they'd taken where they'd met. "So, I've got to do interesting things now, so I'll have something to write about later. I was born rich, and you can't imagine how boring that is."

"Right. I thought maybe you just wanted to shock your family."

"Those repressed snoots? They gave up on me after the first few piercings and Internet lovers from the wrong side of the tracks."

"I admire you so much for being so sure about what you want and don't want."

"I'm just a brat. Nothing admirable about being a rich, rebellious brat."

Mandy was with a customer when Lizzy opened the doors, causing lots of little silver bells to tinkle. When the door closed behind her, Lizzy wrinkled her nose and waved her hand because the air was so thick with incense.

Maybe she was rich, but Mandy fitted right in here. She
had bright, bottle-red hair and wore a tight, stretchy black
tank top that didn't quite meet the waistband of her low-rid-
ing jeans. Her eyebrows, ears, nose, belly button and tongue
were all pierced with small ruby studs, and she had a little
rose tattoo above her left breast—of course, almost always,
the tank top was low enough for the rose tattoo to show and
short enough for the ruby in her navel to twinkle. She had
another tattoo on her butt, that one being a cute, smiling
dragon wreathed in scrolls of flowers that showed when she
wore a bikini or low-rise jeans, like today.

"I wish you'd been with me when this big old weirdo with
huge loops in his ears and nose and long dirty fingernails was
tattooing my butt. It was a hoot." Mandy had laughed at the
memory as if she still relished it.

"Have you told your mom that story?"

"Even though she's a connoisseur of art, she might not appreciate it."

Mandy waved at the sound of the silver bells and Lizzy
fluttered her fingers and blew air kisses. Eyeing her friend's
exposed navel with the ruby enviously, Lizzy pushed at her
own waist and squirmed, fighting like the dickens for a sat-
isfying breath as she readjusted Bryce's awful corset. Underneath her flowing Indian red dress, Lizzy was still
wearing sexy French lingerie.

The tight black corset with the little red ribbons on it
made her breasts bulge above it like balloons. She'd laced
the thing up and then had lost her nerve when she'd seen herself in the mirror. When she'd dressed, she'd donned a loose,
flowing red gown that hid her astonishing hourglass curves
instead of a tight sheath that would have made her look, in
her opinion, like a harlot.

The underwear was sexy all right, but was any man worth
this much pain?

Positive thoughts. Affirmations.

Bryce is worth it. I can change. Where there's a will there's a way. I love the new exciting me.

While Mandy waited on her customer, Lizzy hummed, practiced some yoga breathing and tried not to stare at all the crazy stuff in the shop. Impossible. The huge vivid posters of women dressed as dominatrices that lined the walls grabbed her attention and held it like magnets.

Glancing anywhere but at those posters, her gaze fell on the counter beside her that was stacked with boxes of edible underwear that apparently came in all sizes, chocolate sculptures of body parts to be nibbled on, bright red vibrators and books about naughty things.

When Mandy's customer began to shyly whisper about a chocolate phallus, Lizzy jumped away from the counter and headed to the rack of sexy costumes in the back of the store. After all, she'd come here to buy an outfit that would make her look so wanton and desirable tonight that Bryce could not resist the new, exciting her. Forcing herself to concentrate on the filmy scraps of material on the hangers, she thumbed through transparent blouses and skirts slit to the waist.

Just as she was thinking that there was no way she'd allow herself to be caught dead in any of this stuff, Mandy's voice floated from behind her.

"I pulled a few things for you that will be perfect, especially since it's Halloween." She held out her selection. "I thought this would work. Think theme—"

"Theme?" Baffled, Lizzy turned.

Mandy was holding a sequined cowboy hat and cowgirl dress that would have been perfect for the notorious stripper in Houston who was auditioning to be her stepmother.

"Definitely not that!"

"But you're from Texas—"

"There's a lot you don't know about that—"

"Fill me in. I'm all ears. I've got—" She glanced at her black watch with blue rhinestones. "I've got a witch costume with a slit up the thigh."

"I can't do this."

"We've got until two. Do we eat first or shop for your costume?"

"Eat. No way can I buy something like this on an empty stomach. I need courage."

Mandy laughed. "That domineering daddy and strict mama really did a number on you in Texas. You've got to break out. You've got to show people what you're really capable of."

"I need a salad…organic." *I love the new, exciting me. I love the new, exciting me,* she repeated silently.

"But isn't it my turn to pick the restaurant?" Mandy asked innocently.

"You picked last time." *I love the new, exciting me.*

"I did?"

"Spicy pasta, remember?"

"Hey, I know this darling new little sushi place," Mandy persisted.

"Raw fish?"

"It's upstairs. Nobody knows about it. Wonderful service."

"Okay," Lizzy said, even though it was her turn to pick and she couldn't stand sushi.

I love the new, exciting me, she repeated, trying not to dwell on the sushi.

They didn't really take turns picking the restaurants. They always ate where Mandy wanted to, which worked out for the best since Mandy was a real grump if she didn't get to eat exactly what she wanted.

Better to brave sushi than deal with Mandy complaining endlessly and abusing the waiters.

The restaurant, which had white walls, golden oak floors and low tables with soft little cushions to sit on was as quiet as a tomb. Mandy led her to a table by the window so they could watch traffic and people stream beneath them.

"I love this city, don't you?" Mandy said, staring at the endless flow of people as they sat down. Then she called the waiter over and ordered hot tea. "So, am I still on to take Vanilla to that Halloween block party tonight? Say 'yes.'"

"Yes."

"And you'll actually let her spend the whole night with me?"

"To tell you the truth, I sort of need a break."

"I can't believe you trust me with that precious little angel."

"But you're great with her."

"I raised all my little brothers and sisters."

"Do they all have dyed red hair, piercings. No—don't tell me."

Mandy laughed. "Hey, kiddo, I'm the only one who got into an ivy league school. Isn't that a hoot—me the family genius?"

The waitress came, and Mandy ordered for both of them as she always did. "Okay, so I'll come by for her at six tonight," Mandy said.

A few minutes later the waitress brought something that looked alarmingly like raw octopus on little crackers served on two black plates.

Lizzy stared glumly at the window, repeating to herself, *I love the new, exciting me.*

"So, kiddo, you said Bryce just moved out? How come?"

"It doesn't matter."

"Of course it matters." Mandy dipped an octopus tentacle into brown sauce and began to chew. "You two were great together."

"We…we used to laugh about the same things."

"He couldn't commit? Is that it?" Another octopus tentacle was lifted toward Mandy's mouth.

"Why does there have to be a specific reason? Can we talk about something else?"

Mandy's brown gaze drilled her. "You don't look so hot. Hey, you're not eating—"

"Go ahead and eat my octopus if you want to."

"You sure?"

Lizzy nodded. "Okay, maybe he couldn't commit. We were good together at first—and then slowly…everything changed."

"You should never have brought the baby to New York, kiddo." Mandy paused to devour another tentacle.

"Maybe. Look, I could think about this forever and never figure it out. My plan is to get Bryce back. There's a wild party tonight that we were both invited to. We sort of quarreled about it. He's going, and I need something to wow him at the party."

"And if this fails, is there a plan B?"

Lizzy shook her head.

"So this is all or nothing." Mandy got quiet for a moment. "You know, I've always thought the lure of makeup and new stylish outfits is that deep down we all want to be an exciting, new woman." She paused. "I've got an idea, kiddo, if you've got the guts."

"I'll do anything."

Mandy laughed. "A girl after my own heart."

Anything—except sushi, Lizzy thought as Mandy chomped another tentacle.

I love the new, exciting me.

Six

There should be a rule: no rain or snow on holidays. Joanne associated Houston with wet, drippy days like this. The sky was the color of moldy pea soup, and the air was close and dense. If the weather didn't improve, tonight would be dreadful for trick-or-treaters.

The rain wasn't why she felt as if her blood had turned to sludge as she sat wearily in the plush leather back seat of Gigi's golden Lexus. Still, it was good to be out of the dreadful, prisonlike hospital, to be driven home through the thick traffic that snarled the freeways by a capable chauffeur to her favorite friend's mansion in River Oaks.

Thank heavens Gigi had been the first to call to invite her to move in. Gigi Banks was discreet and kind and very popular. Not only was she a beautiful brunette, she was one of the richest and most glamorous widows in Texas. When her husband and son had died within months of each other several years ago, she'd all but collapsed. When she'd finally pulled herself together, she'd called Joanne and said in her deep, throaty voice, "I've decided it's time I really did something that matters."

Gigi loved the arts and halved her time between Houston and Manhattan. She was immensely popular in both places as she spent the bulk of her time giving her vast fortune away with no strings attached. She funded entire ballet seasons and did wonderful things with trees and children's programs to enhance run-down inner city neighborhoods. She'd been very helpful, working with Walker in the planning of the Golden Spurs Ranch Museum.

No sooner had the Lexus swung into Gigi's wide drive beneath towering lush pines shading a well-groomed, verdant lawn and beds of bright petunias than Gigi herself burst from the back door of the red-brick, two-story home like a golden genie popping out of a bottle. Forgetting to stay off the wet grass, she skipped lightly across her lawn in designer heels to greet Joanne as eagerly as a young child to welcome a favorite playmate.

Joanne smiled in spite of herself and pressed her fingertips fondly against the window. Then the chauffeur opened her door, and instantly the two friends were in each other's arms.

"I flew home the minute I heard," Gigi said.

Gigi had a brand-new Lear jet. "I can't believe how much easier the jet has made having two homes that are so far apart." Gigi laughed then. "For ten million dollars, don't you think it should?"

Joanne clung to her friend. "Thank you for having me. You inspire me."

"A package was here waiting for you when I got in," Gigi said, taking Joanne's hand and leading her up a sidewalk that was lined with perfectly carved jack-o'-lanterns. "Delivered by private courier. It's heavy and rather mysterious looking really." Gigi was clearly intrigued.

"Mysterious?"

"It's from Nicaragua."

A chill went through Joanne. Six months ago, Electra had been strangled in Nicaragua while on one of her photo shoots.

"Went there once," Gigi was saying. "Dreadful place.

Nobody in their right mind should vacation there. Who in the world do you know in Nicaragua?"

"Not a *living* soul," Joanne whispered truthfully, remembering the rainy afternoon when Caesar had scattered Electra's ashes under the Spur Tree and then, when she'd objected, had thrown Jack up to her as he frequently did when he felt guilty.

"You look awfully tired all of a sudden, ill almost," Gigi said. "Before you open your package, why don't we have tea? We'll chat and rest a little. You must tell me all about Caesar. This is just so dreadful."

"He collapsed. A stroke. He can't do much more than stare at me. And he looks...strange, scary almost."

"Will he get better? Do the doctors offer any hope at all?"

"When I touched his right hand this afternoon, I think he moved his little finger."

"You only think?"

"He hooked it around my little finger and wouldn't let go."

They exchanged a look.

"Oh, my dear. Poor Caesar. Poor *you*. He loved you. In spite of what he did with that awful Houston stripper, he loved you."

Joanne wished she believed that. But how could she? "We'd been talking some lately," Joanne said.

"Men are such idiots."

That was so true. But I've been an idiot, too. An idiot to marry anyone—especially Jack's brother—after Jack.

"What about the Golden Spurs? Won't there be a power vacuum?"

"Trouble was brewing even before this. But let's have tea and talk of happier times."

They had tea in a bright corner of Gigi's white and yellow kitchen, and then Gigi led her through charming rooms filled with bookcases that housed her collection of Irish silver and large, overstuffed furniture upholstered in happy prints. Hand in hand they went up a swirling staircase to a lovely red bedroom furnished with a high-poster bed and antiques. A maid had placed Joanne's bags on luggage racks and hung her clothes in the closet.

"I'll see you at dinner," Gigi said with a smile before leaving her.

A fat brown package tied with lots of string lay on top an antique desk near the window. More than anything, Joanne wanted to collapse on that wonderful bed and just lie there and maybe never get up.

Instead she moved stiffly across that wonderful room and picked up the mysterious package.

It was heavy, and when she shook it near her ear, it was so solid nothing rattled.

A book?

She studied the slashing handwriting. How had anybody known where she would be when she hadn't known herself?

She shivered when she read the Nicaraguan postmark. Even before her trembling fingers began to undo the coarse strings and peel the brown paper off the cardboard box that was inside, she felt goose bumps prick her flesh.

This was bad.

Manhattan
Lizzy

"Trick-or-treat, kiddo!" Mandy said when Lizzy answered the buzzer.

"The door's open," Lizzy replied. "Come on up."

No sooner did Lizzy hear Mandy's footsteps on the stairs, than Vanilla began to clap. A few minutes later Mandy burst breathlessly into the tiny apartment wearing a harem outfit that wasn't much more than a gold bustier, a thong bikini bottom, and transparent, hot pink pants. Every tattoo and ruby piercing was visible. To complete her costume, Mandy wore a yellow satin mask with black feathers.

"It's a gorgeous night, kiddo, and the city's wild. I never saw more people in the streets. I just love Halloween!"

Vanilla hid her face and began to cry.

"Oh, no." Mandy ripped off her mask and handed it to Vanilla, who stopped crying in midbreath. "See—it's just me—Mandy."

Vanilla sucked in another big sob-filled breath and then smiled through her tears as Lizzy came into the room, holding a pair of glittery earrings in one hand and a glass of Chardonnay in the other.

"Wow, look at you!" Mandy said. Turning to Vanilla, she added, "Does your aunt look hot or what?"

Lizzy blushed when Vanilla gazed uncertainly up at her. Then she caught a glimpse of herself in the mirror over the table by the door. Sure enough, she'd gone all out, at least for her, for Bryce's Halloween party.

"Are you sure about this...costume?"

Silently she forced her affirmation. *I love the new, exciting me.*

"Kiddo, you're dynamite."

"I can barely breathe."

Lizzy was stuffed into Bryce's corset again, and the torture contraption had her bulging in all the right places. The slippery, little, red jersey number trimmed with black lace that Mandy had loaned her barely covered her hips. The red strappy sandals had her teetering every time she took a step.

"Didn't I tell you, you'd look great in my black mesh hose?"

"I look like a hooker."

"It's called a costume. Tonight you're Bryce's fantasy woman. The dress and the shoes go with his lingerie. Trust me, he'll love the exciting you."

"He'd better."

"Hey, what happened to your eye?"

"I was sipping Chardonnay…trying to relax because the outfit has me so nervous. I got too much black liner on one eyelid. Then I tried to do the other one to match. I'm not very good with makeup."

"Give me the eyeliner. I'll just thicken the other eye."

"Better idea. Why don't I just scrub it all off."

"Because the heavy eye makeup goes with the lingerie. So hold still, kiddo."

When Mandy finished painting her eyelid, they both looked at Lizzy's reflection. Her face was so white, her red lips and heavily made-up eyes seemed garish, at least to Lizzy. Lush breasts swelled invitingly above the shiny red fabric. Her waist was incredibly tiny, her hips wide and curvy.

When Lizzy looked woeful, Mandy smiled reassuringly. "If I didn't know you…I wouldn't know you." Mandy moved behind her and began to fluff Lizzy's wild, corkscrew curls. "Am I good, or what?"

Every time Mandy made her hair poof out another inch, Lizzy pressed her hands onto it and mashed it flatter.

"Quit—" They both spoke at once.

Lizzy took a deep breath and stared at herself in the mirror. Usually she looked so innocent and wholesome. But not tonight.

"Now, give me those earrings and the bracelets," Mandy said. "This is fun, kiddo."

"For you maybe."

"This was your idea, remember?"

Lizzy handed her the jewelry, and soon the gypsy earrings and bracelets flashed against her ears and throat.

Lizzy groaned. "I look so cheap."

"Sexy. Say, I look sexy. Affirmations. Positive thoughts."

I can do this, Lizzy thought, taking another sip of Chardonnay. *I can do this.*

But could she?

I love the new, exciting me, she repeated.

Mandy scooped Vanilla into her arms. "Gotta go. And so do you, or you'll be late."

"Walk down with me…at least as far as Columbus," Lizzy said. "I'm afraid to go out like this alone."

"Finish your wine. Definitely finish your wine…"

Lizzy bolted what was left in the glass.

Downstairs, in the crisp, cool twilight, Lizzy shivered because of her inadequate clothing. At the same time she could feel the faint warm stirring inside her that had to be the effects of the wine. She hoped that soon she would relax and see this as a game.

But it wasn't a game. Her heart was broken. Like a desperate gambler, she was rolling the dice in a last ditch, all-or-nothing shot to get the man she loved back.

"Work the hips, kiddo," Mandy whispered as Lizzy stepped onto the sidewalk. "Work 'em."

Just as she began to make her hips sway, a tall, dark, lean, male figure in the shadows of the building a few doors down took a step toward her and then tensed the instant she saw him.

Although she could only see his outline, something about him *felt* vaguely familiar. The air felt thin suddenly. Even when she looked away, pretending to ignore him, her nerves fluttered so badly she could barely breathe.

The man stood up straighter, and she realized he had to be well over six feet tall. He was broad-shouldered, much bigger than she was. She felt his eyes sweeping her from head to toe.

Don't look at him.

Even so, she knew he was looking at her, and the skin on the back of her neck prickled. Then heat rushed over every bare inch of exposed skin.

Had he been watching her door, waiting for her?

Ridiculous thought. Still, she continued to observe him out of the corner of her eye as intently as he watched her.

Yes, there was something vaguely familiar about him.

A crowd of teenagers in masks and costumes raced together on the opposite side of the street toward Columbus Avenue. Somewhere an ambulance screamed. The sounds seemed magnified, but at the same time they were hazy and unclear. Was that the wine dulling her senses? *Making her vulnerable?*

Mandy, in her harem girl costume that was cut so low in the back her dragon tattoo was clearly visible, was carrying Vanilla and taking such long strides she was getting ahead of her. Not wanting to be left alone with the stranger, Lizzy called to Mandy and ran to catch up with them. Not that it was easy wearing high heels that made frightened little hollow taps on the concrete.

When she heard heavy footsteps behind her, her stomach muscles constricted. *Oh, God.* In a panic she pulled her flimsy red shawl over her breasts and knotted both ends.

The dress was for Bryce. Not for some tall, dark stalker who might take her for a real street walker. The party was a long subway ride from her apartment. Why hadn't she brought a coat or something other than her flimsy shawl? What if he caught her before she reached the party?

"Mandy, I think someone's following us," she whispered breathlessly.

"Will you quit with this nervous little girl routine? How are you ever going to seduce Bryce if you don't play the siren, kiddo?"

"I'm serious."

Mandy laughed and then turned around to check. "Nobody's there, silly. Would you relax?"

Lizzy turned around, too. Mandy was right. The man was

gone. Across the street a pumpkin and a large gorilla were walking behind the teenagers.

She sighed. As usual her imagination was running away with her.

"It's just a costume," Mandy said. "Have fun with it. A lot of girls dress like that all the time. They come in the shop. You wouldn't believe the things they buy."

"Like edible undies?"

Mandy shot her a look that said grow up. "Do you want Bryce back or not? Guys like Bryce want a nice girl to show off in public and a whore in the bedroom."

Lizzy, who didn't want to be a whore anywhere, closed her eyes and prayed for courage. Repeating a few more affirmations, she lifted her chin and squared her shoulders and kept walking.

At Columbus, there were hordes of people on the sidewalk, some in really weird costumes. The pumpkin was hailing a cab. The gorilla was leaning in a doorway studying his handheld PDA.

Nobody even looked at her. Feeling a little less spooked, she hugged Vanilla and told Mandy goodbye. But the instant they were gone, she felt unseen eyes watching her again.

She stared wildly at the crowd rushing past her searching every face for a glimpse of the tall dark stranger. The pumpkin got in a cab without looking back at her. The gorilla was still clumsily studying his PDA. Three ballerinas crossed the street together.

Nobody was paying the slightest bit of attention to her. Then a cool breeze blew over Lizzy's hot, damp skin, reminding her again of just how little she had on. Goose bumps pricked, and she felt her imagination begin conjuring stalkers again. She couldn't let go of the uneasy feeling someone was watching her.

She had to get to that party and find Bryce fast.

Houston, Texas
Joanne

In college, Joanne had been fascinated by her friend Electra, who'd been so willful, exciting and daring. Dread filled her now as Joanne peeled off the last of the brown paper. Slowly she lifted the cardboard lid. Inside was a leather-bound book. No, not a book exactly. A photocopied manuscript.

Not a manuscript exactly, either. She flipped a page and recognized the loopy handwriting as that of her former best friend, Electra Scott.

Somebody had sent her a copy of what appeared to be Electra's journal. But who? Why?

She was mortally sick of Electra. Sick to death of her.

As she thumbed through more pages, a photograph of two young girls with blond hair fell out. Next she saw that some passages had been highlighted with a yellow marker, so that even if she didn't read the entire journal, she wouldn't miss these.

She began to read. "Twins. Girls."

At first Joanna thought she was talking about Mia and Lizzy, who hadn't really been twins at all even though she and Caesar had told everyone they were fraternal twins. But the dates on the pages didn't match the dates when Lizzy and Mia had been born.

No… These girls were a little younger.

Electra wrote about Caesar coming to Columbia to rescue her when she'd been kidnapped. She'd been weak and vulnerable, and Caesar had saved her. Neither had been able to resist the other even though they'd tried.

In the end, she'd slept with the lover of her youth again. The daring rescue had taken a week. Caesar had stayed with her a whole week. They'd made love constantly, which Electra wrote about much too vividly Joanne thought.

While I was home alone…not alone…raising our children.

Afterward, when Caesar had gone home to his wife, Electra had given birth to twin girls, but she'd never told Caesar.

Joanne looked up from the journal.

Caesar had betrayed her. Cherry wasn't the first. What else had Caesar done?

Joanne slammed the journal shut. She had tried so hard to make their marriage work. Had Caesar ever really tried at all?

Where were his other daughters now?

What did this mean for the ranch? For her own children? Lizzy had been enough to swallow.

Electra. Always Electra and her camera. *And to think, I brought her here to the ranch. They met because of me.*

Then Jack had died, and Electra had gone away. Joanne had found out she was pregnant and had told Caesar. He, in turn, had learned Electra was pregnant and didn't want to raise the baby herself or to marry him. At the time, a marriage of convenience had seemed the best solution. She and Caesar would raise both children as their own. They had sworn it would be a real marriage and that each of them would view both children as his.

Those promises had been easier to make than to keep. Having her own children had made Joanne know how differently she felt toward all others. Especially her rival's. Although Electra had once been her best friend, she'd been so vital and colorful, Joanne had felt diminished when around her. There had always been an element of competition in their relationship, as well.

Joanne clenched her hands. Oh, my God. Caesar, how could you? How could, when you promised…

Joanne opened the book again and studied the dates. She remembered those two weeks all those years ago. Caesar had said he needed some time alone to think about their marriage. When he'd come back, he'd said he'd keep trying. Joanne had thought he'd been in Houston or Dallas. When she'd pressed him for details, he'd refused to talk.

Twins?

They were out there…somewhere…and someone knew. Maybe lots of people knew. What would Caesar's secret daughters want when they learned of their heritage?

What could she do about it?

For no reason at all, Joanne felt furious at Lizzy.

Seven

Manhattan
Cole

Behind the hot gorilla mask, Cole felt like his eyes were sticking out on stems. He was rock-hard, riveted. His carefully planned speech to Lizzy about her dad was blown to smithereens by the city… No. Admit it—by that tight skimpy red dress. By her breasts and legs. His brain, never in perfect shape these days, felt scrambled. He forgot his purpose. He couldn't focus on anything else but her.

The city's roar blasted him like the blows of a giant, angry beast as he leaned back against a corner building and watched Lizzy through the slits in his gorilla mask. The blare of horns, the squeal of brakes, the hustle-bustle of heels on concrete and of too many bodies jostling for position on the sidewalk made him wince. At the same time he felt like an ant trapped in the maze of an alien ant bed jammed with too many self-important ants all desperate to get somewhere.

He was used to wide-open spaces, to big skies, to grass blowing in the wind, to silence. Didn't any of the people here get it? They were all going nowhere.

How the hell could he ever figure out now how to tell Lizzy about her father when he couldn't get past the way she was dressed? For the life of him he couldn't quit staring at her breasts and legs—even though doing so had him hard and pissed because he figured the other guys who saw her got hot for her, too. He felt jealous and possessive even though he had no right to.

Why the hell didn't Lizzy just unzip that tight red dress, shimmy out of it and get naked right here on Columbus and 69th? Some guy would jump her. Cole would attack. He'd prefer a brawl like that to this infernal traffic and his raging lust.

Cole frowned. With her teased white-blond hair, glittery bangles, bulging bosom and long shapely legs in black mesh hose, Lizzy didn't look a thing like the shy, sweet girl he knew.

One minute Lizzy was hugging her cheap-looking girlfriend and Vanilla. Then in the next, the redhead with the tattoos on her breast and all the piercings sashayed off, up Columbus Avenue toward The Plaza.

With Vanilla!

Vanilla! Lizzy didn't show a shred of concern about the baby.

Confused, he took a step after the baby that was supposed to be his daughter and then stopped. Hell. He had to trust Lizzy's judgment when it came to baby care.

He'd come to see Lizzy. To tell her about her father. Only how he'd ever manage that now, he didn't know. All he knew was that he'd better stick with Lizzy. She seemed vulnerable, and dressed like that, she could damn sure get into trouble. The girlfriend could definitely handle herself.

Why hadn't he buzzed her apartment the minute he'd gotten there and told her about Caesar? Because he knew how close she was to her father, because he hated the thought of how the news would affect her, because he'd needed time to work up his nerve to talk to her.

If he'd known she was going to prance out of those double doors dressed like a hooker, he'd have bounded up those stairs like a jackrabbit first thing.

The plastic gorilla mask was beginning to make his face drip with sweat. His wet hair felt plastered to his head, and his jeans were too tight.

Maybe the mask was uncomfortable, but he was glad as hell he'd bought it along with that canvas hat with the long black ponytail from that fast-talking vendor in Central Park, who'd grabbed his arm and all but forced him to buy both disguises for Halloween.

Lizzy suddenly glanced straight at him and Cole started. She squinted and stared at him harder. Quickly he lowered his head and typed on his PDA so clumsily he dropped it.

When he knelt to get it, she bolted down the stairs that led to the subway. Dashing after her, he kept to the middle of the throng, bought a subway pass, and managed to catch the same train.

Every time they stopped at a station, he jumped off and watched for her. When he began to perspire underneath the gorilla mask again, he took it off and put on the canvas hat with the long black ponytail.

She got off in the Village, so he did, too. Blending into the crowd again, he followed her down streets and sidewalks that were jammed with laughing, shouting people, who wore garish makeup and masks.

Music blasted from most of the bars and crowded restaurants. The Village pulsed with people and holiday spirit. Girls in sparkly dresses undulated together outside one bar to the heavy beat of drums while a crowd of young men clapped and ogled.

Lizzy paused near a streetlight and studied a piece of

paper in her hand. When she glanced up at the street numbers uncertainly, her gaze swept over him and then returned, lingering even after he'd stepped deeper into the shadows. She continued to stare into the darkness. The streetlight froze her heart-shaped face with a cold marblelike clarity that made his heart pound. He wanted her, and he hated himself for the weakness because he knew how she felt about him— probably for good reason. He grimaced, not liking the role he was playing very much.

Her huge eyes told him she was scared, but she was so damned beautiful, he couldn't stop looking at her.

Lusting after her, asshole.

When he turned, pretending an interest in a violin for sale in the shop window, she ran.

He'd scared her. He hated that, but he kept up easily, relentlessly, following her down the dark streets.

A stalker was after her! If only she could find the party and find Bryce; then she'd be safe.

Lizzy was so tired from running in the tight corset and heels, she was gasping for every breath. Her heart had been racing ever since she'd spotted the tall man in the shadows.

He was like a vicious cat stalking a mouse. No matter how fast she ran or how cleverly she'd tried to evade him, his legs were longer, and his body powerful and his mind focused on her with the deadly determination of a true predator.

Suddenly, she found herself halfway down a blind alley. When she turned, she saw him at his end of the alley, standing statue still. When she cried out, she thought he laughed.

Not that he came closer. He knew he had her. Like a cat, he savored her fear. He was playing with her. But surely she was close, very close to the address on the invitation. Maybe…maybe…

At least he didn't seem to be in a hurry. He just stood there, almost patiently, waiting for her to give up.

Good—the delay gave her time…a chance…to think…

Her eyes climbed the brick buildings on either side of her. They were tall, at least five stories. Tall enough to shut off all moonlight. Since there were no streetlights, it was very dark. In the utter blackness, she couldn't see much of the man who had chased her through the ever-narrowing streets, but she heard his slow, measured tread on the asphalt when she ran deeper into the alley. Stumbling into a doorway before she got to the end, she prayed again that she was at least on the right street. Or maybe someone on the other side of this door would let her in and she could call the police.

Leaning against the rough, unvarnished door, she stood still, gasping for every ragged breath even as she listened to his heels clicking, the hollow sounds growing louder as he moved slowly toward her.

She began to beat against the door.

"Open the door!" she screamed.

Above her cries as she pounded the rough wood, she heard running footsteps in the alley.

She screamed. The door opened, and a beefy fist snatched her inside. The last thing she heard above the deafening roar of the music as she was pulled across the threshold was a sexy, vaguely male baritone, drawling her name.

Then the door slammed and she found herself in a small room with a man who had heavy features, leering black eyes and a cold grin. If the stalker hadn't been outside, she would have bolted.

"The password?" the door man said.

"I don't know it."

"Do you have an invitation?" The man leered at her breasts, causing her to pull her shawl higher.

Indignantly she handed him the invitation she'd retrieved

from the garbage after Bryce had walked out on her. "Am I at the right place?"

Loud knocks boomed against the outside door, and he broke off, nodding abruptly. "You just got lucky, sweetheart. Go on in." He pushed a button under a counter, and a door he'd been blocking with his huge bulk swung open.

She heard the gatekeeper behind her demand the password of the stalker. Rock music and the howl of musicians blasted her as she read the purple graffiti above the door.

Dark Entry—Where Wild Things Happen…

The crowded room was so huge, she immediately wished herself safe and snug at home. The beat of the music shook her. Hundreds of guests screamed in laughter as they gyrated and shouted to each other. Some were dancing; some embracing. All were in costumes and masks. A lot of the women wore skimpy costumes that looked like lingerie.

The party was so noisy, she put her hands over her ears. The strobe lights were so bright and flickering so fast, she had to squint and shade her eyes. The place was packed, and she didn't see a soul she knew, not even Bryce.

As she moved toward the bar, the evening took on a wicked, surreal quality. The man in the alley had scared her to death, but the party scared her, too. She didn't belong here. If only she'd stayed home with Vanilla. If only…

Bryce was right—she was hopelessly dull.

On her way to the bar, she bumped into a woman with long, shiny black hair and a mask covered in hot pink sequins. The woman smiled, lifting her glass so Lizzy could ooze past her.

"Welcome to hell." The woman giggled and turned to kiss her burly date who was dressed like a pirate. Lizzy looked away. Flames leapt in massive fireplaces against one wall to give the illusion of hell, she supposed. Not that the fires gave off any heat. Even with all the people, the air felt icy.

"Lizzy…"

She twisted her head, hoping Bryce had spotted her. But he wasn't there, so she hurried on toward the bar.

On the opposite wall of the vast room, draperies hung from the high ceiling. Just as Lizzy was wondering what they were for, a man in a tiger suit grabbed a girl dressed like a yellow butterfly and threw her onto a low couch. The butterfly squealed in delight when he pulled the thick drape around their couch, creating their own private boudoir.

Lizzy slipped through a doorway into a smaller room filled with couches and plump pillows and plush Oriental carpets. Finally, at last, she found herself standing in the line at the bar. She licked her dry lips. It came as a surprise that she was very thirsty.

She glanced around. Along one wall there were doors of different rainbow colors—yellow, green, blue, pink. From time to time a man or a woman or a man and a woman together opened one of the doors and vanished inside. For what purpose, she wondered nervously. The party felt wild, much too wild for her. She shivered.

Then suddenly Bryce was standing in front of the blue door, holding hands with a pretty, young blonde in a black bondage costume. They were talking earnestly. Bryce was holding her whip and appeared to be pleading with her.

Pain shredded Lizzy's heart.

"What's behind those doors?" Lizzy asked the woman in front of her, who was dressed like black jaguar.

"Your wildest fantasy, sweetie."

Lizzy felt her jaw drop a notch.

"You open a door and go inside with someone you find attractive…man or woman. Anything can happen. There's a bed…a tub… You're obviously dressed like a hooker. If that's your fantasy, find a guy to sell yourself to. You make him pay. Then you do whatever he wants."

Lizzy gulped. *Whatever* he *wants.*

Lizzy reached the bar just as Bryce opened the door and vanished inside, his nervous date running away.

Lizzy's heart began to pound again. What if she opened that door and played the whore for Bryce? Would that really change anything? Would things be worse? Doubts besieged her. Would he want her to go to more parties like this? Could she?

"You having tonight's special, honey?"

When she nodded absently, the bartender placed an icy drink in her trembling hand.

Play the whore? How could she? Even for Bryce? Her eyes glued to those doors, she felt herself losing her nerve, so she bolted the drink. It was sweet and thick and made her thirstier. Her heart began to beat like a drum.

"My, you were thirsty." The bartender laughed and handed her another. "Slow it down," he advised. "Those are potent."

Sipping the second drink more cautiously as she wondered what to do, she walked slowly toward the doors like a sentenced person going to her execution. Her mind blurred. Yellow, green, blue, pink.

By the time she reached them, her temples were throbbing painfully. She felt hot and tingly and strange, not herself at all. What was wrong with her? The rock music pulsed along every nerve ending.

The doors seemed to grow larger, brightening into fierce rectangles of glaring light and then disappearing from sight altogether. She swayed, feeling a little dizzy when they reappeared. She couldn't help thinking about Alice falling into that rabbit hole.

She blinked. *Where am I? What am I doing here?*

Bryce—she had to get him back. She loved him. She had to show him that she loved him, that she could be the woman he'd fallen in love with that first night.

She could be a sexy New York girl—even if it killed her!

Still, she stood there for a long moment, fanning herself with her hands. She was fine, she told herself even as the doors began to spin.

The air felt close, too close. It smelled of sandalwood and incense and exotic perfumes. She didn't want to play the whore, not even for Bryce. Deep down, she knew that. All she wanted was to sit down or lie down, just for a little while until she was herself again.

But Bryce was in there. And the stalker might still be somewhere near looking for her. Fear had her heart thudding even faster than the music. It was now or never.

When she put her hand on the green door, she wasn't sure which door. So, she moved to the blue door. No... Bryce hated blue. Which door? Which door? Dear God... The music was so loud she couldn't think.

Choose.

She gulped in air and opened the green one. If he wasn't inside, she'd simply go to the next room. And then the next...until she found him. Until she showed him that she wasn't dull, that she was exciting. Until she made him realize he still loved her.

But when she stepped inside the dark room, she was so rattled by the sudden hush after the roar of the party, she forgot to close the door.

She heard footsteps. Then a shiver of air caressed her shoulder blades as the door slammed behind her.

"Bryce?"

A bolt clicked.

He'd locked them inside.

For an instant she felt like a bug trapped in a jar.

"Bryce, is that you?"

"Liz—"

"Thank God—Bryce! For a minute there...I wasn't sure which door...which color...I mean."

Ann Major

He said nothing. In the dark nothing felt real. Not even Bryce's voice had sounded real. But who else knew her name?

"I—I know you don't like surprises. You're not angry, are you...angry that I came?" she whispered.

"Lizzy, I've got something important to tell you." His low, gruff tone sounded as muffled and unsure as hers.

She had to talk fast before he got mad. She'd come here to show how much she loved him, to show him she was a new, exciting woman.

"No! Me first!" She held her breath for a second. "I—I love you," she began in a low, cottony, raw voice. "I know you want me to be wild and sexy. So, I wore the lingerie you bought me. A girl told me that these rooms are designed for us to indulge our wildest fantasies. D-did you give me that lingerie...b-because you want me to play the hooker? I will, Bryce. I'd do anything to get you back."

He didn't answer, but she could hear his breathing grow raspier.

"I'll play the hooker for you, darling. I'd do anything," she repeated.

"Anything, darlin'?" drawled that slow, deep voice that was so sensual and male, it made every nerve in her body tingle.

"You don't sound like yourself," she murmured, feeling confused.

"Neither do you," he said, but she felt him come nearer.

"Touch me," she pleaded. "I'm aching to be in your arms. Just touch me. I—I'm so scared."

"Don't be." He hesitated. "So, you're a woman of the night here to please me?"

She gasped. "Yes, oh, yes. I'll be your wildest fantasy."

"Whatever I want—you'll do it?"

"Yes. Y-your wildest fantasy."

"That won't be hard," he whispered. "You always were. You always will be."

"So, w-what exactly do you want?"

"You're a hooker, right?"

"Y-yes."

"Well, I want your mouth on me everywhere."

"All right."

"Then I want to strip you and kiss you and lick you everywhere."

She gasped.

"How much will that cost?" he whispered.

"M-money?" she squeaked, horrified.

"My fantasy…remember? You're the hooker. I'm your client. I pay. You deliver."

"Oh, y-yes…darling." She named a price.

Leather slid against fabric. He got out his wallet and counted out crisp bills. He took his time, pressing the dry wad of bills between her plump breasts with warm, probing fingers.

"Don't you want to turn on the light and make sure you didn't overpay me?"

"Don't worry. I'll make sure you earn every penny. I paid for the whole night."

When she felt a callused fingertip slide down her cheek to her throat, she shivered and jumped back. "I feel so hot and strange, not myself."

"Good, pretty lady of the night. That's the way I want you."

"I—I think I'm drunk, and I know I'm new at this. If I don't quite have the role down, please forgive me."

When he laughed again, she felt him move nearer in the darkness.

"Lizzy. Oh, Lizzy."

Something in his lazy, drawling voice sounded of Texas

and touched her heart. Desire swept her even before his hard, possessive mouth closed over hers. Then his powerful arms wrapped her so tightly, she couldn't think. She could only feel. And oh, how unexpectedly powerful those feelings were.

Something was very wrong, and yet very right. Strange. Bryce had never felt so good. Tonight her lover's arms were hard and strong, his grip tight and firm. He felt so good, she began to shake. She felt young, a girl again. He felt as good as…as good as Cole used to before she'd realized he hadn't really wanted her for herself.

Cole. The mere thought of him sent a pang of sheer, visceral longing through her. Vivid images struck her. Cole making love to her in the oak mott on a threadbare quilt. Cole making love to her on the beach behind the beach house with the pelicans flying overhead. Cole looking so ill and pale and lost after Mia's death, all his dark anger gone.

Cole. Cole. Cole. Her heart beat his name like a tattoo even as she fought to push him out of her mind.

Cole was a million miles away in Texas where he belonged. Bryce was here, kissing her, holding her. Bryce was finally on fire for her, and just because she was on fire, too, the way she used to be with Cole, she had to quit thinking about Cole.

Then her lover's tongue slid inside her lips and a hot, crazy thrill rushed through her. One taste left her reeling. One taste was all it took for her to know deep down in her bones who the man kissing her really was.

Nobody tasted like that except Cole.

What was he doing here?

Later she would wonder why she hadn't fought him. He had never wanted her. He'd only wanted the Golden Spurs Ranch. But in the heat of the moment, even knowing who he was and what he really wanted, she was too hungry for him to care.

Always, always he'd deceived her. Tonight he'd let her think he was Bryce, and she didn't even care about that. Later, she would, of course, but for now, she clung to him, kissing him back, giving him her tongue as she wound her fingers in his thick black hair.

It had been so long—years of lonely separation. And she had been lonely, lonely even when she'd pretended to herself that Bryce was perfect. No matter what she'd told herself to the contrary, she'd missed Cole. Somehow she'd continued to deny this simple, undeniable reality because his marriage to Mia on top of everything else had hurt her so terribly.

She slid her arms around Cole and pressed her body against him. When she felt his lower body harden against her, the world seemed to spin crazily on its axis.

It couldn't be. *It couldn't be.* She hated him. She loved Bryce. She'd run away from Texas to forget him.

And she *had* forgotten him. She had.

Until he'd married Mia and her sister—for reasons known only to her—had put her Golden Spurs stock in his name. Then she'd truly learned to hate him. Or had she? What was that old cliché about hate being the flip side of love? Hadn't that marriage shown her what she really wanted?

Even knowing who he was and how she really felt, she still wanted Cole right now, this very minute, more than she'd ever wanted anything else—more than she wanted New York or Bryce or any other man. She knew all of Cole's faults; she knew all the unforgivable things he'd done. He'd forced Mia to marry him. He'd accepted her stock as his due and received even more stock when Vanilla had been born. Even so, right now Lizzy still wanted him.

"You're not Bryce," said a tiny voice that had to be hers.

"No," he admitted roughly, stealing another swift kiss.

"You followed me here? You tricked me."

"Or maybe you tempted me."

I should slap you. Tomorrow I know I'll never forgive myself for this.

"Cole?" she whispered against his lips. "It's you. Really you."

He didn't deny it. "I wouldn't have let it go too far without telling you who I was."

"Like I really believe that."

"It's the truth."

Cole. Here. It was almost too much to believe. "How did you get past the man at the door?"

"I waited until a couple arrived who knew the password."

When he kissed her again, she wrapped her arms around his waist, glued her body to his and held on tight. She couldn't stop squeezing him or kissing him. Desire built inside her like a burning tide, and she put her hands on each of his cheeks and touched her mouth against his again and again.

He groaned raggedly.

God, how she'd missed him, longed for him, and hadn't wanted anybody to know, least of all herself.

Her hands dug his shirt out of his jeans and she slid her arms around him, needing, compelled to touch his hot brown skin.

"I vowed to hate you forever," she said.

"You pretty much stuck to that vow," he reassured her with a rueful laugh.

"Until now."

"Until now," he muttered. "Don't start hating me again tonight, darlin'. I'm sorry for whatever I did."

The real Cole wasn't sorry. But right now Lizzy was too far gone to care.

She tore his shirt from his body and ran her mouth and tongue up and down his torso, lingering over his nipples and navel, kissing him until she felt like molten flame.

What was she doing? Was she drunk? Why this crazy, wild combustion of emotion and passion for a man she hated? And yet in his arms, she felt like she was shooting sparks, bursting, completely alive—for the first time in years.

She remembered the first time he'd been inside her. That night she'd told herself she'd love him forever. But so much had happened. He was a Knight, and she was a Kemble. She'd run away from him and Texas to make it in the big city.

He'd left south Texas too after their breakup. Only he'd returned with a pilot's license and enough money to start his crop-dusting business. Then he'd married Mia.

He loved the land and cows and the big sky and the big silences as much as she hated them.

But she hadn't been as successful in New York as he'd been at his pursuits.

Cole Knight, bad as he was, vengeful as he'd been, was the only thing I was ever good at.

Was it the icy drinks and the bizarre circumstances and the sexy game she'd played with him that had her so confused? Or had these games opened doors to her truer self?

She didn't know. She didn't care. She only knew that she needed more…more…more of him. Like Alice, who'd fallen into that rabbit hole, this dark little room and her desire for Cole had become her new reality.

His mouth found her nape and sent more hot ripples through her.

"I want you naked," he said on a shudder. "But not here. Not like this. You said you were drunk. I won't take advantage of that."

"I don't understand— You just paid me—"

"Not like this," he growled, sounding as stubborn as she remembered him being.

"Cole— What's happening to us? I hate you. Or at least I'm supposed to— And you hated me…or at least you did…before the amnesia." Her words tumbled out as she tried to gather her thoughts and emotions.

"Lizzy… Oh, God, Lizzy. I don't remember, but I don't hate you now. I couldn't hate you, darlin'. I want you too damn much. I came here because—"

"But you married Mia."

"Mia? I don't even remember Mia. I never think about her or dream about her. Only you. You haunt me, darlin'. Not Mia. I want *you.* Not *her.*"

"I'm a mess, Cole. My whole life's a mess. You couldn't want me. Not if you knew."

"Trust me on this." His large, rough hands covered her softer, smaller ones. "I want you, darlin'. I want you very, very much." Slowly he brought her fingertips to his lips. When he kissed each one, she tingled all the way to her toes.

She felt breathless. And crazy.

He wanted the ranch, and he'd married Mia to get his foot in the door. Was he after her now for the same reason?

Bryce was here at this party. Her whole world was going up in flames, and she was too mad with desire for Cole to care.

One thing she knew—before morning, before her conscience or sanity or the prude in her kicked in and told her not to, she was going to sleep with Cole Knight.

Why shouldn't she have him? Just one more time. Even if her life was a mess. Have him here in New York. Why the hell not?

He might want her for the ranch, but so what? She was on to him. Tomorrow morning she could turn into the New York girl of her dreams and send him packing.

In the meantime, why shouldn't the new, exciting her console herself with a night of unforgettable sex—after all she'd been through?

He opened the door to the room and rock music bombarded them. "Hold on to me, darlin'," he said.

"My God," she whispered, clenching his hand.

If possible, the party seemed a whole lot wilder than it had when she'd first arrived. A girl in a beige satin bikini, who looked nude in the half-light, was chained to posts and writhed to the beat of the music. A man in a toga rushed onto the stage, unchained her, and carried her off on his shoulder screaming.

Everywhere men and women were dancing to the wild music and drinking and laughing.

Lizzy had never been to a party like this, but Cole seemed suddenly enraged at her that she was here. Frowning, he folded her close against his great body as he heaved himself through the mass of humanity.

"How about a foursome?" a man in a red satin suit with horns yelled at them.

What if Cole said yes?

"Maybe later," Cole retorted grimly, causing Lizzy to flush.

A woman painted silver with flowers clinging to each breast threw herself at Cole. Lizzy's breath stopped, but Cole deftly evaded the wanton's embrace and kissed Lizzy instead.

"Had enough?" he growled into her ear.

Before he could hustle Lizzy away from the woman, her date squeezed Lizzy's bottom. Lizzy had had too much. Without thinking, she jabbed her high heel into the man's ankle, and he doubled over, yelping in pain.

Cole laughed. "Don't commit murder. We're almost to the exit, darlin'," he said.

She looked up and she felt giddy with relief when she saw the door ahead. What had she been thinking of to come to such a party?

They were nearly to the door when she saw Bryce nursing a drink at the bar. Before she lowered her head, he saw

her. His face lit up, and he grinned. When he waved and
beckoned her to come over, she was stunned she felt nothing for him. Absolutely nothing.

Bryce called her name and she gripped Cole's hand as if
it were a lifeline and dug in her heels. When Cole stopped,
she tried to drag him toward the exit.

"You know that guy?" Cole demanded.

"I—I used to," she admitted, panicking.

"He wants to talk to you."

"I want to be with you. Just you."

"You sure, darlin'?"

No. She wasn't sure of anything. Her world had just
turned upside down, and she didn't have a clue as to where
she should go from here.

Definitely nowhere with Cole, said a voice.

Not that she paid the least bit of attention to it.

Eight

A short while later, Lizzy squinted against the bright glare of the overhead lights in the café. Or maybe she did so because Cole was so handsome in his cowboy uniform. As always he wore jeans and boots. The only thing missing was his Stetson.

His white long-sleeved shirt made him look very bronzed. His hair and eyebrows were as black and thick as ever; his cheekbones as high and slashed. He was cruelly, sensually handsome. Just looking at his carved jaw made her tingle.

"What's the matter?" Cole demanded. "See anybody you know?"

Shading her eyes so as not to stare at him so directly, Lizzy scanned the café for a familiar face and then shook her head. She pulled her shawl higher. After running into Bryce, she felt a little spooked.

"Have you dated anybody…since Mia?" She covered her mouth with her hands. She couldn't believe she'd blurted that out.

"No." He paused. "You come here often? With other guys?"

"Never. Which is good. I'd die if somebody I knew saw me like this."

He laughed. "You're shy about coming here and you went to *that* party?"

"Sometime maybe I'll explain."

The air smelled of old bacon grease and coffee brewing. She sighed with relief as she glanced around again, glad that the café wasn't one she usually frequented.

Thank goodness there weren't many diners to see her in her costume. The plump waitress with the long red hair looked too tired to be interested in anything but getting off work and going home. The woman was leaning over the counter and scribbling something on a tablet. Dishes clattered noisily behind the swinging doors to the kitchen.

"I feel so ridiculous drinking coffee in this costume," Lizzy said, relaxing a little as she lifted the cup to her lips.

Cole's dark eyes glinted with sexual mischief. "Then we'll have to get you out of it—first thing, just as soon as you sober up."

"Why are you here? I mean, in New York?"

His face darkened, and he drew a deep breath. He looked away as if he were suddenly as uncomfortable as she was. "If I had a reason, you damn sure derailed me." He eyed her again. "What the hell were you doing at a party like that? Dressed like that?"

"Oh, God." She still felt funny and warm after the drinks and all their kissing. Not that she was about to confess to him that even after a cup of coffee his dark, rugged face was still zooming in and out of focus.

"You're not going to tell Daddy about this, are you?"

His frown deepened.

"Did Daddy send you to bring me home or something?"

He didn't deny it.

"Oh, God!" She covered her face with her hands.

"What if he did?" Cole blurted.

"I—I can't go home…even though I've made such a mess of my life here."

"Your life isn't over yet," Cole said gently. "You've still got a lot of time to fix it."

"So, Daddy sent you?"

Cole's large, tanned hands knotted. His mouth thinned. A muscle ticked in his jawline. "Lizzy, there's something…"

She drew a quick breath. "No! I don't want to hear the reasons why he sent you or even talk about him right now. Maybe I can't make my life work, but I won't have Daddy running it. Never again. Can you understand that?"

"Sure." He looked away again as if he had things on his mind that were bothering him too. "If you'd answered your phone when they called—"

"I want to be independent. To do something, anything on my own. They call all the time."

"So you took your phone off the hook?"

She nodded. "I had the most terrible day of my life. I just couldn't talk to them."

He stared out the window. "So here I am," he said softly, dread in his low tone.

God, his classically chiseled profile was as handsome as the rest of him. Suddenly she wished they'd stayed in that snug little room at the party where nothing had been real. She'd wanted him so much then. Now she was beginning to feel really scared.

"Please, let's don't talk about my parents."

It was his turn to nod silently.

"Cole, you said on our walk to this café that you won't touch me until I'm sober." She set her coffee cup down. "Why do I have to be sober before we can have sex? Most guys want to get a girl drunk."

"I'm not like most guys, I guess."

"What if I don't want to do it when I'm sober?"

"Then we won't."

"And you wouldn't care?"

"Is that really what you think of me?" His gaze drifted to her mouth. "Of course, I'd care. Too much." His dark eyes grew so hungry, they seemed to scorch her. "I think you know exactly what you do to me."

She gasped. He didn't even have to touch her to make her blood heat and her pulse pound. "You're so different now."

He frowned. "Look, I know what it's like to have your mind messed up so you can't think straight. You do things and you feel things and you don't know why. That's why I don't drink much now."

"You really are so much nicer with amnesia."

"Other people have told me that, too."

"And I hate that about you. I really do."

"I hate the bastard I must have been," he said, a bitter edge in his voice.

"Shhh."

She'd distrusted him being nicer because it had weakened her resistance to him when she'd visited home. "You were so dark and brooding before. It was so much easier to dislike you."

"But we were friends…"

More than friends. Lovers. She nodded.

"Lizzy, what did I do to make you hate me?"

"Not tonight." She was still determined on that night of unforgettable sex. Talking about her father or what Cole had done would ruin everything. Tomorrow when she booted him out, she could explain if he still wanted to hear it all again. "Can't we just go home and hop into bed?"

"Drink that whole cup. Then we'll hop."

She sipped as quickly as she could, but it was so hot, she burned her tongue. Thus, she was forced to take her time while he watched her. Even as she began to sober up and feel more like herself, her desire for him increased. When she finished the cup, he got up and paid the bill.

They went out into the brisk night air. "Are you going to make me walk the whole way back to my apartment?"

"You're in charge of getting us home, darlin'. After all, you know the way."

When she stepped off the curb to hail a taxi, two cabs skidded across the street toward her, one eventually claiming the coveted spot in front of her.

Cole leaned down to open the door to the cab and helped her inside. "I see I'm not the only guy who digs your hooker costume. Hey, don't forget I paid for the whole night."

Music wrapped Lizzy like liquid, sensual velvet sounds as she swayed back and forth in the pool of moonlight.

He was right…sobering up had changed the mood…

Oh, God…. What was she doing? Stripping for Cole? In her own apartment?

She tore her shawl off and threw at him. Cole snatched it out of the air with his brown hand and laughed.

Lizzy felt stiff as she tried to dance to the music on the radio while at the same time she unzipped her red dress and eased it over her shoulders. Even as she tried to make her hips undulate, her legs began to freeze, and her hands started shaking. Then she made the mistake of looking at Cole from beneath her lashes.

He was sprawled on her couch watching her, holding her shawl coiled around a brown fist. In his other hand he held the rose that had been in her bud vase.

What was he thinking? Did he have doubts about what they were about to do, too?

Her fingers went numb, and she thought, *I want him so much. Too much. But…why is he here?*

Strangely, being alone with him in the familiar setting of her apartment made her more nervous than she'd been in the dark, impersonal little room at the party. Her desk with its books and laptop and her telephone that was still off the hook reminded her of the job she had just lost. Her mantel crammed with family photos of her father and mother and Mia made her think of her roots back in Texas. Maybe her daddy had sent Cole. Maybe they got along a little better now. But Caesar would want to kill Cole if he ever found out what was happening between them.

"I can't," she whispered in the exact moment her red dress surrendered to the force of gravity, falling from her breasts. Losing her nerve, she tried to grab it, but the silk slid down her hips and oozed over her legs, pooling at her ankles in rumples of red that glowed in the moonlight.

Oh, God....

Mindlessly, she continued to sway in a provocative, sensual dance. Cole leaned forward, his dark face intent, his brilliant dark eyes burning her and making her feel new, reborn, and excitingly sexy.

She wanted great sex tonight, wanted it to erase all her failures, wanted it to reassure her that Bryce was wrong and that she was still sexy.

"I—I can't do this," she whispered brokenly as she stopped dancing. "I'm too dull and boring." On a moan that betrayed how truly miserable she was, she covered her breasts with her hands.

"Sure you can," he murmured. "You're doing great. Oh, darlin', you're the last thing from dull."

She blushed as she realized what she must look like to him with her half-naked breasts bulging above the corset, with her thong panties, garter belt and the black stockings.

"This isn't the real me," she murmured forlornly.

"No—it's a fantasy. You look wonderful. Gorgeous. Wild."

She touched the red ribbons of her corset with trembling fingers. "I'm afraid I'm not very good at this. Not with you looking…at me like that."

"It's sexier if you're not very good at it."

"I don't under…"

"Your innocence appeals to me."

"I'm supposed to be a hooker not an innocent…dull…"

"Hush, darlin'."

"Maybe we should forget about me stripping for you and just get into bed."

"So you can hide from me under the covers?" He laughed, and the sound warmed her. "I paid," he drawled sexily. "I'm your john, remember. Your first. This is my fantasy. You promised you'd strip. I'm not going to hurt you."

Burning color washed her face, and his eagerness made her shake. "I—I didn't know how shy and ridiculous I'd feel."

She whirled, turning her back to him. Then realizing that her buttocks were almost totally exposed to his avid gaze by her revealing, black lace thong panties, she spun back around again. Only now, his eyes glowed even hotter, and her cheeks were on fire, too. "I—I need more time," she squeaked.

"Maybe the music needs to be louder," he said gently, turning up the volume. "Maybe you'll feel better in the dark." She saw his powerful arm move, and heard the sound of the chain on the lamp beside the couch. Then the living room melted into velvet darkness lit only by shimmers of moonlight.

"How about some different music?" Deftly he switched to a rock station that had a hard, jungle beat.

She stomped her feet several times before she realized doing so made her breasts jiggle. "I still can't. I just can't. I'm sorry. I'm no good at this."

"So—I can't say you didn't warn me. Do you want me to go?" He got up slowly. "Because I will."

He was so different, so thoughtful. He replaced the rose in the vase and stepped toward the door.

"No, dance with me," she whispered, reaching for his hand across the darkness, even as her heart began to knock in her throat. "Hold me."

The minute his fingers wound around hers, she felt okay again, better than okay, alive, pulsingly, achingly alive.

"I can't believe this is really happening," she said as he folded her into his hard, strong arms. His hands slid into her hair, stroking the silken mass.

"Neither can I." His thumbs caressed her temple and then her eyebrows. "Do you have any idea what you do to me?" he demanded huskily, lowering his mouth to her nape. "When I came here, I never imagined something like this."

His lips and warm breath on her sensitive skin made her shudder long after he ended the kiss. She reached up and began a tentative exploration of his handsome face, tracing his mouth with a fingertip, which he sucked inside his lips.

He shifted his weight, and their bodies settled closer. Soon his holding her began to feel more natural. He was tall, much taller than she'd remembered. He was solid, built of muscle that felt like warm, living steel.

No city boy—Cole. He'd worked hard; he *was* hard. Hard and stubborn. And right now she didn't mind that at all.

He bent his dark head and his lips found hers, his tongue sliding instantly inside. Like always, he was a flawless kisser. Which was good. This was what she'd wanted and needed, his lips, his body, the physical simplicity of it. Slowly her shyness receded.

As they held on to one another, swaying back and forth to the music, her body remembered his and responded to him. When the song finished, he did not loosen his grip. Indeed, he went on holding her, staring at her, and as the moment lengthened, she felt shudders of emotion spiraling through her.

His hands found the red ribbons of her corset. Expertly he began to unlace her as she watched his face. When her breasts were free, he stopped and lowered his dark head to kiss each nipple until they were berry-hard. At the first slight contact of his wet mouth, fiery heat spilled through her in waves.

The music began again, but she barely heard it. She was floating in a sensual dream, her blood warmed by his lips on her breasts and the intensity of his mood. He kissed each nipple again and again with a reverence that stunned her. Her hands dipped into the black satin thickness of his hair, and she moaned, arching her body against his.

He was hard and fully aroused as he continued to kiss her. Slowly his mouth moved lower, down to her belly. Then she felt his hands clasp her thong panties and pull them down her thighs a little way. He parted her legs, and he knelt before her. She felt his warm breath first. Then his hands cupped her buttocks, pulling her closer. Last of all he kissed her *there*.

Her fingers dug into his scalp on a gasp as he began to lick her. "Take me to bed," she pleaded. "Now."

She wasn't drunk, and yet all she could think of was sex. Sex with Cole. With Cole, who'd betrayed her and then married her sister. With Cole, who some said had even killed her sister. He hadn't, of course. She would never believe him capable of anything like that.

"Why are you here?" she said.

"Somebody must have known you needed a guardian angel on Halloween," he whispered. "So, here I am—your very own gorilla man."

"I have to explain about tonight. I—I dressed like this…because my boyfriend left me. He said I was too dull."

"Then forget him. He's a jerk. An idiot."

"I wanted to prove…that I was wild."

"Darlin', you're wild. Trust me."

"You know that guy who spoke to me as we were leaving the party."

Cole nodded. "Darlin', how long do we have to talk about this jerk?"

"He was the guy."

"The right guy showed up, and you still left with me. Why?"

In a burst of emotion she flung her arms around his neck and kissed the top of his black head. "I don't know why any of this is happening."

"Maybe because it just is." Cole stood up. His arms circled her waist, and he kissed her long and deeply. Then he said, "I'll leave right now if you think it's best."

"Are you out of your mind?" She laughed. "I embarrass myself by being a failure as a striptease artist, and you don't want to make love to me and console me."

"Consolation, huh? That's what you want? Okay, darlin', I'll console the hell out of you." Before she could think up a flirtatious reply, he picked her up and carried her to her bedroom.

He kicked the bedroom door open and then kicked it shut, moving swiftly, silently to her bed before he put her down.

Moonlight streamed through the shades, gilding his dark body with silver. Without taking his eyes off her, he sat down and removed his boots and then his socks. One by one, the boots clunked onto the oak floor. Then he stood again and unbuttoned his shirt, ripping it out of his jeans and shrugging out of it, all the time devouring her with his hot gaze.

She gasped at the sheer perfection of him. He was all dark, sleek, rippling muscle—his arms, his broad shoulders, his sculpted torso. When she gasped, he caught her in his arms and quickly stripped her remaining garments off her. The eager trembling of his hands told her that he burned with desire as he undid her garter belt and hand-rolled her stockings down to her toes. Then he slid her thong panties the rest of the way down her legs. Last of all, he finished unlacing the corset, peeling it off her, inch by inch.

Strangely, when she was completely naked, she didn't feel the least bit shy anymore. Eyes shining, she reached for him, running her hands over his lean, muscular torso. When she found the zipper of his jeans, her hand slid inside to circle him, and he groaned aloud. When she unzipped him slowly, teasingly, and he yanked his jeans off. Next came his boxers.

For a long time they simply stared at one another. Then he took her in his arms and folded her close, so close their bodies fused, or so it seemed in her heightened state of arousal.

He kissed her mouth, her cheeks, her ears, her throat slowly, so slowly. He kissed her until she was breathless and shaking, he kissed her until the bedroom was spinning around her.

This is dangerous. Really dangerous, she thought as he lay beside her on the bed, facing her.

"I never imagined this would happen," he said, caressing her cheek.

"Are you glad?" she whispered.

"What do you think?"

"I'm glad, too," she said.

"Then that's all that matters."

"And tomorrow?"

"To hell with tomorrow." He pulled her closer. Then his rough hand moved between her legs. Parting them, he touched the delicate feminine folds and explored her while she caressed him just as eagerly and tenderly. When they had each other so wild they could barely breathe, his large body slid over her slim one, and he plunged inside her. Her body welcomed his, arching against him. He went still for a long, utterly perfect moment, savoring their being joined. Then he withdrew from her, slowly, teasing her until she begged for more.

"Please. Please…"

When he plunged inside her again, she screamed in pleasure. Again he was still for a long time. Finally, he began to rock back and forth, at first gently and then more violently, filling every inch of her with exquisite, molten sensations.

Her emotions built and built as his kisses grew hungrier and more frantic. She clung, crying out his name as he drove into her that last time. They exploded at exactly the same moment. Wave after wave of ecstasy enveloped her as they lay still, fused, their hearts pounding.

Afterward, when he released her, she lay in his arms and felt totally relaxed, limp, utterly complete in a way that she hadn't in years. *Cole. Cole.* She couldn't believe what had happened.

At last she found the strength to roll onto her side and run her hands and lips over his warm body in wonder. Even with his skin gleaming with sweat, he was gorgeous. He was athletic, lean and hard. Perfect. Too incredibly perfect. It was as if her body had been a missing part of his, as if all this time spent without him, she'd been incomplete.

She continued to stroke him, liking the way his flesh quivered beneath her fingertips. All too soon, his manhood grew engorged again, and this time she mounted him. He made love to her more gently, rocking his hips so slowly as he thrust, she thought she'd die from the bliss of it. So slowly every cell in her being began to throb in expectation until finally the slightest movement was too much.

She wasn't dull. She wasn't. She was a magical, fiery, sensual being. At least she was with Cole.

Afterward, she lay wrapped in his arms again, staring up

at the silvery ceiling. How could she have ever thought herself so in love with Bryce and feel like this for Cole? Had she only been with Bryce because she'd been so lonely without Cole?

Yes, Bryce was wrong about her. She *was* wild. Just not with him.

Maybe she couldn't feel like this with anyone except Cole.

He'd married Mia.

But he wasn't that man anymore. He didn't remember Mia. He remembered *her*. Only her. Was that the truth? Or was he just saying that?

All she knew was that no one had ever excited her even half as much as Cole. She didn't want to believe he was solely driven to acquire a bigger percentage of the ranch, or that her life was an even bigger mess than she'd thought.

Cole was the one thing she'd been good at. *The one thing.*

Still, no matter what, she had to send him away in the morning. Somehow she had to. She simply had to. There was too much bad history between them. If she was ever going to make her life work here in the city, she had to find herself before she got seriously involved with Cole Knight again.

Yet closing her eyes and nestling closer to him, she wished tomorrow would never come.

Nine

Cole woke up first. The bed was too soft and the woman tangled in his arms and legs too warm. It was dark outside, but city sounds and the wail of a nearby siren disoriented him. Then he smelled the sweet scent of roses and saw Lizzy's silver hair gleaming in the moonlight on his pillow.

Lizzy. New York. Caesar.

You should have told her about her father first thing!

He was a horny, no-good bastard. When she'd pranced out of her apartment in those stilettos and that tight red dress with her breasts bulging and her legs encased in black hose, his untrustworthy brain had gone south on him again.

He'd barely noticed Vanilla and her friend. He'd gotten hot for Lizzy instantly. Visions of her naked and lying beneath him that had felt too damn much like memories had knocked him off-kilter.

When he'd followed her into that little room at the party, intending to tell her why he'd come, she'd blindsided him by coming on to him. When she'd kissed him like a wanton, more baffling images and feelings had bombarded his mind and heart. Soon he'd felt crazy with lust and desire—and tenderness, too. He hadn't understood any of his emotions, but he'd felt on the verge of remembering something so important, he'd had no choice but to follow her lead.

Her mouth on his in the darkness, her nearness had felt familiar and right. Nevertheless, he should have told her about Caesar then. Period. Now he was swamped with guilt that he'd used her to explore the dark, mysterious recesses of his mind. And to satisfy his lust.

Mia. Where the hell did Mia fit in any of this? When he'd begun to get better after the accident, yet hadn't been able to remember his wife and child, he'd started asking questions. Joanne and Caesar hadn't been much help. At first others had been equally reluctant to talk, but after a while, a few of the hands had filled him in.

Eli had been mucking out a stall when he'd finally lost his temper at being pestered and said, "I'll tell you once, so listen up, boy. You sprung from the cradle with a chip on your shoulder a mile wide. I never liked you much until after the accident. All you ever talked about was how five generations of double-dealing Kembles had stolen land either by rustling cattle from the saintly Knights or buying Texas Rangers and politicians or lawyers until finally they whittled your daddy down to his last fifty thousand acres. Then old Caesar tricked him out of that in a drunken card game. Whine. Whine. Whine.

"So you wanted the Kemble Ranch, pure and simple. All of it, if possible. That's why you bedded naive, bumbling Lizzy. Only Caesar finally outsmarted you and made her see you only wanted his land, not her. When she dumped you and ran off, you ran off, too. Only you came back a few years later with money in your pocket, more arrogant than ever. First thing you did? You got Mia pregnant."

Cole frowned, not much liking the man Eli had described. Was that really what had happened? Had revenge and greed been all he'd cared about? If he'd only wanted Lizzy for the ranch, why did she haunt him day and night?

When Lizzy had offered herself to him last night, he could no more have stopped from making love to her than he could have stopped himself from breathing. Ever since the plane accident, his one ambition had been to remember his life. He wanted his life to make sense. He couldn't remember Vanilla or Mia. Only the land and horses and cattle and planes and Lizzy sparked something incredible and powerful in him. Somehow Lizzy was the key.

So, had he used her last night? Would she think that? Or would she think worse—that greed for the ranch had driven him? His thoughts made him queasy. He knew she lacked self-confidence because Caesar had been so hard on her. He would never forgive himself if she thought he'd used her.

Making love to her had seemed so natural, familiar and wonderful. But although he felt nearer to some vital truth, he was still lost in the dark.

He pulled her closer and nuzzled his lips against her throat. "Forgive me," he whispered. "Forgive me."

While he lay huddled against her until dawn, he berated himself for having gone to bed with her. He wouldn't blame her if she believed the worst when he told her about Caesar in the morning.

Hours later Lizzy awoke to sunlight and traffic sounds outside. She blushed when she opened her eyes and saw Cole's tanned arm draped across her paler breasts. His other dark hand was wrapped around her waist.

Bryce had never liked to snuggle or spoon, and she felt vulnerable and deliciously warm and cherished to be lying like this with Cole. Suddenly she felt far too vulnerable to face him in bed in the cold light of morning.

Carefully, she disentangled his arms and slid out from under him and raced out of her bedroom. Flying across the living room on her tiptoes to the bathroom on the other side of her tiny kitchen, she closed the door and stared at herself in the bathroom mirror.

The slut in the mirror with the wild platinum hair stared back at her in wide-eyed horror.

"Oh, God. He can't see me like this," she whispered to her reflection, grabbing a brush and vainly attempting to run it through her matted hair. She had to shower and dress.

Vanilla! Lizzy glanced at her watch. In an hour Mandy would show up with Vanilla. She had to be dressed, and Cole had to be gone before then.

But she didn't want him gone.

A genuine kick-ass New Yorker couldn't lose her nerve now. With shaking hands, Lizzy turned on her shower and stepped under the warm flow from the spigot. The water felt so delicious, she forgot to hurry. She was washing her hair, when she heard the door open and the shower curtain stir against her naked bottom.

"Mind if I join you?" Cole murmured, his low voice tenderly enticing as he pulled the shower curtain back and wrapped his arm around her waist.

When he started to step into the shower, she screamed and shrank against the tile wall, struggling to elude him. His hand caressed her soap-slick body although he seemed to have abandoned his attempt to enter her shower space.

She grabbed the edge of the shower curtain and wrapped the plastic primly around her body. "No! Go away! I'm not in the mood!" *But she was.*

"I didn't mean to scare you," he said gently, his eyes on her face. "I forgot you're not a morning person."

"You don't know me anymore."

"After last night, I know plenty. And I like what I do know."

"That was just sex."

He laughed and brushed her nipple through the plastic curtain, as if to tease her out of her bad mood.

"Don't! Last night was an…an aberration."

"That's a big word to use on a cowboy, darlin'," he drawled sexily.

"Mistake."

"Maybe for you."

She groaned. Stepping out of the shower, she reached around his naked form and grabbed a towel from the rack. "For your information, I don't even like you." *Liar.*

"Ouch."

"I mean it!" She wrapped the towel around her body and towel-dried her hair with another one from the rack.

His expression darkened. "That's a little hard to believe…after last night. You slept with me, remember?"

"It was a one-night stand, okay? Grow up. That's a common event in this city."

"No, ma'am. Not for you. Or me. I don't buy it."

"Well, maybe I don't care what you buy."

"I bought you, didn't I?" His quick, flirtatious grin was white and so adorable, she wanted to kick him.

"Look, you can have the bathroom. Wallow in the tub to your heart's content. Or shower until you use up every drop of hot water. But I'm going to my bedroom. I intend to dress and get ready for my day. When I come out, you'd better be gone."

He swallowed. "So, that's how we're going to play it."

"What did you think? Last night was sex. Great sex. But that's all."

"Oh, really?"

"Really," she insisted. He looked…hurt…and that got to her so much her heart began knocking in her throat.

"Why am I even surprised? You're the great Kemble heiress."

She had to finish this now. "And you're the upstart Knight with a grudge against my daddy and my ancestors because we're not drunks and…"

"And what?" he prompted angrily.

"Revenge is why you courted me in the first place. It's why you married my sister. It's probably why you did what you did last night."

"Which is?"

"You seduced me."

"The hell I did. Darlin', if anybody seduced anybody, *you* seduced *me*. Not that I'm complaining. I enjoyed every minute."

She stomped past him and was halfway across the living room, when he yelled after her, "Last night before you derailed me, you asked me why I came here—"

In spite of herself, she froze. "I know why you came, why you've done everything you've ever done—including last night. Revenge. Greed. I was a fool, okay? I was lonely. I needed a...*good time*...which you provided. Right now, I— I just want you gone."

"You should have answered your damn phone then. Your daddy's sick, girl."

"What?" Her knees went limp with shock as she turned to face him.

"I didn't come because I wanted to see you." His eyes flashed.

"What?" Her hands began to shake violently.

"Your mother asked me to bring you home." He slammed the bathroom door.

Lizzy forgot she was naked except for the towel she held around her body. "What's wrong with Daddy?"

When he didn't open the door or answer her, she stalked back across the living room and pushed the bathroom door open so hard it banged against her tile wall. "It's not nice to slam doors when someone's trying to talk to you!"

Cole turned toward her. "He had a stroke."

"He had a stroke?"

"When he was in bed with Cherry."

"And you didn't tell me this until right now? How bad off is he?"

Cole's bleak, hopeless eyes told her more than she wanted to know.

"How's Mother?" As if she even needed to ask. Her heart ached as she remembered all the phone calls. Her wise, stoic, chilly, depressed mother was frantic. *And he hadn't told her until now!* She would have called her last night if only she'd known.

"She's in Houston. He's getting the best possible care there."

"How could you not tell me for hours and hours?" she whispered, her own guilt mushrooming as she wiped at the hot tears stinging her eyes.

"It wouldn't have made any difference," he said dully. "We couldn't leave until this morning. I called the airport. The weather's great all the way to Texas. You need to pack— fast. Where the hell's Vanilla? Call your friend. Get her—"

"Selfish bastard!" Lizzy hissed, stomping toward him. "You knew he was ill and you— You wanted to use me. You wanted to sleep with me so badly, you didn't tell—"

"No—"

"I hated you already, but I'll really hate you forever for this. Do you understand? Forever!"

"So what else is new, darlin'?"

"I could have called Mother!" Even before she rushed him, his dark face went chalk white. She read guilt and regret on his handsome features.

She remembered the way she'd thrown herself at him last night and she began to pound at his wide brown chest with her fists. When the towel around her body fell to the floor, she stopped her attack long enough to lean down and retrieve it. Not that she wrapped herself with it. She balled it up and shoved at his shoulders.

She didn't care if she was naked. She didn't care if her body writhed against his and her nipples became instantly tender and erect. Her eyes blazed. "You cad. You beast. You slept with me! And all the time—"

"Stop it!" He grabbed her shoulders and pushed her into the white tiled wall, which felt cool against her burning skin.

"For God's sake, Lizzy, just stop it." He drew a deep breath. "I should have told you, okay. I'm sorry. But things happened so fast. And then later it seemed pointless to make you worry about Caesar an extra day. He's stable. And he's damn sure not going anywhere. But we've got to hurry now."

Suddenly she was aware that the combination of her fury and grief and her body being mashed into the heat of his was arousing them both. Enraged, she let out a low animal sound. "Let me go!"

His hands fell from her shoulders and he backed up a step.

Still carrying her towel, she raced into the living room.

"This isn't all my fault you know," he said, following her. "If you'd answered your damned phone, your mother wouldn't have had to send me. We wouldn't be standing here naked in your apartment having this idiotic quarrel. I didn't want to come, you know."

The logic of his statement served only to make Lizzy feel angrier and more guilt-ridden, so naturally she made him her scapegoat. "Well, you certainly made the most of it."

"So the hell did you. What results did you expect with that hooker act?"

"I don't have to take this!"

"Joanne told me to bring you and Vanilla home. She needs you to help her run the ranch until your dad's better…or this divorce thing is resolved. She's at her wit's end. She needs you there."

"Me? Run the Golden Spurs?"

"*You.*"

The situation was worsening by the second. "I don't know anything... What about Hawk or Walker?"

"Your father kicked them off the ranch. He doesn't want them."

"Anybody would be better than me."

"Not as long as your father's alive. Look, you know more than you think. Ranching is in your blood. Your daddy spent years training you. You have that college degree. I'll help you. Lots of people will help you. The suits in San Antonio are full of ideas."

Dazed, she shook her head. "I don't believe any of this. You fly up here and then you don't tell me about Daddy... Just for the record, I don't want any more help from you. You've done more than enough to screw my life up royally."

"For what it's worth, I'm sorry, Lizzy. Sorry for everything. For last night, too, since you regret it so much. But believe me, I intend to keep my distance from now on. I don't like waking up in the morning to a fight. I'm in here over my head, too."

Something in his low, sincere voice, maybe compassion, touched her heart more than she wanted it to.

"You go to hell, Cole Knight," she whispered, hoping he wouldn't hear her fear and the aching need beneath her bluster. She felt like a scared, heartbroken little girl who needed to bawl her eyes out in his arms. She was mad at him, but she needed him, too. She almost hated him for making her feel pulled two ways.

He swallowed. That muscle in his jaw ticked furiously.

Good. He hadn't seen through her. She'd managed to hurt him.

"Get dressed! Now!" His face changed. "Or would you rather me do it for you?"

"What?"

"Hey, maybe we could start the day with a dress-tease. Get the juices flowing so to speak."

"How dare you! I do hate you!"

"You're repeating yourself, darlin'."

"Don't call me—" Just as she was about to launch into a rather passionate and in-depth explanation as to why she disliked him so much, her doorbell buzzed.

Lizzy gasped. "Oh, God. Mandy's downstairs with Vanilla. They're early."

"No kidding. Guess she got tired of baby-sitting. My first thought was she didn't much look like the baby-sitter type."

"Nobody asked you."

Cole strode toward her and pressed the button that unlocked the doors downstairs. "I'll stay here and get the door. You get dressed."

"But you're stark naked."

"So the hell are you, darlin'."

They stared at each other. He was broad-shouldered, tanned and virile—a hunk if ever there was one. Blood pounded in her throat. In spite of herself, she shivered.

"Too bad we don't have more time," he said knowingly. "You look good. Too good. And your soap smells like roses."

"You swore you'd keep your distance, remember?"

"Thanks for the reminder."

His black gaze raked her. Not that she cowered like a Victorian maiden or even covered herself with her towel—much as she was tempted. No, she stood frozen like a deer caught in a pair of headlights and endured his knowing, insolent eyes as he assessed her charms. She endured his slow, appreciative grin, too.

Not that she grinned back. But she looked at him with equal fascination.

Finally he broke the spell by leaning toward her and snatching the towel she'd been holding. As he tightened the thick cotton folds around his waist, he shot her a smile that was so sexually charged, she almost kicked him.

Not wanting to give him the satisfaction of knowing how much he goaded her, she gritted her teeth.

She did not want him. She couldn't.

"If looks could kill," he teased, grinning charmingly at her again as he finger-combed his black hair.

"Exactly. You're a cad."

"Cad? That word's old-fashioned. You need to expand your vocabulary when it comes to insults—city slicker."

"If you stick around, I probably will."

"So, there's a chance for us?" He winked at her.

"No. Hell, no."

"Darlin', we both know all I'd have to do is touch you."

"Shut up. Just shut up. And you'd better remember to stick to your promise to keep your distance."

"I hear your friend. They're almost up the stairs," he said warningly. "You're still standing there naked."

Lizzy scampered into the bedroom at the exact moment he opened the door for them.

"Where's Bryce? Who the hell are you?" Mandy demanded upon seeing Lizzy's handsome, towel-clad guest.

"Cole Knight. Bryce is history. I'm here to take Lizzy home to Texas."

"Well, you're fast. I'll give you that. Did you two meet at the party or what?"

"You know Lizzy—never a *dull* moment."

Lizzy sagged against her bedroom door and groaned.

"Hi, there little darling," Cole murmured, his voice so sweet and tender, Lizzy ached. "Do you want to come to Daddy? Long time no see, little love."

You don't even remember her—cad.

Think up another word.

Jerk. Jerk. How's that for a more modern word?

The last thing Lizzy heard as she dug through the clothes heaped on her floor for something decent to wear was Vanilla clapping.

The little traitor!

BOOK TWO

Smart Cowboy Saying:

Don't worry about bitin' off more than you can chew. Your mouth is probably a whole lot bigger than you think it is.
—Anonymous

Ten

"Hi there." Cherry's voice sounded soft and excited.

He smiled at her as he pushed the door open and walked inside her small, rented apartment. No sooner had he shut the door than the dingy walls seemed to close in on him. He preferred open spaces to cities. He would never have come here if it weren't necessary. A man had to do what a man had to do.

Cherry was wearing her glittery cowgirl outfit and her silver sequined hat just like he'd told her to. The only bit of brightness in the drab room, she was so pretty, it was kinda sad. All she'd ever wanted was to be a star. How she'd loved the media attention she'd gotten as a result of her engagement to Caesar.

She was too pretty and too young to die.

"I put these on just for you," Cherry purred, wiggling so that her breasts bounced.

She damn sure knew all the tricks.

"You look good," he said as he turned on the music just in case something went wrong. "Now, will you take them off—just for me, too?"

"I can't wait, baby. Did you bring the money?"

He held up his briefcase. "You did good."

"How is he?"

"Later, baby." He turned the pounding music even louder. "Dance for me."

She began to strip, slowly, the way he liked it, showing her big boobs first, jiggling them for him, and then her silver, Texas-shaped pubic hair. Flirtatiously she combed the hair with her fingers.

When she was naked, he told her to come to him, spread her legs and sit on his lap, which she did.

She began to kiss him, first his lips, then his throat. Next she stood him up and pushed him against her wall, pulled his jeans down and licked his erection with her velvet, pulsing, talented tongue. She kissed him everywhere until she had him breathing hard.

She was too pretty to die.

Then he thought about his mother and all the boyfriends she'd had when he'd been a kid. That got him angry.

He carried Cherry to the bed, yanked his jeans and boots off, put on a rubber and buried himself inside her.

"Oh, baby, that feels wonderful," she said when he began to pump.

Soon they were writhing to their own rhythm separate from the music. She made all the right moaning and cooing noises. Her pelvis arched in ever quickening spasms.

"Don't fake it," he growled, seizing her wrists and pinning her down as he pumped even harder.

"I'm not."

"Just don't—I want this to be real. This time, it has to be real."

He thought about Caesar. He liked fucking her because Caesar had fucked her. Following in the big man's footsteps, so to speak. But then wasn't that the point? Hell, he'd selected her for Caesar. It was her rotten luck she'd looked so much like Electra.

"Who's better? Me or old Caesar?"

She grinned. "Guess?"

As his hands moved into her hair, he felt her relax and get wetter down there as he pounded ever more violently into her. When he felt himself on the verge of ecstasy, his hands slowly circled her throat, gently, caressingly, so as not to alarm her.

She began to squirm to free herself, but he was stronger, far stronger. And he'd planned this, planned it so carefully down to the last detail. He was on top of her, his muscular body holding her down. The more she fought him, the more excited he grew, until the exquisite sensations were almost unbearable.

His hands tightened. When her eyes grew huge with terror, he loosened his grip on her throat ever so slightly.

"Relax, baby," he whispered, kissing her quivering mouth. This was the part he liked the best, giving them hope. "I'm not going to hurt you."

He eased off on the pounding, but only to make the thrill of it last. Only she felt so damn good, so hot and wet, so tight he couldn't control his passion. He was furious—furious at her for using her whorish tricks to make his body shudder too soon.

His fingers became talons. Gripping her neck again, he squeezed with all his might.

Her mouth opened. She bucked against him and tried to scream. But he was stronger.

No, this was the best part, when he knew they knew. When they knew he was all powerful. In the end, all she could do was gurgle helplessly and stare up at him with dumbfounded, frantic eyes that knew.

"It's okay, baby. It's okay. It's okay." It was so much fun to lie to them.

He stared into her eyes, plunging again and again, harder and faster until he finally exploded, filling the condom at the exact moment the blank terror in her eyes glazed over and her hands and legs went limp.

He felt alive and all powerful, on the edge of something vast and grand. He lingered over her inert body, his member still swollen and rock hard inside her. When finally he pulled out of her, he stared down into her open, dead eyes for a long, delicious moment.

Then he kissed her mouth one last time, wondering what it would be like to do it to a dead woman.

He'd never done *that* before.

But he had work to do.

Eleven

"You're practically kidnapping me," Lizzy said gloomily as she heaved herself into the seat behind Cole's in his twin-engine Cessna. His pilot, John, who had spent his entire time in New York near the plane, was standing on the tarmac, going over the flight plans.

"Drama queen," Cole bit out. "Make my day, darlin'—fly commercial."

She snapped the ends of her seat belt together defiantly.

"Did you ever reach your mother?" he demanded.

"While you and John were talking to the weather guy. She was very understanding when I explained why I took my phone off the hook."

In truth her mother had been the cool, distant mother Lizzy remembered from her childhood—icily polite, but on some deep level utterly rejecting.

Lizzy popped a white rectangular piece of sugarless chewing gum into her mouth and chomped guiltily. "I'll never forgive you for last night, though. If you'd told me earlier, I would have called her sooner."

"Fine. Blame me."

"Why didn't you just tell me about my father?"

"Why'd you dress up like a hooker if you didn't want some chump to seize the bait? Maybe you were lucky it was me."

"Ohhhh!"

"Besides, darlin', I couldn't tell you. I had to catch you first, remember? I went into that room intending to tell you, but you came on to me like a real hooker, offering to indulge my wildest fantasies. Let me clue you in about the male mind, sweetheart. A man like me can have the best of intentions, but when a woman does something like that, she derails a guy—big-time."

"I don't want to talk about last night."

"Then why do you keep bringing it up?"

"You didn't have to sleep with me," she muttered.

"Neither the hell did you."

"I didn't know about Daddy. You did."

"Right." Cole turned around and began checking the instruments.

In response, she clenched her hands together in utter exasperation.

It never occurred to her he might be on a guilt trip, too. He took another long breath. When he looked over at her again, his eyes were blazing blue. "So, is the baby buckled up? Does anybody besides me want to get this mother airborne?"

John climbed inside and began discussing technical questions with Cole. Lizzy faced forward, notched her chin up and chewed her gum. Every time she caught a glimpse of Cole, his face was even darker and more closed than it had been during their quarrel before Mandy's arrival earlier. He was more like the old Cole—guarded, demanding, less giving. Everything he'd said and done in the past two hours had been abrupt, mechanical and cold.

He'd made her pack in such a hurry she'd probably

forgotten everything she needed. He'd put up walls—against her.

Good. This is good. She wanted walls. She unclasped her hands. She munched her gum a little too loudly, liking it when it annoyed him so much that a muscle in his jaw jumped.

She was too susceptible to that other Cole—the sexy, teasing Cole of last night. She didn't want to go back to Texas. Not with the vengeful, bitter Cole when she couldn't forgive herself for last night.

When he turned to check Vanilla, who was buckled into a car seat as well as the airplane's seat belt, his face softened. Vanilla put her hands together and beamed at him adoringly. If he'd been a marshmallow roasting over a bonfire, he would have dripped white goo all over the ground.

"You gonna clap for me, little darlin'?" he whispered playfully, patting his hands together.

When she did, he clapped, too. "Patty-cake," he said.

Vanilla batted her eyelashes at him and squealed in delight.

When Cole looked at Lizzy again, the warmth in his dazzling blue eyes froze. When he turned back to John without another word to Lizzy and focused on the plane and what the two men had to do to get it airborne, Lizzy's throat constricted. She wished she could tune him out as easily, but every time she cast a furtive glance his way, the sight of his square, determined jaw unnerved her.

What was he thinking? Would he brag to every hand on the ranch that she'd thrown herself at him? Would he share the embarrassing details of her costume and racy underwear with Kinky and Eli?

She remembered Cole coming into the shower. How incredibly warm and tender his big, rough hands had felt gently caressing her breasts. Against her will, a vision of his sleek, brown, muscular body arose in her mind's eye. The memory of the sexual gleam in his eyes as he'd stared back at her taunted her, too.

She sighed, despising herself. First Bryce, and now Cole Knight—again. She didn't know which was worse.

Swallowing, she tightened her own seat belt and stared straight ahead. If he could ignore her, she could try to do the same.

John took off without incident. For the next few hours the two men continued to concentrate solely on flying the airplane. Fortunately cars and apparently planes put Vanilla to sleep, so the baby didn't distract her.

Determined to ignore Cole, Lizzy looked out her window at the blue sky and puffy clouds and the rumpled green earth beneath them, as if she found the view fascinating.

Despite the vastness beneath her and the sunny skies, she felt trapped inside the small cabin and too dependent on Cole. She remembered that night almost a year ago when her daddy had called and Cole's plane was lost over the gulf. Cole had been on his way to Mexico to check on a herd of prize-winning cattle owned by a friend down there. Caesar had told her he should have been on the plane, not Mia, who'd just had a baby the month before. He'd even hinted at murder and sabotage.

Then Cole had been found by shrimpers. There had been an investigation. Cole had been exonerated, and gradually the talk had died down. But his memory of the event—or any leading up to it—had never returned.

Cole flew the entire trip to Texas without speaking to her again. Thus, it was a surprise when they landed in Houston, and he pointed grimly at a crowd swarming in front of their private hangar. Sy'rai and Kinky Hernandez, the ranch cook and foreman, were surrounded by the milling throng.

"Who are they?" she asked.

"The press." His low tone was flat. "They smell blood. Yours. Your father's. Maybe mine, too."

She inhaled a shaky breath.

"Stay put. John and I will unload the luggage and the baby and then come back for you."

They got their bags and carried Vanilla off the plane. Lizzy pressed her hands to the glass as she watched them stride through the crowd and hand the baby to Sy'rai, who hugged Vanilla close. To Lizzy's profound relief Cole soon returned for her.

As he guided her from the plane and toward the reporters, she realized how much she needed him to lean on. If her father didn't get well fast, and she ended up working on the ranch for weeks or maybe months, she, Cole and his daughter would share the same house. She'd have to see him constantly.

Last night wouldn't be over for weeks, maybe months.

She'd barely cleared the plane when Texas newspaper, magazine and television reporters stampeded toward her. Microphones were pressed to her lips. Cameras snapped. Flashes exploded in her face.

"Are you home for good, Miss Kemble?"

"Who will take over? Another more experienced member of the family? You? Or an outsider?" They stared at Cole, too.

"Miss Kemble, do you know anything about Cherry Lane's disappearance?"

"Cherry?" Lizzy shuddered. "Excuse me?"

"Miss Lane didn't show up to dance at work last night," one of the reporters supplied. "Her apartment was unlocked, and her bed stripped. Her Toyota is still in the carport. But she's gone. Nobody's seen or heard from her."

Cole interrupted them. "Miss Kemble is tired and worried about her father."

"Is it true the board asked your father to give up Cherry or resign?"

Lizzy felt Cole's big hand tighten on her arm as he propelled her toward Sy'rai and Kinky and Vanilla, who were waiting for her inside the ranch's big black SUV.

"Miss Kemble—"

Somehow Cole got her inside the big vehicle. Kinky started the engine and rolled up the tinted windows. Soon the SUV glided forward, leaving the chaos behind them.

There were more reporters outside the hospital, who repeated the same question: *Where was Cherry Lane?*

Cole led Lizzy past them to the ICU waiting room, which was filled with family members.

Everybody was there except for the two people she most wanted—her brothers, Hawk and Walker. She doubted they'd even heard about Daddy's condition. Her mother looked tired and wan in jeans and a checkered shirt.

They embraced stiffly and Lizzy felt fresh guilt. And all the time, she felt everybody watching them, watching *her.*

Uncle B.B., Aunt Nanette and her sons, Sam and Bobby Joe, were in the hospital waiting area. Dear, sweet reliable Sam smiled politely enough. Sam's shy younger brother, Bobby Joe, even attempted a smile, too. Still, Lizzy felt walls and new tensions. In contrast to her own mother, Aunt Nanette—who had dyed her hair auburn—was dressed flamboyantly in a flame-colored silk Western shirt, leather pants, boots and half a million dollars' worth of diamonds. A younger cowboy, who was tall and dark, stood behind her, saying nothing. Aunt Nanette's new lover?

"It's such a shock," Aunt Nanette said, twirling one of her diamond rings on her finger. "Caesar's not himself. But you'll see soon enough, dear. A lot of times I thought my brother was meaner than a skillet full of rattlesnakes, but I wouldn't ever have wished this on him."

A false note in Aunt Nanette's tone filled Lizzy with dread.

Sam came up and hugged her while Bobby Joe stood back and merely watched. "How are you doing, Lizzy girl?"

"I'm a little tired." She clung to Sam's wiry, solid frame. He wasn't as tall as Cole, but he was just as strongly built. Next she greeted Uncle B.B. and his wife, Aunt Mona.

"Nothing is the same," Uncle B.B. said sadly. Like her mother, he wore jeans, boots and his regular white work shirt.

Aunt Mona looked exactly as one expected ranch royalty to look. She was tall, slim and stunning in black jeans and custom-made boots. As always, her gold jewelry was done in a Western motif. Today, golden horses dangled from her ears, and a miniature gold horse was pinned to her collar.

"If we pull together, we'll be okay," Uncle B.B. said.

Lizzy stepped back, not quite trusting her uncle for some reason. Uncle B.B. and Aunt Mona had always resented Caesar's control. They'd constantly sent Lizzy's parents and the board a barrage of registered letters filled with their demands, letters that couldn't be read without an attorney to interpret them.

Lizzy felt all mixed up. Being with them and not with her father only made Lizzy miss her father all the more. Desperation began to build inside her until Lizzy wanted nothing except to see him. Wringing her hands, she looked toward the door.

"What's this about Caesar wanting you to run things?" Uncle B.B. demanded while Aunt Mona frowned.

Bobby Joe moved closer so he could hear every word.

"You've been gone for years," Uncle B.B. said. "Who's he to say who should run things anyway after the stunts he's pulled lately? Hell, because of him the Kemble name is a joke."

"It will be rough going for you, Lizzy," Sam said with genuine concern. "You haven't lived here for a while. The

Golden Spurs is in the process of creating a whole new identity for itself. Our operation is more about money than cattle or hunting."

"That's not what Daddy said the last time we spoke."

"A long time ago the family made a vow to keep the ranch together," Joanne said softly.

"Why do I have the feeling the ranch is breaking up then?" Lizzy murmured as she looked at each one of them.

"Because we're experiencing some growing pains," Sam said calmly. "These are new times. Your father wants to stick to tradition while some of the rest of us feel it's time for a new vision."

"To hell with Caesar!" Uncle B.B. thundered. "If he hadn't had a stroke he would have married that stripper. He's done more to bring the ranch down than anybody else."

Joanne moaned.

Bobby Joe stormed out.

"When can I see him?" Suddenly Lizzy was worried about her father, only her father. She'd always felt overshadowed by all these larger-than-life characters. She couldn't deal with them—not now.

Cole, who was standing apart from them, strode toward her. When he took her hand, Lizzy, ridiculously glad he was there, squeezed his fingers.

How could the only thing that felt right in her life be the presence of the one man who couldn't belong in it? But right now he made her feel cared for and safe.

"She'll feel better when she sees Caesar for herself," Cole said gently to the others. "The unknown is scarier than the reality."

When the others nodded, Cole took her hand and led her out of the waiting room, across the hall and through the double doors that opened into ICU. Since Cole knew the way, all Lizzy had to do was follow him.

When they reached a green curtain, a young nurse in pink scrubs and running shoes with a long black braid hanging down her back looked up from a clipboard. "You family?" she barked.

"His daughter," Cole said.

The nurse nodded brusquely. "I haven't seen *her* here before."

The woman's pointed stare struck Lizzy like a blow. Daughterly guilt consumed her. She swallowed. "I live in New York."

The young nurse's pen was tucked over one ear. She looked so efficient. When she set her clipboard down and swept aside the green curtains that concealed Caesar's hospital bed from the rest of the unit, Lizzy felt awkward and utterly useless.

"Normally visiting hours are eight, twelve, four and..."

Lizzy was aware only of the prone figure on the bed. His eyes were wide, and he glared fixedly up at the ceiling tiles. She couldn't believe this rigid lump of flesh covered up with tubes and surrounded by gurgling machines was her once proud and powerful father. If ever a man looked like he'd fallen face down in a sticker patch and been stomped to death by rampaging bulls, her daddy looked that way.

"Daddy?"

His grim expression contorted.

"Daddy...it's me—Lizzy." Hesitantly she leaned over him. "I'm here, Daddy."

She brushed his cheek ever so softly with the back of her hand. "Remember you asked me to promise I'd come home, if anything happened." She strangled on a sob. "Well, I—I'm home."

Not knowing what else to say after that, she lapsed into silence. The only sound was the hiss and murmur of the machines.

She watched all the little lights on the various monitors flicker. The hospital felt so alien. Oh, if only she could say or do something to make him better. She felt helpless and awkward and guilty for being whole and well herself.

She leaned over his tanned face again, unaware that tears streamed down her cheeks.

"Daddy, I just wish I could talk to you. I wish… I— I…wish…that I could have made you proud of me…just once. But I never could. Everybody else always could. But Daddy, I wanted to. You'll never know how much I wanted to. It was just that… Did you ever do anything you were ashamed of?"

His gaze flickered.

More words wouldn't come. The pain of not being worthy of him was unbearable. Her shoulders slumped. "Now I'll never get the chance to make you proud of me."

When she finally left him, she found Cole waiting for her in the hall outside the double doors of the unit.

"How was he?"

"Worse than I expected." She barely recognized her own voice.

"The same then."

"Why do people get sick like that?"

"They get old. They wear out."

"But he's not old."

"All it takes is one weak link. He pushed himself mighty hard. The ranch. The divorce."

"What do you mean?"

"We're like chains. His vascular system was the weak link that broke and caused his swing to crash to the ground."

"I want him like he was before."

"We all do. But we've got to go on from here."

"Do you think he'll ever be all right?"

"I don't know, Lizzy. Maybe."

"Not knowing what will happen next isn't easy."

"But then that's how life is. We don't ever know what's around the next bend in the road."

Twelve

Never before had Lizzy felt so helpless. Day after day as she sat in the ICU beside her father, who continued to stare up at the ceiling, she prayed for a miracle.

Please, God, make him well.

One afternoon when her brothers were in with Caesar, Lizzy opened her eyes in the waiting room after saying such a prayer, Cole was there beside her. As always, he wore crisply starched jeans and a long-sleeved white shirt with the top two buttons undone at his dark throat.

Her heart leapt. "I—I didn't hear you come in."

His quick, gentle smile unleashed a torrent of unwanted emotion, so she closed her eyes again, hoping he wouldn't see.

"I'm leaving later today," he drawled when she trusted herself to look at him again. "Now that Hawk and Walker are here, I'll be taking Sy'rai, Kinky and Vanilla back to the ranch."

"You're leaving?" The thought brought utter desolation.

"There's a board meeting in a few days," he said. "I'll be back to fly you to San Antonio, if you want to go to it."

"Of course. Thanks." She forced a smile. "I feel so helpless here. If only there was something I could do for him."

He slid a thick black briefcase across the floor toward her. "Your daddy wanted you in charge if something happened to him."

She ran her trembling fingers over her father's initials that were engraved in gold into the dark leather.

"He had these documents inside this case when he had the stroke," Cole said. "I had the minutes and reports from all the board meetings from the past six months copied for you, as well. I also included some stuff about plans for the ranch museum's opening. If you get through even half the papers, at least you won't go to the meeting blind."

"Thank you."

He shrugged. "It'll give you something to think about when you have time on your hands here at the hospital and are afraid you can't do anything for him."

She nodded.

"Sam told you that the ranch is searching for a new identity for itself," he continued as he arose to go. "We're redefining what we think the ranch and family should stand for." He moved toward the doorway. "I think if you read this stuff—"

She barely heard what he said. All she could think of was that he was leaving, and she felt too overwhelmed by her father's illness to face anything else. "I've never been to San Antonio without my father…alone."

"You'll be with me."

"You're the last person I should want there."

"Just read one document at a time, and you won't be so overwhelmed," he said gently before he left her.

It scared her a little that he understood what she was feeling so well.

A norther gusted into Houston that night, snuffing out the last of the Indian summer. The skies above the glass skyscrapers and tall pine trees became gray and dark. In the late afternoon when she left the hospital, the weather was humid and drizzly. As if her father's condition, her mother's remote unfriendliness, the dreary weather and the board meeting looming in the future weren't enough to worry her, the front pages of every newspaper ran inch-high headlines about Cherry Lane's mysterious disappearance.

The police suspected foul play. The last vehicle a neighborhood teenager remembered having been parked in front of the stripper's place was a black truck. The kid had given them a couple of numbers off the license plate. The kid had been fascinated by Cherry because of her profession. He'd seen that truck there before—lots of times, usually late at night.

The morning three days after Cole had left, Lizzy and her mother were dressed to leave for the hospital when Gigi tapped on Joanne's door. "That pesty detective is pacing up and down my living room again."

Joanne snapped her purse shut.

Lizzy remembered the man too well. Detective Joe Phillips was a short man with an abrasive manner. Just mentioning his name was enough to make Lizzy's mother bristle.

"The gall of that insufferable idiot! The moron actually thinks I had something to do with that bitch's disappearance. I wish I had!"

"Mother!"

"Go on to the car. I won't be long."

"Don't antagonize him."

They descended the stairs together. When her mother headed toward the living room, Lizzy realized she'd forgotten her father's briefcase upstairs. The board meeting was tomorrow. Since she wanted to go over several documents again, there was nothing to do but rush back up to her bedroom.

When she dashed back down the stairs again, her mother's raised voice stopped her cold.

"I can assure you, Detective Phillips, I never met that awful woman. No, I can't explain about that truck. No, I don't know why someone scrubbed her apartment walls and vacuumed. Look, my husband's ill. My driver's waiting."

"Did you ever speak to Miss Lane on any occasion?"

"Either accuse me of something or leave! I will not sit here and answer any more of your ridiculous questions without my lawyer present."

"This will only—"

"Good day, Detective," she said curtly.

"It's only natural that you disliked her immensely."

"I never met her. Good day."

When her ashen-faced mother stumbled into the hall and caught Lizzy eavesdropping, Lizzy blushed and held up Caesar's briefcase. "I—I forgot this upstairs.

Detective Phillips stalked gloomily toward the front door.

"Disgusting little man," her mother said.

"What did he want?

"Nothing really. A black truck was seen at Cherry's place. He says the license plate of one of our ranch trucks happens to start with the same three numbers. As if that's proof of something."

"Who could have been driving the truck?"

"Who cares? He's blowing the whole thing out of proportion. Cherry probably ran off with another lover." She opened the kitchen door. "Oh, damn. Not more rain."

On the porch Joanne's hands shook so badly as she tried to open her umbrella that Lizzy had to do it for her.

"Horrible man," Joanne said as her big black umbrella finally snapped open.

"*Did* you ever talk to her?"

Joanne didn't answer immediately. "You're as bad as that detective."

"You didn't answer my question."

During the silent drive to the hospital, each of them stared out their own windows at the rain-slick freeway. When they finally arrived, reporters charged their Lexus, screaming questions at her mother, who used her umbrella like a battering ram as she dashed through the middle of them.

Lizzy's mother refused to leave Caesar's side until late that night. By the time they got home to Gigi's, Lizzy was exhausted.

To prepare for the board meeting, she had read and reread the thick stack of minutes in her father's briefcase. Not that all the reports made sense to her.

But they would, she told herself. *I can do this!*

A hand-written memo from her father to Leo Storm, the board's CEO, had caught her attention. She'd gone over it dozens of times. And each time, her heart had raced fearfully.

If anything should happen to me in the near future, put Lizzy in charge. Caesar.

That was all. Still, something about the memo frightened her. It was as if he'd had a premonition, as if he distrusted someone on the inside of the ranching operation.

Why had he written it? Was it a power play on his part to get her home? Or did he really think she could do a better job than the others? Or was there some other reason? What if she let him down?

I can do this! she affirmed, gripping her father's note.

The next morning Lizzy still felt tired as she drank black coffee with her mother in Gigi's bright yellow kitchen before she left for the airport to meet Cole.

"I want you to go home to the ranch after the board meeting," her mother said, getting up from the little table where they'd been sitting together.

"What about Daddy?"

Joanne opened the dishwasher. "He'd want you at the

Golden Spurs. He wanted *you* to take charge. He wrote Leo a memo and he read it, at the last board meeting." She began removing dishes. "And there's Vanilla. She's a baby. She needs you. If you're going to stay in Texas, you need to wrap your mind around her care, the daily operation of the ranch, and the museum opening."

Strangely, the thought of caring for Vanilla made Lizzy's life feel more purposeful.

"I feel so unqualified."

"Your father chose you." Joanne opened a cabinet.

"But why?"

Her mother's hands shook as she placed a stack of saucers onto a shelf. "If I knew that—" She broke off and, crossing her arms beneath her breasts, turned to face Lizzy. "Obviously I am the last person your father confided in."

Lizzy couldn't meet her gaze. For some reason Lizzy had always blamed herself for the inexplicable tension in her parents' marriage.

"Mia was such a natural at everything I do so badly," Lizzy whispered in an attempt to make peace. And yet, even as she said the placating words, she felt it was unfair she always had to praise Mia to win favor with her own mother.

Her mother's jaw tightened. "Yes, she was, but she's gone." Just thinking about Mia seemed to soften her. She uncrossed her arms. "A lot's been happening, Lizzy. Too much for me to go into right now. Your father was under a lot of stress. If only we could have put off that museum opening." Her mother went back to the dishwasher and removed several glasses.

"You're not telling me everything."

"Maybe because I can't. Or, maybe I don't know how." Slowly, carefully she set the glasses in a shelf.

"We were never close. I used to wish you'd talk to me the way you talked to Mia. I'd watch you two together. I'd hear you laughing. Then when I walked into the room you both would go quiet."

"Don't—" Joanne sighed wearily and sagged against the counter. "Just go home to the ranch after the meeting. You promised him, Lizzy." She drew a long breath. "This isn't about you and me. This is about you and your father. He called me and told me that in our last conversation."

"I thought your lawyer told you not to talk to Daddy until after the divorce."

"How could we run the ranch or prepare for the museum's opening and the celebration without talking? We talked. We were talking more and more lately. Maybe we didn't have the best marriage, but surely it was better than anything he could have had with Cherry. I—I know this is ridiculous, but I was beginning to think maybe he was going to come to his senses before it was too late. Now, we'll never know, will we?"

"He hurt you so much. Do you hate him?"

"When cops show up to grill me about vehicle license plates and I have to face those reporters at the hospital, I don't exactly feel the same enthusiasm I felt the day I married him."

In spite of herself Lizzy smiled. "I'm sorry."

"Go home. That's what he'd want. Take a look at the museum and see what Mark and Jim have been doing."

"Mark and Jim?"

"Mark is the painter who's doing the murals. Jim's the sculptor. Walker hired them and was overseeing their work before he left."

"Why did Daddy get mad at Walker?"

Her mother went back to the dishwasher and began stacking plates on the counter. She sighed heavily. "And...and if you wouldn't mind too much, look in on my darling birds. Eli feeds them, but he doesn't go inside the aviary and talk to them. They like to be talked to."

Why wouldn't her mother tell her about Walker?

* * *

The international headquarters of Golden Spurs Inc. occupied the top five floors of a tall brick and glass building in downtown San Antonio.

When Cole and Lizzy arrived by limousine from the airport, reporters rushed them as they tried to enter the building, asking the same tired questions.

"Mr. Knight, don't you usually drive the black truck the police think was seen at Ms. Lane's before she was discovered missing?"

When Lizzy shuddered, Cole shielded her with his body and grimly pushed past the screaming throng. Then they were in the reception area that was decorated with mirrors, huge paintings of the ranch itself, antlers and hunting trophies from all over the world. A full-size elephant and a giraffe stared at each other through a fake oasis of potted palms.

Cole pushed her into the elevator which was a gilded, glassy cage. As it shot upward, she continued to stare down at the giraffe and elephant in the trees of the lobby.

Only in Texas! Lizzy thought.

"You all right?" Cole asked.

"A little nervous," she lied, still staring down as the people and trees and even the elephant grew smaller. She was way past nervous. "Yourself?" she managed to add.

When she locked eyes with his, he didn't answer. His mouth was tightly set at the corners.

"You can do this," he finally said.

"Mind reader." She smiled. "That's *my* affirmation."

He grinned. "Don't tell me you're into that self-help bullshit."

She blinked innocently. "Not me!" She balled her hands into fists. "*I can do this!*" she said, winking at him.

In no time they were in the cherry-paneled boardroom that

looked down on the Alamo and a serpentine curve of the fashionable River Walk that was lined with tall cypress trees, posh shops, restaurants and bars.

Not that Sam, Uncle B.B., Aunt Nanette, Hawk, Walker and other members of the family, who were seated at a long table with Leo Storm, the CEO, even noticed the view. Everybody was talking rather heatedly until she entered. Then a hush fell.

Lavish refreshments had been set up on a long table by one of the tall windows, but no one had served himself anything other than coffee or a soda.

When he saw her, Leo moved across the beautiful room to shake Lizzy's hand. Tall and as dark and fit as Cole even though he held a corporate, indoor job, Leo towered over her. As always he was dressed beautifully in a navy blue suit, Italian, probably. His silk tie was expensive and conservative, his perfect smile white and professional.

"I hope we didn't keep you waiting," she said.

He eyed his watch. "You're exactly on time. We were enjoying coffee." He pressed her hand again. "I'm so sorry about your father. I know how close you two are."

The sincerity in his low tone caught her off guard, and she was barely able to keep her lips from quivering. She'd caught a glimpse of herself in a mirror downstairs and imagined that she probably looked stiff and pale and very young to him in her simple black sheath and a long strand of white pearls. She'd tried to look grown-up by drawing her unruly hair back from her slender face into a chignon, but the hairdo had been a mistake. Untidy strands of platinum silk kept falling against her cheek, and she kept pushing them away.

"Would you like some coffee?" Leo said.

Oh, God, she couldn't do this.

She had to do this.

She nodded too quickly. "Black, please." Unable to face

sitting down at the table yet, she turned and found Cole standing beside her.

"Why don't you take a seat beside your brother, Lizzy, while I pour you a cup?" Cole said.

Even though he wore jeans and a long-sleeved white work shirt, he looked every bit as tall and commanding as Leo did in his fancy Italian suit.

She nodded.

You can do this. You can do this.

When she eased herself into a chair, Walker took her hand briefly and touched it to his lips. Everybody else smiled and greeted her. Trying to hide her insecurities, she did the same, but she either talked too fast or mumbled her answers.

You can do this, she repeated silently even as she thought that everyone in the room, including Walker, seemed far more confident and poised than she.

Cole brought her her coffee and she sipped it gratefully.

Leo seated himself at the opposite end of the long table facing Lizzy. "Are we ready to begin?"

Somehow she resisted the urge to squirm in her leather chair. Cole stood at the refreshment table.

"At the last board meeting we asked your father to give up Cherry or resign," Uncle B.B. said without preamble. "He refused to give us an answer that day. Because of him, the ranch has suffered a great deal of negative publicity. Our bottom line is suffering. Since his stroke and the media's fascination with Miss Lane's disappearance, it has only gotten worse. In short, we believe that it is in the best interests of the ranch for us to have a strong leader to steer the south Texas ranching operation during his convalescence."

Feeling defensive, Lizzy sank lower in her chair. "Someone other than me?" she said.

"Uncle B.B. doesn't mean to be unkind, Lizzy," Sam said gently.

"Caesar read us a memo saying he wanted you, but, dear, you *have* been absent from the ranch for years," Aunt Nanette added.

Hawk was dark and silent. Walker leaned back in his chair and said nothing, as well.

"I believe you should step down and let a more experienced person fill your father's position until…he returns," Uncle B.B. finished.

"If he returns," Lizzy said, forcing herself to sit straighter.

"Good," Uncle B.B. said. "I'm glad that's settled. The important thing is for us to choose the right person." His broad shoulders seemed to expand. He smiled warmly at everybody.

Cole was so busy slathering salmon and cheese on a cracker, he didn't return Uncle B.B.'s smile. But when Lizzy glanced nervously at him, he beamed and waved his cracker at her. When he offered her one, she shook her head so fiercely several more flyaway tendrils came loose.

"What kind of man do you think we need, Leo? What is the biggest challenge facing the ranch right now?" Lizzy asked, pushing the strands of hair out of her eyes, only to have them fall back again. "I know we've got the museum opening and the celebration coming up."

"That won't be a problem. I've come home to take charge of that," Walker said.

"Which everybody is thrilled about." Leo smiled. "You asked about leadership, Lizzy."

Before taking the helm of Golden Spurs, Leo Storm had been the CEO of an immense ranch and agribusiness in Montana for more than eight years. Had he ever doubted himself in his whole life? Probably not, Lizzy thought. After all, he held a degree from Harvard.

From what Lizzy had read about him in the reports Cole had given her, he was an extremely able executive. Nevertheless, someone, possibly a ranch insider, appeared to be sabotaging everything Leo did and everything Caesar had done.

"We'll need a man who understands the new technology involved in ranching operations," Leo said. "Then there are environmental values to consider. Not to mention that consumer demands and tastes change constantly, and we must change to meet them. Then there are crises like mad cow disease. So, we need someone strong and flexible. But I guess the biggest challenge—at least in south Texas—will always be the weather. It's usually too damn hot and too damn dry for anything other than rattlesnakes to thrive down there."

"Maybe we should market rattlesnake meat," Lizzy said. Everybody laughed.

"You didn't tell her we need to play hardball with the oil company," Uncle B.B. said.

"He means Sheldon Oil," Aunt Nanette chimed in.

Uncle B.B. frowned. "We're being paid for old gas and new gas. We think Sheldon is paying old prices for new gas, which means lower prices, and we've got to do something about this."

"Why don't we sue?" Aunt Mona suggested.

"All I want is more money," Aunt Nanette said.

"A lot *is* going on," Lizzy said.

Uncle B.B. smiled. "Believe me, we've only touched on a few of the high points."

"Lizzy, you don't have to worry your pretty head about any of this," Sam said kindly. "You can just leave it all to us."

It would be so nice to lean on Sam. *Dear Sam.* But strangely the part about not worrying her pretty head made her feel defiant instead of comforted.

Lizzy stunned herself as well as the others when she stood up. "You may be right, Sam. But Daddy did ask me to take over for him. Suddenly hearing what he's been up against, I feel called to serve…at least temporarily."

There was an audible gasp. In the ensuing silence, she took a deep breath herself. Seconds ticked by, and everybody in the room except Cole and Walker seemed to tense. Walker toyed with his pen while Cole appeared totally absorbed in spreading thick, gooey Brie onto another cracker.

"I'm going to ask Cole if he'll help me—if I do take over." She glanced at him just as he chomped a rat-size bite out of his cheese and cracker sandwich, but he turned his back to her and stared out the window.

Everybody at the table except Leo rose and began to object at once. Aunt Nanette even pounded the table.

"But Lizzy," Uncle B.B. yelled louder than the rest. "We had it all worked out before you showed up."

"Obviously she and Cole had it all worked out, too," Aunt Mona said.

"I appreciate all your hard work, Uncle B.B.," Lizzy offered softly.

"Why do you want to do this when you've always hated ranching?" Sam began. "Did Cole put you up to this?"

Because something's wrong here. And because you don't think I can.

"It's not that I want to do it," she said. "I'm sure I'll come around to your point of view very soon. This is simply something I've got to do right now. For Daddy. He's so helpless. I want to help him. It's the least I can do."

"But can *you* do it?" Uncle B.B. yelled. "That's the question."

Cole wiped his mouth with a paper napkin and strode to Lizzy's side. "She asked me to help her—and I will," he said. When she looked up at him, seeking support, his handsome face was dark and closed.

"A Knight? Are you kidding? Your father would roll over in his grave," Uncle B.B. said.

"Daddy isn't in his grave," Lizzy said.

Yet, someone amended silently.

Leo listened to everybody. Finally he said, "All right. We could talk all day. I propose we try this for ninety days. We can see how things go. After all, Lizzy grew up on the ranch, Caesar taught her everything he knew. Besides, she'll have Cole."

There were audible groans.

"It's Caesar's wish," Leo added. "For all his faults, he was a hell of a rancher."

At that, everybody, Hawk, even Uncle B.B., shut up and stared at Lizzy so intently, she began to tremble.

But one of them had murder in his heart.

After the board meeting she followed Cole and Leo into Caesar's lavish office. Cole was moody and silent, but he took meticulous notes while Leo worked out the details with her for their new arrangement. Leo suggested Cole give her a tour of the ranch first thing and bring her up to date. Meanwhile, Cole sat down and typed his notes into his PDA.

Leo also showed her an outline of the speech about the ranch's history and future that Caesar had planned to give at the museum opening and asked her if she would deliver it. Even though she wasn't a gifted orator like her father, she agreed.

When she and Cole finally found themselves in the elevator alone together again, their briefcases bulging with documents, Cole's scowl was darker than ever. He stood as far from her as he could possibly get in the gilded cage that whisked them to ground level.

They were both flying back to Houston with John, and once she'd been dropped off in Houston, Cole and John would continue on to the ranch. Hawk and Walker had plans to see Caesar. Lizzy wanted to check on her father one more time and have dinner with both her brothers in Houston before she drove to the ranch. Gigi had promised to loan Lizzy her daughter's car.

When their elevator reached the lobby, Cole held the doors for her and said he was hungry and intended to catch a quick bite on the river. "You take the limo to the airport, and I'll catch a cab later."

"But—"

He wouldn't even look at her.

"Are you mad at me, Cole?"

He shook his head too fast. "See you in an hour and a half, okay?" Then he practically bolted out of the elevator.

"Since we're sharing a limo, maybe I should just join you for lunch? Is that all right?"

He turned slowly, his glittering gaze too sharp as he studied her. "Suit yourself." But he didn't smile.

With him stiffly leading the way, they strode single file along the crowded river bank. He walked so fast, she had to run to keep up with him.

He chose a French restaurant that wasn't too packed. Since it was a nice day, he asked for a table outside by the river where they could watch barges and tourists stream by their table.

The day was bright and crisp, and the river sparkled beneath the cypress tress. When the waiter brought menus, Cole didn't even let him set them down. "We're in a hurry. We'll take your specials."

Then he ordered drinks, which came almost immediately along with a wire basket of bread and assorted butters.

"Why the rush?" she whispered, fearing his reason was that he wasn't pleased she'd joined him.

"The specials here are wonderful," he said, evading her real question as he smeared butter on a piece of bread.

"Thanks for saying you'd help me, Cole."

"You could have asked me first, you know. You really put me on the spot in the boardroom."

"You offered to help in New York."

"And you told me to keep my distance. Doing both is going to be tricky."

"Okay, I—I didn't know I was going to ask you until I did it. I'm new at this, okay?"

"Okay. I don't know when I'll have time to do the tour," he replied coldly.

"I can wait."

"So, what about New York?"

She blinked. Now it was her turn not to want to look at him or answer. "What about what?"

"To be blunt—the sex? You've been mad as hell at me ever since. Like I said, I was told to keep my distance. Now we're to be housemates and business partners?"

"Well, I'm still not exactly happy about New York."

"But—"

"I see no reason why one stupid little incident—"

He lifted his beer mug to his lips. "The hottest sexual *aberration* of my life, to be more exact."

"Well, only because your memory is not too good at the moment."

He scowled. "Don't keep throwing that up at me."

"Fine." She emptied sugar packets into her tea, squeezed her lime juice into the tall glass and made a fuss of stirring. "I don't see why one idiotic mistake made during a horrible period in my life needs to ruin our business relationship, Cole."

"Oh, so that's what we have now? A business relationship?" He smiled grimly.

"Partners." She dinged her iced tea glass with the long spoon and set it down. "You said you'd help."

"And I will."

"And you'll keep your distance, too...just like you promised in New York."

"Since we'll be living in the same house, I assume you mean sexually?" His silver-blue eyes drilled her.

"Hands off! That's what I mean."

He leaned a fraction of an inch closer over the table. "What about lips?"

His soft voice and his hungry glance got her edgier.

"Don't!"

"Where do you stand on a little light flirtation?"

"No."

"You're not going to ask me to marry you to make this a real partnership, so people won't question my leadership, are you?"

"Marry you?" She regarded him warily. "Whatever gave you a crazy idea like that?"

"Before you propose publicly, ask me in private first." His voice was hard.

"I would never want to marry you! I don't want anything of that nature to do with you. Don't you get it?"

"Got it," he snapped.

"When you asked me to lunch—"

"I didn't ask you, darlin'. You invited yourself."

"Because I was trying to thank you for agreeing to help me, you big, handsome lug."

"Handsome. Well, finally—a compliment."

She pushed her chair back and picked up her purse. "I didn't want to start a fight, so I'll go."

When she started to stand up, his tanned hand closed over her wrist. "No! Stay."

Even after she quit struggling to pull free, his hand lingered on her wrist. She felt his thumb making warm circles on her soft skin. "I'm inviting you to lunch with me now." His blue eyes were intense.

Mesmerized, she sank back into her chair. "Since we've already ordered," she relented.

"When we get to the ranch, I'll leave you the hell alone," he said cheerily. "You can count on it."

"Great." But her throat constricted. The idea of him leaving her the hell alone, as he put it, depressed the hell out of her. Oh, this whole thing between them was crazy.

Neither of them spoke for a while, but the day itself was a sensual joy with the sunlight sparkling in the trees and glittering on the surface of the water. The air felt balmy against her skin. Couples walked by, arm in arm, laughing and talking.

It was nice out here, having lunch with him. Almost she could imagine they were real friends, like those other couples. And as much as she hated to admit it, it was nice to be home in Texas.

Home. Funny how being here with him felt so right in some way.

"You sure know how to stir up a shit storm," he said after he gobbled down a second slice of bread. "People in that meeting were furious at you."

"What are you saying?"

"You were poetry in motion, darlin'. I admired the way you led them to believe you'd step down." He snapped his fingers. "Then just like that, you pretended you'd changed your mind."

"I did change my mind."

"Be careful playing your games. These people are rich and spoiled. They're all jealous as hell of you, too. Not to mention, there is a lot of money involved. Hard decisions have to be made. The ranch is facing big challenges. There's no telling what some of those people might do. A lot of weird things have happened lately. One of them could be sabotaging the operation. Just be careful."

She remembered her father's memo and lifted her brows. "What do you mean?" she whispered.

"Lizzy, you're playing with fire."

"You're scaring me."

"Good." His face darkened. "You grew up with a silver spoon in your mouth. You were Daddy's favorite, his spoiled darling. You had it so easy—you don't know what it's like to really want stuff."

"Yes, I do." Her voice was barely audible.

"Listen to me, darlin'. Some people will do anything to get what they want. *Anything.*"

She drew a deep, shuddering breath. "Would you?"

"Don't be ridiculous." Suddenly his dark face was guiltily closed.

"Am I being ridiculous, Cole?"

Anger flashed in his eyes. Maybe he would have stood up and left her then, but their waiter arrived with their food.

Cole's tension lessened as soon as he stabbed his mesquite-smoked quail with a fork.

Hers did not. Barely touching her vegetable entrée, she watched him uneasily.

How far would he go to get what he wanted?

Thirteen

Dr. Sanson's office was a mess. The desk, the maroon carpet and the oak bookshelves were piled high with medical journals, prescription pads, papers, stacks of charts and giveaway pens from drug companies.

Cole checked his calendar in his PDA to see if he'd remembered everything he was supposed to do today. Then he picked up a pen and fiddled with it. He wished he were anywhere else. But he had to know the results of his latest tests. It had been nearly ten months since the accident, and he was still having the blackouts.

Some people will do anything to get what they want, he'd told Lizzy. *Anything.* His remark worried him. *About himself.*

Who was he really? What was he capable of when he lost time? Detective Joe Phillips kept calling, wanting to know about his truck. He'd suffered a few lengthy blackouts. Had he been at Cherry's? Hell if he knew.

At the sound of approaching footsteps, he pitched the pen onto the doctor's desk and sat up straighter.

"Sorry to keep you waiting." Dr. Sanson sidestepped several piles of medical journals and sat down, facing Cole across the tangle of papers on his desk.

Dr. Sanson had to be in his sixties, yet he looked younger. He had a kindly, red face and flyaway white hair in need of a talented barber. A jumble of pens made the ink-stained pocket of his white medical jacket sag.

Dr. Sanson opened Cole's chart and read it before glancing at him. "You said you had some questions?"

"The blackouts? I don't know what I do…or who I am…when I'm *not here*."

The doctor smiled genially. Cole did not smile back.

"Is that all?" Dr. Sanson snapped Cole's chart shut and tossed it onto his desk. "I wouldn't worry too much. As I explained, I've reviewed your most recent EEG, your CT scan of the head and MRI. I consulted with your neurologist and neurosurgeon. Everything looks great."

"But I'm still having blackouts."

"Your plane went down in the Gulf of Mexico. It's a miracle you're even alive."

"I understand that—"

"Do you?" The doctor leaned forward.

"Is my condition permanent?"

"We don't know. I'd say it's a good sign that these episodes are less frequent."

"A good sign? Is that all you can say?" Cole stood up. "Do you have any idea what it's like find yourself somewhere, doing something, maybe having a conversation, and you don't remember the last hour—or several hours? I'll come to and find myself in the middle of a poker game or a sentence I don't know how to finish. I bluff and try not to look like a total idiot. If I'm lucky, the other person will repeat himself and I can fool him. But a lot of times, I can't. I never used to lose at poker, either."

"I wouldn't play for big money then."

Cole didn't laugh.

"Look, you had a severe closed head injury. Think of

your brain as being a computer. When your plane hit the water, your computer was smashed. A lot of your connections have been shaken up."

"But will I ever be all right again? Can't you do something?"

"I could prescribe another different, expensive medication, but nothing you've taken so far has helped. I'd say it's mostly a matter of time."

"I get so frustrated not to be able to think. I have to rely on lists and my PDA to keep my life straight."

"Join the club."

"Sometimes I'll be doing paperwork, and I'll lose my focus." He thought about Lizzy. He didn't want to hurt her or put her at risk. "When will I be able to fly alone again? To drive on a highway?"

"I repeat—give it time."

"Things are tough at the ranch right now. A lot's been happening."

"I heard about Caesar. And I read about his stripper friend's disappearance. Tell Joanne I'm sorry." The doctor stood up and extended his hand. "All of you have been through a lot. Too much."

Lizzy's heart was beating with excitement when she drove through the trees and saw the familiar, three-story stucco house with its tall red roof and wide wraparound verandas. As a girl, she hadn't felt she could ever belong here. Today she felt a powerful nostalgia. She braked Gigi's daughter's silver sports car so fast, thick clouds of white caliche dust swirled around the little car, and the house vanished from view.

When the white dust finally settled, she got out and looked up at the six flags of Texas flapping lazily above the long roofline. Tall, wavy grass stretched endlessly to the east and south, and an immense, cloudless blue sky loomed above her. Her gaze wandered from the huge mansion, to the glittering spurs on the Spur Tree, to the antique dinner bell. She sighed, hugged herself and let the eerie quiet wrap her in its kindly, welcoming embrace.

No tall buildings. No freeways. No noisy traffic. Just the land and the sky and the animals and that special sensation of wildness that was always in the air here. Due to the big ranches, this part of the country was one of the last wildernesses in the United States. Until she heard the popping of several hunters' guns in the distance, it was so quiet she could hear herself breathe.

Unafraid, a deer and a faun, their dark velvet eyes watching her, ambled softly across the lawn to nibble timidly at the grasses under the Spur Tree. Lizzy inhaled deeply again. Until this moment, she hadn't realized how much she missed all this—even the hunting. Finally she was home.

The land was greener, the grass high and lush and the cattle, deer and turkeys fat. Kinky had told her the weather had been wetter than usual for more than a year. Which was wonderful.

She stared toward the distant horizon. Normally, few places were more difficult to raise cattle for a profit than south Texas. Much of the ranchland was made up of dense, tangled brush, which had to be cleared at great expense every few years. A practice that upped the cost of maintaining acreage.

The region was a semiarid desert, too. Droughts were so frequent, a rancher needed twenty acres to feed one cow. Ranchers—even big ranchers like the Kembles—who were lucky enough to be without debt, were still land rich and cash poor.

She dawdled on the front lawn so long Eli came out, greeted her and unloaded her bags. With an eye out for wild

critters, she headed toward the house. Not that she needed
to worry all that much. Even during a drought when the
grass would need more water if cut short, her father always
ordered that the lawn to be sheered as close to the ground as
possible near the house as a prevention against rattlesnakes.
When she reached the bottom of the stairs, she waited, scan-
ning the porch again. Not that she was looking for Cole's
dark head or broad shoulders.

I'll leave you the hell alone. You can count on it, he'd said.

Suddenly, Lizzy thought about Mia and instead of enter-
ing the house, turned around and headed to the Spur Tree.
She was touching Mia's spurs and wondering about Cole's
relationship with her sister when the front door opened behind her. She whirled, smiling expectantly. But it was only
Sy'rai coming out to welcome her.

"Hi."

Lizzy lifted her hand and waved, and Sy'rai, who had
Vanilla in her plump arms, was all smiles. Wing Nut,
Joanne's black Lab, trotted from the back of the house bark-
ing.

Despite her extra weight, Sy'rai looked much younger than
a woman in her early fifties. Her gorgeous, olive skin glowed.
Her big dark eyes sparkled with warmth and affection.

Vanilla clapped, held out her hands to Lizzy and began
to wriggle to get down. Wing Nut circled Lizzy, sniffing her
ankles and wagging his tail.

"Welcome home," Sy'rai said as she descended the stairs
with the baby.

Lizzy touched Mia's spurs one last time and then Uncle
Jack's, making them jingle. As she pulled her own spurs off
the tree, she saw a new bronze marker on the ground that
read, Electra Scott. There were two dates, the birth date and
the death date, which was fairly recent. Lizzy wondered
why neither of her parents had mentioned the new marker.

She bit her lips and took a deep breath as she backed away from the tree and headed for the house. When she reached Sy'rai, Vanilla held out her arms again and made cute little monkey sounds that meant she wanted to go to Lizzy. So, laughing, Lizzy took her.

"You looked like you were expecting someone else to walk out of that door," Sy'rai said with a knowing look. "Now let me guess who that might be."

Lizzy kissed Vanilla's brow. "D-Daddy. I miss him. That's all."

She wasn't about to admit, even to herself, she wouldn't have minded seeing Cole—just for a minute or two, just to say hi. After all, he'd promised to work with her.

Well, lucky her. He was nowhere around. She could settle in without being distracted.

But it bothered her that he didn't turn up when he heard she'd arrived, and she knew he'd been notified because she'd overheard Kinky talking to him on his cell at exactly 10:40 a.m. about some dumb old bulls. Kinky had said, "Yes, she got here about an hour ago. She's fine. Just fine. Pretty as a picture and playing with Vanilla. How'd it go at Dr. Sanson's? Okay? Great! Guess who pulled up and took her first step? Yes, she did! I swear! Our Lizzy set her spurs on the kitchen table and Vanilla was after them."

Just listening to Kinky talk to Cole had her heart beating suffocatingly. Once Lizzy knew Cole knew she was home, she spent the rest of the morning unpacking, settling in and playing with Vanilla—all the while half listening for the sound of his boots and the jingle of his spurs. She changed into a white lace blouse and black slacks that were becoming on her slim frame.

When Cole didn't appear at lunch or dinner, either, she realized he must have been very serious when he'd said he'd leave her the hell alone. His making such a point of it began to grate on Lizzy's nerves. After all, they were business partners. Wasn't it only natural that they confer first thing?

After putting Vanilla to bed, Lizzy ate alone at the long polished ebony table in the dining room. Without Cole at the other end of the table, the dining room seemed huge and dark and far too quiet. Her only companions were the family portraits of her pioneer ancestors, who stared disapprovingly down at her from their golden frames.

Suddenly she missed her dad and her mother and Mia and her brothers. Big houses weren't meant to be lived in alone.

She went upstairs to her room, but left her door cracked so she could hear better. The house had been built around 1930 and was like a drum. The tiniest sound on any floor carried throughout the entire building. Hours passed and still Cole didn't come. Finally she went to bed, still wondering where he was.

And why had he been to see a doctor? Was he ill? Had he been injured? Could he be alone somewhere hurt? Could he have been putting a difficult horse in a trailer and been kicked in that hard head of his? Had a snake bitten him? Did he have a date?

Do not think about him. Do not.

An hour later she picked up the phone and dialed Sy'rai.

"Yes," Sy'rai said and rather smugly, Lizzy thought. "He had a doctor's appointment, but that was early this morning. How should I know where he is now? I reckon he'll be back when he feels like it. The sooner you turn out your lights, all the lights, the sooner that man will be home. He be scared of you. That's what he is."

"Scared of me?"

Sure enough, the minute Lizzy turned the lights out, she heard a door click softly on the ground floor and his boots falling heavily on the stairs. Dog tags jingled.

She went to her door and stood there, holding her breath

when Cole paused on her floor. Wing Nut trotted up to her door and barked. Her heart beat wildly until Cole resumed climbing the stairs. Nails scraping the oak floors, the black Lab bounded after him. When she heard Cole's bedroom door close, she went out into the hall and clasped herself tightly, no longer feeling quite so alone in the vast house, and yet feeling suddenly restless as she thought of him upstairs in his bedroom, undressing and crawling into his bed. She returned to bed and spent the rest of the night tossing and turning.

The next morning Lizzy had her oatmeal downstairs in the kitchen, which was made up of several rooms that took up at least half the huge ground floor. Sy'rai came out of the pantry, put both hands on her ample hips, set a plate of purple grapes on the counter and told Lizzy without her even so much as asking that Mr. Cole had already gobbled down a big plate of *huevos con chili roja.*

"That man—he have huge appetites."

"I don't care about his appetites or where he is," Lizzy said in a carefully neutral tone.

"Then you don't care to know he lit out of this house in boots and chaps and his oldest white shirt and in a dead run."

Trying to act indifferent, Lizzy popped a purple grape into her mouth and chewed it until it burst and turned to mush.

"Or that he's heading out on Ringo to the Cameron pens?"

Grape number one was followed by two more that melted juicily in Lizzy's mouth. Not that she even tasted them. "I don't care a whit."

"Wonder what's got that man in such a hurry to get out of this house—since you got home?"

"What do you mean?"

"You two gonna be in a snit the rest of your lives? Usually Kinky gives the men their orders. Cole, he stays and watches the weather forecast and flirts with me a spell."

"Kinky better not find out about that."

"My Kinky is a mighty understanding man."

"Because he understands the best thing he ever did was marry you. Oh, Sy'rai, it's good to be back even if…" *Even if she was totally confused about everything since she'd slept with Cole, and especially about Cole.*

Sy'rai embraced her. "It's good to have you back, honey. It's the best thing that's happened around here in a long time. Except for Vanilla," she amended. "Which reminds me, I'd better go check on her. With that little rascal thinking she can walk, no telling what she'll get into, even if she's in her play pen supposedly taking a nap."

"I'll do it."

"You know Cole asked about you, too."

Lizzy glanced at her in quick surprise.

"For a girl that isn't interested, you look mighty interested. Something happen in New York that I don't know about, girl?"

Lizzy shook her head way too briskly. Her feelings for Cole were powerful and personal. Her father had been against him. He'd married her sister, and yet she could feel herself growing more dependent on him and attached to him by the day. Still, it was all too new and threatening to share with others. Nobody could know about New York. Country people made it their business to know everybody and everything about everybody. There was no such thing as a secret. Gossip flew across fences and huge pastures from house to house even faster than wildfire.

After bathing and feeding Vanilla, Lizzy left her with Sy'rai and pointed her borrowed sports car in the direction of the Cameron pens. When she reached the pens, cattle bawled and dusty trucks were parked everywhere.

Cowboys in leather chaps and boots, some old faces and some new, grinned and yelled good morning to her and then went back to the hard work of weaning calves from their mothers. A few horses, including Ringo, were saddled and tied to a nearby fence.

Because of the recent rains, the job had been postponed for two weeks. Still, all the cattle and men were as muddy as pigs. Cole was the dirtiest one of all and yelling the loudest.

Kinky tapped Cole's broad shoulder and gestured to where she was getting out of her car. Lizzy was surprised when he stopped what he was doing and strode right up to her. Wing Nut trotted behind him, his tail wagging.

"Sorry I'm so dirty," Cole said in that slow easy drawl of his, his blue eyes intent as he studied her face and figure.

"I just wanted to say hi." She felt shy, strange. She was wishing she'd taken more pains with her appearance. "Haven't seen much of you."

"It's what you want, Lizzy."

"Yes. Of course. It's what I want."

"Good. 'Cause all I want is to make you happy."

She bit her lips. Wing Nut stuck his head under her hand and she patted him absently.

"I heard you went to the doctor yesterday. You're okay, aren't you?"

He went still, and that warned her.

"Just a routine appointment," he said, but he bit out the words.

Her eyes searched his for secrets.

"I told you—it wasn't important," he insisted.

When she wouldn't quit looking at him, his black head jerked and he turned away abruptly. For a while, he just stood there as still as a carved stone statue, with his back toward her.

The cowboys, who'd stopped their work to stare at them, got back to work the minute the boss glanced at them.

"If I left you alone, it was because I was giving you

breathing room," Cole said after a lengthy spell. "Because you want it that way, damn it."

"Thanks," she muttered, not feeling the least little bit grateful he was following her rules.

She couldn't think of anything else to say, so she watched the men, too. His nearness made her heart beat so loudly, she was scared he'd hear it.

Not that he looked at her again. Still, she was glad he stayed beside her. It felt nice, almost right, just standing with him like they belonged together—like maybe someday they could be friends. Which was strange, him being who he was, and them having their history.

The cattle were bawling as they were herded with electric prods and chased by cow dogs that nipped them into increasingly narrow corridors until they reached the final weaning chute, where they could only fit single file. A young cowboy in a baseball cap with spurs fastened to his duck boots opened and closed the quarto, a swinging door which sent the animals to separate pens.

Another cowboy was rinsing mud off his hands with fresh water and drying them before returning to the task of roping one particularly stubborn calf and pulling the almost six-hundred-pound animal to the weaning chute.

"New York," Cole said in a grim, low tone. "I've thought and thought about it. Guess it doesn't have to mean anything, unless we let it."

"Right," she muttered, suddenly so furious at him she wanted to kick him.

"Maybe we should wait a few days before I give you that tour," he continued.

"Anytime."

When he didn't reply, she just stood there beside him, tongue-tied, until he and the Lab left her to check on Ringo and get to work. She watched them a while longer until she reminded herself she should spend more time with Vanilla instead of this frustrating man and forced herself to drive away.

Two more days passed without Lizzy seeing Cole even once. Although he and Lizzy shared the same house, it was easy for him to hide from her in the vast, sprawling, multi-floored mansion. For one thing, Cole lived on the third floor in a suite in the southern wing while Lizzy was on the second in an immense suite on the north wing.

By the time she got up in the morning and came down for cereal and bananas or oatmeal, Cole made sure he was long gone to his crop-dusting office or the range. He never came home until well after supper. Sy'rai always made him a heaping plate of food, which he warmed up before he climbed the stairs and went to bed.

Lizzy could tell he hadn't bragged to the hands—or even to Kinky or Eli—that he'd bedded her because they treated Lizzy more deferentially than ever, asking her about Caesar first thing every morning. So she had nothing new to complain about where Cole Knight was concerned other than the fact he ignored her. And that became a maddening torment.

She couldn't get her mind off him. Was it the sex that had made her feel this profound connection to him? She liked the fact he hadn't boasted to the men. Did it mean he cared? Oh, how she hated the way she analyzed everything he did or didn't do.

When he was gone during the day, she wondered where he was. In the evenings when he was home and kept to his suite with his door closed, she felt restless and too distracted to read or write in her journal or watch television. No matter how many affirmations she made to erase him from her brain, she thought about him more every day that passed instead of less.

Thank goodness she had Vanilla to occupy her time during the day. But after she put Vanilla to bed, she would go to the window and stare out into the darkness, feeling extraordinarily jumpy and nervous. Sometimes she'd go out and walk the long gallery in the moonlight and stew over Cole.

Why didn't he spend more time with Vanilla? Why was he always so cool and distant when Lizzy and he chanced to meet? If only she could feel aloof about him, but he had only to look at her and she'd be flooded with hot reckless emotions that she didn't know how to deal with.

She knew she should go to her father's office and at least begin to work on the pressing ranch paperwork and return his phone messages, but some part of her kept hoping she'd get a call from Houston that he was coming home to take over again. So, she kept putting off going to the office. After all, Cole and Kinky were tending to what had to be done.

Her mother phoned her every other day. Her mom was so depressed, Hawk had stayed in Houston just to be with her. Walker, on the other hand, would be returning to the ranch soon to help work on the museum.

Then one night when Lizzy had given up on ever seeing Cole or having him react to her, much to her surprise, Cole turned up in the dining room on time right after Sy'rai rang the big ranch dinner bell. He'd showered and wore a clean white shirt and pressed jeans. As he entered, his eyes swept the room and caught hers. When she raised her eyebrows at him but felt too shy to speak, he smiled.

He sat down and unfurled his napkin with a flourish. "I thought maybe tomorrow we could start that tour of the ranch Leo suggested. I could show you how things have changed."

"Like I said before, *anytime.*"

He shot her a quick smile, and she felt her skin heat. "6:00 a.m., then?"

"Anytime," she agreed, wanting to say so much more, but biting her tongue instead.

His eyes shone as he grabbed a biscuit, and she felt her face grow even hotter. Slathering it thickly with butter, he ate lustily. When she remained silent, he did not attempt any more polite conversation.

She wanted to speak to him so badly she hurt. Her heart beat painfully in her throat, but all she could do was sit there, mute as a statue, in that tall, dark room, unable to think of a thing to say.

They had slept with each other, and yet they couldn't talk to each other. Why? What were these feelings that threatened to devour her? What did they mean?

Why was everything going so terribly wrong?

How could she ever sort any of it out when he wouldn't even talk to her?

Oh, if only Daddy would get well!

If only...

Lizzy got to the garage before six the next morning. Cole's truck doors were wide-open, and he was in the front seat, slinging all sorts of things out of it onto the ground.

She yelled hello and then jumped aside when he threw a trailer tire out.

"Hey—don't hit me!"

"Sorry...." He stuck his head out and grinned sheepishly. "Excuse my lousy housekeeping. My truck's my office. I was trying to clean it up before you got here—to make a false good impression."

She smiled. "Daddy's truck was the same way."

Before they could get in, Cole had to scoop wire cutters, pliers, his cell phone plug, and assorted sales slips from hardware and feed stores that had been stacked on the passenger seat into a bag and stuff it behind the seat. Then he got out and threw everything on the garage floor except the trailer tire into the trash.

"Would you mind driving?" he asked in an offhanded manner.

"No," she said, even though it seemed a little odd. Then she remembered he hadn't flown the plane by himself. Without making a comment, she took her place behind the wheel.

As they drove off, he said, "We don't have any hunters during the first part of this week, so we'll tour some of the hunting camps to start with."

"Great."

"Since there's not much profit in ranching right now, we have to make money any way we can. We use the latest technology, and where we used to focus on cattle, we simultaneously manage ranching, hunting and wildlife touring enterprises."

"Wildlife touring enterprises? Like birding?"

He nodded. "We're not seeing the growth in hunting that we're seeing in ecotourism."

The truck's tires whooshed and crunched on the rough caliche road as they drove, and for a while the countryside on either side of the road was lush and green. When they came to a large artificial lake, ducks burst into flight. Everything was beautiful until they crossed the wooden bridge that spanned the pond. On the other side the earth was blackened and the mesquite and oak stunted.

"What happened over here?"

His face was grim. "Last fall we chained this pasture, but then in January, our burn got out of control. We nearly lost the camp you're about to see."

"Who was responsible?"

"Me."

"How did it happen?"

His hands clenched. When he didn't answer her, she didn't press him.

"Your father accused me of doing it on purpose," he said.

"Did you?"

"I don't know."

"What does that mean—you don't know?"

"Look, I'm sorry this came up. I wish I hadn't said that, okay? Forget it. Just forget it."

They drove in silence across the scorched land until they reached their first stop, which was the hunting lodge he'd mentioned. It had been remodeled and expanded since Lizzy had last seen it.

They crossed a creek, and she saw a wall of salt cedar at the edge of green lawns that surrounded the camp. The metal roofs of the buildings glinted through the trees. The sight of so much greenery after the blackened pastures was a welcome relief.

"It's gorgeous."

"Your high-end hunting experience," he replied, his mood lightening a little as they drove up to the camp and parked in front.

The low white building with long porches and antlers hanging on its roofline looked both rustic and comfortable, and yet matched the historic architecture of other buildings on the ranch.

Jimmy McBride, the camp manager, a tall thirtysomething eager-looking fellow with a thick mane of blond hair, sprinted out of the lodge and extended a brawny hand to help her down from the truck.

"Cole said to give you a tour."

She smiled, and McBride began to deliver a speech he'd obviously given before. Dutifully he expounded on all the hunting camps and their corporate lessees. Then he went into brush control and told her about the different grasses he was planting to encourage wildlife. But what really excited him was the grant proposal he'd just written to try to promote much-needed quail-management research.

"Nobody knows why quail populations vary from year to year," McBride explained.

"Not that people around here don't have strong opinions on the subject," Cole inserted dryly.

"We're having a boom year, but on the whole, quail are declining everywhere all over the country, even here in south Texas where we have more than anybody. We need to find out what's happening to these birds before it's critical."

"And I thought hunting was the salvation for ranchers," she said.

"That's past history. Hunters are declining," Cole replied.

After the tour, they had coffee. Then Cole and Lizzy got back into his truck and drove over the flat land for hours. He talked about the ranch's different soils, about how clay soil encouraged cactus, such as prickly pear, and how they didn't use herbicides to treat it.

"But then you know that already, don't you? You've got that fancy degree from A&M."

She smiled warily. "Nobody was too impressed in New York."

He laughed. "Goes to show you—what do *they* know?"

He took her to see several five-thousand-acre pastures that were under a newly implemented, four-pasture, sixteen-month grazing system.

When he told her to stop the truck, he said, "Three herds are rotated between four pastures, leaving one pasture free to recover."

She nodded.

"With one pasture lying fallow, we have a program to improve land. Brush can be cleared or the land can be reseeded or grass can have time to grow."

"How's it working?" she asked.

"Better than we'd hoped. We don't have to move cattle as much, so we cut down on labor. And the cattle have higher pregnancy rates even during drought conditions."

"Impressive."

They resumed their tour. When they reached a pasture where brush was being cleared, he helped her out of the truck so she could watch an enormous yellow roller chopper that looked like a bulldozer plowing heavy mesquite and hackberry trees.

"You've seen this before, but the driver's got a computer in his cab. He's got GIS data, and he's leaving oak motts according to a map on his computer screen."

"Do you reseed after you chop?" she asked.

"No. We let the brush lie where it falls for a while so it can dry out before we try to get a burn. I've been having trouble getting my guys to build the perfect brush pile." His expression darkened. "Last time I think maybe the piles burned too hot."

His handsome face looked haunted. She didn't believe he'd let the burn get out of control. At least not deliberately.

What was really going on? What was he hiding?

He led her back to the truck. "Sometime I'll take you up so you can see what pastures like this look like from the air. It's pretty amazing."

"I can't wait."

They drove all over the ranch, not that they covered even a tenth of it. They agreed to meet at six the next morning again, but when she went to the garage the next day expecting Cole, she was acutely disappointed to find Kinky there instead.

"Leo called late last night, so Cole and John flew to San Antonio."

"But why?"

"Cole didn't say. More trouble I expect."

"He should have taken me with him. I was left in charge, and we're supposed to be partners."

"You'll have to take that up with Cole. You ready, girl? I don't reckon I'm as much fun as Cole, but I'll certainly do my best."

She frowned. Were her feelings for Cole so obvious?

On that note, what exactly *were* her feelings for Cole?

Kinky took her to the Golden Spurs Research Center, the museum and the horse barn. They talked to experts about environmental research, cattle breeding, quarter horse bloodlines, and wildlife habitat, but during the long day when she became bored and dispirited, she realized she missed Cole.

Oh, God. What was happening to her?

The roar of Cole's plane's engine on the flight back to the ranch was so loud he couldn't hear himself think. John sat on his left, but Cole was hardly aware of him. Ahead, a brilliant sliver of burnt orange sun hung above the wild brush country and set it ablaze. Thorny brush that had been sculpted into graceful, flowing shapes by the roller choppers glowed amber, pink and violet and cast flickering dark shadows across the pastures.

Hell, Cole wished he was down there chasing a wild bull. If only his life could be that simple again. But things were getting more complicated by the minute.

What Leo had told him in San Antonio was highly disturbing.

In the hope of coming up with an answer, he relived the meeting.

"There've been too many accidents centered around you, Cole," Leo had said over black coffee as soon as they'd sat down together.

"First, there was the plane crash that took Mia's life. You

and Caesar, not Mia, were supposed to be on the flight," Leo reminded him.

"So?"

"I've got a hunch that you and he were supposed to go down without a trace. Not Mia. Now all of a sudden Caesar's out of the picture. Very convenient for somebody."

"You're not saying that I—"

"Maybe."

Cole shot out of his chair.

"Maybe not. I want your brain on this, not your emotions. Ever since the plane crash, you've been in one hot spot after the other. Ever wonder why?"

"How the hell—"

"You started that burn last January."

Cole, who had returned to his seat, flushed. He hadn't told anybody, not even Leo, about his blackouts.

"The piles got too hot for some reason."

"You nearly died. Maybe you were supposed to."

Cole didn't say anything. When he'd come to after starting the burn, he'd been trapped in a firestorm and had had to run for his life. If the creek hadn't been running, if the fire had been slower, he would have died for lack of oxygen.

"Then there were the two truckloads of cattle you shipped to market that vanished two months ago."

Leo's black gaze drilled him. Suddenly Cole felt like a bug in an airless bottle. Pressure built in his lungs until he had trouble breathing.

"What the hell are you getting at?"

"Relax. If I was sure you were behind all this, we wouldn't be having this conversation." Leo paused as if he were choosing his words carefully. "Here's the real bomb, old friend. TSCRA's computer system discovered that the brand and tag data sent to them from a cattle auction in Crockett, Texas, matched our missing cattle's brands and tags."

"This is great news."

"Except for the thief." Leo's black eyes were so intense again, Cole's gut clenched. "You'll never guess who the seller is."

Cole's bowels turned to water. "It isn't me?"

"You got it."

Cole shot out of his chair again. "You wait just a damn minute—I didn't steal those cows!"

"No, *you* wait. Like I said, I need your brain, not your emotion. If I thought you'd do something that stupid, you wouldn't be here. Still, we'll need to do an audit of your records, including your bank accounts, as a step toward clearing you. I'll want to know about any trips to Mexico or anywhere else out of the country you've been."

Cole's heart was still pounding as he sank back into his chair again. "Sure. Anything."

"Now the plot really thickens. Yesterday a Houston detective, Joe Phillips, sent a local officer by our offices. He said they've run the plates on your truck and they think it's the one that was seen by one of Cherry Lane's neighbors before she vanished."

"That's bullshit. They've got two or three lousy numbers. Why would I go near her?"

"Let's look at this from another angle? All our trucks are black. Suppose someone switched license plates with you for a spell. Would you have noticed? What if somebody's trying to set you up?"

"To get rid of me you mean," he muttered, his voice harsh and cold.

"Maybe you've got more enemies at the Golden Spurs than you realize. Mia's dead. Maybe somebody wanted you dead instead of her. Or maybe somebody blames you because she is dead. A lot of people don't like the way you got Mia pregnant and forced her to sign over her stock as the price of marriage, either. Now it appears you're getting friendly with Lizzy again. Maybe somebody thinks you're becoming too powerful. You're a Knight, you know."

"Not to be trusted," Cole said bitterly. Not that he had much sympathy or liking for the bastard he'd apparently been, either.

"Is there anything you have to add that would help me clear your name?"

Cole shook his head. No way was he about to confess about the blackouts.

"Then watch your back, old friend."

Usually flying took his mind off his worries. Not today.

Had he gone back to Cherry Lane's during one of his blackouts? Had he deliberately torched thousands of acres? Had he sold the cattle and put the money in a secret account in another country or something? If he'd done those things, what else might he do?

Who the hell was he really? A monster? He hated doubting himself. One thing he knew—he had to stay the hell away from Lizzy.

As always the sun sank too quickly in this south land. John and Cole were flying low over stubby green mesquite, hackberry, huisache and stunted oak trees. The land beneath them was unremittingly flat and usually so dry and harsh a man needed quite a few acres to run a single cow. Still, Cole loved it, especially from up here where he felt free and could really see it. Prickly pear cactus, spiny yucca, populated with cougars and coyotes and bobcats—he loved it all.

In addition to the blackouts and the mysterious accidents there was his tension about Lizzy. Every time he was with her, he wanted her more. The thought of seeing or not seeing her drove him crazy. Ever since they'd had sex, she was on his mind all the damn time. He was like a rutting teenager, and she wanted nothing more to do with him.

What the hell was sex, anyway? Why the hell couldn't his fucked-up brain just forget it? Hell, it damn sure forgot everything else.

He'd screwed her, and he still wanted her. She didn't want him.

So, get over it. Find another woman.

He didn't want another woman. One of the flaws in his nature was he was stubborn and tenacious. He knew what he wanted.

The self-serving bastard he'd been before the plane crash had always known what he wanted, or so Eli and the rest of the big mouths on the ranch told him every damn chance they got.

His daddy had been a no-good drunk, who'd lost his family's ranch to Caesar Kemble, and Cole had wanted a stake in the Golden Spurs. A big stake. Fortunately he'd been better at poker than his daddy. He made part of the money to start his own business by winning at poker. He'd married Mia. He'd fathered Vanilla. He had lots of stock in the ranch now. Lizzy had virtually given him full command of the place, as well.

But the Golden Spurs wasn't enough anymore. He wanted Lizzy.

Forget her. For her own good, forget her. There were grave reasons why he should stay away from her.

He stared down at the land to distract himself, but all he thought of was her. The trouble with empty country was it put a man in touch with his soul—and made him see more clearly.

In cities, which Cole normally detested, a man could go to the theater or out to dinner with friends, or merely roam the streets on foot or in his truck. He could distract himself. He could visit bookstores or pace in malls or drink in bars. Here, the nearest town of any size was forty-five miles away. Not that Chaparral even approached being a city.

There was a town square with a historic courthouse, a few lousy bars, a movie theater with uncomfortable seats that were falling apart, a grocery store and about ten gas stations and fast food burger places. Forget shopping. There wasn't even a Wal-Mart.

Why did it always have to be this way for him? All his life he'd been labeled a villain and had had some hunger eating him alive.

There was no future in wanting Lizzy. Maybe she had come home for now, but she wouldn't stay here. She wanted bright city lights and a sophisticated man like that no-good Bryce character, who'd been dissatisfied with her.

Not that Cole was right for her. He knew that.

He had to leave her alone, damn it—if it killed him.

It was because he had to leave her alone, he'd made a date tonight with a willing woman—Susan Johnson, the sexy secretary who worked at the private airstrip where he kept his plane. Suz was Hal Johnson's daughter, and she loved the ranching life as much as he did. Suz had lovely dark hair and a sweet smile, and she'd been after him ever since Mia died. She was good with kids, too. Vanilla clapped every time she saw her.

He was supposed to have dinner at Suz's house at seven tonight. This morning before he'd flown to San Antonio, she'd made quite a point of telling him Hal was away for the whole weekend. No doubt she'd try to entice him into her bed.

Good. Maybe he'd let her. Maybe sex would take his mind off New York and Lizzy.

Two hours later when he got home, Sy'rai told him Walker had shown up and gone down to the museum to check on the progress on the mural.

"Finally," he told her. "I need all the help I can get with that. I don't know much about art, but Walker's a genius in that department."

"You eating here tonight, Mr. Cole?"

"I've got a date."

Sy'rai raised her eyebrows and smiled, coaxing him to say more, but thankfully she didn't ask for details. Still, to avoid prying questions, Cole quickly marched upstairs, only to pause as he always did on *her* floor. This evening, though, it was a mistake because he caught her scent, and it got him hard and hot—and not for Suz.

Storming up the rest of the stairs, he slammed his door, sank against it for a long moment before he ripped off his clothes and headed into the long cold shower.

Dressing quickly again, he strode over to his mirror and ran a comb through his wet, black hair. As usual he wore clean, creased jeans and a long-sleeved, starched white shirt. The only thing he'd done differently was to put on his best boots. He was sliding the comb into his back pocket when he heard the tentative knock on his door.

A soft voice that sent a shiver through him merely said, "Cole?"

But that was enough to make the skin on the back of his neck tighten.

Lizzy? What the hell was she doing up here?

Knowing she was there electrified him. In two long strides he was across the room. His hand went to the doorknob, but then as if he were afraid of her, he just stood there. *Damn.* Almost angrily he flung the door open so hard it would have banged if he hadn't caught it at the last second.

At his unexpected violence, Lizzy jumped back from him and then stood in the dark hall, looking white-faced and young and very sexy in skintight jeans and a blue-checkered halter top. Her bluish-lavender eyes were huge and luminous even though she couldn't seem to meet his gaze. Her shiny platinum hair fell loosely about her shoulders.

Was there anything more attractive in the whole world than a pretty blonde?

"The telephone rang a while ago," she said. "It was for you."

Damn if he couldn't see her nipples under the thin material of that halter. "I must have been in the shower," he said grumpily, scowling at her.

"Somebody named Suz," she whispered, flinching a little and backing away from him even more, her hand involuntarily covering the breast he'd been staring at.

He tore his eyes from her. "Thanks." He tried to shrug carelessly, but his body felt huge and awkward. His manhood hardened. Hell, she had him in knots. "I'll give Suz a call. First thing."

"She left a message. Do you want to know what she said?"

Hell no. He wanted to end this impossible conversation before he acted on his feelings and did something wild—like kissing her.

"Shoot," he said, his low voice cool and indifferent.

"She's running late. She says not to come over until seven-thirty."

"Thanks."

Lizzy stepped closer so that she was standing in the pool of light spilling into the hall from the lamp in his bedroom. It lit up her hair, turned it to silver, made her look so sexy and ethereal…like the wanton creature from one of his wet dreams. With a slim fingertip she began to play with a silken strand of her hair.

Even her hands were gorgeous. And he could smell her. Lavender tonight, he thought. Not roses.

Aware of the bed behind him, he felt a strange pull from her soft form and fought the almost overwhelming urge to move toward her, to touch her, caress her, first her hair and then her body.

She was so damned beautiful, he couldn't stop staring at her. He wanted to seduce her, to make love to her for hours.

"Walker's here," she said.

"I know."

"Have you seen him?"

"Not yet."

"He's having dinner with Mark," she said.

"Right, the guy, who wears pink shirts and is doing the murals."

"I went over there to check them out today," she said. "Mark's very good."

"Right. Well, he should be." Did this conversation sound as stilted to her as it did to him? "He's got quite a name," Cole muttered.

Willing her to leave, he assumed a hard, insolent expression. When that didn't work, he took a long slow breath followed by another.

"Oh, and a sheriff's deputy, Jay, came out and asked Kinky a lot of questions about your truck. He wanted dates as to when it's been off the ranch. He wanted to know when you've been off the ranch, too. Wanted to know if you ever loaned it out."

A chill went through him that left him feeling so cold and drained he wrapped his arms around himself defensively. "Do you think I'm a criminal now on top of all my other sins? Do you think I did something to that stripper? Do you?"

"No. Of course not. Why do you even ask?"

"All right. Then do you have something else on your mind?" he rasped.

Unconsciously she bit her lower lip, which seemed to be trembling all of a sudden, maybe from his harsh tone. She shook her head, but she kept standing there just the same.

"Well, then, darlin'?" He leaned down toward her pretty

face, his very nearness an unspoken threat that he might kiss her. *Lord, he wanted to*. He wanted to so much he didn't trust himself this close to her.

When she didn't speak or move, he said, "I guess I'd better finish getting ready for my date."

She licked those swollen, trembling lips of hers and refused to budge. He forgot about the sheriff's deputy and his date with Suz.

"What do you want from me, girl?" he mumbled. "What the hell do you want?"

"Just to tell you…"

He held his breath.

She couldn't seem to go on.

"You shouldn't be up here, you know. I might get the idea you want more from me than you say you do. I might even think I should do something about it."

Do you want me to do something about it, darlin'? Is that what you want? He took a step toward her.

Tearing her gaze from his, she ran lightly down the hall toward the stairs without another word.

He drew a long breath to try to recover his sanity. His hands shook by the time he closed the door. The ridge of swollen flesh against his fly hurt like hell. A full sweat broke on his brow, and he began to pace, swearing under his breath.

Before he knew what he was doing, he was stripping again. Unbuckling his belt, he ripped it out of the loops. He undid the buttons of his shirt and tore his shirt off. Next he yanked off his boots and jeans.

Then he was in the icy shower, jumping up and down and then beating the tiled walls with his fists as blasts of liquid, icy needles stung his overheated skin.

For her own protection, she'd better leave him alone.

Fourteen

"Hello, fantasy girl." Cole pushed Lizzy ahead of him into the gilded elevator and then grabbed her slim wrist, which he lashed with a red velvet rope to a bronze hook on the wall.

Dry-mouthed and terrified as she stared at the wall, and yet sizzling from head to toe, Lizzy didn't fight him when he tied her other hand to the opposite wall. Nor did she scream for help before the doors closed, and she was alone with him.

"What have we got here?" he whispered from behind her, caressing her neck with his lips and causing her to feel even more bone-deep heat. "How much is it going to cost me this time, hooker?"

His hands cupped and squeezed her breasts, his blunt fingers burning the tender mounds of plump flesh through the thin silken fabric of her sheer gown. "Beautiful. You're so beautiful."

Lingeringly he kissed the hollow of her throat until she begged him to take her. Then he ripped the gown from her body, leaving her naked and exposed. But only for a moment. In the next, his big hands were all over her again, and his tongue was between her legs.

Spreading her thighs wider with his hands, he kissed her

there for an endless time before standing up again. Then he yanked his zipper down and plunged inside her.

At that first delicious contact, Lizzy sprang awake, shivering even though it wasn't cold at all.

"Oh, my God." She felt shamed to the core. But also she felt a soul-deep emptiness and loneliness that he wasn't in bed with her, too.

It was 2:00 a.m. How could she dream she was a hooker, selling herself to Cole Knight? Enjoying it? Wanting him still?

She drew a deep breath. No doubt he was lying in the arms of that other woman this very minute. Suz Johnson, wasn't that her name? Oh, God. And she, poor foolish Lizzy, was dreaming of the handsome devil's warm mouth between her legs. How could she be wet and hot and dying for him?

Her stomach heaved.

It was only a dream. But why had she had it?

She'd gone up to his room to give him a simple message. When she'd seen his bed and read the blatant desire in his eyes, she'd actually wanted him to kiss her and take her to bed.

Glancing about the darkened bedroom, she felt disoriented as she made out oddly distorted shapes. She buried her face in her hands and rocked back and forth. No way could she go back to bed and risk another revealing dream like that.

Galvanized, she switched on her bedside lamp, got up and put on her jeans and T-shirt. Racing out onto her veranda, she began to pace. The quarter moon lit the sky with a brilliant sliver of silver fire. Zillions of stars looked like diamonds sprinkled on black velvet.

The night was alive with the music of cicadas and frogs. Smiling, she leaned over her balcony and listened to the roar of tens of thousands, maybe millions, of darling, adorable frogs.

Because of all the rain, there were ponds all over the

ranch. The frogs were croaking so loudly, the ponds seemed to purr like giant wet cats. It was a wonderful sound, a sound from her childhood that reminded her of plentiful rain and good times. The sound was pure country, and it spoke to her troubled soul.

She remembered collecting tiny frogs after the rain and keeping them in jars with holes in the lids, marveling at the wonder of so many little frogs in the grass and on the sidewalks.

But she wasn't a child anymore. She was a woman, and she'd gone to bed with a man, planning for it to be a lark. Only it wasn't, and she couldn't let go of her emotions for that man. She was obsessed by him.

Her mistake had been to fall for the liberated woman propaganda. Sex was not something all women could play at like a game. For her, it was too deep and too personal. But how could she—with her values—have a bondage dream? The mere thought of letting a man tie her up made her hate herself.

I like myself. I like myself.

That's a bold-faced lie, and you know it.

Don't criticize. You like yourself.

This isn't working.

Oh, just shut up.

She could not undo having gone to bed with Cole or having made a fool of herself tonight when she'd gone to his room. All she could do was learn from her mistake, make the best of it and go on.

Silently she ran her shaking hands through her hair, sat down in a wicker rocker and willed her mind to go blank. An hour passed, and still she stayed in her trancelike state with the frogs singing all around her until a truck crunched caliche in the drive.

So, Cole had finally come home.

She got up. She could not go on like this, thinking about him constantly, dreaming tormenting dreams. She didn't have to. Her hour of meditation had made her realize she had something very important to do.

For the first time since coming home, she knew what she *had* to do and why. For her own sanity, she would tackle the mammoth job her father had given her with a total determination. She would be a real business partner to Cole.

Tomorrow, she'd talk to Kinky, the foreman. She would call Leo Storm. She would ask Cole how she could best help him. She would get busy, so busy she wouldn't have time to dwell on Cole.

When she heard him climb the stairs and close the door to his bedroom, she leapt up, grabbed her father's key ring from her purse and raced down the stairs, heading for the ranch offices, which were outside.

The world wouldn't miss a baby frog or two. The watcher, who'd been standing in the dark shadows of the Spur Tree squashing little frogs with the heel of his custom-made boots until their bodies popped, jumped back when Lizzy bolted from the house. Her sneakers fell so lightly on the asphalt driveway, she barely made a sound as she raced toward the offices.

He stepped deeper into the shadows and stared at the black truck parked in the driveway. What the hell had gotten into her at this hour?

A few minutes later, lights came on inside the old ice house which now served as the ranch offices. He stood there for a long time, observing her slim shadow leap against different window shades as she moved from room to room.

Whatever the hell she was doing, she had no right to be there. Maybe she was Caesar's chosen one, but she was a foolish, ignorant girl, who knew nothing about the Golden

Spurs. If she ran it for long, she'd destroy everything he'd been trying to build.

He remembered Electra, who hadn't pleaded for her life, and then Cherry. Without any warning, he felt the despicable hunger to enjoy a woman beg while he rutted on top of her. He swallowed several deep breaths, despising himself for panting like a dog. His appetite was growing stronger. No. It was *her* fault, not his. Lizzy shouldn't be out here flaunting herself when he could go only so long now in between women.

Not Lizzy. He liked Lizzy.

Lizzy was in the way. And she was pretty.

They had to be pretty. He couldn't get hard otherwise.

Still, Lizzy was special. He didn't want to kill her.

She should have listened to reason.

Inside her father's very masculine office, which was decorated with hunting trophies, Lizzy hesitated, wondering how and where to begin.

"Oh, Daddy, I don't belong here. I'm not up to this."

Slowly she sat down at his desk and leaned back in his leather chair until it creaked, her gaze sweeping his immense desk, his computer, gold pens, notepads, the stacks of yellow sticky notes, the files and ledgers on the metal shelves above his desk, the deer mounted heads and the framed photographs of wildlife that hung on his walls.

The photos were signed Electra, with flashy swirls of gold ink. Lizzy remembered her curiosity about the bronze marker under the Spur Tree. Electra had died recently. She must have meant a lot to her father.

When Lizzy was old enough to read handwritten script, she'd asked her father who Electra was.

He'd been at his desk. He'd looked a little startled at first, but he'd glanced up at the pictures and said, "Nobody important really."

She hadn't quite believed him even then. "But who is she, Daddy?"

"Electra Scott, a famous photojournalist," he'd barked, shuffling his papers. "She visited the ranch once. A long time ago. Before you were born."

"What's a photojournalist?"

He wadded several papers up. "Somebody who tells wonderful stories with pictures, and writes."

"I like to write."

"You're gonna be a cowgirl not a writer," he'd snapped. "Get that in your head."

She'd asked him more questions and received more terse answers.

"Don't you like her, Daddy?"

"I like her," he'd said. But he'd looked odd and a little sad, and angry, too.

Unlike the stuffed heads that seemed so dead, Electra's pictures were wonderful. Somehow with her camera she'd caught the soul and purpose of each animal or object she'd photographed.

There was a wonderful picture of shiny ibis birds roosting in a barren tree while cattle grazed. There was a great shot of tack drying on mesquite trees as the sun set, painting the world with its magic light. There were several more shots of big blue sky and the thorny flat land beneath it.

Lizzy knew each windmill on the ranch Electra must have climbed to get her pictures 'cause her daddy had climbed them with her to point out his favorite views. Electra's pictures always gave her the exact emotion she felt when she was awed by the same sight in real life. Electra hadn't lived here, but she had captured what the ranch was about.

Lizzy ran a hand through her unruly hair. Oh, God, she felt like a child sneaking into her daddy's office again, or worse, an impostor in her daddy's office. As her gaze drifted over the photographs, she remembered how her father used to bring her here to his office, carrying her high on his shoulder.

Caesar had shown her off to all his secretaries. The women would get up from their desks and circle her, paying homage as if she were a princess. They'd complimented her platinum hair, her clothes, anything. And they'd given her candy, which her stern, domineering father hadn't allowed her to eat.

She fingered her father's mouse and thought about turning on his computer. Like Cole, and then Kinky, who'd continued the tour, had told her, ranching technology was changing fast.

"It has to because the margin of profit is so small, Lizzy," Cole had said.

The calves she'd seen weaned a week ago were definitely wonders of modern technology. Ranchers like her father used DNA fingerprinting to pinpoint genes for tenderness and marbling. Ultrasound could determine a rib eye's exact size. Not so long ago, ranchers went to auctions and used videos to buy more stock. Cattle buyers now logged onto the Internet.

A financial report lay in the middle of Caesar's desk. As she began to thumb through the pages that were filled with columns of numbers, she realized what an enormous responsibility she'd asked Cole to assume. Hundreds of people depended on the ranch and the corporation that owned other businesses. She'd been smart to ask Cole for help, but she had no idea if she could trust him or who else she could really depend on.

I trust Cole. Even after New York. How can that be?

Slowly she began to read the report. It made more sense to her than it would have if she didn't have that degree from A&M in ranch management. Still, she was rusty and no whiz at numbers. After she finished reading it, she was exhausted, and yet somehow not willing to go back to her bed, either. Despite a wonderful year weatherwise along with low feed prices, and high cattle prices, the Golden Spurs had done worse and worse each quarter. Why?

There had been a number of strange accidents. Her father had told her about some of them over the phone, and she'd just read about more of them. There had been the burn last January that had gotten out of control. A barn full of valuable livestock had mysteriously burned on the Chaparral division, as well, when Cole, Uncle B.B. and Bobby Joe had been there. Several truckloads of cattle on the way to market had vanished into thin air. And of course, there were the ongoing lawsuits.

She began opening the drawers of her father's desk, her fingers rustling through the various supplies she found. In the top drawers there were reams of paper; boxes of diskettes, staples and index cards; scissors and more pens. When she got to the bottom right drawer, it was locked. When no key on Caesar's ring would fit it, she pulled at the handle several more times before giving up.

She stood and began rummaging through the files on the shelves above his desk, pulling them down one by one and thumbing through them. Apparently these files were his active projects. Several had to do with the museum. But Walker was here now to supervise that, so she thumbed through the pages about the opening, about the hiring of the designer for the building and the artists, reading only key words. She kept going through files until the words and figures began to blur.

Intending to rest for a minute only, she laid her head down on Caesar's desk. Hours later she awakened to the delicious smell of fresh coffee. Opening her eyes, she pushed her head off the tumble of files that littered the top of her father's massive desk. Steam curled above a mug of dark brew.

"Working late or working early?" Cole murmured dryly as he raised the shade.

She blinked at the bright sun and then shielded her eyes with her hand.

In an instant she imagined her dream about the elevator when she'd been naked and his mouth had been between her legs.

Annoyed at him, she sat up with a jerk and rubbed her neck in the hopes he wouldn't notice she was blushing. "Ouch," she whispered, speaking around a yawn.

"You look awful," he said, grinning down at her in a friendly, rather than sexy, fashion. "Really bad," he teased.

"Don't be rude. I have a crick. You're the last person I'm in the mood to see first thing this morning."

"Forget the coffee. You look tired. You'd better go straight to bed."

When he reached for her coffee, she grabbed the coffee mug and sipped possessively. "How was your date?" she asked, not really wanting to know.

"Great!" He shot her a dazzling smile. "Suz is a nice woman. Pretty, too. Do I dare flatter myself that you're jealous?"

"Of course not!"

"I thought maybe when you came upstairs last night…you were chasing me."

"I was delivering your girlfriend's message," she snapped. "I'm glad you two had fun."

The corner of his sensual mouth tightened. "Well, you damn sure don't sound like it. You sound grumpy as hell. I'll bet Suz—"

"What do you want from me?" she muttered, her nerves going raw.

"That's the last thing you want to hear, darlin'," he teased, his gaze lingering on her body. "Or is it?"

Her breath caught. Was he flirting with her?

He looked at his watch. "*Hell.* I'm late. The hands headed out for the pens an hour ago. After San Antonio I'm way behind." He stalked across the office to the door.

"Cole, what was your meeting about?"

His shoulders tightened, but he didn't turn around. "That's between Leo and me."

"I'm supposed to be in charge."

"Then, so long, boss lady. Don't let me keep you." He tipped his hat and then slammed out of the office.

She stood up and stomped her feet a dozen times until she felt better.

"Good. This is good." Better for him to be mad and me to be mad back than for me to be dreaming about his mouth between my legs.

When her gaze fell to the locked drawer again, she remembered the scissors she'd found earlier. Pulling them out, she jammed a pointed tip into the lock and jiggled it. Before she was done, she'd destroyed the scissors, broken a nail and her coffee was cold. But she'd successfully unlocked the drawer. Chewing on her nail, she yanked the drawer all the way open and began digging through its contents.

Feeling a little guilty, she lifted a large manila envelope with the word Confidential scrawled across it in her father's bold hand. Underneath the fat envelope lay a thick stack of letters tied together with a wide, blue, satin ribbon. The postscripts on the envelopes were from all over the world, and they were addressed to her father at a P.O. box in Corpus Christi, a city ninety miles north of the ranch, rather than to the ranch itself.

Had her father been carrying on a secret correspondence?

A tremor went through her as she opened the first letter, which was from Kenya. She was right.

Slowly she began reading words that had been written

years ago in a strong, loopy hand. When she finished the first paragraph, Lizzy's heart was pounding in her throat.

Darling,
Had a second and thought I'd dash you a note. The pictures you sent of our precious little Lizzy are so wonderful. You truly have the gift of composition.

Like you say, she takes after me more than she does you, at least, in physical appearance, poor dear. But, she is so beautiful, it almost makes me wish I could be with you both. But it wouldn't have worked. No matter how much we might have wanted it to. You know that.

I'll photograph lions today and write a really good description of my adventures here in Kenya for you. Last night a lion came up to my tent and actually slept against the tent right beside me, only he was outside and I was in the tent. I could feel his body warmth all night. It was really quite exhilarating.

Send more pictures and keep me posted on all of Lizzy's adventures. I'm sorry about that awful beast biting the tip of her little finger off. Poor little dear. Kiss it for me, and don't worry—you'll make a true cowgirl of her in the end. I'm sure, you will, even if you did fail so miserably with me. I'm so proud of you both.

Must go before I lose the last of the light. You know how I love early morning and late evening light. The big cats will be out, too.
Love, Electra

When Lizzy finished the letter, her heart was still thudding violently. Slowly, carefully, she folded it and put it back in its envelope. With exquisite care, she tied the letters up exactly as they'd been in the fat blue ribbon and laid them on top of the desk.

Then she shut the drawer. Before standing up, she traced the scratches she'd made on the wood with her fingertip. They weren't really noticeable unless one looked closely.

Gathering the envelope and Electra's letters, she walked toward the door and stepped out onto the porch, which was lit by magical, golden light. Electra's light. For a long time Lizzy stood in the long dark shadow of a column, clutching the letters and the manila envelope against her heart, feeling connected to the light in a new and different way.

She barely noticed the two pickups, one with a trailer for horses driven by Cole followed by another pulling a trailer for cattle driven by Kinky. They were probably heading for the pens.

Electra Scott was her mother—not Joanne Kemble.

All her life, Lizzy had felt that something was wrong with her, that she didn't belong here...that she wasn't a true Kemble. Now she knew why. No wonder Mother had favored Mia.

Not Mother...Joanne.

No wonder Joanne and Mia fit. No wonder her father had been so determined to make Lizzy prove her mettle.

She was his bastard from some sordid affair like the one he'd had with Cherry. He'd forced Joanne to raise her. He'd forced her down everybody else's throats. Cole had said everybody was jealous of her. How many of them knew the truth? No wonder she had wild, shameful dreams. Her mother had been some sort of artistic, free spirit.

Oh, God...

The early, brilliantly lit morning air suddenly felt so chilly, she shivered.

* * *

From where Lizzy sat in the middle of her big bed as she talked to Mandy on her cordless phone, she could see herself in the gilt-framed mirror over the dresser. Her skin was pale, her lavender-blue eyes huge. Never had she looked so small and defenseless.

"Incredible," Lizzy said. "I can't believe you know who she is."

"I went to Princeton, kiddo. Electra Scott's, like, really famous. Not to mention supercool. They had an exhibit of her stuff at the Met when you lived here. You're her daughter? Way cool!"

"You mean you went to her exhibit?"

"Yeah. They were black-and-white close-ups she'd done of kids and animals all over the world. She loved children, all colors and shapes."

"Then why did she ditch me so fast?"

"She had special gifts. She made a choice. Life's all about choices. It's not like she threw you out to starve."

"But I'm all mixed up. I always have been because of what she did."

"Did you never have to make a hard choice where there was no perfect solution?"

"Who made you such a guru?"

"You called me, kiddo." She let that hang. "Hey, I gotta go. A customer just walked in. Looks like a live one, too. You should see her. Black bondage outfit. Diamond piercings. Oh, she just stopped at the edible undies section. Gotta reel this baby in, kiddo. Did I tell you the manager put me on a commission? You're gonna figure this out, so lighten up."

"Nice to hear your voice at least. And thanks for keeping an eye on my New York apartment. I don't know if I'm ever going to get back there, but at least it's in good care."

"No problem, kiddo."

When Mandy hung up, Lizzy felt restless and out of sorts and abandoned. Her thoughts turned to Cole.

He was the next person she wanted to tell about her real mother. Why was that? Why did he have to pop into her mind all the time? Like he was someone special to her?

When she called Joanne to find out how her father was, Lizzy felt more awkward with her than usual. "S-so, how's Daddy?"

"More or less the same, but they're moving him out of ICU."

"Thanks—Joanne."

She had never called her that before.

"Are you all right?" Joanne asked.

"Fine."

The line fell silent long before each of them hung up.

After lunch Lizzy put Vanilla down for a nap and took a walk, wandering to all Joanne's favorite places for reasons she didn't fully understand. Joanne drove everywhere in a golf cart, so there were paths cut through the brush for her cart. Lizzy followed the path that led to the fenced garden and Joanne's greenhouse.

Inside the greenhouse, thorny plants burst out of terracotta pots. Lizzy flipped through a gardening book that told how to grow things and how to kill weeds without poison. Weirdly shaped sticks, interesting bones, turkey feathers and rows of antlers had been precisely lined up on low shelves. There wasn't a speck of dust anywhere. Joanne was a naturalist and an environmentalist, as well.

Lizzy had come here as a child when she'd been curious about her mother and wanted to feel close to her. She lifted one of the antlers and turned it over, studying its graceful shape. Who was Joanne really? Had the war between her parents been about her? Mia and she had been the same age. Had Daddy gotten two women pregnant at the same time?

Why had Joanne and Daddy married if they hadn't loved each other? Would she ever know? Were one's parents always a mystery?

The last of Joanne's retreats that Lizzy visited was the aviary. Joanne had put wire mesh in a stable and then had knocked a hole in the back wall of the barn and had had a huge screened aviary built when the birds had multiplied.

Cole found her there, cooing like an idiot to seventeen white fantailed pigeons.

"Your mother's babies," he said as he let himself through the screen door. "She started out with four. You know. If she doesn't start giving birds away, she's going to have to add on again."

He took off his Stetson and propped a shoulder against the rough wood wall. Crossing his legs, he leaned back, his gaze traveling over Lizzy.

"Don't look at me like that!" she said, frustrated by his heated perusal.

"Like what?" His black brows went up in feigned innocence.

"You know."

He chuckled. "Sorry. Couldn't resist. It's really your fault you know."

"How is it my fault?"

"For looking so sexy."

"I thought you had a new girlfriend."

"If you say so."

Wild turkeys silently picked at the ground outside the aviary. Dragon flies sparkled like jewels in the air. The wind was light and balmy. Even with Cole here, and the aviary feeling smaller by the second because he was inside it with her, Lizzy felt a sense of peace she'd never once felt in Manhattan.

He leaned toward her. "Missing your mother, are you?"

His deep voice was so gentle her throat constricted. More than anything Lizzy longed to tell him about Electra. She'd read all her mother's letters.

In her own way her real mother had loved her. She'd kept up with her through the years. Her father had clearly been proud of Lizzy, too. Lizzy felt good about that, and she wanted to share her feelings with Cole. She felt a new confidence in herself now that she knew her true story.

Why was it becoming harder and harder to remember why he was so wrong for her?

"Are you okay?" he asked, his low tone, huskily protective.

She felt herself softening toward him again.

"I'd better go," she said. "Like you said, you have a new girlfriend. So, I'm sure you've got lots and lots of better things to do than to waste time with me."

"Not really. But I get it. I know a brush-off when I hear one."

He slammed out of the aviary so hard there was a wild flurry of white wings. Pigeons flew about her face in a mad rush to reach the safety of the rafters overhead.

"Cole!"

When she ran after him, he turned.

"You scared them," she said.

"Sorry." His black hair gleamed in the sunlight. Never had his shoulders looked broader or his hips leaner. But he looked hurt and confused, too, and that made her feel even more vulnerable to him. Oh, why did he have to be so dear and so dazzlingly handsome and look like he cared? Suddenly she forgot to worry about Suz or Mia or New York or his old greed and quest for revenge.

"Sorry—you looked so lost and sad, I forgot the rules," he muttered. "Won't happen again."

He turned his broad back to her and plopped his battered

Stetson on top his head. Squaring his shoulders, he strode down the golf cart path toward the big house.

"Cole!"

He sped up without looking back.

It was dark. Caesar hated the dark, hated the long nights when all his visitors went home and he couldn't sleep.

His tiny, prisonlike hospital room reeked of antiseptics. Caesar couldn't move, not even to twist his head. Joanne was gone. So was Hawk. Thus, he was alone with his thoughts and regrets. All he could move were his eyelids, so he glared at the ceiling tiles.

Electra Scott was dead. She'd taken up such a big place in his heart for so many years it was hard to imagine her dead or murdered or believe that all that was left of her were her ashes that he'd scattered under the Spur Tree. So, he didn't think about her being dead, maybe because he couldn't bear it.

Nothing had turned out as he'd planned. He remembered the day they'd met. He'd been in a foul mood because Joanne, the girl from the ranch next door, had slept with his older brother, Jack, who now felt duty bound to marry her.

Jack had wanted to elope. Joanne had wanted a big wedding. As usual Joanne had won. The next thing everybody knew, Joanne's best friend from *The University* in Austin, as that school was so arrogantly called, at least, in Texas, had been asked to be maid of honor and was on her way to the ranch to help plan the wedding.

A few days later she had landed on Caesar's doorstep. Bold as brass, arms crossed under her ample breasts, her triangular chin thrust willfully in his face, she stood pale and tall, a warrior goddess, not his type at all. She had thick platinum hair that flowed to her waist in silken waves and a lush red rose that matched her red clingy dress tucked behind her ear. Her bright lavender eyes burned a hole through his heart.

His preference ran to small, soft brunettes, not Amazons who didn't know how to dress and he was tempted to tell her so.

"Hello. I'm Electra Scott. You must be Jack." She licked her lips as if he looked delicious enough to eat.

"Sorry to disappoint you," he muttered, furious at her because of her instant power over him.

"Who says I'm disappointed? Who the hell are you, cowboy?"

"His little brother. Not that it's any of your business."

She laughed. "Well, I'm glad you're not Jack."

"Why?"

Her eyes went hotter than ever. "Because it wouldn't have made any difference."

She was right. He'd known from the first minute he'd seen her, before he'd even touched her, that she was the woman he'd been waiting for all his life.

Her eyes locked on his again and stole a piece of his soul. She knew she had him.

"It wouldn't have mattered? You're *her* best friend," he lashed.

"Last I hear God doesn't hand out a rule book. Until he does, I'll make my own rules."

He frowned.

"And you don't care. Not the least little bit," she said.

He was furious at her for being amused, furious at Joanne for bringing this force of nature into his life because even then he sensed Electra would consume him.

"Joanne's inside." He stormed past her out to the barn.

Instead of looking for Joanne in the house like a proper maid of honor, Electra stalked him to the barn stall that smelled of oats, molasses, hay and horse.

When she closed the door, locking them inside the stall together, a drum began to beat in his head. He had never felt so overwhelmed by the virile male beast that raged inside of him. He'd intended to saddle Raven and disappear until he regained his own will.

Barns and horses could calm him as nothing else could. He loved grooming them and riding them. Just watching them drink through their lips that seemed to be closed or watching them gobble great mouthfuls of grain or chase the pile of kernels around their feeding tubs could make him smile.

But not tonight. Not with her here, too.

"I came here to be alone. If you're smart, you'll stay away from me," he growled as she approached him.

"Sometimes playing dumb is way more fun." She removed the rose from her ear and slid the soft petals against her cheek, then lower down her own swanlike throat. Then she pulled a strap of red gown down and caressed her breast.

The stall still smelled of fresh hay and horses, but now of *her* and of that damnable red rose that she slid between her teeth, too.

"So that's how you want to play it," he said.

She lifted the rose to his lips and slowly, languorously teased his flesh with those sweet velvet petals until he wanted to scream.

The next thing he knew, red silk was sliding off her voluptuous body, and she was gloriously naked.

Instinct told him not to touch her, that she would not be a trivial affair, that if he so much as laid a hand on her, she would own him forever.

But he was a man possessed. Even when she began to laugh, he had to have her.

He seized her and threw her savagely against the wall of the stall. "What's so funny?"

"Life isn't a serious affair, or haven't you heard?" She stared at him, her lavender eyes blazing. "Why are you just standing there like a big old bull, snorting and panting? Hasn't anybody ever taught you to make love, cowboy?"

"Is that what you're going to do?"

"I'll bet you're a fast learner. Talented, too." She took his big rough hands in hers and moved them over her body, holding them against her breasts for a long time, smiling whenever he touched her in a way that gave her the most pleasure. He ripped off his clothes.

"There's no hurry," she said.

She'd made him wait. She made him be gentle. She began by licking him everywhere and running those soft rose petals over his arms and legs and engorged penis.

Finally, when she let him take her, and her body was twisting and writhing beneath him and she laughed no more, he knew he could never let her go. When he exploded inside her and told her how he felt, that he loved her, that he would always love her, she wrapped her arms around his neck and held him close as though she could never let him go, either.

To his surprise, she began to cry.

"Why aren't you laughing now?" he murmured.

"Because some day I will have to let you go. Because I could never live here for long or belong to any one person— even you. And you can never live anywhere else."

"What are you saying?"

"The truth. I love you. I will always love you. But in my own way. Which isn't your way, my love." Her voice was so sad, it made his own heart feel heavy.

"You're wrong."

"I'm never wrong about me. I tried once to live as others do, but I hurt people. In time I always have to be free."

That night he hadn't believed she was the woman she said she was. He'd believed what they'd shared—what they'd felt—had been bigger than both of them and that in time, she would change for him. For how does one let go of one's own soul and go on living?

But they had.

When he'd finally understood her and realized that there was a wildness in her that was like the wildness of an untamed creature. Not a vicious wildness, just something free and true that was her nature. She could no more be domesticated and live happily than a panther or a deer or a javalina. She was no bronc to be tamed to the saddle, nor a tree with roots. She was like the wind that blew freely.

In the end, he'd loved her enough to let her go.

There were footsteps in the hall. The door opened. He felt a whoosh of air, and a cone of whiteness from the hall flashed across the ceiling tiles.

It wasn't Joanne or his nurse because they always spoke to him.

"Goodbye, Caesar," said a harsh, yet familiar and beloved voice.

His tension eased until he heard rustling near his IV tube. Then alarms went off inside him. In vain he struggled to twist his head.

What was going on?

"Surprised? Well, don't feel self-righteous. You killed for the ranch, too. You killed your own brother, Jack, didn't you?"

No!

Caesar felt a strange, stinging heat in his veins, and he knew.

"I set you up with Cherry to ruin your reputation, so you'd be removed from your position. Too bad for you they kept you on."

He was going to die.

Images flashed before him. He saw Lizzy as she'd looked leaning over his bed, her hair falling softly against his cheek.

He'd thought she'd looked more like her mother every day. He saw his sons and Mia, and then Joanne. He saw Jack's broken body in the dunes.

Then he saw Electra. She stood in a circle of pink light at the end of a brilliant tunnel, and she was holding out her arms to him.

There was a roaring sound, and he was rushing toward her.

A voice behind him called, "Adios, Caesar."

Then he heard laughter.

The murderous bastard was laughing at him.

I trusted you! Caesar wanted to scream, to cry out a warning, but his lips seemed made of stone and wouldn't move.

Slowly, slowly, the ceiling tiles above him dissolved and were lost forever in the darkness.

BOOK THREE

Smart Cowboy Saying:

If you find yourself in a hole the first thing you do is stop digging.

—Anonymous

Fifteen

Electra Scott. Lizzy couldn't think about anything else except that the woman was her real mother.

Lizzy's back hurt and her shoulders felt numb when she got up from the computer. She rolled her shoulders forward and then backward before beginning to pace.

After breakfast Cole had shown Lizzy exactly how to buy and sell livestock on the Internet. Then he'd left her a list of livestock that needed to be sold and asked her to e-mail the owners of a couple of bulls he was interested in buying. Not that she'd been able to concentrate with her mind on Electra. Still, she'd tried. But when she'd finished e-mailing the bull owners, she'd typed Electra Scott's name into the search engine and hit Enter.

A wealth of stories about her famous biological mother abounded on the Internet. Electra had had shows everywhere and numerous grand openings. All her photographs showed her dressed as a gypsy—just as Lizzy preferred to dress—and she was always laughing.

More than anything Lizzy wished she could hear her mother laugh. Lizzy had discovered that she'd done a series of extraordinary photographs during her stay on the Golden

Spurs, and had them published in a book. She wondered if maybe one or two would be suitable for the museum, which was about the history and life on the ranch. She would probably have to fight Joanne. Still, it was something to think about.

Electra Scott had traveled the world doing her thing. Nothing had stopped her except a murderer, who'd assaulted her in the primitive hut where she'd been camping in Nicaragua while she photographed endangered tropical birds. The camp had been in a remote area. Somehow she'd been raped and strangled without her staff hearing a thing.

With growing dismay, Lizzy read two more stories about her mother's death.

"Why did you have to die before I ever got to meet you?"

Lizzy felt sad until she remembered that her mother had always known where she was and had never taken the trouble to meet her or even call her. Then anger washed away her sorrow.

The phone rang and Lizzy jumped. Sam was calling her from his cell phone.

"I can barely hear you," she said.

"I've been in San Antonio in a meeting with Leo. Bobby Joe and I are on our way back to the Chaparral Division. Thought maybe we'd stop by for lunch, if you were going to be in. We want to check out the progress on the museum."

"That would be lovely, Sam. I'll look forward to seeing the two of you."

"It looks incredibly historic," Sam said after he finished reading the plaque in front of the museum. "I can't believe after all that's happened—I mean the fires, Cherry and Caesar—that it's this near completion. I wish Bobby Joe hadn't decided to stay at the ranch house. He loves history."

Lizzy smiled. "It's the old carriage house, you know. Joanne said it would be perfect for the museum."

"Gussied up a bunch."

"The wonders of paint," Lizzy said.

"And money," Sam countered with a warm smile.

She tucked her arm through his. She'd missed Sam. That was the trouble with growing up. You left people who were dear to you behind. When neither person was good about keeping in touch, you lost each other.

The white, two-story museum beneath the shade of the tall live-oak trees looked inviting as they walked up the sidewalk arm in arm, their faces dappled by the spreading shadows of the live-oak branches.

"I like the courtyard area," he said, noting the grassy lawn shimmering in the sunlight around back.

"We're going to put some old buggies and wagons out there. We'll have information stations, similar to those found in zoos that will tell the history of the ranch as visitors wander the courtyard. Just wait until you see the murals."

When they went inside, the wooden floors creaked. Lizzy expected Walker or Mark to greet her, but the three large rooms painted with brilliant, lively murals that depicted the ranch's history, were empty. They went through the rooms, their eyes lifted, staring up at the paintings.

"They're wonderful," Sam said. "Impressive."

"Mark's a very sensitive artist. He studied in Mexico."

"Looks like he was influenced by Diego Rivera. Too bad so many of the ranch's artifacts are in archives or in other museums," Sam said.

"Well, for now we have the sculptures of the family, an audio tour and a video. It will take a visitor two hours to tour the museum. Oh, I found a wonderful book of photographs of the ranch in the library by Electra Scott. We're going to put the book in a lighted case and leave it open. Each month the curator will flip to a new page."

Looking back, Lizzy would never be able to remember

the exact moment she realized that she and Sam weren't alone in the building. Maybe she heard a voice or a whisper. Maybe she simply *knew*. Maybe Walker simply chose this moment and this way of telling her himself.

As she approached the little room that was to be the museum office and stock room, which was near the glass case that would hold the items to be sold, she heard whispers. Then papers rustled, and a chair squeaked in the stock room.

"Hello?" she called, her voice echoing strangely.

A chair crashed to the floor. Suddenly Mark and Walker emerged, their faces darkly flushed. Mark's shirt wasn't buttoned all the way to his throat.

Lizzy swallowed. Had Daddy caught them together like this?

After a long moment, Lizzy went up to them and took their hands in hers and spoke as if nothing was wrong. "The murals are too wonderful for words. You've both done a great job."

Walker's eyes met hers. She saw his love for her as well as his love for Mark. For the first time, she saw the man he really was.

She leaned into her tall brother and whispered against his ear, "Nothing has changed. Not really. Not for me." Then she smiled at Mark.

"You're wrong," Walker said gently. "Everything has changed for me. I don't have to live a lie. At least not with you. And that's everything to me. Too many people are forced to live lies."

She turned to introduce Mark to Sam and was surprised that Sam had left without her.

Feeling rejected and embarrassed for Walker's sake, she ran toward the door. This sort of thing must be harder for men, she thought. But truth was truth. One had to accept it.

"Sam?" she called out when she didn't see him.

Cole drove up in a swirl of caliche dust and jumped out of the black truck. His face was dark with strain. "Lizzy. Finally. I've been looking everywhere. Called you on your cell."

"I guess I left it in my car."

"It's your father—" he said and broke off.

A thick silence fell between them, but he said nothing more.

"Is he—" She couldn't finish her question.

His handsome face blurred as dread slithered through her.

"But they moved him out of ICU!" she murmured. "He was getting better!"

When Cole still didn't answer, she sucked in air as panic raced through her. Then she hurtled into his arms.

"We aren't supposed to touch," he muttered.

"Damn you. Just hold me."

"There, there, Lizzy," he murmured, stroking her hair. "You wouldn't have wanted him to go on the way he was, now would you?"

"My mother's dead and now Daddy, too."

"Joanne's fine. I just spoke to her."

"You don't understand. You don't know," she wailed.

"Know what?"

"The truth. About my real mother. Electra Scott."

He stiffened. Then she told him everything she'd learned about her biological mother through broken sobs, and he went on holding her and caressing her. Finally, when she quieted, she let him go.

"I'll call Mother…. I—I mean Joanne, as soon as I pull myself together." She wiped at her eyes and cheeks with the back of her hands.

"But are you going to be all right?" he asked.

"Yes."

Ann Major

Then Sam came around from the back of courtyard, and she jumped guiltily away from Cole. Not that it wasn't natural for him to comfort her under the circumstances. Even so, she felt her cheeks flame as Cole told him about Caesar.

"You tell Walker, and I'll drive Lizzy back to the house," Sam said, his tone grave.

Lizzy started to object. She wanted to be with Cole. More than anything she wanted to be with Cole.

But she turned and followed Sam to his truck.

Lizzy slipped into the darkened horse barn and then stood still, unable to see much inside the closed building after the bright sunlight outside. So, she just stood there, waiting for her eyes to adjust, listening to the familiar sounds of the horses blowing and snorting inside their stalls.

Although she knew her father was dead, the reality of it hadn't really sunk in yet. Her mind and heart were numb. Even so, she knew that something terrible, something irrevocable had happened to him, and she felt an overpowering need to be with him, a need to run into her daddy's strong arms as she had when she'd been a frightened little girl.

He'd loved the horse barn. It was his favorite place on the whole ranch. If his soul was anywhere, she would find him in the barn.

Apparently Kinky had reacted to the terrible news the same way she had because he was mucking out a stall, a job he never did. When he heard her, he came out with his pitchfork, took off his hat and smiled at her sadly.

"Your daddy's got some big boots that need filling, girl. It'll be a spell before people get used to his being gone."

She moved farther inside the barn. The names of the horses were on the doors of the stalls. She paced back and forth, touching each name with her hand: Ringo, Sleepy, Drake and Star.

"Which one is Star?"

"Star is that sweet gray gal with the white star on her forehead."

Lizzy turned and smiled at the mare, who was watching her, too.

"Like a lot of women, she loves attention," Kinky said. "Pet her."

Lizzy went up to Star and began stroking her. "Remember how I was always so afraid of horses when I was a little girl," Lizzy said.

"You took more than your share of falls."

The mare nuzzled Lizzy's hair. "She won't bite, will she? I haven't got a finger to spare."

"She's the gentlest, sweetest mare we got. You just keep on talking to her and petting her, and she'll treat you right."

Lizzy went on stroking the animal. "Do you need me to do anything?"

"You could make sure everybody has water. The buckets are over there by the door."

"Sure."

Lizzy left Star and did barn chores for nearly an hour, glad to have physical work like carrying water buckets to distract her. When she was done with that task, Kinky tied Star to a post so Lizzy could brush and comb her and spray her for flies.

"She'd let you do that all day," Kinky said when Lizzy set the brush and comb down.

"What if I took her out on a short ride?"

"Mr. Cole wouldn't like it."

Lizzy bristled. "But Daddy would. Remember how he always wanted me to be a good rider."

"But you haven't ridden in a long time, honey. I don't think you ought to ride alone, especially not the first time…and when you're upset. Besides, your uncle B.B.'s got some brand-new hunters on his lease."

"I've got to do this for Daddy."

"If you're set on this, at least let me go with you."

"I need to be alone right now, Kinky."

"Sometimes you're as stubborn as your father, girl. It wasn't his best trait, you know."

His eyes narrowed and his bottom lip protruded when she lugged Star's equipment from the tack room and began to tack her up. Nor did he offer to help—not with the saddle blanket, nor the saddle, not even when she struggled to lift it. Nor with the bridle or the bit, either.

When she kissed Star on the nose before slinging herself into the saddle and urging the animal out of the barn, Kinky growled, "I hope you know what you're doing."

"Thanks for all the help," she teased above the clatter of hooves on concrete as she leaned forward and patted Star on the neck. "And don't you dare tell Cole."

"Keep her away from water, you hear? Don't try to swim her. Water's the only thing that spooks her. Took her to the beach once. Boy did the surf make her crazy."

Naturally Lizzy was a little nervous because she hadn't ridden in so long, and because she harbored a secret prejudice that horses were stupid and tricky and hated her. Kinky's being so against her riding and his warnings didn't help any.

Soon, however, the feel of the leather reins lying lightly in her fingers reminded her of whom she was supposed to be—a Kemble, Caesar Kemble's daughter. She dug her feet into the stirrups, thrust her chin out and sat a little straighter in the saddle.

I can do this!

The sight of Star's gray ears flicking back and forth, the powerful neck bobbing in front of her and her mane bouncing as the mare's easy, rhythmic gait carried them along began to feel so good and so right she wanted to lift her face to the sun and shout, "Look at me, Daddy! Look at me! I can do it!"

Maybe he could see her. Maybe he knew.

"You be back before dark, you hear," Kinky shouted from the barn, "Or Mr. Cole will have my hide."

"Don't you dare tell Cole. He's not in charge of me. In fact he wants nothing to do with me."

"He wants too much to do with you, girl. That's his whole damn problem."

It was a beautiful afternoon, warm and bright and still, so still sounds traveled well. Lizzy chose to follow one of Joanne's meandering golf cart trails that cut through thick tangles of brush. Occasionally they came to a break in the trees, and she spotted javalina once, then a cautious red fox. She saw deer, cattle and a flock of turkeys, too.

Her instinct to ride out alone in the brush country with just the brush and the grass and sky turned out to be just what she needed. The emptiness of the wildness felt so elemental, she could almost breathe in the power off the land. The smell of the woods and grass and the sightings of the critters lifted her and made her know that her problems were pretty small in the scheme of things. She remembered how Daddy used to ride out alone when he was tense, and how he'd always come back in a better mood.

She began to relax a little. Maybe because she was alone and without a judgmental audience, Lizzy enjoyed riding for the first time in her life. As a child, she'd always had her father along, an instructor, or Mia, or someone else who constantly told her what she was doing wrong.

Always she'd been compared to Mia, who'd been fearless and show-offy. Mia, who'd always angled to ride the boldest horse instead of the gentlest. Mia, who'd been a faultless rider. Well, Mia was gone, and so was Daddy.

"It's just you and me now, Star. We don't have to compete with Mia or please Daddy. We can just be ourselves and ride the way we want to."

Star plodded doggedly along the golf cart trail.

What if we went faster? What if we cantered? Could I?

Lizzy's heart did a double backflip. She'd always hated to trot or canter.

I can do it!

Taking a deep breath, she dug her feet into the stirrups and Star surged forward. The mare trotted a short distance and then sprang into an all-out gallop. Fifteen seconds into the mad run, Lizzy remembered to breathe. Another fifteen seconds, and Lizzy's fear evaporated. Instead of fear, she felt exultation.

She was flying on Star. They were floating, soaring, and Lizzy was grinning from ear to ear like a thrilled kid. Her hair came loose and streamed behind her. Her T-shirt plastered itself against her breasts even as it filled and ballooned up and down the length of her spine.

"I like to ride so fast, I get bugs in my teeth," Mia used to brag.

Yes! Yes! I can do this! I'm doing it! Just like you, Mia!

Mesquite and live oak whizzed past Lizzy in a gray-green blur as the mare's hoofs thudded against the hard earth. Instead of reining Star in, Lizzy let out a couple of Indian war whoops.

Then suddenly she heard the thunder of hooves pulsing on the trail behind them. Instantly Star's head turned and her ears pricked backward. Then a terrified whinny rang out.

Someone was chasing her, probably Cole. No doubt Kinky hadn't wasted a minute tattling on her on his cell phone, and Cole had come after her.

She swiveled in her saddle and shouted, "Cole?"

But he didn't answer her, and she didn't spot him because the brush was dense. Perhaps he wasn't that close after all. She turned back around, feeling nervous suddenly.

What if it wasn't Cole? For some reason the thought

spooked her. Leaning forward, she stood up in her stirrups and urged Star faster.

A shot rang behind her, and bits of bark burst from the trunk of the oak tree beside the path and hit her cheek, causing drops of blood to spatter on her T-shirt. Had she accidentally ridden onto Uncle B.B.'s hunting lease? Another shot hit a mesquite tree.

She splashed through a shallow creek, and Star rolled her eyes back and ran like the wind.

She heard the unmistakable crack of a gun a third time.

Terror zigzagged through Lizzy as she fought to hang on.

"Is that fried chicken I smell?" Cole said, forcing a smile into his deep voice as he entered the kitchen. The truth was he was worried. He didn't know where he'd been or what he'd done since he'd left Lizzy and Sam at the museum. When he'd come to his senses he'd been sitting in his truck parked along the side of the private, rarely traveled ranch road near the Cameron pens.

He'd wanted to stay with Lizzy after he'd told her the bad news. Now he was glad he hadn't.

"I'm so hungry I could eat a bear," Cole said. He pulled back a chair and sat down at the table, staring gloomily at the checkered tablecloth. "Where's Lizzy?"

Sy'rai came out of the kitchen and put her hands on her plump hips. "Don't you have eyes in your head, Mr. Cole? Is that mud and sand I see on my freshly mopped kitchen floor?"

Cole frowned at the bits of mud and grass all over the glossy red concrete floor and got up.

It hadn't rained in a spell. Where the hell had he been? What had he done?

"Sorry," he muttered. "I'll get a broom."

When he'd come to in his truck, his glove compartment

had been open, and he'd been staring at a ticket to Nicaragua with his name on it. According to the ticket he'd flown to the Central American country last April—six and a half months ago.

How could he forget something like that?

"No, I'll get a broom," Sy'rai was saying huffily as she slapped a knife on the table in front of him. "You'll take this and go outside and scrape your boots."

"Where's Lizzy?" he asked again.

"Kinky said she went riding."

"Riding? On a horse?"

Sy'rai stared at him. "What else?"

"*Alone?* And Kinky let her?"

Cole didn't understand the sudden dread that consumed him, the same dread he'd felt when he'd stared at the ticket. It was like he knew something he didn't know. "When?"

"Four o'clock. He offered to go with her, but she wouldn't let him. She was pretty upset about Mr. Caesar."

So the hell was he, Cole realized, surprised. Joanne had said the doctor said it was weird the way Caesar had died. But she hadn't elaborated.

He glanced at his watch. "And she's not back?" He stared broodingly out the window. The last rays of the sun were pink in the clattering palm fronds. It would be dark soon.

Without another word, he stormed out of the kitchen, punching the number of Kinky's cell as he went, not caring that he was leaving bits of caked mud and sand in his wake or that Sy'rai was shaking her head at him again.

When Kinky answered on the fourth ring, Cole barked, "Get to the barn and see if Lizzy's back yet."

"I can tell you she ain't because I'm at the barn, and Star's stall is empty. Funny thing, though, somebody took Ringo out and didn't unsaddle him. He's lathered up, too."

"I don't give a damn about Ringo. Just get as many men

to the barn as you can. I want some on horseback and some in trucks. We'll need flashlights and floodlights. We've got to find her fast."

"She's on Star. Anybody can ride Star."

"Then why the hell isn't she back?"

A wind had come up that made crashing sounds in the brush. The palm fronds were rattling, the live-oak branches were crackling. Hell, even the long grasses murmured as they were flattened beneath the brute force of the gusts.

"Lizzy? Lizzy!" Cole had called her name so much he was hoarse. It was 2:00 a.m. and he was saddle sore, exhausted and starving, but he wasn't going to give up looking for her if there was a chance he might find her. He kept on riding Ringo through the rough brush country, shining his flashlight in all the darkest places until he got Kinky's call on his cell phone.

Cole's heart stopped at Kinky's shaken tone. "Mr. Cole..."

"You sound worse than death itself. What's wrong?"

"Eli and me, we're sitting in Eli's pickup with our headlights shining." His voice faltered. "W-with our lights shining on a saddle blanket and gray horse leg that's sticking up out of the stock tank right behind The Cowboy Cemetery."

A cold chill licked its way up Cole's boots. "What about Lizzy?"

"The water's too murky to see much."

Cole turned off his flashlight and the roaring darkness seemed to close over him like a coffin lid. "Get everybody there," he said in a low, muffled voice, even as horrible images he associated with the airplane crash in the gulf started to bombard him for the first time since the crash.

One minute that fatal day had been bright, the clouds powdery and the gulf blue and serene. Then the clouds had thickened until they were cliffs and chasms. Next the sun vanished above him as did the waves below him, and they were lost in the suffocating swirls of turbulent black clouds that tossed them about as if the plane were a toy.

He remembered Mia had glanced at him worriedly as he'd struggled to fly the plane. Just when he'd begun to calm down, the plane had been jolted by two explosions. The engines had shuddered and missed. For the first time he had noticed that the fuel gauge was inexplicably low. There had been nothing for it but to go down through the clouds until he could see the waves.

"What's happening?" Mia had yelled as the altimeter began to unwind inexorably.

"We're going down!"

The clouds had swallowed them then. All he had seen were his instruments inside and the smothering folds of inky cloud outside. Down, down, they'd gone. Ten feet above the water, the clouds had broken, and he'd seen frothing white caps rushing up to meet them.

Mia had screamed.

"Give me your shoe!" he had yelled.

He remembered opening his door and wedging her fancy, red high-heeled boot into it, so he'd be able to open it again after they'd hit the water.

Then the plane had slammed into the dark, gray waves and rolled over.

When he had regained consciousness, water was pouring into the dark cabin. They'd been belted in and sinking fast.

Don't let Lizzy be drowned like Mia!

"I can't hear you! I can't hear nothin' but the wind!" Kinky screamed, bringing Cole back to the present.

"Call the sheriff. Tell him…hell, tell him he may need to send Jay and some men out to help us drag the pond."

Cole remembered fighting his way out of the cockpit and dragging Mia after him.

But that's all he remembered until he'd regained consciousness on that shrimp boat.

Working in the lights of ten pickup trucks, the cowboys and Jay, the sheriff's deputy, speculated on how such a gentle mare that hated water could have let herself be ridden into the pond in the first place, let alone have thrown her rider.

"I could see one of our wild broncs doing it, maybe," Eli said. "Maybe that youngster, Buster."

"The hoof prints are carved mighty deep in the sand right where she went in," Kinky said. "Hey, there were two horses. Looks like they was running at a hard gallop."

Cole strode over to Kinky.

The wind had picked up some and had become a mad, howling gale. Cole removed his Stetson, so it wouldn't blow away, and his hair whipped his brow.

"It was dark. Why would Lizzy be running her so hard?" Eli said. "Lizzy hated even a fast walk on any horse."

"Star didn't like water much," Miguel offered. "Get her close to water, and every time she'd roll her eyes, turn and pitch."

"Some horses that don't take to water just turn on their sides and sink like a rock if you even try to make 'em swim," Kinky added.

Cole's throat tightened as he thought about Lizzy being in that deep dark water with her pale hair streaming about her white face, but he said nothing. He thought about Mia then. Had both sisters gone to watery graves—because of him?

Feeling tired and old, he knelt beside Kinky and shone his flashlight onto the hoof prints in the mud and wet sand and wondered who in the hell had been with her.

Where was the other rider?

Where had he been when this had happened?

The next couple of hours were filled with silent tension despite the screaming wind. Cole stood with a knot of cowboys along the muddy edge of the pond, waiting, waiting. Finally, at 4:00 a.m. there were excited shouts from the boat.

"Got somethin', Jay. A woman I think."

Cole stiffened.

Then the sheriff's men dragged a woman's body from the tank. Even from where he stood at the edge of the pond, Cole could see that she had long pale hair that shone like spun silver. She was slim, but her clothes made her body so heavy, it took three men quite a spell to pull her into the boat.

Lizzy. Dear God. Lizzy.

Just like Mia.

Guilt and self-loathing crept over him. Hadn't the accident taught him anything? He should have been more careful. This was his fault. He should have kept Lizzy safe. He shouldn't have followed her stupid rules and kept his distance.

He should have realized how upset she'd be over Caesar. He should have stayed with her.

Where the hell had he been to let something like this happen?

Where the hell had he been—period?

He'd been lost in another damn fool fog at best. He was a cripple, maybe not visibly, but he was a cripple just the same.

But at worst? Had he caused this deliberately? Was he some kind of monster?

Dread filled him at the thought of looking at her cold, dead face. He simply couldn't. Not tonight when his grief and guilt and fear were too raw.

The body was bloated and unrecognizable as Lizzy, Eli warned him.

"What was Lizzy wearing?" someone yelled.

Their voices blurred as they began to argue.

"Shut up! Just bring her here," Cole yelled. "You can work out the details later."

When they brought her to him and laid her on the ground, he made them cover her with a blanket before he knelt beside her body. When he laid his Stetson on the ground, the cowboys hung their heads and backed away to give them some privacy.

Slowly Cole lifted her cold, bruised hand. He turned it over. Nothing about the swollen, lifeless hand, especially not its puffy shape, reminded him of his vibrant, sassy Lizzy. She'd had long, slim fingers. These fingers were bloated and yet somehow shrunken in death. But he went on holding her hand because it made him know for sure *his* Lizzy was dead and gone forever.

Maybe because of him.

The wind ruffled the blanket the cowboy had laid over her body, and Cole took great pains straightening and tucking it around her body before he got up and left without saying a single word to the others.

He turned and looked back once. Jay's steady gaze was boring a hole through him.

Guilt washed Cole again. If he'd done this, there was no way out for him.

Sixteen

The speedometer on the dashboard hovered between seventy-five and eighty. Cole was driving the black pickup so fast over the rutted, caliche, ranch road he and Lizzy had toured together that he was jounced so hard his head hit the ceiling. Pain knifed down his neck. Not that he cared.

Ahead, the cruel, twisting road cut through open pasture land, gleaming like a sodden rope of silver.

Two horses. Why two horses? Who the hell had she been with?

Where the hell were you when she died? Where were you, you stupid, crazy, sick bastard? His inebriated brain screamed questions, but the walls in his mind were up and shut tight.

Disturbing facts worried at his mind. Ringo had been ridden by some sick fool who hadn't bothered to unsaddle him or even take the bit out of his mouth. Cole had left a trail of mud and sand on the kitchen floor.

He clenched the wheel tighter.

He would never have hurt Lizzy. He would have saved her. He wouldn't treat any horse, much less Ringo, so badly.

How the hell do you know who you are or what you do when you black out?

He took a long swig from his Scotch bottle. The truck veered off the road and bounced over rocks and cactus.

Hell. Without removing his foot from the accelerator, he maneuvered the truck back onto the road. The front wheel hit a rock, and the truck went into a wild, careening skid. He began to laugh as he struggled to regain control.

When the truck finally straightened itself, he was almost sorry. If she was dead, he wanted to be dead, too. He took another pull of Scotch.

He'd kill himself if he kept this up. So the hell what?

He stomped harder on the accelerator. When the truck sped up to ninety, it seemed to him that the road bucked beneath him more spastically than a crazed bronc.

Lizzy. Staring at the bleached ribbon of caliche winding its way through the rough country, he remembered how she'd looked under him in her bed in New York when she'd climaxed. God, how she'd dazzled him in the shower the next morning. God, how he still wanted her.

She'd been so soft and sweet when she'd been outside the aviary, he'd almost begun to hope that someday they could have a normal relationship. That she could forgive him for the man he'd been in the past.

Everybody he'd ever cared about was dead or gone: His father, his brother Shanghai. *Lizzy.*

His memories were both sharp and vague, but it seemed to him he'd always loved Lizzy. Too bad he'd been such a damned pigheaded, hard-hearted fool. She'd loved him, too. At least Kinky and Sy'rai had told him so.

He slammed on the brakes and banged his forehead against the wheel again.

Ringo had been ridden and left in the barn with his saddle on. Lizzy was dead. Had the same person who'd ridden

Ringo been with her at the time of the accident? Had that person deliberately hurt her?

Cole didn't want to believe he'd ever deliberately hurt Lizzy. So far whenever Cole had come out of a blackout, he'd found himself performing whatever task he'd been doing perfectly, with no one the wiser anything was wrong with him. Once he'd been roping wild bulls in the brush with Eli. He'd come to just as the noose had slid around the angry beast's neck and Eli had let out a war whoop.

But if he hadn't ridden Ringo, who had ridden him and left him in his stall like that?

What did it matter? What did anything matter if Lizzy was dead?

Slowly Cole opened his glove compartment and pulled out the envelope that he'd hidden there earlier. Ripping the envelope open, he glanced at the airline receipt for the flight to Nicaragua that had his name on it.

He shook his head as he jammed the cigarette lighter into the dash and waited for it to heat. When it sprang out of its socket, he yanked it out and pressed the livid orange coils the corner tip of the receipt until the paper curled and blacked as smoke and flame exploded. Before he could burn himself, he opened the door and threw it out. The wind caught it, and he watched it flutter down the road, shooting sparks and ash into the darkly ominous night.

Exhausted and sick at heart, he lay back on his seat and swigged more Scotch. Usually he never drank. He'd made a pact with himself because of his father's problem. Since the accident, the last thing his brain needed was any extra dulling or confusion by a drug like alcohol.

What difference did his drinking or not drinking make now? As he lay there in a haze, a half-remembered memory flickered through the mists in his mind.

He was standing outside his crop-dusting office, and the

sun was so hot it burned him even through his shirt. He looked up and saw Lizzy riding down the runway toward him on Pájaro, whose hoofs were tap-dancing.

Lizzy's hair was shining and she held herself erect, looking almost sure of herself on the horse.

"My hat's not even mashed," she'd quipped as she'd dismounted and handed him the reins.

"What are you doing here?" he grumbled.

"I heard you'd come home."

"And what else did the gossips tell you?" he said as he tied Pájaro to a low mesquite branch.

"What else should they have told me?" she'd whispered softly.

"This." He thrust his left hand in her face and brandished his gold wedding band.

Her lips went white.

"I'm your new brother-in-law, darlin'. Mia and I eloped."

She was standing utterly still, staring up at him with huge, lost eyes, clouded over with pain. "But why? I don't understand. Why'd you go and do a thing like that behind my back?"

"She's pregnant. I had to marry her."

The mists swirled around Lizzy, but he fought to hold on to the memory.

"Oh, God, Daddy was right," she said, her voice raw with pain. "You know something…I hate that about Daddy, him being such a know-it-all. Don't you just hate him sometimes?"

"I love *you*," he growled.

"It doesn't matter. It's too late."

"It's all that matters. Things aren't the way they seem. I can explain."

Before he'd known what he was about, his arms circled her and his lips fell hard on hers. She opened her mouth, yielding, her kisses filling him with a surging tide of warmth.

His tongue was inside her lips, and he felt her nails in his shoulders and the wild tremors in her young body.

"Lizzy, I love you. I love you. You have to know how much I love you."

"I love you, too." Her rapturous expression changed to one of self-disgust. "We're a fine pair aren't we—*brother-in-law?*" She pushed him away, and her enormous eyes were wide and blazing. "Well, I can't stay here now. That's for sure."

"Lizzy, you've got to let me explain." He reached for her again, but she seized Pájaro's reins, mounted him and ran.

Was the memory true? Their conversation had felt real, yet he couldn't remember his feelings at the time. Had he loved Lizzy even when he'd married Mia? If so, why had he slept with Mia before he married her? Was it as Kinky and Eli said—that he'd wanted the ranch more than anything, even Lizzy?

With Lizzy dead, did that even matter now? When he didn't know if he even wanted to go on?

Right before he passed out, Cole's future loomed ahead of him like an empty, meaningless void. Nothing meant anything to him but sharing his life with Lizzy. And that dream had died when he'd touched that dead, bloated hand.

When he awoke, it was still dark outside and his cell phone was vibrating in his pocket. His head hurt. He ached all over, and his stomach felt queasy.

He wasn't in his truck. For a second or two, he didn't know where he was. Then Ringo whinnied, and Cole smelled hay and horses and sawdust. He was flat on his back on a cold concrete floor.

The barn. But how in the hell had he gotten there?

In a daze he answered the phone.

A woman said, "Cole?"

Every nerve in his body buzzed. "Lizzy?"

No, he thought numbly as he stared upward at bare rafters. *Lizzy's dead. I held her horrible dead hand.*

"Cole, you've got to help me. Somebody chased me."

Lizzy's voice or the impersonator's was badly garbled in static. But she damn sure sounded exactly like Lizzy.

"Lizzy's dead! Who the hell are you? Speak to me!" He bolted to a sitting position.

His joints were stiff, and a pulse in his temple pounded so painfully he was afraid his brain might explode.

Ringo whinnied again. Cole realized he'd lost time— again. Only this time, the spell wasn't over. He was hallucinating that Lizzy was alive.

The static on his cell phone cleared for a second, but the voice that sounded exactly like Lizzy's kept on talking.

"I'm in the camp house you showed me on that tour. A hunter shot at me and spooked Star. I was thrown. I couldn't call before because my cell phone kept saying no service or I'd get that awful busy signal. Oh, Cole, come quickly. It's dark, and I'm scared out of my mind. I—I need you so much. I never needed anybody the way I need you now."

He could barely hear her, but unless he was insane, Lizzy *was* alive.

In his excitement, he forgot everything except Lizzy. "Darlin', Uncle B.B. called me the morning you left and canceled the hunt, so no hunter shot at you. But there's a key under the flowerpot by unit four. McBride keeps the electricity and the hot water heater on in that unit, too."

"Thanks, Cole," she said. "But hurry."

"You hold tight, darlin'. I'll be right there."

Lizzy was alive. But if she was alive, who was the dead woman they'd pulled from the tank?

Trying to calm her frazzled nerves, Lizzy stood in unit four's shower, hot water streaming over her body as she sponged herself with a washrag and bath gel. She'd rinsed out her dirty, damp clothes and hung them up on the towel racks. A door slammed, and she jumped, her heart racing in fright even though she was expecting Cole.

Still, just in case, she turned off the water and dried herself off quickly. "Cole?"

"It's just me, darlin'."

She took a couple of quick breaths and fought to get a grip. Winding a towel around her wet hair, she pulled on the thick white terry-cloth bathrobe she'd found in the closet. The sleeves fell over her fingers and the robe dragged the floor. Opening the bathroom door, she stepped into the living room because she wouldn't feel safe until she saw him.

"You look like a lost, little waif," he muttered gruffly, watching her from just inside the door as if he couldn't believe she was real.

"Believe me, I feel like one, too. You don't look too hot yourself." The cold tile floor stung her bare feet and sent chills up her legs. The room smelled a little musty. "I—I thought you'd never come," she whispered as she began to shake.

She wanted to run to him and throw herself into his arms and tell him scared she'd been. But his face was dark and grim. His white shirt and tight, threadbare jeans were wrinkled and dirty. No telling what he'd been doing when she'd called. He probably didn't want anything to do with her. Now wasn't the time to tell him how frightened she still was.

So, she bit her lips and clutched the edges of her robe together at the throat and said rather primly, if not nervously, "Thanks for coming. Unit Four is so charming and cozy I may never want to leave it."

"I just can't believe it's really you," he whispered, appearing to be somewhat dazed.

They were staring at each other from opposite sides of that

large sitting room that had a lovely stone fireplace flanked by a pair of brown leather sofas. Above the fireplace hung an immense portrait of Caesar, and it unnerved Lizzy a little that wherever she stood, her daddy's eyes followed her just as they had when he'd been alive.

There was a bedroom, a bath and a small kitchen, even though most hunters probably preferred to be fed and waited on in the main lodge.

"I'll try to find you something to wear home," he said as he turned from her and began to open and shut all the drawers.

How could he be worrying about clothes—now—when she was so afraid? And so glad to see him? So glad to be alive?

"I—I don't want to go home," she whispered and felt herself flush all over when he glanced up abruptly to read her meaning. "Not yet anyway."

That's right. The rules have changed, cowboy. I want to be here alone with you.

Yesterday she'd learned for certain her brother was gay. Then she'd learned her father was dead. And when she'd thought it couldn't get worse, she'd been chased and shot at. Cole's presence was the only thing holding her together. Did she want to go home? Not hardly.

When he slammed the last drawer shut without finding anything, he turned, and she saw that his dark cheeks were as red as hers probably were. "You hungry then?"

"Starved." How could he act so normal? She was looking directly at him, imploring him to read her mind, to care a little, to feel *something.*

If he did, he was loath to let on.

"Me, too." His voice was hoarse.

"The only thing here is a jar of instant coffee," she said shyly.

"Then I'll go down to the lodge and find something to cook for us here."

"Don't leave me!" Like a terrified little kid, she scampered after him when he opened the door. Her eyes lingered on his face. She wanted so much to touch him, to be held and comforted, to feel safe.

"What the hell happened?" he whispered, reaching for her. Pulling her close, he brushed his hand across her cheek where the bark had hit her when she'd been shot at.

"I—I…" She stopped, clamping her teeth together. If she tried to tell him, she'd fall to pieces and maybe weep hysterically.

"Just hold me. Don't ever let me go."

"I thought you were dead," he murmured gravely, hugging her. "I've been through hell. I'll tell you about it later."

"I nearly was dead. But just hold me." She was still trembling as if she had the chills.

They stood together at the door for a long time, locked in a tight embrace.

"You smell a little funny," she said.

"Sorry about that, darlin'." Without further explanation, he turned his face from hers even as he pressed her even closer.

He was warm and tall and strong. After a while her teeth stopped chattering, and her knees quit feeling so wobbly.

"Feeling better?" he asked gravely, frowning when he saw her hands poking out from under her thick sleeves. Slowly he lifted her fingertips and turned them over to inspect the red scratches on her wrists and palms.

"Oh, my God! You're hurt!" He whistled when he saw all the cactus needles imbedded in her left palm. "What are these?"

"Needles. From a cactus."

"I mean—how'd you get them?"

"They're not that bad." She fought to pull her hand free, but he held on to her wrist.

"The hell you say! I'm going out to my truck to get a pair of pliers."

"No!" She jumped closer to him.

"Now don't be scared. I'll be right back. Lock the door behind me."

She nodded. When he was gone, she stood right by the door, hugging herself for a while. When he didn't return as fast as he'd promised, she began to pace. Where was he?

Her restless gaze skimmed over the rooms. The kitchen was immaculate except for a few bits of paper in the trash can.

Odd, that there should be any trash if no hunters had been here.

Curious, she knelt and retrieved the torn white fragments. When she pieced them together, they formed a credit card receipt from a local hardware store in Chaparral dated yesterday that was signed by Uncle B.B.

When she heard Cole's footsteps again outside, she wadded the receipt and slipped it into her robe pocket. Then she ran to the door to throw it open for him.

He was loaded down with cans of chili, chicken, tomatoes, tuna, pliers and a bottle of brandy.

"You were supposed to only get the pliers."

"I couldn't very well let an injured woman starve, darlin'."

"Or yourself."

"I was thinking of you, darlin'."

She gathered a few cans off the top to help. In the kitchen he found a glass and poured a single shot of brandy.

"Here, Lizzy. This will warm you even better than a fire or hot food, and dull the pain in your hand, too."

"Aren't you having any?"

"I've already had my share tonight."

"So that's why you smell funny," she said.

"Sorry."

She bit her lip. "What…what does Suz mean to you?"

"I see her at work." He sighed. "I had one lousy date with her."

"And that's all?"

"That's all."

He knelt before the fireplace and struck a match to the kindling beneath the stacked logs in the fireplace. When the fire roared to life, she moved closer to the yellow flames and swallowed the brandy, which sent more dizzying warmth through her veins.

Feeling better but still tired, she sat down on the couch. He turned on a lamp and sat down beside her and pulled the needles out with expert ease. Each needle stung as it slid out and he placed it on the table, but the brandy helped.

"You want to tell me how you got these?" he said, staring at the pile of needles.

She told him about being chased and shot at and thrown from Star, about crawling over thorns and about burying herself under high grass to hide. She told him about the rider who'd left her and had raced after Star.

"Did Star get home okay?" she asked.

His face had darkened at the question, and his whole body tensed. Suddenly she felt afraid again.

"Is Star…?"

"Did you get a look at him?" Cole demanded. "The rider?"

She shook her head. "I—I tried to call you when I was sure he was gone, but my cell phone wouldn't work. So I walked through the brush for hours, it seemed, until I found the road and headed for this hunting camp. I kept thinking…he'd come galloping back and shoot me."

"Thank God he didn't." Cole's face had never looked so lined and grim as he stared at her. He didn't glance up again until he finished removing the last of the needles and set the pliers down beside the little pile of thorns on the table.

Getting up and sitting down on the couch opposite hers, he said, "It's late. You'd better wash that hand. I've got an ointment for it. I'll cook us something easy and fast."

"All right," she whispered, feeling vaguely disappointed at his formal manner as she took the ointment and headed to the bathroom.

When she came back, she watched Cole set the table; she watched everything he did, devouring his broad shoulders and tall lean body with her gaze. Being alone with him in such a romantic setting seemed truly wonderful after the horror that had gone before. If she hadn't nearly lost her life, she might have wasted months being too stubborn to realize how much she cared about Cole. Just looking at him made her temperature rise and her skin tingle. She felt safe and happy and treasured. Which was crazy. A maniac had tried to kill her.

Cole. Cole. Cole. He was everything.

Every step she'd taken across rough wild country tonight had felt like a step back to him. Lying in that grass after her fall, she'd known he mattered more to her than anything else in her life. The past was forgiven. Yes, he'd married Mia, and Lizzy didn't know why. And he didn't seem to, either. She simply didn't care why.

He was different now, and so was she. Those events felt like ancient history—she knew they had happened, but all emotion surrounding those happenings was long dead.

After they'd eaten and pushed their plates aside, he made her recount every excruciating detail of her misadventure.

"You know something," she said. "For the first time in my life I wished I had a gun. Daddy used to be adamant that I strap on my pistol when I rode, but I never wanted to. I used to tell him he didn't always carry a gun. You know what he said?"

Cole shook his head.

"He said I was prettier than he was."

Cole smiled as he got up from the table and began to pick up their dishes. On his way to the kitchen, he said, in a cold, formal tone she hated, "It's late. Why don't you go to bed. I'll do the dishes and find sheets for the couch."

Instantly she felt bereft.

He was gallantly giving her the bedroom when all she wanted was to be wrapped in his arms and held close. Yet she didn't know how to tell him.

"All right," she whispered, getting up but feeling miserable and awkward and shy as she headed to the bedroom alone. Her eyes met his and she had the fleeting thought that maybe he felt just like she did.

Later, as she pulled back the thick down coverlet and got into bed, she tried not to think about him in the next room, but, of course, she could think of nothing else. Death was somehow related to sex. The loss of her father plus her own recent brush with death had made her want Cole with an unbearable, undeniable need. She knew that someday she would die for sure, and she wanted to make every moment count. And she knew that the moments that would count the most for her were the moments she spent with him. More than anything she wanted to feel alive, and Cole made her feel that way.

She lay tossing and turning. He was being the perfect gentleman. He was being the Cole she'd always wanted rather than the dispossessed bad boy next door who wanted what he wanted regardless of other people. But he was rejecting her.

Or was he simply showing her by considering her feelings how much he did care? She had to find out.

Hardly knowing what she did, she got out of bed and padded slowly into the sitting room. At the sound of her door opening, he came to the doorway of the kitchen.

He was watching her, and she saw the desire in his eyes even though his low voice was casual. "Something wrong?" he whispered huskily.

"The bedroom was so cold," she said, lying as she rubbed her arms.

Very slowly, hardly knowing what she was about, she fluffed her damp hair with her fingertips so that it flowed freely over her shoulders. His blazing eyes made her feel powerful and exciting.

Then slowly, rhythmically she began running her hands through the silken platinum. Even though he was still fully dressed, she lowered her hands and shakily undid the sash of the robe and let it slide off her shoulders to the floor.

"I felt lonely, too," she continued softly, closing her eyes as if to savor her own touch. "Without you." She batted her long lashes and smiled at him. Then she glanced up into her father's painted eyes.

"I don't think this is such a good idea," Cole said, but his warm gaze said something else. "You're not yourself tonight. Hell, I don't know who I really am most of the time. You said New York meant nothing. You told me to stay the hell away…"

"Shhh. I know what I said. And I know what I want. Can't a foolish woman change her mind, cowboy?"

"Sure she can," he whispered on a ragged note that tore her heart.

Lizzy smiled when he strode across the room faster than she'd ever seen him move. Then his strong arms were around her and he was holding her so close she could barely breathe. Their bodies were fused, and she melted into the heat of his. The next thing she knew his mouth was on hers, hard and yet soft and warm and wet, too, exactly right, as always, and soon she was drowning in his frenzied kisses.

"Don't ever let me go," she begged as he lifted her into his arms and carried her to the bed.

"Not a chance. Not tonight. Not ever. Oh, Lizzy, Lizzy, oh, my darlin' Lizzy. I thought I'd never hold you like this again."

"One more thing! Would you take Daddy's picture down. I don't want him watching this!"

Cole laughed. "Neither the hell do I! It'll just take a minute."

He crossed the room, removed the picture and stood it so that Caesar's painted face was against the wall.

She ran into his arms, and he kissed her.

"You're alive," he said. "I can't believe you're really alive."

Seventeen

Pink light sifted through the windows and slanted across the bed. Beneath the covers they were naked. Lizzy closed her eyes and pressed herself against him, reveling in the hard contours of his long body as she began to explore him with her hands.

"What do you want now that you've got me all hot and bothered?" he murmured, running his palm between her thighs.

"I'm easy. Just another night of wild, unforgettable sex."

"Like New York?"

His body heat drew her like a magnet. Snuggling closer, she parted her legs.

"Wanting you like this shows me New York meant something…meant a lot, at least to me," she said.

"To me, too, darlin'."

"I nearly died. Oh, Cole, make me feel I'm glad to be alive."

"Wanting you has damn near made me crazy," he said fiercely, his hot whispery breath falling on intimate places that made her quiver when he lowered his head and went down on her.

"It has?" she squeaked when his mouth nuzzled her there.

"What did you think, woman, that I was made of stone?"

"Only *that* part of you." She giggled.

"Do you want to talk *or*—"

"Definitely…*or.*"

His mouth had begun stroking the delicate folds of feminine flesh, sending lava warm tingles flowing inside her. He kissed her and licked her until her body writhed. Until her hands tore the sheets. Until she begged him to take her in frantic, breathless whispers.

"Not yet. Maybe it's your turn to return the sexual favor."

She rolled him onto his back and rose above him. Her tongue moved down his lean, muscular body, circling him with her lips, taking the large, satiny hardness inside her mouth and flicking her tongue in circular motions until he groaned with pleasure.

Then he lifted her head and pulled her forward until she was on top of him, straddling him. He paused at the pulsing brink for a long moment before easing her gently down and thrusting up inside her.

She bent forward, lowering her breasts against his wide chest, savoring the feel of fur covered muscle against her aroused nipples. As they made love, their bodies moving in perfect harmony, all the old hurts dissolved even as fragile new hopes flamed to life.

Then she shuddered quietly while he exploded, yelling her name and gripping her fiercely. Later he wrapped her in his arms and held her close.

"You are so beautiful," he said. "So perfect."

She blushed, pleased. "So are you."

"Let's get married," he whispered.

Maybe, she thought. *Maybe.* Then she remembered Mia lost forever in the cold, dark gulf and pulled away from him uneasily, the old doubt welling up inside her.

Was he attracted to the Kemble name or her?

"Maybe we should just enjoy what we have for now."

"Whatever you say." But his voice was tense, his mood as changed as hers was.

He was lying beside her, his eyes wide-open with her at a loss as to what to say next when his cell phone began to vibrate in the pocket of his jeans, which she'd tossed into a heap when she'd stripped him.

"Don't answer it," she murmured when he rolled away from her.

Frowning, he leaned over the bed and grabbed his jeans.

"Always so responsible?"

"You make me sound like the bad guy."

"I fell in love with the wild bad boy, remember?"

"Right. The real me." His jaw tightened.

She swallowed. His sudden tension reminded her he didn't like thinking of himself in that light. He was different now, she realized. So different. Wonderful.

She caught a glimpse of his stark profile as he stalked out of the room, his cell phone pressed against his ear, and she thought the nice Cole was the real Cole.

Life had twisted the old Cole and made him bitter. He'd believed the only way he could be whole was to get even with the Kembles. He'd schemed to use her. Then he'd schemed to use her sister. Without the bitter memories of his youth, he seemed to be the man he would have been if life hadn't been so hard on him.

She remembered how he'd saved her when Pájaro had run away with her. Even that first afternoon she'd felt a truth between them that was more profound than his hatred of the Kembles. Her father hadn't seen the good in him, of course. None of her family had, except maybe Mia, and now Joanne.

Maybe the past, even Mia, didn't have to matter if she didn't let it. Her father was dead. Her leadership was resented. Somebody had shot at her yesterday afternoon. Happiness was precious. Life was lived moment by moment. One had to seize the happy moments and make the most of them.

She needed Cole. She had to believe in him. She simply had to. How hard was it to see the good in a person instead of the bad?

"All's well that ends well," she murmured to herself drowsily, closing her eyes as Cole shut the door as he began to talk to whomever was on the phone.

"Cole, it's Cherry Lane's body," Jay said. "Not Lizzy's."

The shock of hearing the deputy's voice even before he understood what he was saying sent a jolt through Cole. For a second or two he'd been so disoriented, he didn't know why Jay would be calling him or even who Cherry was.

"Tried to call you before, but you didn't answer."

The mists in Cole's brain parted, and the sudden vision of a silver-haired woman being lifted out of the pond felled him like a paralyzing blow. He sank onto a leather couch, which was so cold against his bare butt, he sprang to his feet and began to pace.

Again he felt that stiff, swollen hand in his when he'd thought he'd been saying goodbye to Lizzy.

What in the hell was wrong with his brain that he could forget something like that...even for an hour, even if he'd tied on a few drinks? Only an idiot needed to jot a note to himself in his PDA about an event of that magnitude to jog his memory.

But as soon as he'd seen Lizzy, he'd focused entirely, utterly on her. He ran a shaking hand across his perspiring brow. Would he ever be himself again?

"She's been dead a while. But my guess is she wasn't in the pond long. A Detective Phillips is flying down from Houston tomorrow. He wants to question you. And he wants permission to search the ranch. Says if he doesn't get it, he'll get a warrant."

"Tell him I'll give him his own personally guided tour."

"How did Cherry Lane get in your cattle tank?"

"For God's sake, how in the hell should I know?"

Cole hung up just as the bedroom door opened. When he saw Lizzy, looking soft and rumpled from their lovemaking, he tried to smile.

"You look awful," she said.

"You'd better get dressed."

She flew across the sitting room into his arms. "What's wrong?"

"They found Cherry Lane's body in the tank behind the cemetery."

"Oh, God, do you think she was so upset about Daddy dying, she came here? But how could she just drive through the gate without anybody seeing her? And how could she hike to the cemetery and fall into our pond? Do you think it was another accident?"

He didn't answer.

"What was she doing here?"

"She was already dead," he said in a low, flat tone. "Somebody carried her here and put her body in that pond. Whoever it was killed Star, sweet gentle Star, to make sure her body would be found."

"Oh, no!"

She was thinking about her father's death—and her mother's. She'd been chased and shot at. "I could be dead, too," she said softly. "Maybe her murderer was after me, too."

The realization slammed her. For a long moment she couldn't speak. Neither could he.

"Probably," he said. He stared into her eyes, and even though they'd made love, she felt a dark chasm between them. There were mysteries to be solved, questions to be answered, a murderer to be caught, the ranch's good name to be restored, she thought. And somehow, she had to learn to trust Cole.

Cole's strong arms tightened around her, and for a long moment, she clung and wished she never had to let him go.

"I don't want to face the real world," she said.

"Neither the hell do I."

"I'm afraid," she whispered. "I'm so afraid."

"I've got to get back," he finally said. "I can't leave you here alone."

She nodded wearily as he let her go.

The November afternoon had been unseasonably warm when the sun was out, so Lizzy hadn't worn a sweater over her black silk dress for her father's memorial service under the Spur Tree. Now dark clouds obliterated the sun, and a chilly breeze picked up the strands of her hair, blowing them about her face.

She was hugging herself and shivering as she stared at the enormous sprays of red roses, yellow daisies, orchids and irises circling the silver urn that stood at the base of the Spur Tree. The drone of the preacher's voice as he read Caesar's favorite scripture was somewhat comforting. Aunt Mona and Uncle B.B. looked as elegant as always. Aunt Nanette and Sam stood apart from the others. Several times Aunt Nanette raised her hand to stifle a yawn. The rest of the family stood on either side of her.

Only the family, the cowhands, a few neighboring ranchers, longtime friends, a few key players in the cattle industry and Texas politics and the detective, Joe Phillips, attended the private memorial service. Not that the boisterous press wasn't camped outside the ranch's front gate, demanding to know how Cherry Lane had come to be in a cattle pond on the Golden Spurs.

Joe Phillips stared holes through everybody, especially Joanne and Cole. The detective had been furious when he'd ordered an autopsy on Caesar's body only to be told the body had already been cremated. He'd blamed Cole and Joanne.

Lizzy wished the man wasn't here. He cast a pall on the sacred service and made her feel guilty. She was sure she went deathly white every time he looked at her and then at Cole, who was standing beside her.

Cole didn't do anything wrong. Oh, God, why can't you see that?

When the preacher finished the reading, Joanne stepped forward and knelt, opened the silver vase, and held it against the ground. With a shaking hand, she poured Caesar's ashes onto the ground near the bronze plate with his name on it that lay a few feet away from Electra Scott's, and all the while Phillips's gaze drilled a hole through her.

When Joanne finally stood up, she met the detective's eyes and smiled. Lizzy's throat tightened. What was going on?

Only vaguely was she aware that the service was finally over—that people were drifting past her to their cars or toward the big house so they could take part in the family meeting that was to be held in the library. Against Lizzy's wishes, Leo had insisted on the meeting today since so many Kembles would be at the ranch.

Not wanting to face everybody who would be in the library, she lingered by the tree for a while. But family and friends circled her there, their hands clasping hers. They embraced her and offered their condolences. Many said what a shame it was to lose Caesar before the upcoming celebrations and the holidays.

Numbly she endured their kindnesses and managed the appropriate responses. She felt as if her grief was a wall that locked her inside some private hell. Now Cherry was dead, too, and the press saw the ranch as the center of a real-life, lurid soap opera.

Once she caught Cole staring at her as if to see deep inside her. Did he think she doubted him? When she looked at him, his own gaze softened, and she felt comforted by his glance.

Joanne came up to stand stiffly beside her. More than ever before, Lizzy felt cut off from this woman she'd believed to be her mother. When Joanne touched her waist, Lizzy pulled away.

"Your father loved you. He loved you so much."

Why couldn't you have told me the truth? About who I was? About why you couldn't love me?

But these thoughts that tore at Lizzy's heart went unspoken.

Joanne then went up to the tree and hung Caesar's spurs by his brother's. Tears burned Lizzy's eyes, and she didn't know what to say as Joanne touched Uncle Jack's spurs. Suddenly Lizzy felt her control slipping.

"I'm sorry—Mother," she whispered.

For a long moment they stood there together. Lizzy closed her eyes. Thus, she wasn't aware of the exact moment Joanne left. When she opened them again, the wind had picked up and she was alone. She watched the ground where Caesar's ashes blew about, some scurrying over Electra's bronze marker.

Were her parents together now? She wanted to think so.

"Oh, Daddy, did you know what I was getting into when you asked me to take over?"

The clouds grew darker, and the wind made her shiver.

"We'd better go," said a hard voice behind her.

Joe Phillips put his hand on her arm. She nodded. Without a word, he led her toward the house. When he opened the front door for her, the noise from the library hit them.

"Leo said I could address the family before your meeting," Phillips said quietly.

Raised voices erupted from the library.

"Are they always this noisy?" he asked.

"Yes, but the house has terrible acoustics. It magnifies sounds."

When she entered the library on the detective's arm, everybody fell silent. Then Leo rushed to greet them and introduced the detective.

"Joe Phillips has a few words to say to everybody," he explained.

Cole, who had been slouching near the fireplace, straightened; his dark face tensed. Uncle B.B. got up from the couch where he'd been sitting beside Aunt Mona and shut the library doors. Suddenly, despite the crowd, despite all the lit lamps and the fact it was two-thirty in the afternoon, the library seemed filled with shadows. Tall table lamps beamed in the corners, and the brass chandeliers above everybody cast a warm glow. But the room was huge, the ceiling high, and the leather furniture and tall cherry bookcases, heavy and dark.

Nobody had remembered to switch on the lights above the portraits. Maybe they would have helped some, but Lizzy didn't want to draw attention to herself by doing so.

"Three people connected to this ranch are dead," the detective began without preamble. "Electra Scott. Caesar Kemble. And now Cherry Lane."

Furtive glances flew, but nobody said anything. Lizzy watched Cole run his hand briefly through his black hair.

"Ms. Lane didn't drown. She—like Ms. Scott—was raped and strangled," the detective continued.

Leather and wood creaked as people shifted uneasily in their chairs. Again, they glanced at one another warily.

"Besides the murders, there have been a number of accidents on this ranch. I think Caesar Kemble is the key to all this. His brother died in an accident, too, which is how Caesar came to power. Now, Caesar himself is *conveniently* dead."

He shot Joanne and Cole an ironic smile. *Conveniently cremated, too.*

"If anybody here today knows anything or thinks he knows anything and wants to talk, call me." He waited a few seconds for his words to sink in. When nobody said anything, he pulled several business cards from his jacket pocket and flung them onto the library table.

"Call me," he repeated, leaning over the table so that he was on eye level with them. "Your name could be next on the killer's hit list."

A trace of a smile crossed Uncle B.B.'s mouth. Under his breath he said, "For a cop, he damn sure has a flair for the dramatic."

Aunt Mona laughed.

A cold chill gripped Lizzy. She remembered gunshots peppering the tree trunks behind her as she'd run for her life through the brush. Only yesterday she'd stood beside Cole as Star's stiff gray carcass had been loaded onto the bed of the huge truck and hauled away.

Was she next on the killer's hit list?

Eighteen

"We need new leadership. Strong leadership. Now." Uncle B.B.'s hard gaze bored into Lizzy, who was standing beside Sam.

"You gave us ninety days," Cole said, moving to the other side of Lizzy.

"And what the hell have you accomplished? Cherry Lane's body in your cattle tank. An expensive quarter horse dead. We've got lawsuits to fight. Not to mention Sheldon Oil and gas."

"Yes! Even though gas prices are up, has it made one bit of difference in my royalty check?" Aunt Nannette demanded.

"We're still being paid old gas prices for new gas," Uncle B.B. said.

"We have a team of accountants and lawyers on this problem right now," Leo said. "Sheldon Oil offered to settle, but we think we can do better."

"You didn't get on to this until I told you to. We need somebody at the helm who is willing to lead. Not an ignorant girl."

Lizzy bristled.

"Someone like you?" Cole placed a protective arm around her waist.

There wasn't a sound in the room. Uncle B.B. straightened his tie. Then he glanced at his rapt audience. "All right. Yes. Someone like me. Someone who wouldn't be so set on sinking as much capital into a losing investment like ranching."

"Maybe we'd be better off with a professional running the ranch—rather than another family member," Lauren Capp blurted. When everybody looked at her, Lauren blushed and hid her face. "Oh, I—I probably shouldn't have said anything. I don't know much about ranching."

Lauren was a younger cousin of Lizzy's who lived in Colorado and worked in an art gallery in Denver. Like a lot of Kembles, she'd never dared to speak at a meeting before, and Lizzy felt a little sorry for her.

But Leo's face was grave as he contemplated her suggestion. "I agree with Lauren. Not that I don't think Lizzy's up to the job. Also, she's Caesar's daughter, and that has a lot of symbolic meaning."

"At the same time, I think the position may have become too dangerous for any family member to hold," Cole said. "Especially for Lizzy, *because* she is Caesar's daughter. This thing is beginning to have the feel of a private vendetta."

Lizzy gasped.

"Sorry, Lizzy, but I agree," Sam said.

Stunned, Lizzy whirled on them. "What if I don't want to step down? My father wanted me in charge. He wanted *me!* Not some stranger. Not Uncle B.B."

"We don't have to decide today," Leo said calmly. "I hear your dissatisfactions and opinions. I say we go on as we are until the celebration and museum opening are behind us. We're only talking about a couple of weeks. Asking Lizzy to resign would just cause more unfavorable publicity."

To Lizzy's surprise nobody objected.

"Before we adjourn," Leo said, "Detective Phillips asked me to hand out a questionnaire. He wants an hour-by-hour accounting of your time on the two days before as well as the day Cherry's body was discovered in the pond. It's a fill-in-the-blank situation."

When everybody had their papers and had begun to write, Lizzy noticed Cole staring at his paper almost angrily, his pen jabbing a hole in the paper. Then he wadded it up and left the room.

Why didn't he write something like everyone else? Didn't he know where he'd been?

Furious, she wondered what his real motivation for wanting her to step down was.

Her heart began to pound in her throat.

Lizzy sighed nervously as she picked up the phone in her bedroom and dialed. She didn't have the slightest idea what she'd say if Mr. Jamison or one of his clerks starting asking why she was suddenly so curious about her Uncle B.B.'s purchases or told her his doings were none of her business.

Jamison answered in his gruff, no-nonsense voice, and she forced herself to speak.

"Mr. Jamison, I—I was wondering what my uncle B.B. bought in your store yesterday." She hit her forehead. Why hadn't she asked him how he was or how his wife Mabel was? Anything to soften him up?

"Shotgun shells. Bullets. Nails. A wrench. Why do you want to know?"

"I—I found a receipt. I was trying to figure out if his purchases were tax write-offs…or if I could just throw it away. I—I hadn't seen him. I—I didn't realize he was at his lease."

"It wasn't Uncle B.B. that came in. It was your aunt

Mona. Hey, isn't he out there for the memorial service? How come you don't just ask him yourself?"

Aunt Mona?

Wing Nut left Joanne's side and dashed headlong down the golf cart path to the aviary after a small brown rabbit. Joanne whistled and yelled his name. Vanilla clapped her hands as she toddled gleefully after the big dog. When the rabbit disappeared into a hole, the black Lab barked and pranced excitedly around the dark mouth in the earth as if entreating the animal to come back out in play.

Joanne was glad to have escaped the house. She'd felt like she was suffocating during the memorial service and the meeting afterward. When the rabbit stayed put, the dog sniffed around the hole for another minute. Then tail wagging, he sprinted back to Joanne and jumped up, muddying her jeans and windbreaker with his enormous paws. Not that she cared.

His sudden return had caused Vanilla, darling Vanilla, who'd been following him so trustingly to plop onto the short, clipped grass too hard. Joanne flew to catch the baby in case she cried, but Vanilla, who was as tough as Mia had been, looked up at her grandmother and smiled. Then she began to clap, pleased to find herself the center of utter adoration.

"Oh, my darling. My darling." Joanne knelt and picked up a brown oak leaf.

"Leaf. Leaf," she said, looking into Vanilla's huge, blue eyes.

Vanilla grabbed the leaf and turned it over clumsily.

With rapt attention, Joanne watched her study the leaf and then set it down and smash it with her tiny fist and then pick it up again. Joanne had never loved anything or anyone as she did this baby. Was that because Vanilla was all she had left of Jack and Mia? Or was this just the natural love she would have felt for her first grandchild?

"Leaf," she whispered as she hugged the child again fiercely. *Oh, darling, if it weren't for you, what would I do?*

Being with Vanilla after the memorial service and the meeting made Joanne feel almost sane again. As she'd stood beside Lizzy and placed Caesar's spurs beside Jack's on the Spur Tree, she'd thought about Electra and Jack. Then she'd rethought her whole life.

Had it all been for nothing? Were all lives for nothing? She'd married the wrong man, a man who'd betrayed her on every level. She'd tried and failed to mother his daughter.

Then in the library when Phillips had hinted Caesar might have had something to do with Jack's accident. She'd started shaking so badly she'd been afraid someone would see.

She remembered the first time that idea had entered her head. She remembered who'd said the words that had filled her own heart with doubt about her husband.

Until then she'd believed what Caesar said—that he had loved and admired his brother and had grieved for him as she had, that he had given his own life to the ranch, that the good of the ranch was what he cared about.

Until then she'd had such high hopes for their marriage and what they would accomplish together. Until then she'd tried to be a real mother to his daughter.

Yes, she remembered the exact words that had been said to her to plant the seeds that had made her see that her marriage was an illusion. She'd been standing companionably under the Spur Tree with Aunt Mona, someone she'd trusted, even if they didn't get along perfectly.

"The history of this ranch is soaked in blood," Mona had said as the spurs had jingled in the wind.

"All that was a long time ago."

"Was it? Jack was killed under mysterious circumstances, wasn't he?"

"Jack? I never thought so before. He was breaking a horse," Joanne had said a little too passionately.

"He rode out one day and the horse came back lame without him. Caesar found him, didn't he? There was a single blow to the head. It was *assumed* he'd fallen, but they'd always been rivals, hadn't they? Their father had forced them to compete, to make men of them," she'd said. "Caesar came into power because of that accident, didn't he?"

Doubt and dread had filled Joanne. "What are you implying?"

"Nothing." Aunt Mona had laughed. "Maybe I shouldn't have said anything."

Joanne had turned and stalked back to the house abruptly. But the damage had been done. The doubt had festered over the years.

She had tried never to think about that conversation again. But what one decides not to think about is sometimes the very thing that shapes ones life in a new and terrible direction. Doubt became a poison inside her. She had gone cold in Caesar's bed, and that had proved fatal for their marriage.

She stroked Vanilla's dark hair. Did she really regret her marriage?

She'd grown up a poor rancher's daughter, motherless but ambitious. She'd loved the outdoors, animals, nature. When Jack had fallen in love with her, she'd known marrying him would be like marrying royalty. And she'd wanted that. Even after he'd died, she'd still wanted it. God help her, but she had. But had she sold herself to the devil to get it?

The baby's skin was so soft, as was her hair. Joanne smiled. Vanilla had been born with the thickest head of hair, and Joanne had been conceited about Vanilla having such beautiful hair even as a small baby.

Vanilla. Thank goodness for Vanilla. Vanilla calmed her, made her feel that she still mattered.

She picked the baby up and carried her to the aviary where they stood outside together and talked about the birds. Or rather, Joanne talked and Vanilla watched and listened to her and the birds, lending the awful afternoon the magic of her trusting innocence.

The birds were peaceful as was the wind in the tops of the trees. Joanne wanted to teach the baby to love everything that she did. When Joanne opened the screen door, the white birds soared above Vanilla and her.

"Birds," she said. "Birds. Aren't they wonderful, darling? God is in each and every one of them."

Joanne lifted her gaze and watched them, her eyes filled with as much awe as Vanilla's.

The detective had scared her badly. He had warned of more killings. Would someone in the family talk to him? Tell him what he wanted to know?

She hadn't gotten around to reading the rest of Electra's hateful journal yet. Just skimming it that first day and reading about the twins had upset her too deeply. She hadn't wanted to lug it to the hospital, and when she'd come home at night to Gigi's, she'd been too exhausted.

Then Caesar had died. Since then, she hadn't had time or the emotional energy.

But she'd brought it with her to the ranch to read, and had hidden it in her lingerie drawer.

I'll read it later. Maybe tonight after I put Vanilla to bed.

Lizzy felt Cole's eyes on her as she pushed his bedroom door open and entered without knocking. He got up from his computer and came toward her. "Lizzy?"

She swallowed. Despite his having humiliated her at the family meeting by suggesting she should step down, his husky voice saying her name warmed her through. He'd supported her more that most of her family had. She'd overheard Aunt Nanette complaining about money, which she needed for plastic surgery and for remodeling her own ranch house. And Joanne had told her Uncle B.B. wanted to impress Aunt Mona, who felt he'd been passed over too often.

Too late Lizzy realized she should have tackled this conversation in a less intimate setting than his bedroom.

She brought her chin up. "Why did you turn on me like that—in front of everybody?" Not wanting to, she glanced toward his bed.

"All right. I felt weird tensions in that room. Somebody tried to shoot you. Two women are already dead. What if you're next on a madman's hit list? I don't want to find you strangled and raped. You've got to leave the ranch until I figure out what's going on."

"Until *you* figure out? Caesar put *me* in charge."

"I held Cherry's stiff, icy hand thinking it was yours. Do you have any idea what that was like?"

"I hope I am next. I can use that to trap —"

"You'll get yourself killed," he said. "That's what you'll do."

She backed away from him. "You still think I'm a scared, incompetent, little girl."

"Your father would want you gone. He'd want you safe."

"He wanted me here."

"Why can't you see I'm right," he said.

"Why can't you see this is something I have to do?"

"This isn't a career move you can mess up on."

"Oh, so that's what you think I'll do?"

"I didn't mean it like that," he snapped. "This is life and death. *Your* life."

"You want me gone, just so you can be in charge?"

"Damn you. Sometimes you're the most stubborn—"

"Me? All you've ever wanted is the ranch."

"Maybe…in the past. But now I want you alive. I want a future with you."

"I refuse to step down."

"Then marry me, Lizzy, so I can protect you."

When she didn't answer him, he grabbed her. "I don't want to lose you. Not when I've lost everybody else."

Something hot in his eyes leapt from his soul to hers, and still she couldn't trust him. Even as his mouth came closer, a voice warned her not to let him kiss her or take her to bed.

But when his lips touched hers and her arms wrapped around his waist, a power beyond herself made her his for the taking. Her skin tingled all over. A few blazing seconds later, she was naked on his bed. He stripped, and she watched him as avidly as he'd watched her. Then she held out her arms and pulled him down on top of her.

She circled his neck with her hands, and soon, long before he entered her, she was melting, moaning. As always, when they made love, everything felt wonderful and right and true.

"Marry me," he said a long time later when he could breathe again.

"What happened to the gentleman in New York who wouldn't bed me when he thought I was drunk and not thinking clearly? Now I'm drunk on your kisses."

"This is different. I love you. And you love me."

"You're awfully sure of yourself."

"Not really."

She saw the pain in his eyes. Then she rolled on her side and traced the pattern of moonlight on his sheet. "Where were you when I was thrown and Star galloped into that pond?" Her voice was casual, but her heart was thundering.

She felt him shudder violently. Then he grabbed her by the arm and yanked her back against him so that she faced him in the dark.

"Do you think I tried to kill you?" His fierce whisper cut her like a knife. "Is that what you think?"

"I simply asked you a question. Where were you?"

Pushing her away, he heaved himself off the bed. She watched him move across the darkness to the window. He lifted the blinds and peered out as if he were straining to see something, he couldn't see. Then he snapped the blinds shut.

"You don't know, do you?" she accused softly, switching on the lamp to study him more closely.

He grabbed his jeans off the floor and yanked them on. His jerky movements were hostile. Sliding his feet into a pair of leather loafers, he picked his shirt up off a chair and thrust his arms into it.

"Answer me," she said. "Your silence is scaring me."

"No!" He whirled. "All right? Are you satisfied? *I don't know!* And it's killing me because I don't! I don't know why my plane went down, either! I blame myself for Mia, too! For Vanilla being motherless! For not remembering them! For being alive even! For loving you. But, God help me, I can't change any of it!"

His passionate outburst surprised her, touched her. "Oh, Cole, don't torture yourself like that."

"I don't want your fake sympathy. You started this. Why didn't I die, too? I remember the storm and an explosion and the plane suddenly spiraling downward. I remember being upside down in that wreckage underwater and barely conscious. I had a concussion and my leg was broken, but I remember unbuckling Mia's seat belt and dragging her out of the plane. But that's all I remember. I don't know if she was dead or alive, or if I let her drown. The next thing I knew I was lying on a shrimper's deck. His mouth was on mine and suddenly I was spitting water in his sunburned face. I didn't know where I was or how I got there. I didn't ask about Mia once. I didn't remember there was a woman in the plane, much less my wife, until your mother started asking me about her. Why the hell am I alive? Why me?"

"You just are."

"I lose time, okay? And I hate it! The doctors don't know why, and they can't seem to do anything about it. None of the medicines they've given me do any damn good. But I want you to know that if I had anything to do with what happened to you in the brush or to Star or even to Cherry, I don't want to be alive. Understand?"

"You're not a monster. I know you're not. Don't torment yourself by thinking like that."

When she got up to comfort him, he backed away from her.

"No. You started this, remember."

"Cole, come back to bed." She held out her hand to him.

"You should leave the ranch until we find out what's really going on. I don't want to hurt you...*accidentally.*"

"You won't."

"I don't know that, and neither do you."

He ran out of the room and the door slammed behind him.

The instant he was gone, she felt hurt and wanted him back. Not that she was sorry she'd asked her questions. She was changing, willing to face things, willing to demand answers, determined not to be a people-pleaser every minute of her life. She thought about her uncle B.B. and aunt Mona. Nothing was what it seemed.

Wearily she began picking up her own clothes. A few minutes later, back in the safety of her own bedroom, Lizzy stripped again.

Too nervous to sleep, she eased herself into her big claw tub and took a long bubble bath hoping it would relax her. It broke her heart that Cole doubted himself so much he thought he might be capable of monstrous acts.

She couldn't leave the ranch. Why couldn't he see that she

wanted to be a full-fledged person in her own right, and that to do that she had to stay? If she really was next on some murderer's hit list, she had to lure the real killer into the open for Cole's sake as well as her own.

How she loved him! How different he was than the bitter man he'd been when she'd first fallen in love with. And yet, she'd loved him then, too. She felt selfish about her feelings now, as if she had a right to them—to him. She couldn't leave and risk losing him.

It wasn't entirely pleasant to want him as she did. She ached to be near him all the time. She felt vulnerable and overly emotional.

Their relationship was long and complicated. They'd dated each other from the time they'd met until she'd graduated from college. He used to drive up to College Station on the weekends, when she'd attended A&M University. They'd been together every holiday when she'd come home. She sank underwater in the tub. When she emerged, she toweled her face off. Lying back and closing her eyes, her mind flashed back to the afternoon when she'd broken up with Cole—after her father had finally convinced her that all Cole Knight would ever want from any Kemble—even her—was revenge.

Like the other times he'd tried to name all the reasons why she shouldn't be with Cole, her father had chosen his words carefully. "Your precious Mr. Knight can't live with the loss of Black Oaks Ranch. Hell, girl, maybe I couldn't live with it, either, if I was him. But mark my words—he doesn't love you. He feels dispossessed and humiliated."

"He does, too, love me."

"No. He's just using you to recoup his family's fortune and to restore the Knight name."

"I don't believe you!"

"Just ask him the next time you're with him. Unless you're scared to."

"I'm not scared. I know Cole. I don't have to ask him!"

But later, when she'd met Cole at the ruins of the old Knight headquarters where they went sometimes to make love on a blanket in one of the deserted rooms, she'd refused to go into his waiting arms. Maybe her daddy's words had finally worn her down. Maybe she wanted to put an end to his bad-mouthing Cole once and for all. Whatever the reason, that day she'd attacked. "My daddy said you wanted me because of the Golden Spurs. Is that true?"

"No, darlin'," but he hadn't met her gaze.

"Look at me. What did you want that first day when Pájaro ran away and you saved me?"

He hadn't answered.

She'd swallowed. "Oh, God. You wanted the ranch."

"Darlin', you've got to understand. I'd just buried my father. I blamed your father for his death. Back then…"

"Back then, what?"

"All right. I was born wanting everything that had been ours. Then my daddy threw what was left away. Lizzy, I grew up on stories about how all of it should have been mine."

"You used me."

"I love you."

"No, you love the ranch." She'd hesitated. "Which do you love more—me or the land?"

"What the hell kind of question is that? That's like asking me if I'd rather eat or breathe when I have to do both to live."

"Choose. Let's leave this place and go away together. To a big city. We'll never come back."

His dark face went white. "This is all I know. This is who I am. But I want you with me, always. This is the generation where we'll make things right between our two families."

When he'd reached for her, she'd run. From him, from her

father, from the ranch, from everything and everybody, who made her feel like she wasn't anything without the grand Kemble name.

For a long time after that it had seemed vitally important to be more than just a Kemble. She'd fled to New York, vowing that the next man she loved was going to love her—just her.

Ironically, Cole had left, too. Probably because he hadn't seen a way to get what he really wanted with her gone.

Only he'd made good and she hadn't. When he'd returned, he'd wasted no time in marrying Mia.

The water was cold when Lizzy stood up and got out of the tub.

Was Cole really so different now than he had been then? She thought so. Did he truly love her?

She wanted to believe he did. But, deep down was she really sure? She was willing to die for him, and yet she wasn't willing to marry him.

Joanne's hands froze when she touched the tangled satin slip in her drawer.

Someone had been in her room and gone through her things.

The slip fell through her fingers. For a long time she stood motionless over her open lingerie drawer. She was tidy to a fault. Tonight her lacy bras were scrambled with her panties and slips, all of which should have been neatly folded.

She would have to remind Sy'rai not to put her things away, that she would do it. But how strange that Sy'rai would forget when she never had before.

Joanne began to dig underneath the silky undergarments and then went utterly still as a second shattering realization dawned.

Electra's journal was gone.

Her clean lingerie was neatly stacked on top her dresser, as always, where Sy'rai had left them. Sy'rai had not done this.

Someone else had invaded her privacy and stolen the journal.

Her blackmailer?

Why?

Lizzy heard the blasts from Sam's and Cole's rifles long before she reached the skeet range. She was licking the top off a chocolate ice-cream cone as she stepped out of the brush into the open just as a clay pigeon arced against a clear blue sky. Cole's rifle tracked it for mere seconds before he pulled the trigger and blew it to bits.

"Good shot," Sam said as clay sprinkled onto the brown grass.

"Your turn," Cole challenged.

Sam blasted several clay pigeons in rapid succession. Lizzy wasn't surprised. Sam had always been an expert shot.

"I remember when we used to ride around in Daddy's pickup in the evenings with Hawk and Walker and Mia. You used to shoot everything that moved—skunks, raccoons, coyotes, even cute little bunny rabbits," she said.

Sam laughed. "You used to cry, too. Except when I killed rattlers. We tried our best to toughen her up, Cole. We really did."

"Didn't work, though," Cole said, his voice gentle.

"That's about to change," she retorted crisply. "Cole, I came out here today because I want you to teach me to shoot."

He drew a deep breath. Suddenly she knew he was remembering their quarrel last night.

"I thought you hated guns," Sam said, oblivious to the undercurrents between them.

"You used to say they were a necessary evil. So did Daddy. Maybe I'm just taking you at your word."

When Cole started to hand her his gun, she shook her head. "No. I want to practice with my revolver. I got it down out of my closet. I found several boxes of bullets, too."

"What do you intend to shoot with that?" Sam asked when she pulled it out of her jacket pocket.

There was a long silence.

"I'm not rightly sure," she said, holding her cone awkwardly while spinning the empty cylinder at the same time. "Whatever gets in my way, I guess." She didn't mean that. She didn't want to shoot anybody or anything—ever.

"Didn't anybody ever tell you it's dangerous to carry a gun in your pocket?" Sam said.

"Especially when you're gobbling ice-cream cones?" Cole added.

"Lots of things are dangerous. But they are more dangerous if you don't face them." She took another long lick of chocolate and smiled when she caught Cole watching her with that special gleam in his eyes. Oh, if only she was as brave or felt as playful as she pretended.

Sam lifted his brows. "You're changing—fast."

"All right then," Cole replied. "We'll get some empty soda cans and drive to the pond. Nothing like shooting cans in a pond to improve your aim with a revolver. You wanna come along, Sam?"

"Sure. But I'll join you later. I have a couple of phone calls to make. You two have fun."

"Always," Cole said under his breath, grinning at her as he leaned down close enough to kiss her.

"Want a lick?" She held the cone up to his lips, but he drew back.

"Tease," she whispered, glancing up at his chiseled lips with way too much hunger.

"Can't have you getting too conceited about your power over me," he murmured. "You're not as irresistible as you think."

"Just 'cause you had me last night." She hesitated. "Cole, I'm sorry about last night."

"Me, too." He grabbed her and kissed her hard.

She laughed. "See, I am, too, irresistible."

He grabbed her cone and painted the tip of her nose with it lightly.

"Cole!"

"You shouldn't have pushed it," he said. "A man can only resist so much. Chocolate ice cream looks mighty tempting all of a sudden."

She laughed again, and he kissed her again so thoroughly she tingled all the way to her toes. Then he grabbed her cone and bit off the top.

Cole drove to the far side of the pond where the brush and grass were blackened by fire, and she was reminded anew of the mysterious accidents and the murders—and why she was practicing her shooting.

"We need the wind on our backs," he said as he threw the cans out.

She smiled, understanding when they began to float away from them.

"Don't shoot until I tell you," he said.

"You're the boss."

"Out here, maybe. If I was really the boss, you'd marry me."

She felt her pulse flutter with illogical longing. "Don't…"

She turned away and began to fire rapidly. Her first three shots missed, but the ripples in the pond showed her that each succeeding shot hit closer to the can than the one before. Her last three bullets sank the two cans. Hitting what she aimed at scared her a little.

"Not bad," he muttered, clearly impressed. "For a girl."

"For a beginner," she corrected.

"Are you ever going to trust me?" he said, taking the revolver and showing her how to reload it.

"I trust you," she murmured.

"But just so far," he said, handing the pistol back to her. "Not enough to marry me."

"We're having an affair. Why can't that be enough now?"

She took aim just as Sam's blue truck rumbled over the bridge.

"Hold your fire," Cole said, placing his hand on top the barrel of her pistol and lowering it as the truck roared up to them.

"Hey!" Sam yelled as he alighted from his truck. "How's she doing."

"Don't sneak up on her in the dark. She's a natural."

"Wouldn't think of sneaking up on a country girl." Sam winked as he loaded his pistol. Then all three of them took turns shooting. The men were sure and fast and so cocky about their ability they gave her pointers. Very soon, she was sinking every can with a single bullet. When she got a little cocky herself, they took full credit.

"We're just good teachers," Cole said.

When they were out of bullets, they returned to the big house for lunch. Without greeting them Sy'rai slapped a Houston newspaper onto the table as they pulled chairs out from under the table.

"Do you believe this?" she said.

"That's helluva welcome."

Cole frowned as he picked the paper up.

"Kinky drove Joanne to town this morning," Sy'rai continued. "They brought this when they came back. The guy writing this piece thinks Caesar was murdered along with Electra and Cherry. Joanne got so upset, she locked herself in the bedroom. The phone's been ringing off the wall, too. Everybody who's anybody in this here state wants to come to the museum opening now. Joanne caved and ordered a second tent. She's decided to expand the guest list for the celebration dinner. She said, 'If everybody's talking about us, I think we need to let them all come and gawk.'"

"If we expand the guest list, we'll need a lot more security," Sam said in a concerned tone.

Cole set the paper aside. "What's for lunch?"

"How can you think about food right now?" Lizzy said.

"Easy." Cole arched a brow at Sy'rai. "You didn't answer my question."

"Fried chicken."

"My kind of woman."

Lizzy shot him a mock scowl and everybody laughed. Nobody said much during lunch, but from time to time Lizzy thought Sam watched Cole rather warily, as if he sensed the change in their relationship. As the men were finishing homemade apple pie, while Lizzy sipped coffee, Cole got a call on his cell phone from Leo and excused himself from the table.

Lizzy set her mug down. "I'd better go see what Vanilla's up to."

As she stood up, Sam said. "Stay a sec."

"What's the matter?"

"I'm worried about you."

"Don't be."

"Maybe you should leave the Golden Spurs for a while," Sam said.

She notched her chin higher. "What are you saying?"

"Maybe you shouldn't be taking shooting lessons or living here with Cole right now. Uncle B.B. asked me to talk to you. He said maybe you should go back to New York. Take Vanilla. Stay away…at least until we get this celebration out of the way. There's going to be a lot of people. In the confusion, anything could happen."

"Sam, surely you don't agree that I should be afraid of Cole."

"He hasn't been himself since the accident, now has he? You heard that detective. A lot of weird things have been going on. Phillips suspects him. Apparently, Cole won't tell him where he was for several critical hours the day before and the day after Cherry was found dumped in our tank. Phillips says he's going to want DNA samples."

"Cole didn't kill Cherry. Why would he?"

"Maybe she knew something."

"He won't hurt me, either. You must believe that."

"He's a Knight. He used to hate us. Maybe he still does."

"Things are different now," she said.

"Are they?"

"But he married Mia. He fathered Vanilla. He owns stock in the ranch. He works harder for the Golden Spurs than anybody."

"Maybe he killed Mia."

"Don't say that!"

"She's dead, and if he marries you, he'll own even more stock, won't he?"

"Do you think he wants to marry me or kill me? You and Uncle B.B. can't have it both ways."

"Why can't we? He may have married and killed Mia. Listen to me. Two women are dead. Two women your father was involved with. Now your father's dead, too. Did Cole tell you he flew to Nicaragua, shortly before Electra Scott was murdered?"

"How do you know that?"

"The police. Phillips got his name off the airline's roster."

"I don't believe you."

"Ask Phillips, then."

When she said nothing, Sam stared at her, concern and what looked like pity lighting his soft, dark eyes. He had always looked out for her.

"Cole wouldn't hurt me," she whispered.

"I damn sure hope to hell you're right 'cause I'm tired of people dying around here."

Nineteen

Whenever Lizzy was nervous she frequently sought refuge in the nursery by playing silly games with Vanilla. Today, she was trying not to worry about Cole as she inserted a Teletubby DVD into the DVD player and switched on the television.

Vanilla, who'd been sitting on the floor in the nursery shaking her music box and playing nursery rhymes, dropped the music box and toddled to the screen, laughing when the soft round tubbies appeared. Then Vanilla turned to see if Lizzy was watching, too.

Joanne had redone Mia's old room into a nursery. The walls were painted in pastel colors, pink, yellow, green. Each wall had been painted in a different color. The nursery floor was carpeted with plush squares that had pictures of animals and big fuzzy numbers and letters on them.

The tubbies began to sing what seemed to Lizzy a silly song, but Vanilla found their gentle voices inviting and their pastel fairyland that looked a lot like the nursery nonthreatening.

Rocking back and forth in time to their tune, Vanilla watched them entranced. When the tubbies broke into dance, Vanilla hopped up and down so excitedly until she fell on her plumply padded bottom.

Lizzy laid her yoga mat down and was doing her warm-up stretches when the phone rang.

She answered it and immediately stood up straighter when she recognized her old boss's voice.

"Liz?"

"Nell? Hi."

"I'm sorry about your dad."

"It was nice of you to call, Nell." Lizzy sank into a rocker.

"I've been reading about the Golden Spurs. Sounds pretty impressive. And you're running things down there?"

Lizzy didn't smile. "Being run over by them mostly."

Nell laughed. They talked for a while, about New York, about Lizzy's new life at the ranch, and all the time, Lizzy rocked back and forth, wondering why Nell had called.

"I'm sorry I wasn't here at the station when you came to pick up your things," Nell finally said.

"I was pretty upset."

"That's understandable. I'm sorry, Liz. Um…er…well, I don't know how to say this exactly, but if you ever decide to move back to the city, come by and see me." She hesitated. "I'd like to give you another chance. I feel really bad about what happened." She paused again. "You could have told me who you were."

"I did."

"Right. I knew you were a rancher and a Kemble. I just didn't know you were one of *the Kembles*."

"Oh." Lizzy felt the beginning of the glow inside her dissolve. "I didn't think it was relevant."

Nell laughed. "I don't think I fully appreciated what an original you are—a famous person, who doesn't want to be famous."

Lizzy remembered Nell was a celebrity hound.

"Well, I just thought I'd call and let you know we're hiring again," Nell said brightly.

"Sure." Lizzy spoke through her teeth. "Thanks. I'll think about it."

"No hurry. The job's open. Anytime."

Not for me. For a Kemble.

Nell chatted some more, and Lizzy listened numbly, a little surprised that the prospect of making it in Manhattan on the Kemble name didn't excite her nearly as much as it excited Nell.

A week passed, and the weather grew colder. Although Lizzy and everybody else were nervous and watchful, nothing untoward happened. Detective Phillips harassed Cole by phone as often as possible. He gave Joanne and Sam and Leo a hard time, too, which kept the tension level high. He wanted DNA samples, and was busy making the necessary arrangements.

There were no breaks in the case and no more suspicious accidents, either. No missing cattle shipments, no fires.

Yet, still the ranch felt strangely oppressive, and everyone was on his guard. Lizzy couldn't shake the feeling that any minute there would be a new disaster. As a result she found herself wandering out to the Spur Tree much too often, as if some profound question could be answered there. She practiced using her revolver.

Kembles from all over the country, including Uncle B.B., Aunt Mona, Lauren, Nanette and Sam, began arriving and moving into the big house to prepare for the museum opening and the celebration. Although some came by private jet, most flew commercial. Sam, of course, had only a short drive.

Thus, there was the constant, daily excitement of more new comers. Nearly every day another Kemble from some far-flung locale had to be picked up from the Corpus Christi airport. At the end of the week, the big house overflowed and took on a dude ranch atmosphere. The urban Kembles strutted around the place in their fancy Western outfits and brand-new Stetsons.

At night the dining room was so jammed, Sy'rai had to hire extra help to cook and clean. Lizzy's depression lifted now that the house rang with voices and laughter, and there was so much to do and to look forward to.

During the days everybody worked to spruce the ranch up and work out the details for the parties and decorations and events that were to be held. Lizzy spent long hours in the library reading history books to perfect her speech. Joanne, Sam, Walker and Leo would be giving speeches, too.

Lizzy felt that she and Cole were living on borrowed time. Thus, every night when the house was dark and the family had gone to bed, Lizzy stole up the carpeted stairs to lie in his arms. They would make love with a sad kind of desperation. Afterward he would hold her close. And always he would demand that she leave the ranch or marry him.

On one such night as they lay entwined, their bodies still slick with sweat, he said, "Why don't you take Nell's job, go back to New York, at least for a little while."

"We've been over this and over this."

"But I can't quit worrying about you, darlin'," he murmured. "Whoever chased you and ran Star into that pond is probably sleeping under this roof right now just waiting for his chance."

Lizzy shivered. "Cole, did you ever think that I might not be any safer, even in New York? My mother was murdered in Nicaragua."

His big body tensed.

She stroked his back. "What's the matter, Cole?"

"Nothing." But he tried to pull away.

She rolled on top of him and stared into his eyes, so that she could read him. "Did you go to Nicaragua…before my mother died?"

Agony scrawled itself across his dark face before he could hide it. Then he pushed her aside and sat up. Next he jerked a pillow under his head. "Why? What if I did? Does that mean I killed her? Is that what you think?"

"Did you go there or not?"

He inhaled deeply and stared straight ahead.

"Why won't you answer me?"

"Maybe because you've already made up your damn mind."

"If I had, would I be here in bed with you?" She hesitated. Then she said softly, "You don't remember, do you?"

"Okay! Damn it, I found a ticket to Nicaragua with my damn name on it! And it scared the shit out of me! But I don't remember going there and I've never blacked out for the amount of time it'd take to fly to Nicaragua and back. So I don't think I did. Now, there, you know what I know. Are you happy?"

She went very still.

"Do you think I killed her, and then Cherry? Is that what you think?"

She chose her words carefully. "The Cole I know isn't capable of murder."

"But what if I'm someone else, too?"

"You aren't." She wanted to believe that. She wanted to so much.

He raked a hand through his black hair. "I hope to hell you're right. Look, I know I used to be a single-minded, whiny, egotistical jerk with a chip on my shoulder a mile wide. I hated your father. I know I hurt you, too, Lizzy. I hate the man I was, but I'd rather be him than be some sicko like a Dr. Jekyll/Mr. Hyde combo."

"Don't think that! That's not what's going on."

"Are you really sure? Maybe my head injury did permanent damage, and I'm some sort of freak."

"You're not."

"That's why I want you to leave. Okay, don't go to New York. Go somewhere I can't find you."

"I'm sorry I asked you that question."

"I'm glad you did." After that he didn't say anything more.

His dark mood was her fault. She'd asked. Now she had to get his mind off this terrible subject.

She ran her hand down his lean torso, feathering her fingers through the dark matted hair at his chest. "Make love to me now. What's your wildest fantasy?"

"For you to love me forever and to marry me."

"Even if I'm not ready for marriage?"

"You want to know what I think?" His voice was suddenly low and harsh. "I think you're afraid to marry me…because deep down…you believe…just as I fear…I might be that monster."

The breath went out of her. "When you say that I feel like I'm living in a nightmare."

"Welcome to the club, darlin'."

She couldn't think of anything else to say or do that would make things better between them. With each beat of her heart, the silence in the dark room thickened.

At last he sighed. "We're not getting any sleep, either one of us, and we've got a lot to do tomorrow to get ready."

"I don't care about tomorrow."

"Well, maybe I do. You know, I'm beginning to think we should give our relationship a rest."

"What are you saying?"

"I'm saying I want you to go. I'm saying you're a Kemble and I'm a Knight…and maybe worse. Hell, maybe I'm a certifiable monster. I'm saying don't knock on my door tomorrow night, darlin'—or ever again for that matter."

"But, Cole—"

She tried to put her arms around him, but he shook her off.

"Look, you don't trust me. I don't trust me. Maybe we were damned from the start. All I know is that I'd rather be alone than for you and me to go on like this. Hot sex isn't enough for me anymore."

"Hot sex? Is that all you think we have?"

"Well, we damn sure don't have trust or true love, now do we? I want more, Lizzy."

On a sob, she got out of bed and hurriedly dressed.

He didn't turn on the light and watch her dress-tease, as he called it, the way he usually did. And she missed his eyes gleaming so hotly they lit her entire being.

Instead he rolled over as if he were bored with her and ignored her completely.

The nursery radio was playing hard rock. Lizzy had turned it on to drown out her sorrow about Cole's sudden desertion and because Vanilla loved music. Ever since their quarrel, Lizzy's heart had felt like it was breaking.

Vanilla stood on the dresser and was jumping up and down to the beat in her ballerina dress while Lizzy ran a silver brush through her snarled hair.

"Hold still, Vanilla. Don't you even care that cocktails are to be served at six-thirty sharp outside on the lawn and your aunt Lizzy is supposed to be a hostess for the museum opening gala?"

Vanilla giggled.

Lizzy's cell phone that was clipped to her belt rang, and she answered it, hoping it was Cole.

"Where are you?" Joanne demanded. "The party's started."

"I'm with Vanilla."

"Hurry."

They both hung up.

"Of course, you don't care that we're running a little late, you little minx, now do you?" Lizzy said to Vanilla, who patted the mirror on her dresser.

Lizzy didn't care, either. In fact she dreaded going to the party now that Cole was so determined to avoid her. Some part of her doubted him and he knew it.

She hadn't seen much of him lately, and she was almost glad the long day's back-to-back activities had left her breathless and tired. She'd given her speech at the museum and listened to the others' speeches, especially the one Leo had given in honor of Caesar. Then Joanne had talked her into hosting a two-hour bus tour of the ranch. But what had really worn her out was having to make small talk with the endless visitors who'd come, especially to mingle with the family. Part of her job was to smile, answer questions and try to be positive about the ranch.

Watching the baby dance on her dresser as Lizzy brushed her hair made it impossible to believe there was real evil or murderers who strangled women in the world.

"Be still. You can hardly walk and already you're trying to dance—on your dresser, no less!"

Vanilla jerked her head away from the brush and then tried to grab it.

"Too bad. I'm done. And you're beautiful."

Lizzy felt pretty and feminine as she stared at herself and Vanilla in the dresser mirror. Lizzy wore a black silk Western shirt, tight black jeans and black custom-made boots. Vanilla had on a puffy pink chiffon dress with satin slippers. The little girl stopped dancing and smiled flirtatiously at herself and then at Lizzy's reflection. Growing bored, the baby began to tug at her pink satin bow.

"Don't, Vanilla, dear."

The little girl stuck out her lip and yanked harder, laughing mischievously when the bow came undone. She began chewing on the long pieces of ribbon until they were sodden with saliva.

"It would make more sense to dress up an orangutan," Lizzy said.

Vanilla dropped the limp ribbons and clapped at her reflection. Then she stretched her hands out to Lizzy and made appropriate monkey squeals that meant *pick me up*.

Grinning, Lizzy swung the happy little girl up into her arms. Together they descended the stairs down to the dinner that was being held under two immense white tents on the back lawn, to celebrate the museum opening.

Every time Lizzy thought about Cole, she fought to distract herself. She forced herself to note how beautifully lit and gorgeous the house looked as she carried Vanilla through the huge rooms downstairs. Wood floors and furnishings had been waxed or oiled, the Oriental rugs taken up and cleaned.

When she reached the front door and stepped outside, she saw the booths that Hawk and Walker had set up on the lawn where guests and clients could learn about wildlife management, cattle management, environmental research and brush control.

It was a beautiful evening with a sprinkling of stars. There would be more stars, of course, as the night darkened.

Tables with long pink table clothes and little copper bowls filled with roses for centerpieces were scattered about on the grass. A dance floor had been set up off to one side, and a Western band was playing under a huge oak tree. A dozen couples were waltzing, and just watching them made Lizzy's heart ache.

As planned, cowboys in jeans and white shirts and black Stetsons sat astride quarter horses that were lined up on either side of the sidewalk from the parking lot all the way to the party. Lizzy glanced at them to see if Cole was among them.

He wasn't.

Joanne wore a long black dress and was playing her role as the ranch's mistress to the hilt. She flew about, seeming to be everywhere at once, greeting first one person and then another. When Joanne saw Vanilla, she made her way graciously through the well-dressed throng to greet Lizzy. Delighted, Vanilla squealed to be taken into her grandmother's waiting arms.

Cole was standing at the bar talking to a pretty, predatory-looking, young redhead wearing a low-cut gown. Even though she wasn't Suz, Lizzy quickly looked the other way.

Without Vanilla to care for, Lizzy mingled freely with the guests and tried to stay as far from Cole as possible. But any time she accidentally caught a glimpse of him, he was surrounded by beautiful women.

Sam found a drink for her. Her throat felt parched, but she set it down. Hawk and Walker brought her a plate of appetizers from the buffet table. Not that she could make herself eat either.

She was as popular with the men as Cole seemed to be with the women. Not that she wanted to be. She wanted Cole. Only Cole.

But her doubts and nagging questions had driven him away. She *had* to believe in him.

Everybody wanted to talk to her about the ranch, about her father and about all the bad publicity that had been in the Texas newspapers and on television, which, of course, was the last thing she wanted to discuss.

"Was Caesar murdered?"

"What about Electra Scott? What's the connection there? Were they lovers?"

"Who's next? I'd be careful if I were you, sweetie!"

Lizzy was polite, if evasive. When the men asked her to dance, she demurred. Despite all the attention from men, she felt bereft because Cole ignored her.

When Aunt Nanette arrived on the arm of a cowboy as young as her sons, Sam and Bobby Joe, and began to make a spectacle of herself on the dance floor, the men stalked abruptly into the house. Aunt Nanette, who was slim, looked far younger in her white leather pants and clingy silk shirt than her age.

Uncle B.B. and Aunt Mona glided up to Lizzy.

"They keep getting younger and younger," Uncle B.B. said, his eyes on his sister.

"Sam and Bobby Joe should be used to it by now," Aunt Mona said. "Still, no wonder Sam lived with Caesar and Joanne all those years. Sam's always seemed sort of lost...like he didn't belong anywhere. And as for Bobby Joe, he can't seem to find himself."

Aunt Nanette rubbed against her lover on the dance floor and Lizzy blushed. "Sam was like my own brother."

"You shouldn't be trying to run the ranching operation, Lizzy," Uncle B.B. muttered, his tone so grim it almost sounded threatening.

"I'll step down just as soon as I can," she said.

When still another man asked to Lizzy to dance, she smiled and almost accepted just to escape Uncle B.B. and Aunt Mona, but a deep baritone behind her rocked her senses.

"She's with me."

She turned questioningly to Cole. "Am I?"

Uncle B.B. scowled at them both. Then a dark look passed between Aunt Mona and him as they moved away to circulate.

"Well, you damn sure didn't look like you wanted to be with *him,* or your aunt and uncle," Cole said in his sexy,

Texas drawl as he led her away. "I always was a sucker for a damsel in distress."

"Which is how we met," she said, feeling shy.

"Do you want to dance? I think we'd better. Your new suitor is scowling at us."

She smiled, nodding. "I guess we have to. But there's no way we can compete with Aunt Nanette."

Then Lizzy was in Cole's arms, being whirled about on the dance floor. There were other couples besides her aunt and her new lover, and yet to Lizzy it seemed as if they were the only two people in the world.

Her doubts had receded in importance. Nothing mattered except being with Cole. Not having him around for the past few days had made her know for sure how desperately she wanted to be with him forever.

He was the only man she'd ever loved. No matter what had gone wrong before. No matter the risk, she had no choice but to take a chance on him. He couldn't be the killer. She couldn't have loved him if he was. She couldn't stand her life without him.

Now that she knew for certain that she couldn't live without him, she couldn't wait to tell him she wanted to marry him.

"Cole, could we go somewhere to talk?"

He looked uncertain and yet her shining eyes must have communicated what was in her heart because a new eagerness lit his dark face. "Sure."

He took her hand and squeezed it before bringing it to his lips.

"Darlin', I love you." The warmth of his lips seeped inside her.

"I love you, too." She hugged him.

"Let's go."

He was leading her toward the golf cart path that led to

Ann Major

the aviary and the greenhouse when suddenly there was an explosion directly in front of them from the direction of the barn.

Next came yelling, screaming and utter pandemonium.

She clung to Cole. Above the trees, she saw white birds soaring and flames licking the inky, star-bright sky.

"It's the horse barn!" Cole yelled. "And the aviary! Get back to the house. Stay close to your brothers." Then he kissed her before taking off in a dead run for the barn and aviary.

Twenty

Orange flames licked the inky night, streaking it with gold. White birds whirled overhead. Cole had disappeared inside the smoke-filled inferno that had been the barn and was unlocking the stalls to free any horses that weren't being used for the celebration and might still be inside. As heat blasted her and ashes blew toward her, Lizzy was filled with panic that he might be overcome by smoke and never get out.

Suddenly there was an unearthly roar above the groaning and crackling of burning timbers. Then the entire south end of the barn shuddered and began to rip apart from the rest of the building.

Explosions rocked the barn. The fire must have reached the gas cans and mowers stored at one end. Sparks shot even higher into the air.

"Cole!"

A horse screamed and galloped out of the barn, racing past her.

Ringo.

But where was Cole?

"Cole?" She was crying his name and stumbling toward

the barn when the south end collapsed in upon itself, spewing sparks high into the air.

Dazed, Lizzy felt tears on her cheeks. When something began to vibrate against her waist, only vaguely did she realize it was her cell phone. When she picked it up, a disembodied voice said, "I've got Vanilla."

Sirens screamed in the distance.

"Too late," she whispered, not really knowing that she'd spoken out loud. Cole had to be dead. Nothing inside that barn could still be alive.

"Lizzy," the caller repeated. "I've got Vanilla."

Even as she felt cold and crazed with grief and fear, her pulse accelerated in alarm.

It isn't Cole. The killer isn't Cole. Cole isn't a Mr. Hyde. Cole is dead.

Not that she felt any relief in that knowledge.

"Come alone, Lizzy, or I'll kill her."

Vanilla. Lizzy's throat went dry. *Vanilla was in danger.*

"Come where?" she screamed, feeling dead and hollow, backing into the shadows.

"If you tell anyone, if anybody else comes with you, I'll set the camp house on fire just like I did the barn. I'll kill Vanilla just like I killed your mother and your daddy and Cherry…and Cole."

How did the monster already know about Cole?

"You know I will," he said softly.

"Who is this?" she hissed.

"Come and see. If you've got the guts, little Lizzy."

"Tell me who this is!"

The caller laughed.

"Tell me," she begged.

More laughter. Then the line went dead.

"Lizzy!" Cole screamed.

One minute, she'd been there, at the edge of the brush talking on her cell phone. In the next, she'd vanished in the smoke.

Fire trucks whirred up and surrounded the barn. An ambulance braked, but its siren kept on screaming.

Cole felt strange, disoriented. White birds whirled above him. Black dots danced in front of his eyes. Suddenly he knew he must've lost time again. He'd gone in one set of doors, but he must've escaped out the back. He began moving toward the trees. He'd been standing so close to the fire, he was bathed in sweat and his hands were blistered.

But where the hell was Lizzy? It scared the hell out of him that he couldn't find her. Had whoever set the fire done something to her?

Firemen rushed up to him, and he went wild, trying to push past them to find Lizzy, but they grabbed him and threw him on the ground. When he fought back, it took three of them to hold him down.

"It's all right. You're in shock," one of them said.

A man in white stuck a needle in his arm. "Breathe deeply and you'll be fine, sir. We're going to take good care of you. Everything is going to be all right."

"Let go of me! Let go! Let go! Lizzy—"

But Lizzy was gone.

Had he hurt her?

The black dots thickened in front of Cole's eyes until they blinded him.

The last face he saw was Uncle B.B.'s.

"We've got to save Lizzy," Cole said. Then total darkness.

It's Uncle B.B., he thought.

Lizzy drew a swift breath as she parked on the road a quarter of a mile shy of the camp house. Then she tucked her loaded revolver into her waistband and got out, climbed a fence and snuck through brush country to the camp. Her black outfit concealed her. She was drenched in sweat and so terrified that whenever a leaf rustled, or a twig broke, or a frog croaked, her heart leapt into her throat and she sank to a crouch. The gun felt heavy and alien against her spine, but the thought of Vanilla in mortal danger was enough to keep her going.

I can do this. I can do this. I'm Caesar's daughter. And Electra's, too. I've got my gun. I'm scared, but I'm strong.

When she finally reached the camp house, all the lights were blazing. For a long moment she stayed in the brush and watched the house, wondering what to do. Then she heard Vanilla's music box start playing softly in the same unit where she and Cole had made love such a short time ago.

Keeping well inside the brush line, she crept closer to the camp house. Through a window she could see that a baby bed had been set up, and a blanket had been thrown over it. The blanket was tented as if a child stood there.

"Vanilla!"

When Lizzy raced onto the veranda and then inside the room, the door, as if caught by the wind, slammed behind her. When she ripped the blanket off the crib, the last thing she saw before the lights went out was a stick of wood on the pillow instead of Vanilla.

The baby wasn't in the crib.

"Vanilla!" she screamed as an explosion shook the building.

She sank to the floor in the suffocating darkness. Holding her breath, she crawled to the door and waited.

Where was Vanilla? She had to get out. She had to find her, and yet she was afraid of what she'd find on the other side of the door.

When the doorknob rattled she wanted to scream but then covered her mouth with her hand. Someone was out there in that blackness. Her mother's killer? Her father's? She felt crazed with grief and fear.

Again she saw Star's carcass on the flatbed truck. Again she saw the barn roof collapse and knew Cole was inside.

In the absolute stillness that followed, she raised her pistol and took aim.

"Don't shoot," a voice said.

"Who?" Her hand holding the gun shook uncontrollably.

When the door slammed open and struck the gun, she accidentally pulled the trigger.

She heard a burst of fiendish laughter.

Then a tall, broad-shouldered figure toppled toward her, and the lights came back on.

His arms outstretched, Cole lay in a pool of blood at her feet.

"Cole." Horrified, she knelt beside him. *"It was you. All the time it was you."*

Surprised she felt no revulsion toward him, she touched his thick black hair. "I—I can't believe it was you." It made sense, of course. He'd hated them. All he'd ever wanted was revenge. He'd probably blacked out again. But she didn't believe it, not really.

"Lizzy, are you all right?"

She looked up as Sam entered the room and ran toward her.

She felt exhausted and defeated. It was wonderful to have someone to lean on. "Sam? Thank God, you're here. I shot him. I shot Cole!" Hot tears burned her eyes. "Cole couldn't have done it! He couldn't have!"

"Uncle B.B. sent me. I saw your car and Cole's truck in the brush. Vanilla's in Cole's truck asleep. She sure as hell looks zonked. He must have drugged her. Lizzy, what's going on? I got a call on my cell phone and was told to come here or else. There's a fire at the end of the camp house."

She stared at Cole, too stunned to move.

"I—I don't feel too well. I'm very tired, Sam. Just call the sheriff. And an ambulance. And the firemen. Then we've got to get Vanilla and make sure she's all right."

When Sam went out to make the calls, Cole's dark head

stirred. His hands smeared blood across the threshold as he fought to lift himself.

"Don't move," she whispered. "Or…or I'll…"

He was so weak he couldn't lift his head and it was agony to watch him struggle. Their eyes met, and she began to tremble all over when she saw his concern and fear—*for her.* He was bleeding. She had to stop the blood, she thought. She had to save him.

"Run," he managed in a thready whisper. "S-Sam… Run!" He closed his eyes.

"Sam?"

A second or two of beating silence passed before he managed in hoarse voice. "Not me. Not me—*Sam.*"

And then she knew.

"Let him go. Put the gun down." Sam's disembodied voice came out of the darkness before she saw him. "Don't forget I've got Vanilla. She's safe and sound for the moment, but not for long. She'll die if you don't do exactly what I say." Sam stepped over the threshold into the lit room.

Feeling desperate, she stared helplessly at Cole's black head. "But he'll bleed…"

"So?" Sam laughed.

"Why, Sam?"

"Why? Why the hell couldn't Caesar have flown with Cole that day instead of Mia? If they'd gone down together, the board would have chosen me for sure."

"You don't know that."

"If you'd only resigned… You had no business…" His voice changed. "Just put the gun down."

The hand that held the revolver hung limply against her side. Slowly she knelt, intending to do exactly what he said.

It was over. She was no kick-ass heroine after all. No brave audacious cowgirl like Mia. No daughter Caesar could be proud of, either. She was a joke. Cole would die because of her. She'd even suspected Aunt Mona—for buying bullets. All hunters bought bullets. She'd shot the good guy, who also happened to be the man she loved.

Her face crumpled. Just as she felt herself surrendering to total despair and her fingers relaxing on the gun, she glanced up desperately, straight into the painted eyes of her father's portrait. Someone had replaced the immense painting above the fireplace, so that he could stare coldly down at her in this moment of supreme stupidity. He looked as arrogant and superior as he had in real life—and as demanding.

"I'm sorry, Daddy," she murmured. "I wanted you to be proud of me." She turned to Sam. "You killed all of those people."

"I did it for the ranch," Sam said. "I want to run the ranch. I don't want to answer to anybody other than the board. I did it for the same reasons your father killed his brother. Down here whoever runs the Golden Spurs is like a king. I tried so hard to make Caesar proud of me. Just like you did. But I was only his nephew, and he wanted one of his children to be his heir. I tried so hard to show him…. Then Cole married Mia, and started to outshine me."

"Daddy didn't murder anybody. He loved Uncle Jack. He's not sneaky like you. He was brave and bold. You're a coward. A real coward. Maybe he saw through you, Sam!"

"Lizzy, put the gun down or I'll blow your brains out."

She stared at Cole again, who lay sprawled before her. Slowly she lifted her gaze to her father's portrait again. For the first time in her life she *felt* his profound belief in her. It was almost as if he were here with her.

"It's up to you," Caesar seemed to say. "Everybody's depending on you. You can do it, Lizzy."

She thought of her mother.

And then it happened.

One minute she was weak and scared and utterly lacking in self-confidence. Her shoulders were sagging, and she was lowering the gun to the floor about to do as Sam said.

And then the wind gusted, the door banged and her father seemed to speak to her again, "Give it all you've got, girl! He's gonna kill you sure as shootin'. Cole will die sure enough. You have nothing to lose, girl!"

Her grip tightened on the loathsome gun. Without thinking she whirled, thrust it upward and fired twice.

Boom! Boom! The gunshots sounded like explosions.

Sam staggered backward, clutching the bullet wound in his chest. "I didn't think you had it in you."

"I didn't."

It was as if someone else had done it. As if Daddy's spirit had leapt out of that canvas and taken charge of her and pulled the trigger for her.

Lizzy fell to her knees. Dropping the gun, almost shoving it away, she gently touched Cole's face. His brow felt cold. So cold. Like ice. Maybe he was already dead.

She'd shot him. She'd killed him. She would never touch another gun as long as she lived. Never!

"No! Don't die!" she screamed. "I'll marry you! I love you! Just don't die!"

Grabbing her cell phone, she dialed 9-1-1. Then she rushed to the bedroom and found blankets to cover both men with. She had to find a way to stop the bleeding.

If Cole lived, would he ever forgive her for believing him capable of murder?

And where was Vanilla?

Lizzy pressed against his wounds with the blanket and held him while she waited.

"Duck! Puppy!" Vanilla made monkey sounds along with real words. Joanne bounced her and pointed at the television set in the ICU waiting room in an effort to amuse her.

Lizzy glanced at her watch. "You two can go. I don't need a baby-sitter."

"Not until it's time for you to go in to see him," Joanne said. "He's going to be fine, you know."

Lizzy was so frantic and guilt-stricken over Cole that she hadn't left the hospital other than to shower and change for the five days he'd been here. Friends and family came to stay with her and to tell her to take care of herself, that she had to keep herself going for Cole.

She barely noticed them coming and going. The few moments when she was allowed inside the ICU to speak with Cole, he lay as still as her father had, except Cole's eyes were closed. He didn't react, not even when she said his name and told him who she was. He simply lay there, the only sounds in his room were those of his machines.

According to his doctors, who constantly reassured her, Cole was in a light coma. Even though his doctors were very optimistic, Lizzy was still terrified that he was going to die. Or if he didn't die, she was terrified he'd never forgive her. When she was with him, she stroked him, talked to him, held his hand, prayed for his love and forgiveness and begged him to stay in this world because she loved him so much.

Joanne only came during the mornings because that was Vanilla's best time. In an effort to cheer and distract her, Joanne always brought the baby. Thus, the three of them were sitting together on the edges of their chairs in the little waiting room this morning.

Never one to be confined, Vanilla was squirming in her grandmother's lap and pointing excitedly at the cartoons on the television. Joanne constantly stroked the wriggling baby's curls as if to reassure herself the baby was all right.

"You saved her," she said simply.

I shot Cole, she thought. "Not really. Vanilla was asleep in Sam's truck the whole time. I don't think he could've hurt her. She was strapped into her car seat. He took her to scare me."

"Thank heavens she was okay."

"It's nearly noon," Lizzy said. "Vanilla's restless. You might as well go. They'll let me into see Cole again in a few minutes." She hesitated. "Did I tell you the doctors say he's getting better? That maybe today, maybe he'll wake up."

"Five times this morning."

"Did you know Sam's doing so well, they're moving him to the county jail today. I'll be glad when he's in jail, locked up I mean. I keep having dreams about him escaping and coming after me."

"I can't believe that Sam did all those horrible things," Joanne said. "He flew to Nicaragua pretending to be Cole. He changed license plates with Cole... Aunt Nanette has taken to her bed. It would be a hard thing for a mother to take. Even her. She ignored him as a child. She paid more attention to her lovers. That's why we took Sam. Poor Bobby Joe still doesn't know what to do with himself. Well...at least it's over."

"It won't be over until Cole pulls through," Lizzy said. "And...and forgives me. If he does."

"You were so brave and wonderful," Joanne said. "You saved Vanilla. Of course, he'll forgive you."

"But I shot him."

"That part was an accident. Cole is going to pull through. He of all people will understand. Remember Mia...and his awful guilt? Sweetheart, your father would be so proud of you."

"Who would have thought that Sam... *He killed Mia,* you know. Not Cole."

"And your father and that woman and two of my darling little birds, as well. I found their little corpses in what was left of the aviary. Vanilla and I buried them in the garden under the roses. All the rest of my little darlings are roosting in the Spur Tree until Eli can build them proper quarters."

"Sam wanted everything that was Caesar's," Lizzy said. "He told Phillips he had always been jealous of me because Caesar favored me over everybody."

"He was even blackmailing me. Although I didn't know it was him at the time."

"Why?"

"He sent me a copy of Electra's journal while I was in Houston. I brought it to the ranch to read, but he stole it out of my room before I got a chance. After the shootings, when I went to get Vanilla out of Cole's truck where he'd hidden her, I found the original on the seat beside Vanilla, and I took it."

"But it's evidence."

"It's private family history. They have enough evidence to put Sam where he belongs for a long long time. The journal is your birthright. You deserve to know about your mother. She was my best friend in school. She came here to help me with my wedding. Your father fell madly in love with her. Only she couldn't settle down. I don't think I ever quit loving Jack. Now I know Caesar never quit loving Electra."

"Tell me about Mia…and me."

"She and I both got pregnant at the same time. Then Jack died, and Electra refused to marry your father. So your father and I eventually married, but our life together was more complicated than either of us ever imagined. We didn't love each other, and we couldn't let go of the past. I think we began blaming each other instead of supporting one another. Sometimes we blamed you and Mia, too. Sometimes we competed through you and Mia. Once when Electra got in trouble, he flew to South America and saved her life. He stayed with her two weeks and got her pregnant again."

"What?" Lizzy felt the room spin.

"Lizzy, it's all in her journal. She wrote that you have twin sisters. The blackmailer or rather Sam said Electra was going to publish it, but I think she kept the journal so that if anything happened to her, you would find out. Only Sam found the journal instead and used it for his own purposes. To stir us all up."

"Sisters? I have sisters? Where are they?"

"I don't know, but there was a photograph of them. They're blonde and look a lot like you. I was too upset to read the journal all that thoroughly, and now the picture's gone. But I have the original journal at home under lock and key. The important thing is that you have twin sisters."

"And I'll find them. When Cole is better, if it's the last thing I do, I'll find them."

"And you and I?" Joanne began before her voice broke. "What about us?"

Lizzy saw a gentle maternal wisdom and an acceptance shining in Joanne's eyes that she'd never seen before.

"Us?"

"Do you think we could start over? And at least try to be friends?" Joanne asked. "A long time ago I made a promise to your father to be a good mother to you." Vanilla looked up at both of them, and Joanne smiled. "This time I'll try really hard."

"And so will I. At least now I understand what you were going through."

Vanilla, who was beaming brightly at them both, began to clap softly.

"You little rascal." Lizzy took her hands and kissed them. "You want us to pay attention to you, don't you?"

Joanne opened her arms, and Lizzy and Vanilla, who cooed and wriggled, came into them.

* * *

Cole heard a woman say his name very softly. He opened his eyes and groggily fought to focus on the woman beside him.

Terrible antiseptic hospital smells made him wrinkle his nose. He made out hazy green walls. South Texas sunlight streamed through a window and lit up a woman's hair so that it shone like spun silver. She was sitting to his right, and since the light came from behind her, he couldn't see her face.

Was he dead? Was she an angel?

Trying to see her better, he moved. Pain knifed through his shoulder in a savage burning thrust.

"Damn!" He hurt too much to be dead.

"Cole?"

"Who the hell are you?" he grumbled, blaming her.

"Lizzy."

Lizzy. She spoke. Then he was alive.

"Will you ever forgive me for shooting you?" she said, touching his hair.

"Shooting me?" He remembered her in the door holding a gun in a wobbling hand. She'd looked scared to death. "Now that's a hard one," he muttered, but he tried to manage a lopsided grin. "The last time I felt like this a foul-breathed shrimper was giving me mouth-to-mouth...."

"I'm serious, Cole."

"Kiss me, so I'll know you're real and I'm real. Then I'll think about it. You shot me, huh?"

She leaned over and cradled his face in her hands. "I've been waiting for you to wake up for days. The doctors kept saying you would. But I was scared."

Me, too.

"I prayed. I prayed so hard. Most of all I prayed you'd forgive me."

Love for her flowed through him, frightening him with its intensity. "Just kiss me darlin'. Make the hurt go away."

She made a choking sound. Slowly their mouths met. His lips were dry and chapped, but hers felt soft and dewy sweet. The kiss didn't last long before his head fell back to the pillow, but it was enough for now.

"You gonna marry me or not?" he whispered.

"Yes. Yes."

"Still think all I want is the ranch, darlin'?"

"I don't care. All I know is that I love you and that I can't live without you."

"I feel the same way," he said as he felt his eyes growing heavy and the darkness closed in on him.

"You didn't say whether you'll forgive me for shooting you."

"I think I'll let you suffer a spell." He closed his eyes.

"Cole!"

When he woke again, he felt stronger. It was dark, but she sat in the same chair beside him, looking desperate and uncertain. He asked her about Sam, and she told him everything.

"He's in jail. Apparently he thought Daddy killed Uncle Jack to get control of the ranch, so he thought the same path to power would work for him, too. Only Daddy didn't kill Jack. I know he didn't."

"So, you turned out to be a kick-ass heroine after all. Shot me. Shot Sam. You're a real cowgirl. Your daddy would be proud. Hell, I'm proud."

"I'm sorry I…I suspected you of murder. If it helps, I suspected Aunt Mona and Uncle B.B., too."

He didn't speak for a long while. "Hell, I suspected me."

"I'll never touch another gun. I swear!"

"Lizzy, I understand why you shot me. You thought whoever was out there had Vanilla and that he'd kill you and then kill her."

"I made a terrible mistake. I should have thrown the gun down. I should've—"

"I've made a few mistakes of my own."

"I—I just want to be myself now. Whatever that is. Life is an ongoing challenge and process."

"Tell me about it. Before the accident I was one person. Then I became another. I'm the same person, and yet I'm different in ways I may never be able to understand."

"I don't care. Either way I love you," she said, touching his cheek with a trembling hand. "I love you so much."

"I have all these images of you in my mind. I've forgotten a lot. But I always remembered you. And you're always so beautiful. I still don't know why I married Mia."

She went very still. "And I don't care anymore."

"Maybe I'll never remember. All I know is that I love you and I always will. And that I never slept with Mia."

"I love you."

He took her hand in his and pulled her closer to the bed, and he saw the depth of her love for him in her shining eyes.

"Lizzy, oh, Lizzy."

Their lips met. A long time later he released her mouth with a sigh. Then he rested his cheek against the base of her neck and continued to hold her.

"I don't ever want to let you go," he said.

"You don't have to."

EPILOGUE

Smart Cowboy Saying:

The easiest way to eat crow is while it's still warm. The colder it gets the harder it is to swaller.
                                        —Anonymous

Epilogue

The wedding march was playing, and the music seemed to soar high above Lizzy as the doors of the ranch chapel opened. Everybody turned. For an instant she thought of her father and those who weren't there—her mother, Mia, Shanghai, her missing sisters. Then she took a deep breath at her end of the red plush carpet and waited for the perfect moment to make her entrance.

Vanilla, who stood at the other end of the little church beside Cole and Mandy and all the other bridesmaids and groomsmen, began to clap and dance when she saw Lizzy in her bridal gown and veil.

You little minx, you're stealing my show. Not that Lizzy minded.

The wedding guests stood.

Holding her bouquet of orchids before her, Lizzy quickly made her way down the aisle.

Vanilla threw her flowers down and dashed toward Lizzy. When the baby reached the bride, she threw her chubby hands up and made gurgles to be picked up and held. Everybody laughed, including Lizzy, who lifted her and carried her the rest of the way down the aisle, not caring if the baby mussed her veil and her satin gown.

Cole's blue eyes stared straight into Lizzy's. Her breath caught. Sensing that she was no longer the center of Lizzy's attention, Vanilla turned and threw out her arms to her daddy. When he took her, she began to clap. Slowly her fat little hands quit moving, and she reached up and touched his face with wonder.

Joanne let out a choking sob, and a stillness descended upon Lizzy as she turned toward the minister. Glancing toward Cole, who was so darkly male and virile and gorgeous that she felt a thrill in her belly, she sighed a deep sigh of utter contentment and infinite longing. Even before she said her vows, she felt truly committed to this man she loved and his precious daughter, and to the land that would be their home.

She felt strong and sure in herself and yet proud of him, too.

"Forever," she whispered. "I'll love you forever."

* * * * *

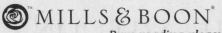
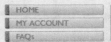